DETROIT PUBLIC LIBRARY

3 5674 05700601 8

✍ **W9-BVP-604**

THE

ALCHEMY

OF

NOISE

DUFFIELD BRANCH LIBRARY
2507 WEST GRAND BOULEVARD
DETROIT, MICHIGAN 48208
(313) 481-1712

APR 0 9 2019

DU

ALSO BY LORRAINE DEVON WILKE

After the Sucker Punch

Hysterical Love

THE
ALCHEMY
OF
NOISE

a novel

LORRAINE DEVON WILKE

SHE WRITES PRESS

Copyright © 2019, Lorraine Devon Wilke

All rights reserved. No part of this publication may be reproduced, distributed, or transmitted in any form or by any means, including photocopying, recording, digital scanning, or other electronic or mechanical methods, without the prior written permission of the publisher, except in the case of brief quotations embodied in critical reviews and certain other noncommercial uses permitted by copyright law. For permission requests, please address She Writes Press.

Published 2019
Printed in the United States of America
ISBN: 978-1-63152-559-9
ISBN: 978-1-63152-560-5
Library of Congress Control Number: 2018956760

For information, address:
She Writes Press
1569 Solano Ave #546
Berkeley, CA 94707

She Writes Press is a division of SparkPoint Studio, LLC.

Book design by Stacey Aaronson

All company and/or product names may be trade names, logos, trademarks, and/or registered trademarks and are the property of their respective owners.

This is a work of fiction. Names, characters, places, and incidents either are the product of the author's imagination or are used fictitiously. Any resemblance to actual persons, living or dead, is entirely coincidental.

Lyrics of "Rockin' Robin" by Leon René (under the pseudonym Jimmie Thomas) are in the public domain.

For Pete and Dillon, always

ONE

IT WAS NOT AN ORDINARY DAY.

It could pretend to be. It tried. The sun rose in the east. Blue jays squawked their usual morning greetings. Lyft drivers shuffled down below, and the coffee pot dinged at the exact prescribed moment. Still, it took only seconds to realize this was not, in fact, an ordinary day.

Maybe it was the drawn curtains—midnight blue and so rarely closed she'd forgotten their shade. Maybe it was the rumpled sheets, tossed in cologne and the scent of warm skin. Maybe it was his head on the pillow next to hers, sweet and breathing, eyes closed and lips parted.

Everything near and tangible gave evidence of something Sidonie Frame did not do. She did not wake up in darkened rooms, next to men, in her home, in her bed; not anymore, not these days. Too much danger in the exercise, too little benefit to the risk. She'd accrued at least that much wisdom in her bracingly instructive life.

Yet there he was. A sleeping man with strong arms and dark brown skin, tucked in a bed made the previous morning with no hint of its erotic disruption in the night to come. She smiled, pleased that life could still surprise her.

As she slipped from the covers and padded quietly toward the bathroom, Chris Hawkins, the unexpected man, stirred, waking just enough to alert him to the parameters of the day. His first assembled thought as he viewed the back of her pale naked form was "This *did* happen," which struck him as both strange and delightful.

Sidonie turned as he fell back into a dream and, gazing upon his peaceful face, felt the flush of something familiar warm her cheeks and quicken her pulse. Could it be happiness? Some form of happiness? Was that possible? She decided it was. Happiness, rare and wonderful, inspiring tenderness for this man she'd known only briefly but whose presence promised better days ahead.

This might be an adventure worth having, she thought before heading to the shower.

In the months to come, she'd reflect often upon that fleeting moment of optimism.

TWO

Four months earlier...

"NO BUSINESS EXISTS WITHOUT CHAOS," FRANK LEHMAN, club owner and Sidonie Frame's longtime boss, once proclaimed. "No ideas are implemented, no plans put to action, no partners assuaged or employees managed without the grit of bedlam. Gird yourself, kiddo."

Embrace of his nihilistic maxim may have been pragmatic, but it did not make her job—head manager of The Church, one of Chicago's buzziest small concert and event venues—any easier to contain. In fact, today, with its gaggle of nonprofit micromanagers bordering on hysteria in her office, she found herself, once again, chafing at the demands of her accidentally chosen profession.

She'd come to The Church the summer between her junior and senior years as a business major at Northwestern University. Confident to the point of arrogance, she'd been certain her foray into nighttime cocktail waitressing, required to keep bills paid and yogurt on the table, would be a brief thing of good money and flexible hours. It was. The tips were surprisingly lucrative, and she worked as often or as little as she liked; it sustained her through graduation, even financed her master's at the Kellogg School of Management. What it was *not*, however, was brief.

Working at The Church ceased being a job over six years ago, when Frank, quick to recognize talent, offered Sidonie the position—and impressive salary bump—of head manager. Given its resemblance to her dream of running a top-notch club of her own, the promotion seemed a wise step, one that, by now, had evolved into a full-blown career. But at thirty-five—divorced, overworked, and currently bereft of any previously held joie de vivre—she found the luster of wrangling celebrated performers and whipping up events for high-maintenance clients to be wearing thin. She was itching to break out, but until her own project sprang to life, she was there. At The Church. Night after long night.

It was when Jasper Zabrinsky, her all-around guy who ran everything stage- and music-oriented, announced the latest kerfuffle that she sensed this night might tip the scales. "He's not here." Wire thin, scruffy in a perpetual two-day beard, Jasper panted as if years of prodigious smoking had left a mark.

"Who's not here?" Sidonie, tucked in a bar booth checking invoices and sipping a lemonade sparkler, barely looked up from her tablet.

"Troy! He took his monitors out last night, had a gig this morning, now he's not answering his phone."

Troy Cleveland was The Church's somewhat-past-his-prime sound manager. In an ill-advised operational quirk, his stage monitors and dedicated mixing board were used to supplement the state-of-the-art sound system Frank built into the room years ago, a cozy arrangement that allowed Troy additional compensation and made both his presence and equipment essential. Sidonie had alerted Frank to the potential conflict of interest, but loyalty issues prevailed: he and Troy had been bandmates in the '80s and those ties never failed to trump logic.

And despite Sidonie's concerns, Troy had been, for the most part, reliable, managing The Church's eclectic lineups and sound demands without a hitch. At least until the last twelve months. Suddenly there were snafus and unpredictabilities of every kind. Drug rumors floated and there was ample evidence of a serious drinking problem, but he'd had a rough patch after a messy divorce, so leeway was given. Now he was unreachable on a day when Susan Brayman, point person for the Chicago Empathy Initiative Gala, a capable woman who could nonetheless snap with the force of a hurricane, was veering perilously close to combustion.

Sidonie finally looked up, the gravity of the situation dawning. "Wait, the monitor system isn't here?"

"No! He took his stuff out last night. Said he had some big thing in Joliet this morning. He was supposed to be here over an hour ago and so far I'm gettin' nothing with either texts or calls." Jasper's eyes had a comical way of bugging when he was particularly stressed, a sort of Steve Buscemi effect that typically inspired mirth; even now, with trouble a brew, Sidonie had to stifle a reflexive grin.

"How worried should I be?"

"We've got two bands coming in for sound checks, and five different speakers on the rehearsal schedule. It's all supposed to start in twenty minutes."

She looked at her watch. "That *is* bad."

"That's what I'm sayin'!" Jasper plunked to a chair as if the weight of the day just hit his bloodstream. "I can't do it myself, Sid, there's lots of moving parts to this one."

"I know. Any ideas?"

"I've got a friend I could call."

"A sound guy, with a full monitor setup, even a board?"

"Yeah, a guy I used to work with downtown. Has his own company, Sound Alchemy. Ever heard of it?"

"No, but it's not exactly my wheelhouse."

"He's got great gear, does a lot of outdoor stuff, but he can rig a room without a problem. He's actually kind of a genius. Odds are he's booked—he's pretty busy—but it's Thursday, so we might get lucky. Should I call?"

Before Sidonie could consider this unexpected option, the shriek of her name echoed from across the room. She turned to see Susan bristling at her office door, head shaking and eyes flaring in her direction. Sidonie's responsive nod was a terse *be right there.*

Jasper's leg was twitching. "What do you want to do, Sid? We don't have time to think about it."

"Call him. If he's available, get him here ASAP. If he's not, come find me and we'll figure something else out. But don't tell anyone—I mean *anyone.* I've got enough fires going without that one."

As Jasper sprinted off, Susan again caterwauled from afar. Sidonie took a deep breath, a slow sip of her sparkler, checked some notes on her tablet, then turned and walked purposefully in the direction of her frazzled client.

THREE

UNDER A CANOPY OF INDIGO CLOUDS AND THE BACKDROP of downtown's shimmering skyline, the rush and hustle of Chicago nightlife surged outside the club. Discreet signage beckoned, the notable hip quotient of The Church a draw to revelers strolling past, and a growing crowd angled for any way in, guest list be damned.

Wind off the lake, brisk and biting despite the timid approach of spring, buffeted the arrivals area with ruffian fervor. Undeterred, gorgeous women in sleeveless couture and gravity-defying stilettos teetered across the slush of Armitage Avenue to make their fashionable entrances. By six o'clock the valets were hopping, the velvet rope was taut, and invited guests, celebrity donors, and an impressive array of print and media personalities jammed the bar. In the adjoining performance room, a dramatic space of cathedral ceilings and artfully hung stage lights, dinner tables extending in from the adjacent dining area truncated a dance floor that was already filled with young, beautiful people getting the party started.

In the midst of the cacophony, reigning from behind a rectangular bar of slick concrete, stained glass backdrops, and racks strung with sparkling Edison lights, was Al Bonnura, The Church's head bartender. A forty-something veteran of the local circuit, with Italian movie star looks and a long history of entertaining Chicago's cocktail aficionados, Al had achieved a kind of regional celebrity. He once confessed to Sidonie that he'd taken career inspiration from the film *Cocktail*, doing little to raise him in her esteem, but she was that rare woman who never warmed to his charms, a status he viewed only as a challenge to overcome. So far he hadn't.

But he did know his way around a bottle, and the shining, glittering women who surrounded his nightly domain attracted the swarm of men who followed. It was a prosperous formula that granted some latitude for his bawdy stylings, some of which, waitresses occasionally complained, bordered on unacceptable workplace behavior. Still, he managed to hold the line, if precariously. Tonight he was in rare form, playing to the phalanx of cameras and eager reporters: bottles twirling, quips flying from one end of the bar to the other; eyes glinting in high-pitched performance as occasional applause left his face flushed and ebullient.

Stepping incongruously into the mayhem was a tall black man, midthirties, with serious eyes, in faded black jeans and a Thelonius Monk T-shirt. Notably dressed down in comparison to the attending crowd, his approach drew Al's immediate attention, who hollered over the din: "You here for the pickup?"

The man looked up, perplexed. "Excuse me?"

"She's out in the lobby. Red dress. Not feeling too good. I think she's headed to River North."

The man's demeanor shifted imperceptibly as he felt a *tick*, reflexive response to the cliché of presumption. He took a quick breath and smiled tightly. "No, not the cabbie. I'm here doing sound for Sidonie Frame. Was hoping I could grab a beer before the show."

Al took a beat, then shot him a chagrined smile, pulled out a Sam Adams and slid it across the bar. "Sorry, man. Been so busy I didn't notice what was going on in there. Can't say I've seen you in here before."

"No problem." The man took a long draught, placed some bills on the bar, and reached out for a handshake. "Chris Hawkins. A friend of Jasper's. Came in tonight to help out."

Al returned a hearty shake and pushed Chris's money away. "This one's on me. Sorry about the confusion." He turned back to his beckoning customers as Chris slid to an available stool, spinning slowly to take in the room.

Al was right; he had never been here before. Lincoln Park was not his usual stomping grounds, though his nights were more often spent working than barhopping. When he did get out, it was typically to clubs further south; smaller, more casual places with good jazz and blues, and the kind of home-style menus rarely found in tony rooms like this. Looking around, he noticed few faces of color in the mix.

But still, it was a nice venue, a prestigious place, and he knew their performance roster was first-rate. Jasper had invited him in on several occasions—when guys like Clapton and Buddy Guy were playing—but so far he'd never taken him up on it. Until tonight.

His availability had been a fluke; the original job fell through after a kitchen fire broke out in the booked venue. He'd been heading to dinner when Jasper called; given his old friend's frantic plea, and the not-inconsiderable emergency wages being offered, he quickly shifted gears. This would be a shoot-from-the-hip kind of night, not his usual style, but after his monitors and board were set up and a rough sound check was managed, he was confident they'd get through well enough.

Meeting Sidonie Frame had impact. He wasn't sure why, but there was something about her that set the night on a different plane. It wasn't just her swinging blonde hair and memorable face; it was the way she made eye contact: warm and direct. She'd been gracious and grateful upon meeting, going out of her way to make sure he had everything he needed. Which wasn't always the case at gigs, certainly not always the case with women who looked like Sidonie Frame. Chris would never say he had a type, and typically he wasn't drawn to white women—dating, briefly, only two in his thirty-four years—but she made an impression: not flashy, grounded somehow; smart and clearly in charge. That she was stunning seemed almost an afterthought.

And approaching now from the undulating crowd was the very woman in mind.

Her face lit up when she saw him. "Oh, Chris, good, I was just looking for you. I'm glad you got something to drink. Have you had a chance to eat? It'll get too crazy later and I don't want you to starve to death."

He liked that she'd thought of him. "Thanks, I'm good. Grabbed a burger a few minutes ago." Just then Jasper flew by and Chris noticed he'd changed into a dress shirt and tie. "I'm sorry I'm not better put together," he remarked to Sidonie. "I rushed over from another gig and didn't realize the setup was so formal."

She stopped scanning the room to note his attire. "That T-shirt will only score you points in this room." She laughed. "I'm just grateful you're here. And listen, if you need to step away during the night, there's a little office right behind the stage. It's really more of a closet, but the door locks, so escape is possible."

Her tablet lit up with a text; she quickly sent a response, then turned back to Chris. "It seems we're rolling. Just do your best and let's be sure to touch base at the end of the night." Her smile radiated a suggestion of what she was like when she wasn't beleaguered.

"Absolutely. You know where to find me."

"Thanks, Chris." She squeezed his hand. "Jasper'll take good care of you, and if my client drives you to drink, just know it's on the house!" With that, she hustled off, people grabbing at her from every angle.

Chris watched her cross the entire length of the room.

FOUR

DESPITE NOTABLE HIGHLIGHTS AND THE COMMENDABLE efforts of everyone involved, the evening was not without its glitches. Two of the guest speakers were ultimately so unnerved by the demands of public speaking they were barely audible, losing meaningful speeches to the din. Conversely, one of the two bands, local headliners poised for a national breakout, persisted on playing so loudly (despite Chris's repeated adjustments) that several of the more elderly donors left early with expressed irritation. Lastly, Susan Brayman, while empathetic to the needs of an "Evening for the Chicago Empathy Initiative," complained often enough that every transition was a battle ("We're *not* serving dessert before the last speaker, I don't care if it *is* soufflé!").

The food was delicious and well received, however; the dollars raised were substantial, and The Church was once again acknowledged as the place for entertaining and event fulfillment, making Frank a happy proprietor. Sidonie just wanted a hard drink and a long vacation, only one of which was available by evening's end. As she sat at the bar sipping the best vodka gimlet she'd had in a long time, courtesy of Al's magical touch, she noticed Susan leaning against the stage in a provocative pose, her smile coy as she chattered away with Chris. Jasper stood across from them boxing microphones, and when Sidonie caught his attention, he rolled his eyes. She waved him over.

"What's up, boss?" Jasper wheezed. She wondered how he always managed to look like he'd just stepped off a hard road trip, even in dress attire.

"What on earth are those two talking about?"

"She's gushing about what a great job he did. I also think she's angling for a phone number."

"For reasons of work or play?"

"Your guess. Chris is a big boy, he can handle her."

"Any word from Troy?" She was reluctant to ask. Several big events were coming up and she didn't have time for wayward employees, particularly of the sound department kind.

"Yeah, a couple hours ago. He was pretty messed up. Said his stuff was stolen out of his van this morning and after dealing with the police and everything, he just got fucked up and lost time." Jasper, like Frank, felt some loyalty to Troy, who'd gotten him the job five years earlier. But, unlike Frank, Jasper was disinclined to minimize the problem. "Pissed me off that he acted like it was no big deal. I let him know my thoughts."

Sidonie could only imagine that conversation. "I'm sorry about his equipment, but what did he think would happen when he didn't show up tonight?"

"I don't think much thinkin' went on."

"So, what's the plan? He comes in tomorrow and we pretend nothing happened?"

"I don't know, Sid." Jasper shifted uncomfortably. There was nothing he liked less than answering for someone else, and he'd had to do that a lot lately for Troy. "He's gonna have to replace everything. He's got no insurance and money's tight for him right now. He said if Frank wants to rent out some stuff, he'll take care of getting it in here and set up, but that's up to you guys."

Sidonie wasn't feeling magnanimous. From her perspective, Troy's sense of job entitlement was severely disproportionate to his value. Her eyes slid past Jasper; Susan was now waving goodbye in her direction—she waved back with a nod and smile, noticing Chris was back on stage rolling cords. "How'd he do tonight?" she asked Jasper.

Jasper looked over. "Chris? Great. Knows his stuff. I wouldn't have suggested him if he didn't."

"I know, I just mean how do you like working with him?"

"He's awesome. A total pro and a great guy. Why?"

Sidonie took another sip of her gimlet. An idea was gelling. "I don't know . . . just wondered. Don't let him leave before I have a chance to talk to him, okay?"

"Yeah, no problem." Jasper jaunted back to the stage area just as Al approached from the other side of the bar.

"Hey, good lookin'."

Sidonie felt a recurring wave of annoyance. She'd asked Al to stick to her name, which for him typically meant her last name, but tonight he was clearly feeling sassier than usual.

"Crazy night." He grinned.

"Yep. A wild one."

He leaned in closer than she appreciated. "Listen, you remember Mike Demopoulos, right?" He motioned to the other end of the bar where one of the neighborhood cops who'd made The Church a watering hole raised a glass in her direction. She had a vague memory of meeting him at some point.

"Not really. Why?"

"Nothing major. He was just commenting on how cute you are, how capable you seem, you know, working the crowd like you do. I think he has a little crush on you." Al winked with enough leer to convince Sidonie the conversation was over.

She popped off her stool. "Thanks for the gimlet." Before he could respond, she turned and walked toward her office, passing the kitchen just as Frank emerged with an overburdened plate of crab legs.

"Hey, want some of these? I think I overdid it."

"I'll say!" She laughed. "I'll pass on the food, but I do want to talk to you about something."

"Come sit, tell me what's on your mind." Frank, good-looking late-fifties, always immaculate in business dress, pulled a couple of chairs up to a table in the darkened dining area and the two of them sat. Sidonie had to smile as he launched into dinner with enough verve to splatter melted butter down the front of his designer shirt. He grinned. "Never fails. It's why I wear a bib at home!"

Sidonie liked Frank. He was a fair boss and ran a classy operation.

He was good to his wife and two college-age sons, treated the staff with respect, and never failed to acknowledge her role at the club as essential. His biggest flaw, beyond misguided loyalty and a tendency toward conservative thinking in both business and politics, was his sloppy eating habits, a deep contradiction to his impeccable grooming. She found the trait endearing.

"We need to talk about Troy. You know what happened, right?"

"Jasper gave me the rundown, including his drunken call of a couple of hours ago. Not thrilled, obviously."

"It's beyond 'not thrilled.' He put us in real jeopardy with a very big client tonight. If Jasper hadn't come through with his friend, I don't know what we would've done. Apparently, he now plans to just walk in tomorrow like nothing happened, without his monitors and board, which he expects you to replace for the time being, and, I have to admit, I'm not feeling generous."

"Okay. What are you feeling?"

"I want to talk to Jasper's friend about stepping in."

Frank looked up. "Temporarily? Put Troy on suspension?"

"No." She hesitated. "Let him go."

"Wow. That bad, huh?"

"That bad. Tonight may be the worst, but it's not the first infraction. By a long shot."

Frank went back to his crab, pondering her proposal.

She continued the pitch: "I'm not sure Chris is available or would even be interested—Jasper tells me he's got a successful freelance business going—but if you're agreeable, I'll at least run it by him. If he can't do it, we'll reconvene on other options. But I'd like to make an offer, even consider a bump on what Troy's making. Really shift gears here. I can't risk any more unpredictability, and there's been too much of that lately. Now, I know you two go way back and—"

"Sidonie, I'm not stupid." Frank looked up from his plate to give her his full attention. "I know he's been dropping the ball. I wanted to give him the benefit of the doubt, as we have—"

"For quite a while, actually."

"Yes, for quite a while, and maybe I haven't been as on top of this as I should've been. But when you're right, you're right. Tonight was a major screwup. I'll leave it to your good judgment. Talk to your guy over there and if he's onboard, I'll be the one to let Troy go, okay?" Frank went back to his plate.

"Okay." She gazed at him briefly, assessing his conviction. "Thanks, Frank."

"Anything else?"

"Nope." She got up quickly. "Just thinking it through."

"Then get outta here. I'd like to be a slob in peace."

She smiled and headed out, surprised, really, at how easy that had been.

FIVE

CHRIS FOUND HIMSELF PAYING ATTENTION TO SIDONIE'S comings and goings throughout the night, and now sensed he was a focal point as she and Frank convened in the adjacent dining area. Despite the few unavoidable snafus, the event had gone about as well as could be expected under the circumstances, status confirmed by Susan's gushing accolades, but he'd learned that clients could sometimes offer unexpected post-gig assessments. As he noticed Sidonie glance his way more than once, he started to get jumpy.

"Hey, Jasper, was your boss cool with everything tonight?"

Jasper looked up from behind the stack of speaker cabinets dwarfing him at the back of the stage. "Sure. She knows the problems weren't on us. Why?"

"Just wondered."

"She did say she wanted to talk to you before you left, so check it out with her."

As if on cue, Sidonie approached from the dining area. "Hey, Chris, can we talk for a minute?"

"Sure." Climbing down from the stage, he walked with her to a bar booth. "Can I get you a drink?" he asked politely.

She smiled at his formality. "Thanks, I hit my one-drink limit about ten minutes ago."

As she slid into the booth, he sat across from her, surprised at how nervous he felt; her cool approach was somehow intimidating.

"First, I want to say how much I appreciated the save tonight,"

Sidonie began. "I'd have been happy just muddling through, but you made the switch almost seamless. I'm in your debt."

He felt a flush of relief. "I know there were a few bumps—"

"Susan acknowledged those were all on her. She picked the bands and the speakers. You guys adjusted about as well as you could. Which actually got me to thinking about something I wanted to throw out to you. I just ran it by Frank and he's open to it as well."

"Okay." He held her gaze in anticipation, intrigued by the lead-in.

"Would you be at all interested in stepping into the position full-time? Beyond the stellar job you did tonight, Jasper vouches for you, which is a big deal to both Frank and me, and we're definitely in need of change around here. I'd normally take longer to find the perfect person, but if tonight were an audition, I'd say you *were* the perfect person." She suddenly noticed the intensity of his eye contact and it rattled her. Which was odd. She was rarely rattled.

"Wow." He sat back, nonplussed.

She quickly filled the gap. "I know you have your own business, which Jasper says does really well, and I know the quirks of this place might not fit your work model. But I'm wondering if there's a way you could balance both. Like, if we worked around your schedule until you could hire more guys for your private gigs. Or if, say, we trained our standby guy to sub in more regularly so you could step away when you absolutely had to. Or we could set up a flex schedule that—" She stopped, her face reddened. "I'm pushing too hard, aren't I? Am I pushing too hard?"

Chris laughed. "A little. But it's nice to feel wanted." Which was true. It was also true that the appealing way her cheeks flushed tripped his own flustered response. "Um, let me grab a quick beer, would you? Can I get you anything?"

"No thanks. Or maybe some water," she said, relieved by the opportunity to regroup.

Standing at the bar, he took the moment to consider her query. *Strange turn of events, this night. What to make of it?* Procuring a glass of water and another Sam Adams from Al, who again refused his money, Chris returned to the booth and her waiting anticipation.

"Here's the thing, Sidonie: it's a great situation for the right person under the right circumstances. The problem for me is that I'm booked solid for the next few months. Beyond that, I honestly doubt you could beat what I'm pulling in on my own. From a business standpoint that's a big component for me, and not something I can afford to jeopardize."

"Of course not. Though we're certainly open to discussing whatever salary demands you might have." Which was largely unfounded, particularly given Frank's penchant for thrift, but she was compelled at this point. "Do you have a number in mind?"

He laughed.

"What? Am I doing it again? Steamrolling you?"

"It's just that I've got so much going on right now, with so many people depending on me, I can't even think about what salary demand would make sense. I appreciate the offer, but, in all fairness to you, I don't think I could rework my obligations to give you guys what's needed around here. But thank you . . . and maybe another time?"

"Absolutely. And I really do understand." She gave him a wistful smile and slid out of the booth. "Thanks again for a great night, Chris, and if anything changes, do let me know—"

"Hypothetically speaking, though, how quickly would you need me if it *was* something I could work out?" His about-face startled even himself, but it suddenly struck him that The Church was a prestige gig. It could raise the value of his brand, bring in a whole new stratum of client. *Shouldn't he at least consider it?*

Sidonie, as taken aback as he appeared to be, sat down without a pause and opened her tablet. "Well, let's see . . . this weekend is easy, singer-songwriter stuff, a light acoustical roster throughout next week. The week after that is sporadic, spoken word one night, a couple of bands over the next weekend—Jasper could manage those with Andrew, our standby guy. But the following week we've got two big corporate events, and both Joss Stone and David Crosby coming in. I'd definitely need the full team by then."

He leaned back, juggling a mix of overwhelm and honest consideration. He once again opted for delay. "Okay, let me go over a few things before I give you a definitive answer. If we can work the money out, and I could ramp up to it rather than leap right in, it might be doable. Can I have the weekend to think about it?"

His earnest expression, devoid of either Troy's snark or Jasper's perpetual beleaguerment, charmed her, inspiring an unexpected tug of feeling. *Bad negotiation strategy,* she thought; now she really wanted him for the job. "Absolutely. Shoot me a text when you've got a number in mind, I'll run it by Frank, and we'll take it from there."

He stood up. "Sounds good. And, thanks, Sidonie. I enjoyed working with you." He took her hand. It was warm.

"No, thank *you!* You quite literally saved my ass today."

He smiled and walked back to the stage area, actively pondering the aforementioned body part.

Before she could slide out of the booth, Mike Demopoulos suddenly appeared at her side, drink in hand. "Good evening, Sidonie. Al tells me you're a gimlet gal and I figured after such a long night you could probably use some libation."

Mike was a pleasant enough fellow, not completely unattractive—average height, a little paunchy; a face most women would characterize as cute—but at the moment Sidonie found him as annoying as Al, who stood grinning behind the bar.

She looked at Mike with an inscrutable expression. "Mike, is it?"

"Yeah, Mike. We met before, remember? Mind if I join you?" Oblivious, he plopped to the seat Chris had just vacated.

Sidonie simultaneously stood up. "Actually, Mike, I've had all the libation I need and was just about to head home. But thanks. Good night!"

As she walked off, Mike gave Al a shrug and headed back to the bar.

S I X

AFTER THE SOUND ALCHEMY VAN WAS LOADED, AND handshakes and goodbyes were exchanged, Chris caught the neon of a 24-
hour market a couple of blocks north and decided to walk over for a
few needed items. Armitage Avenue remained closing-time hectic.
Looking for a more peaceful stroll, he pulled his jacket tight against
the wind, and turned into an adjacent residential area.

Walking at night was a kind of poetic meditation for him. A man
whose head was filled with sound most of the time, Chris gravitated
toward quietude whenever he could find it. He often took longer
routes afoot, content to wander streets he didn't know to get places he
needed to be, fascinated, always, by what was noticed along the way.

Curiosity had been a proclivity of his since childhood. His mother
would chastise him for being a "nosy sort" when he'd stare too long at
passing strangers, or listen too closely to bus stop conversations, but
his inquisitiveness prevailed. The half sentence that floated by; chatter
from an open window; a couple's whispered embrace on a porch
stoop. Even before he had the maturity to articulate or understand it,
those brief intersections sparked a sense of existential connectedness.
His mother told him it was safer to mind his own business. He found
life too intriguing to ignore.

As at this very moment. To his left, across a short expanse of late-
winter lawn, behind a window warmed by amber lamplight, a middle-
aged couple danced closely to the strains of something smooth and
melodic. Chris slowed his pace, wondering who they were to each

other and why they were dancing at two thirty in the morning, imagining their story to be something tender and provocative—

Woot, woot! The strident bleat of a police siren jolted him from reverie as a patrol car crossed the lane and pulled sharply to the curb. The uniformed officer on the passenger side—white, probably late-twenties—leaned out the opened window, training his flashlight on Chris's face.

"What are you doing there, buddy?"

Chris felt a *tick*, the familiar *tick*. He took a breath. "Just heading to the store up on the corner."

"Oh, yeah? Up on Armitage?"

"Yes."

"Then what are you doing on this street? Kind of an indirect route, isn't it? And they don't much appreciate strangers loitering around here."

"Not loitering. Just looking for a quieter walk."

The cop climbed out of the car, hand on his gun. "Where are you coming from?" His approach was tense, wary.

"I worked at The Church tonight," Chris remained still, responding in as neutral a tone as could be mustered. "Just wrapped it up and decided to grab a few things at the store."

"How about you show me some ID?"

As Chris carefully extracted his wallet and pulled out his driver's license, the officer behind the wheel, also white, though likely older, disembarked. Hand atop his gun, he positioned himself on Chris's other side. No one spoke and the moment crackled with frisson. The first cop studied the license, scanned Chris's face, then walked back to the car to run the information. *Tick, tick.* Chris took another slow breath.

"So you work up at The Church?" the second officer asked.

"Yes."

"I hear that's a pretty nice place." He was clearly running the "good cop" angle.

"It is."

"What do you do over there?"

"Ran their sound tonight."

"Huh. You don't look like a sound guy," he remarked.

Tick, tick. "Really? What does a sound guy look like?"

"I'm just saying I wouldn't have expected that."

The first cop came back, nodded to his partner, affirmation of some kind, then handed the license back to Chris. "So why were you looking at that house? That sort of thing tends to make people nervous."

Chris turned back to the window; the couple, oblivious to the drama outside, was still dancing. "I noticed those people, that's all. It caught my eye. It was just . . . I don't know . . . poetic."

The two cops turned toward the window and, for one odd moment, all three men stood watching, their shadows forming an unlikely tableau on the browned lawn. A beat, then everyone shifted back to their assigned roles.

"Okay well, Shakespeare, time to move on," the first cop intoned. "And probably smart to stick to the commercial streets from now on. It's a lot safer that way."

Safer for whom? Chris thought but didn't ask.

Both cops gave him a nod, climbed back into their cruiser, and pulled slowly away. Chris started toward the intended destination, then stopped, deciding there was nothing at the store he needed that badly. He turned and headed back to The Church parking lot.

SEVEN

MONDAYS WERE SIDONIE'S SUNDAYS, MAKING THEM AS close to perfect days as she got. They lent themselves to sloth and serenity, luxuriating in warm blankets, good coffee, day-old *Sun-Times*, scones from A Taste of Heaven, and agendas free of obligation. Patsy Gilmore's presence, therefore—with her charts and spreadsheets, short, stubby legs pacing the room, red hair flying, and voice decibels louder than necessary—was an unwelcome Monday incursion.

"They want visuals, Sid, not just ideas. This is a serious group, with serious funds, and they have serious demands."

Patsy was a brilliant chef, in constant demand for high-end events around the city. She was also Sidonie's former college roommate and the partner with whom she was planning her next career move. They were in the nascent stages of raising capital for the restaurant-club they'd dreamt up years earlier, and with their complementary skills made a good team. Sidonie had an impressive list of business contacts she wasn't afraid to tap; she managed the minutia of putting their offering documentation together and wrote a brilliant and detailed business plan.

Patsy, on the other hand, brought her "sparkling personality," as she so immodestly put it, to her role as the pitch person: she was funny, smart, and charming, and had been successful in convincing seed investors to provide development funds the previous year. Now, with coffers dwindling, they were making another push to raise the capital necessary to actually launch. Patsy had a hot prospect on the line, making her weekly report, typically reserved for Friday lunch, urgent enough to break the harmony of Sidonie's weekend.

"What does that mean: 'They want visuals'? Actual restaurant blueprints? We don't even have a location. How would we do that?"

"We improvise. Remember that place on Halsted we liked? It's been on the market for almost a year. They lowered the price two months ago and it's *still* on the market. Odds are good we could grab it on the low once we have funds."

"So you want to invest in sketches for a *maybe* location? That doesn't seem wise use of the little money we have left."

"All I know is, they want to see some semblance of this grand plan, and I get it—I would too. Since we've identified Halsted as ideal, why don't we sketch a loose floor plan, and if we ultimately don't get it, at least we've got something rough on paper we can tweak later."

"That won't be cheap."

"I've got a friend in the architecture department at Illinois Tech and we've already talked about giving it to one of her master's candidates. They get a grade and a decent stipend. We get cheap sketches. Want me to set something up?"

"Sure, if that makes sense. But if this new guy I'm talking to doesn't take the sound job, I'm in for some serious headhunting. I won't have much available time to meet."

"No worries. I'll give her a call and we'll figure something out." Patsy finally sat down, grabbed a scone, and with an expert twist of her knife, spun jam and honey into an irresistible drizzle that ultimately found its way down her chin. "I'm so good at this food thing!" She laughed. Loudly.

"You are a child," Sidonie retorted, handing her a napkin.

"I think we could actually get this one, Sid. These guys are bona fide, and they really want a presence in Chicago. This might be our team." She leaned in and gave her partner a hard look. "So don't screw it up."

Sidonie recoiled. "What does *that* mean?"

"Oh my God, I'm kidding!" Patsy yelped. "What would *you* do to screw anything up? You're the most toe-the-line person I know. I'm counting on you to wow them with your predictable know-how and expertise!" She laughed again. She was very loud.

Sidonie wasn't thrilled at the assessment of her character, especially since it had crossed her mind lately that she'd become stodgy and uninteresting, a dreaded event to her way of thinking. She also harbored creeping doubts about whether she was as excited about this project as she'd once been. Beyond the many and recurring disappointments inherent to the process of raising money, the energy they expended on it came in fits and starts, determined by the two women's work demands and time availability. Both were busy enough that, despite mutual and stated commitment, momentum often stalled, long enough and frequently enough to dull Sidonie's enthusiasm. But before she could ponder the dilemma further, her phone rang. She glanced at the caller ID, then deadpanned to Patsy. "Theo."

"Are you going to answer it?"

"No."

"Do you ever?"

"No. Why would I?"

Theo and Sidonie had been married for six years, six turbulent, sexy, deeply disturbing years. During that foray he developed an opiate problem, she miscarried a pregnancy, his multimedia production company tanked, and he left her for a young model who left him two months later for a rich mogul. It was both a cliché and a swirling heap of personal failure, none of which was worth rehashing—ever—particularly since its denouement was well over a year ago. Why he'd taken to calling in the last month was perplexing, but so far she'd resisted the bait.

"Aren't you the least bit curious?"

"No." Not true, but all Sidonie would admit.

Patsy cocked her head, disbelief registered. "I'd be dying." Patsy had been the maid of honor at the wedding, a splashy affair Theo deemed necessary to properly fete his new marriage and the prestigious business contacts in attendance, and she reveled in her role as the couple's booster. Sidonie suspected that, despite Patsy's appropriate commiserations of hate and rancor during the divorce, her best friend retained a soft spot for her ex, who, she once cooed, was "one of a kind." It was not a topic they broached easily.

Cuing off Sidonie's reticence, Patsy changed the subject with a glance around the notably minimalistic living room. With its gray, nondescript couch, two wooden Ikea folding chairs, and a coffee table that looked like a back-alley garage sale find, it inspired a familiar re-tort. "I see you're still going with temporary-college-housing motif."

"I am." When Theo left, he took most of the more artful furniture he'd personally acquired during their marriage. It was a point of con-tention at the time, but Sidonie ultimately capitulated, realizing she didn't like most of it anyway. Now she couldn't raise the interest to do anything about the resulting domestic deficit.

"So you're just *never* going to put this place back together? Some decent furniture, maybe a few things for the walls—something, *any-thing?*"

"Ambiance is overrated."

"Philosophy that may contribute to your hovering depression."

Sidonie finally looked around as if noticing the place for the first time. "It is hideous, isn't it? But I honestly don't have time to decorate. Nor do I have the talent. That was all Theo."

"I could argue the point, as I knew you before Theo and remem-ber you having some swell interior design impulses." Patsy got up with a long stretch. "But since I never win those debates, I'm gonna go cook up something scrumptious, and we'll share a nice lunch in this shitty room. That, I guarantee, will brighten your day!"

She was right. Patsy went to the kitchen and rustled up the best meal Sidonie would have that week and, for the moment, that was enough.

EIGHT

CHRIS'S MONDAY WAS SPENT PONDERING THE JOB OFFER. Regardless of how it was parsed, he couldn't figure a way in which it was honestly feasible. He liked his freedom. Liked being able to schedule his life around the clients he chose to work with. He didn't want to be beholden to higher-ups who'd expect things he might not want to give. The entire reason he'd set out on his own was to avoid micromanagement and obligation. He wore entrepreneurship well; what advantage was there to giving it up?

"The money, bro." Diante Robinson, a childhood friend whose South Loop condo Chris had moved into four years ago and never left, sat on the couch in sweats and a dirty work shirt, a burning joint and cold pizza nearby, deep in a video game that involved sharp arm movements and visceral grunting. Despite the activity, he appeared to actually be listening as Chris debriefed the unexpected events of the weekend. "Plus, you're not giving it up—you're adding to it. The Church is a cool room, it sounds like a good gig, and, come on, you can never have too much green."

Diante's general philosophy was that, as forward-thinking black men, they were obliged to go after wealth like miners to the lode. He was in his seventh year at a small, rapidly growing financial management firm on LaSalle, the heart of "Chicago's Wall Street," where he'd worked up the corporate ladder with astonishing speed. Despite being a comer in ways that didn't necessarily align with Chris's more measured life strategy, Diante's financial acumen was unassailable. Chris's concern was that his old pal wasn't taking in the bigger picture.

"I can't just *add* to it, D. Alchemy takes all my time now. This feels either/or, and it doesn't make sense to even consider shelving what I've sweat over for the last five years."

"Who's talking about shelving it? That would be damn stupid. Farm it out. You've got, what, how many guys on call now?"

"I don't know, seven, eight."

"Hire a few more, get them trained up. Be a CEO instead of a grunt. If your teams are tight, which they will be if you hire the right guys, you keep building Alchemy *while* running The Church. Sounds win-win to me."

"Or a whole damn lotta work. And what are the odds they'll offer anywhere near what I'd need to offset what I'm farming out?"

"Sounds like you're talking yourself out of it."

It did. "I don't know. Maybe." The admission deflated him. *Interesting.*

"Bottom line, putting aside logistics, are you interested in the gig?"

"Somewhat. The club's got a big name. It'd raise Alchemy's profile." He avoided mention of the intriguing woman behind the offer.

"Then do this: crunch the numbers so you know exactly what it'll cost to farm out the bulk of your gigs, make sure you build flexibility into your contract with The Church so you're available for any really big Alchemy stuff, then throw out a figure so damn high they either walk away, no harm done, or you bank a serious pay raise."

Impressive prescription. Chris stood up and grabbed his bag. "Not bad, Robinson. I'll give it some thought. Thanks."

"Let me know what happens." Diante suddenly leaned back. "But hey, before you go, I've got something to run by you, too."

Chris, surprised, sat back down. "What's up?"

"The time has come, my man." He grinned.

Chris had no idea what time that might be or why it had come, but he bit. "Okay . . . for what?"

"Jordan's moving in." Diante looked like a boy who'd just won his first trophy.

Chris's response was more muted. "Seriously?" Jordan was one of Diante's revolving posse of women, making this an unforeseen development. In fact, the most salient aspects of Diante and Jordan's relationship, at least from Chris's perspective, were that she was young and staggeringly hot; Diante generally acted stupid around her, and their default rapport was incendiary.

Diante, clueless to his friend's assessment, nodded gleefully. "Yep, we figured it was about time."

"That's . . . random. I thought you were edging away from that one, said she'd gotten too needy or whatever it was."

"I did and I was, but we spent a lot of time talking this past weekend and decided part of why she's so insecure is that she can't tell how committed I am."

"Not hard to understand, since you're still hooking up with Tiana and that other chick you had over here a week or so ago."

"DeDe? Nah, that's all done now."

"Yeah? Didn't look so done when she was bent over the chaise lounge the other night."

Diante flung his remote to the couch. "Why are you breaking my balls, man?"

"I'm just being real, D. You've been through some raucous shit over the years and I don't want to see you go down that road again, that's all."

Diante took a swig of beer, calmed himself down. "Yeah, yeah, I know. I appreciate you lookin' out for me, I do. But, seriously, man, I love this girl and I think the fooling around was just 'cause I was scared. I'm still scared, but I'm more scared of losing her than living with her. Hell, man, I'm thirty-four, been divorced almost five years, and one of these days I want a family. I gotta at least try again, don't I?"

Chris could see the man was struggling. "Hey, if it's honestly what you want, go for it."

"It is. For her too." Diante then paused awkwardly.

"What's the tag?" Chris sighed. "I can tell there's a tag."

"If I'm gonna run with this, I gotta approach it like the real thing. Like we're doing it right, grown people building a home together."

"What does all that mean?" Chris knew exactly what it meant; he just didn't want to deal with what it meant.

"I need the place to myself, bro. I gotta fully take it on, you know? Her and me living together like a real couple, not just hanging out with my buddy in the next room. And, come on, you have got to be wanting your own pad by now, right? I mean, when was the last time you had a girl in here? Jordan was just sayin' that you live like a god-damn priest. What's it been, like, two years?"

Beyond the inaccurate time gap, Chris bristled at the thought of Diante's damn-near-teenage girlfriend critiquing his love life. His last relationship had been with a dancer he'd met doing sound for an Oak Park wedding about three years ago. She was beautiful, incredibly sexy; they dated seriously for two years, then she got recruited by the Alvin Ailey Company in New York, left with promises made, and never came back.

"It's not even been a year and I'm too busy for all that right now, that's all."

"Not even a booty call? Come on, man, you've got to get back in the game! That'll be a hell of a lot easier if you don't have me and Jordan around."

Chris and Diante had roomed together, on and off, since they'd graduated from college. Despite their many differences, both personally and professionally, they'd managed to maintain enough common ground to keep the arrangement workable, one they returned to time and time again while rolling through the process of growing up. The current chapter began about six months after Chris launched his company; Diante was newly divorced, his condo was centrally located, and he had an industrial-sized storage locker available for Chris's sound equipment. When the invitation was extended, Chris was happy to grab it. He was less happy to leave it at this particular moment.

"I know this is a little abrupt," Diante continued, "so I don't expect you to pack up tonight—"

"Well, shit, I hope not!"

"But I do want to move things along pretty quick."

"How quick?"

"Could you be out by the first?" That was fourteen days away.

"What are you doin' to me, D? I just told you what I've got going on right now! When am I going to have time to look for an apartment?"

"I could do some scouting for you, make some calls, and, look, if it takes a little longer, no big thing. You can keep the storage locker. I don't think Jordan'll need it and if she does, I'll help you find an alternative. I would've given you more notice but this just kinda sprang up—"

"You've been seeing her for over a year." Chris was authentically annoyed.

"I mean the living together thing. I'm sorry, bro. We'll make it work—I got you covered."

Diante reached over for a fist bump, but Chris wasn't feeling the solidarity. He got up, his knee jostling the table just enough to splash Diante's beer over his latest skin rag.

"Hey now!" Diante yelped, picking up the dripping magazine.

"Better get rid of that shit, brother. As I recall, Jordan takes competition very seriously."

The wet magazine flew in his direction.

NINE

IN THE THIRTY MINUTES SHE'D BEEN WAITING, SIDONIE mentally assessed every detail of her current surroundings at least twice. She was seated at a table in a pop-up farmers' market, alternately checking her phone and sipping latte on this pretend-spring day, the kind Chicagoans know as the "tease before next week's snow." The ice of mid-March had begun to melt, leaving the adjoining park awash in tiny, misguided buds that crept early from their green shells, all poised to be cruelly glaciated in the next freeze. Still, it was a lovely back-drop: the air was crisp, the sky blue, and every single person she looked at appeared to be part of a couple.

Maybe it was a subverted form of Baader-Meinhof Phenomenon, that frequency illusion where a random concept is suggested and sud-denly it's visible everywhere. But after a year spent reclaiming her "stable singlehood" (as Patsy so charitably put it), focused on identify-ing herself outside the framework of wife or couple, Theo's calls started, and from then on, coupledom seemed everywhere.

Loving twosomes reveling in their twosomeness. Gentle touches and heads teased inward; the gaze of attachment, the soft laughter of shared, easy conversation. Connected and conjoined. Walking down streets with hands held, hips bumping, shoulders leaned; their couple-dom as solid as the ground, the floor, the earth beneath their feet, and upon that foundation all happiness could be built.

Sidonie remembered feeling that way. Being with Theo made her understand for the first time how *institution* could logically be linked with *marriage*. She'd always thought the word made cold and clinical the ultimate romantic gesture of matrimony, but she discovered marriage *was* an institution. It had its own hum, its own rhythm and energy. It was something both inside and outside a couple, both within and around them. It was ephemeral and intangible, yet as alive as skin and muscle and sex and emotion and the very air coursing in and out of breathing lungs.

And when marriage was gone, the institution was gone. The heat, the electricity, the foundation; it all shifted and changed until it finally disappeared, leaving one standing on . . . ground. Just ground. Alone. Detached. Solitary. Nowhere to lean.

Unlike the couples she now saw every damn day of her life.

A fire truck roared by, snapping Sidonie's gaze from the attractive pair cooing across the way. She ceased her inner grousing at their public display of affection and, instead, took in the gaggle of other folks in view, finding comfort in the random loner, the elderly dog walker, the solitary book browser.

This was a popular market typically opened only during the temperate months, but on warmer days of colder seasons they sometimes popped up in defiance of winter, as they had today. Sidonie met her older sister Karen every Tuesday during the more manageable seasons, and this was a perfect halfway point when they did. It also boasted a kiosk that served the best brew in Chicago, where Sidonie was now perched. Waiting.

She looked at her phone for the fifth time since she'd arrived. Nothing. Dammit.

It wasn't Karen's call she was anticipating; given her sister's propensity for lateness, there was little expectation of that. It was Chris Hawkins. Sidonie was disappointed that he hadn't gotten back in touch about the job. She expected a text yesterday, but, if nothing else, sometime this morning. It had now been four and a half days, and she'd presumed the urgency expressed would have compelled a quicker response. Not a good sign.

She also had to acknowledge that she'd been looking forward to talking to him, probably more than she was willing to admit. She didn't know why. Maybe it was the novelty of a new person. Someone to alter the landscape, be interested in stories already told, shift the status quo. Maybe it was just the prospect of a more amenable sound team at the club. Maybe it was the buzz that happened whenever their eyes met.

No, it wasn't that. There probably wasn't any buzz. And if there was, it was probably all in her head: a desperate woman looking for attention from a capable, intelligent, brown-eyed man with sound skills. Interesting to consider, though. If there was a buzz.

She'd briefly dated a black man in college, so there was no cultural resistance to the idea of "intermixed coupling" (as a dorm mate had deemed it). There'd just never been occasion to explore it again. Frankly, she'd had little interaction with any persons of color throughout her younger life, at least until college. Growing up in the homogenized suburb of Palatine, north of Chicago, she and her sister attended schools largely populated by kids from white families. And while neither of her parents expressed overt bigotry, there was implicit expectation that she keep romantic ties within her own race, a notion made verbal when her father met said college boyfriend and remarked, "He's a nice enough fellow, but why do you want to get into the complications of all that?" She wasn't sure what "all that" meant, but hadn't queried further. The circumstance never came up again.

Until this moment, as she pondered why she was so keyed up about Chris's response.

It had to be the job, this interest, because he didn't fit any previous paradigm of who she'd normally be attracted to, who she might date or potentially fall in love with. Though she wasn't sure why. And certainly she wasn't even thinking about him that way anyway. But if she were, the truth is she'd dated and fallen in love with a variety of types over the years, so why Chris, beyond race, seemed outside the scope was confusing.

She'd guess he was younger, and she'd never been attracted to younger men. Maybe that was it. And though he had his own business and was clearly a well-respected man, he had a sort of scruffy, tech-geek presentation she wasn't used to. Theo always looked like he'd just stepped off a photo shoot, and, to be perfectly honest, she'd liked that, so maybe—

"I'm here, I'm here!" Karen rushed up in a lather of familiar apologies—the traffic, her clients, the unexpected phone calls; the usual. Natty in requisite designer wear, sun-tipped coif smartly windblown, Karen was constructed like the quintessential TV lawyer. Two years older than Sidonie, and ten years into a partnership at the prestigious downtown firm that courted her away from a career in criminal defense, Karen led an impressive life in an impressive setting: gorgeous home in Logan Square, tense but enduring marriage to Josh Ritmeyer, a corporate litigator at another firm, and a fourteen-year-old daughter named Sarah who was charming, entitled, and working toward becoming "exemplary and accomplished," as Josh remarked at her middle school graduation.

"Why do you look so depressed?" Karen inquired, now set with a latte and chocolate croissant.

"I *am* depressed."

"Why?" The response made clear just how out of sync the sisters had become.

"Oh, I don't know . . . still smarting from the divorce, still have a stressful job, still drowning in loneliness and lack of joy. But, hey, how are you?"

They'd spent long, meaningful hours talking when Sidonie's pregnancy was lost and as her marriage crumbled, and Karen was exceptional at authentic solace and attention. In fact, she'd literally saved Sidonie during those dark times, bonding them beyond usual sisterhood. Lately, however, they'd talked less. With no new dramas and little change in her life, Sidonie had kept largely to herself, leaving Karen detached from the subtle nuances of her suffering.

"I'm sorry, Sid. Truly. Has it been that long since we got together?"

"Since right after the holidays."

"Well, that's too damn long. I didn't know things were so rough, honey. I thought you were past the worst of it. I would've checked in more often if I'd known."

"You couldn't have known. I've been busier than usual and haven't felt much like talking. It all feels so unfixable."

"Nothing's unfixable."

"Theo's been calling."

Karen stopped chewing and wiped her mouth. She was not fond of the man. "Why's that?"

"I don't know. I never answer. Never call back."

"Good. Keep it that way. He's toxic."

"I know."

"Listen, I went over the information Patsy sent last night and I think this group is promising. I'm not sure about the depth of their capital, but once they throw an offer, I'll be happy to look at it."

"Thanks, that'd be great. I really appreciate you helping us out with all this."

"Happy to do it. Listen, I don't have much time today and we need to talk about something else."

"That sounds ominous."

"Not ominous, just surprising. Mom's moving to Florida."

"With Steve?"

"Of course with Steve! Why else would she go?" Their mother, Marian Frame, had been a divorcée since the girls were in high school and their father left with an aging ski instructor from Wausau, Wisconsin. After a long dry spell in which men, as a gender, were banished from her life, Marian met a welding inspector named Steve Banasiak two years ago and had been dating him since. Steve spent half his time in Florida where his employer was headquartered, which made the concept of Marian moving south not entirely unexpected. Still, Sidonie never figured her mother for life-changing decisions.

"I'm stunned. I thought she hated Florida."

"She does. But she loves Steve, and he's been given an ultimatum to either move to Florida or lose his job. She's making the adjustment."

"Does Dad know?" Their father had remained a distant and largely uninvolved factor in their lives since his move north, which made the question an odd one.

"Fuck Dad. He has zero to do with this," Karen snapped.

"I know. I don't know why I asked that." Chagrined.

"Me neither." A beat, then Karen reached over and patted Sidonie's hand with a forgiving smile. "Anyway, that's her big news."

"Wow. When did all that happen? I haven't heard a thing about it."

"She called last night, the first I'd heard of it myself. Said she needed a lawyer's perspective—I have no idea why, since the condo is paid for and will fly the second she puts it on the market. She has plenty of money, absolutely nothing to worry about, so I think she's just nervous about making that kind of commitment."

"Well, yeah! It'd be one thing for her to move in with him here. It's a whole other deal to relocate someplace she doesn't like, to live with a guy for the first time since Dad, with neither of us around!"

"Trust me, she's as worried about all that as you are. But the woman *is* only sixty, she's got lots of life left, she hates snow, and she loves Steve. She deserves a new chapter."

"She does," Sidonie glumly agreed. Great. Another person leaving her life.

"And she did tell me to share this when we got together today, said for you to call her this weekend, so you haven't been forgotten." She punched Sidonie's arm.

"If that's the best I get, so be it."

"Well, I am her favorite." Karen grinned.

"But I'm her baby, which trumps favorite." They both laughed. It was an old joke.

Karen stood up. "Okay, got to go." She looked around. "Have I told you how much I love this market?"

"Yep."

"Probably be under four feet of snow next week."

"Yep. Have I told you how much I hate winter?"

"Every winter." Karen laughed.

TEN

THE DRIVE FROM STATE STREET TO HYDE PARK, WHERE his mother still lived in their family home, was slow going, giving Chris time to ponder recent conundrums. He'd spent several hours going over his accounts and scheduled jobs, assessing projected budgets, and who and what would be needed for each upcoming gig, and, as Diante advised, came up with a number to present to Sidonie. It was significant, but since negotiations had to start somewhere, he figured he'd throw it out and see where it landed.

As he made his way through the glut of construction cranes and late morning traffic, familiar streets rolled into view. The dusty alleyways and corner playgrounds where he'd spent countless hours of his youth always stirred a rush of nostalgia. Memories entwined in this part of the city were deep and of every kind, some more painful than others, but all poignant and enduring. Pulling up to the curb in front of the home where his parents raised him, his older brother, and younger sister, reminded him, always, of how lucky he'd been.

While some areas south and west of the neighborhood were brambly with crime and blight, not much about this pocket surrounding the University of Chicago, where his mother had been employed her entire adult life and worked still, had changed. With its unusually robust campus police force, and wealthy, prestigious demographic, Hyde Park was a kind of island in the midst of encircling urban grit. The small bungalow his parents purchased shortly after they married was blocks from the more affluent neighborhoods immediately adjacent to the campus, but was, still, a haven of relative peace compared to the streets where many of Chris's friends and classmates had lived not all that far away. The tidy brick house, a survivor of the city's "urban renewal" program of the 1950s and '60s, was surrounded by well-treed curbsides and similar, smaller homes, many of which sufficed now as student housing. It remained pristine and well cared for, his father having been a remarkable landscaper and his mother the fastidious sort. She ran her household like she ran the administration office at the university, taking collective pride in belonging to the community best known as the home of Barack Obama.

Grimy snow resistant to the warmer days of approaching April crusted the front stairway. Only visitors used those steps, his mother typically coming through the side door from the garage, so Chris took a moment to clear the slush away with the porch broom. As he moved up the steps, his eyes caught sight of his mother reading at her favorite chair near the front window. The view comforted him.

Delores Hawkins was an old-fashioned kind of mother. Short, plump, traditional; even at only sixty-two she seemed older, a throw-back to maternal figures who always wore dresses and had coffers filled with good food no matter who was or wasn't around. Maybe it was the job, a position that gave her tremendous responsibility and made excellent use of her organizational efficiency, but there was rarely anything messy or discombobulated in Delores's world.

"Honey!" She leapt up with a smile as Chris came through the door. "I wasn't expecting you. What a nice surprise." She wrapped him in a quick hug and before he could say a word, turned toward the kitchen. "Let me put a little snack together. I just picked up some of those crescent rolls you like."

"No, Ma, it's okay, I just ate. I came by because I wanted to talk to you about something."

"Oh, all right." She sat down, smoothing her skirt with the attentive posture of a student. "I hope nothing's wrong."

"Actually, there's a lot of good stuff going on and I wanted to run a few things by you."

Delores had been a pivotal advisor during the many months of putting Sound Alchemy together, and with her business acumen and prodigious common sense, Chris often relied on her insight. He explained the offer from The Church, laid out the complications of running his own business simultaneously, and itemized the reasons why there was value in taking the job regardless. She nodded throughout.

"I think Diante's advice is right on the mark, son. I also think you need to stipulate that a reasonable opt-out clause be written into your contract in the event it becomes impossible to manage both situations. The one thing I don't want to see you do is jeopardize your business after everything you've put into it."

"That's exactly my concern, so good point."

"When are you going to discuss it with them?"

"Tonight. I'll text the head manager, the woman who made the offer, and see what she thinks. We'll go from there."

"Does that leave you time for dinner?"

"Actually, no. I've got to get downtown to meet with a few of the techs I might hire. But I do have one more thing to ask."

"What is it?"

"Diante's decided it's time to try love again. He's got his girl Jordan moving in and he wants to do it without me around."

"Ah, sweet Diante." She smiled, remembering the wild little boy who shared Chris's childhood adventures. "From the rake to the romantic! I love that he never stops trying." She gave Chris some notable side-eye, which he deftly ignored. "And I don't think you can blame him for wanting the place to himself. If he's ready to make that kind of commitment with a woman he loves, the man needs his privacy."

Chris could barely keep from rolling his eyes. "Yeah, well, I'm not so sure about the love and commitment part—*he's* probably not so sure about the love and commitment part—but whatever it is, I need a new place to live. With everything going on right now, I won't have much time to look, so would you be okay with me bunking here for a few weeks?"

"Of course, sweetheart, this is your home too!" She beamed as if he'd just given her a Christmas present. He couldn't help but warm at how easy she made things for him. Then she added: "It'll be so wonderful to have both my kids home for a while!"

Not good news.

"Vanessa's here?"

"Yes . . . at least every other week." Delores shook her head, lips pursed. "I'm sorry to be the bearer of bad tidings, son, but she and Hermes have separated."

Chris was genuinely shocked. "Wow. What happened?"

"I don't know—she's not telling me much. But it seems neither of them wants to shift the kids in and out of the house, especially during the school year, so they've worked out this convoluted arrangement where he spends one week with them and she spends the other. He has an apartment downtown, and she comes here on the alternate weeks. It's a very tense situation and I can't do anything but pray for them all." She sighed deeply.

"That sounds . . . stressful."

"Oh, honey, you cannot imagine the state your sister's in!"

But he could. It didn't take a separation, a financial crisis, or any other kind of catastrophic event to stir Vanessa's frenzy. She was always perched somewhere near the edge.

Chris and his younger sister did not enjoy a convivial relationship. From childhood on, they'd had little in common, with personalities so disparate as to be combustive. While he faced life with his mother's openness and father's equanimity, Vanessa was all taut surfaces and sharp angles, ever ready to pick a fight. Growing up on the south side of Chicago, even Hyde Park, didn't make it easy for a scrawny black girl with big ideas and a bigger mouth, and her journey to adulthood had been a battlefield of schoolyard tussles and fractious relationships. Now a social worker who spent most of her time at a battered women's shelter not far from the Calumet Heights neighborhood where she and her family lived, she'd become very involved in a local chapter of Black Lives Matter, finding a seamless merge between the two causes. Her activism was admirable, often inspiring, but the causticness of her frequent lectures to Chris about his lack of political involvement was tiresome. He did not relish her particular energy at this moment of his life.

"I'm sorry to hear that. I didn't know she and Hermes were having trouble."

"Neither did I. Not till she showed up about a month ago with her suitcase in hand and bags under her eyes, insisting I keep it to myself. I hope you'll forgive me for not saying anything sooner."

"No worries, I get it. I just feel bad for her . . . for all of them."

"Well, the girl never sleeps, and with all she does on *top* of raising those two children, I doubt she has one ounce of time for that husband of hers. And Lord knows his schedule is just as bad. That never bodes well for a marriage."

Vanessa's husband, Hermes, was a top studio engineer who worked long, unpredictable hours, likely a factor in the separation. He was the person most responsible for inspiring Chris's passion for the art and craft of sound; he was also someone Chris admired for many reasons, not least of which was his endurance of Vanessa's many dramas in the ten years they'd been married. Chris would genuinely hate to lose him as part of the family.

"You know, thinking about it now, Ma, it probably doesn't make sense for me to be here if she's already having a rough time. You know how it gets with us."

"I do, sweetheart, but you're both so busy you wouldn't be around all that much anyway. And you *could* make a special effort to keep things simple for the time being, couldn't you? I would love to have a full house for a minute or two. It's been so long."

Beyond his true need for temporary housing, her wistful plea struck a chord. "Okay, all right. I'll do my best. That's all I can promise."

"That's all we can ask. Now, let me fix you a plate of something."

Before Chris could again protest his schedule, she was off to the kitchen. He checked his watch and decided there was time for an all-too-rare good meal.

He wandered upstairs to his old bedroom. Other than the absence of outdated high school and college memorabilia, packed away when his mother briefly used the space as her office, the room was remarkably unchanged. It was not, and never had been, a paragon of artistry. With its brown plaid bedspread, variegated shag carpet, and vintage wood paneling, it was a monument to questionable '70s design trends. But memorable times had been spent in this room—the mythical discovery of masturbation at ten, the titillation of caressing his first naked breast at thirteen; hours with friends playing video games in high school, and the comfort of that carpet when he curled in agony after losing his father and brother after college. The room's unwavering existence in this house was testament to his private world of growing up and coming back, and it always looked and felt like home.

As he walked back down the hallway, he glanced, as he always did, at the collection of framed photographs collaged across the wall. His eyes went first to the ones who were missing: his father, John, and older brother, Jefferson. Two figures in his life whose deaths still weighed heavy and forever would. They'd died together in a car accident eleven years earlier, when Chris was twenty-three. Just out of college and facing the rest of his life with a mix of thrill and terror, he'd gravitated toward their male pull in ways he never had when he was younger. The three "men of the family," as his mother liked to call them, took to spending a fair amount of time together while Chris was still unemployed. On the night of the accident—coming home from a White Sox game, hit by a drunk Milwaukee Brewers' fan—Chris was supposed to be with them. A hard flu had descended the night before, and while his father and brother enjoyed hot dogs and debating balls and strikes, he fevered with disappointment. He never forgot the irony of sickness saving his life while everything around it shattered.

The deaths of those two seminal figures remained the single most devastating aspect of existence for the remaining members of the Hawkins family. Whatever separated them, wherever they scraped and struggled, the loss glued them together in ways that could not be diminished by time, rancor, or disagreement. Looking now at their smiling faces in one photograph after another, Chris felt the always-familiar pull of grief, the piercing jabs of emotion that sprang anew each time he looked at this wall or spent too much time thinking about them. He found the grief reassuring. He still felt something. They hadn't disappeared. They still had a place here, on this wall, in this house, within this family. In his mind and heart.

He was glad he'd be spending some time at home. He made a vow to extend patience to the one sibling he had left.

ELEVEN

IT WAS A MUCH HIGHER NUMBER THAN SIDONIE ANTICIPATED. On the other hand, it didn't completely surprise her. She knew Chris would have to manage serious logistics and myriad new expenses to make the arrangement work. But still, Frank was unlikely to go that far beyond Troy's salary without her making at least some effort to meet with other candidates. She sat in her spare, uninspired dining room, already wording the ad for the employment post as she called his cell.

"Take it," Frank said, stunning her speechless. "Of course try to knock him down as far as he'll go, but take it." He didn't even hesitate.

"Really? That's so out of character for you."

Frank laughed. "I know. But the fact is, we've got two of the biggest months we've ever had coming up and I don't want to waste time if we've already found the right person. He and Jasper have built-in rapport, he did a great job, he knows the room, and I did some checking around."

"You did?" That surprised Sidonie as well. Frank typically didn't get involved in matters of staff, so this should have either annoyed or impressed her. At the moment it did both.

"I just happened to run into a friend of mine downtown, a guy on the charity event circuit, and mentioned the situation, asked if he had any suggestions. Chris's name was the first to come up, which was synchronistic. Said he'd worked with him on a number of events and thought he was a standout. So take it. I have a feeling he'll be worth the money."

Sidonie was pleased. It made life easier. "He and I are set to meet in about an hour, so I'll get my very best haggle on and you get talkin' to Troy."

"Not looking forward to that."

"No, I imagine you aren't. Did he call again?"

"He texted an apology yesterday. I haven't responded yet. Wanted to settle this first. I'm glad we have. Go sign 'im up, kiddo."

"Okay, I'll call after—"

"Oh, and I've already got a new monitor system coming in tomorrow," Frank interjected. "If there's any way Chris can be here to make sure it works for the room, get it set up the way he'd like, I'd appreciate it."

"I'll ask." She smiled to herself. He wasn't fooling around.

TWELVE

THEY MET AT A COFFEE SHOP OFF CLARK NOT FAR FROM Sidonie's block. It was late enough that only a smattering of booths were occupied, and the relative unhipness of the place ensured it would likely remain that way. Which was fine; it was quiet. They both ordered coffee, and Chris decided to indulge in one of the very impressive layer cakes in the bakery display. As he stood at the counter making his choice—there was some conflict between coconut and carrot—she took the moment to peruse him anew.

He was around six two, well built, muscular, with close-cropped hair and a college-student wardrobe, the general effect being one of geeky athleticism. His open face was too asymmetrical to be truly striking, but he was handsome and his large brown eyes did much to warm the pleasant whole. She liked him. He was calm and easy, the exact opposite of the erratic, high-strung man he'd be replacing.

Once he sat down with his coconut cake—"Carrot felt too much like salad," he said, laughing—they spent the next twenty minutes talking money. She bumped him down a bit, not much, but enough to feel like she'd made the effort. They discussed his contract specifics, all of which she agreed to, and set a time to meet the next day to put the details in writing. After they discussed the incoming monitors, business was done and they were left . . . awkward.

Coffee cups were refilled, the table was cleared, and though there was nothing left to negotiate, neither seemed compelled to leave.

"How long have you been at the club?" he asked, safe entry to further conversation.

Sidonie ran through her resume, from the conclusion of her master's through her various positions at The Church, briefly referencing the project with Patsy while keeping details vague. When she queried about his background, he discussed how his brother-in-law had guided him through the many obstacles and confusions of starting his company; how his grandmother put up the investment capital, and his mother helped write the business plan. Before they realized it, two hours and many cups of coffee had transpired.

"I don't think I've talked this much in years." She laughed. "You are either remarkably—"

Crash!

The front door of the coffee shop was thrown open by a disheveled man in a crumpled business suit, cold air flooding in behind him.

"Hey!" the man bellowed, his pasty white cheeks gleaming with sweat. "Whose piece of shit van is that out there?" Drunk and agitated, everything about his comportment was a cliché, from the rheumy eyes and food-stained jacket, to the greasy, matted hair, and bloated stomach straining against a partially unbuttoned shirt. His level of inebriation clearly stoked the urgency of his mission.

"I *said*, which asshole owns that ratty blue van in the parking lot?" His eyes flitted over each of the few patrons present. Gazing past a young hipster couple who blatantly ignored him, over an older man doing a crossword puzzle who shook his head, and past a middle-aged woman sitting alone with a piece of pie, he zeroed in on Chris. Like a marauding gorilla, he staggered toward their booth. "Is that your van out there, blocking the whole fucking alley?"

Tick. Chris felt it like a jolt. He took a sharp intake, letting his breath out slowly.

The man glared, shaking his head. "What, you just gonna sit there like a goddamn baboon?" he bleated.

"Okay, *that* is just completely unacceptable!" Sidonie snapped. "Why would you presume that's his—"

"Cuz lazy motherfuckers like him leave their crap all over the place—"

"Are you kidding me with that?" Sidonie retorted loudly, her cheeks flaring deep red.

Chris reached out and put a steadying hand on her arm. She stopped. He turned to the panting drunk, jaw set, voice modulated. "It's not my van. I don't know whose van it is. I'm sorry you're blocked, but check with the cashier or the manager and maybe they can help."

Swaying back a few steps, and after a conflicted pause, the man turned and stumbled back toward the door. The manager, intent on circumventing further customer harassment, brusquely led him outside.

Sidonie looked at Chris, chagrined. "Sorry. I should have kept my mouth shut. I didn't mean to embarrass you."

"You didn't embarrass me." His hand, still resting on her arm, squeezed gently. "I like that you stood up for me and my vehicle. I wouldn't be caught dead in a ratty blue van." He grinned.

She was relieved. "Perhaps that should be a regular interview question from now on: what sort of vehicle do you drive?"

"Yes, well, right now, ma'am, I'm in my very cool polar white Sound Alchemy van, but once I'm working for you, I'll be dragging my shitty blue Jeep Cherokee out of storage. That oughta rile 'im up!"

They laughed. Then the air went out of their stress-humor. She pulled her arm from under his hand, reaching for a napkin to clear around her coffee cup. "That was ... bizarre."

"Life in America."

"How do you deal with it?" She shook her head. "How do you keep from putting your fist through a wall?"

"You want to sometimes. But you have to keep it in perspective. My father used to say, 'Take each thing on its own. Don't let it trigger the entire history of racism.' Which made sense to me. Keeps things manageable. If I let every asshole get under my skin, I'd be in a strait-jacket and I'm strictly a T-shirt guy." He gave her a doleful smile, still trying to defuse the tension.

She didn't smile back. "Well, that's shitty."

"Yeah ..."

He signaled the waitress for the bill.

THIRTEEN

HE PICKED UP THE TAB, DESPITE HER INSISTENCE THAT IT was company business, then asked if he could walk her home. Strolling through the trendy Andersonville neighborhood, with its Swedish flair and charming boutique culture, took them from the commercial district of Clark Street to the residential blocks nearby. Chris glanced around as they walked, taking in the ambiance of historic brick buildings and vintage homes surrounded by budding trees and the green of advancing spring.

"Nice neighborhood," he commented.

"It's always been one of my favorites."

"I can see why. Some really great houses. Like that one there." He pointed to a bungalow with large beveled windows and a wraparound porch set with wicker chairs and tables. "Bet there's lots of stories to see there."

She glanced over to the house. "How do you mean?"

"I don't know. It just looks like one of those houses where life would be interesting." He turned to her. "Do you ever do that thing where you walk by a place and your eye catches something, just some little interaction between people inside, or out on the porch, and for a flash it touches you? That thing of 'gazing upon life we don't know and gaining perspective from the view.' I read that somewhere and it stuck with me."

"You sound like some of the philosophy majors I knew in college." She laughed.

"Yeah?" His grin was sheepish. "My mom says I'm just nosy."

"I'd say you have a unique view of life." She stopped for a moment, gazing upward. "My thing has always been the sky. When I was a kid, my friends and I would lay out in this vacant lot near our house just staring up, naming constellations, yelling out whenever we spotted a shooting star. We were regular astronomy groupies."

"That's an iconic childhood picture," he remarked.

"Isn't it?" She started walking again and he kept pace. "During middle school this poetry professor from Northwestern came out to read from her book—she'd just been published and we were *thrilled* to meet someone famous. But when it turned out her favorite poem was this piece called, 'I Tilt Toward the Sky,' I became her little fan girl. Felt like it was written just for me. Her name was Jovana Stanton—did you ever hear of her? She was high profile for about a minute. Oprah even had her on her show once."

"No, but can't say I follow poetry much. Or Oprah." He grinned.

"'I look to my feet to . . . to keep from falling' . . . or stumbling . . . or something like that. I can't remember all the words. Anyway, I still think about her almost every time I walk out the door because I'm one of those people who always 'tilts toward the sky.' It's just a habit now. I even keep the curtains open in my bedroom so I can see the moon and stars at night." She turned to him with a smile. "So I guess we both have our observational quirks."

He looked at her with new appreciation. "That's a nice visual: you wrapped in a blanket, gazing out the open window, stars glittering, moon lighting up the room . . ."

"Now you sound like a cinematographer." She laughed again. "How did you end up in sound?"

"Hermes. He basically opened up that world to me."

"He's your brother-in-law?"

"Yeah. I'd go to his studio and stand at the mixing board listening to him do his thing, and what he could do with great music was undeniable. It was when he worked on something uninspired that he really spun his magic. He has this amazing ability to turn something less, even something completely shitty, into something . . . I don't know, *better.* Maybe even great. That was a revelation to me, that transformational power. He calls it 'the alchemy of noise.'"

"Is that how you came up with the name of your company?"

"With a little spin." He smiled. "Anyway, I think whether you look up, or look around, or run sound, or whatever you do, it's about paying attention to what comes your way, you know? You do what you can to enjoy it, or make it better, or even just notice it. It's a pretty interesting world."

Sidonie watched Chris as he talked, thinking, *He's the most unusual man I've ever met.*

When they reached a row of relatively new townhouses whose curb appeal included ornate iron gates and brick patchwork exteriors, Sidonie stopped. "This is me."

"Nice. Which is yours?"

She pointed to the right. "Second to the last. I've got a really nice couple on the left and a cranky old shrew on the right, but generally it's a good mix around here." She pulled out her keys. "Thanks for walking me home, Chris. I'm really looking forward to working together." She reached out her hand; they shook.

"Me, too. I'll be in your office at nine thirty tomorrow."

"Perfect. See you then!"

He waited as she bounded up the stairs and unlocked the door. A quick wave and she was in. As he headed back to his polar white Sound Alchemy van, he knew he'd be thinking about her the rest of the night.

FOURTEEN

THE STARBUCKS OFF ROUTE 12 HAD TO SUFFICE AS A
meeting spot. Cleaning crews were doing a scrub-down of Marian
Frame's condo before she put it on the market, so there was no getting together there.

Sidonie had decided, despite her unwieldy schedule and the unavoidable battle with late morning traffic, to make the drive up from
the city. Cold drizzle had begun to fall over the last hour, mucking
things up even further, but she was so galvanized by the notion of her
mother leaving the state that she opted to brave it all.

Like many northern suburbs, Palatine exuded an insistently beige,
generic curb appeal—or *unappeal*, depending on one's aesthetics. Growing up there, as self-absorbed as children and teenagers are wont to
be, Sidonie rarely took notice of the town's homogenized ambience
and demographics (which skewed disproportionately Caucasian), but
every time she returned, after years in the grit and diversity of Chicago,
Palatine paled by comparison, literally and figuratively. As she pulled
into the mini-mall parking lot, surrounded by more variations of off-
white than she imagined possible, it struck her that moving somewhere with a wider color palette might, indeed, offer her mother an
epiphanous experience.

Once hugs and kisses were dispensed, Sidonie nursed her usual
latte while Marian, donned in Florida-ready white pants ("Even this
early in the season!" she'd chortled), lit into a yogurt parfait with a
side of croissant.

"I hate to say it," Marian remarked sotto voce, "because I know I should be supporting our local business owners, but I'd rather eat here than that Greek joint down the street."

Beige, Mom, so, so beige. "Papa Yanni's? Have you actually eaten there? It's really good."

"One time and that was enough. Everything tasted like olive oil. Anyway, enough about food. How are you, sweetheart?"

"I'm fine. Busy. The club's crazy, I'm working in a new sound manager, so there's a lot going on."

"And I have no doubt you're handling it like the pro you are! Is anything new happening with your restaurant?"

"Patsy has a prospect on the line. They've got us jumping through some hoops, but it's still early."

"You look tired. I worry about you, honey. Are you making time for yourself? *You* time? So important not to let that go!" Marian was a big believer in the self-sustenance school of discipline these days, not surprising given her twenty-plus years of servitude to a demanding family.

"I'm working on it, Mom. I take walks when I can, I eat okay, whatever. But today is about you. Big news, this Florida thing!"

"Isn't it?" Marian's grin lit up her entire face. Sidonie noted that her mother looked younger than she had in years, manifesting as a remarkably fit, gently aging matron who would blend perfectly in the Sunshine State.

"I'm excited for you, Mom, but I have to admit: I never thought both my parents would end up out of state. We're truly orphans now," she remarked with a wistful smile.

"Well, I can't possibly speak for your father, but I plan on getting back here often enough. And won't it be fun for all of us to have a new place to spend time together? As you know, I've never been that fond of the state with all its retirees and that crazy weather, but I decided— for Steve's sake—to jump in full steam ahead. But I told him I don't care what it costs, I want a big place near the water. After sixty years of snow and ice and tornadoes and all that baloney, I want warm ocean breezes and coral shells. Though I do worry about hurricanes, so we'll just see. But wherever we end up, it's a new chapter for the whole family!"

Sidonie reached out and grabbed her mother's hand. "Mom, just know this is all yours—you deserve it, and I couldn't be happier for you. And yes, it'll be fun to have a reason to get to Florida. I've never been and it's about time. I'll miss you, but we'll set you up on Skype, maybe even get you a Facebook page so you can post all the photos you'll be taking. We'll probably end up knowing more about each other than we do now."

"Oh, honey, that would be so nice. And Steve really is the most wonderful man, that much I know." Again, she beamed.

Though Sidonie and Karen had spent little time with their mother's boyfriend in the two years they'd been dating, what time they'd spent had been pleasant enough. "He seems like a pretty great guy."

"I'm glad you think so. Because if he didn't pass muster with you girls, I wouldn't have a thing to do with him!" She laughed, then leaned in with a tender expression. "And when does Sidonie have a happy relationship again?"

"I'm fine, Mom."

"Are you even dating anyone?"

"No, but honestly, I don't have time."

"There's always time for love."

"Very romance novel, but I really *don't* have time—not even to find someone, much less wrangle a relationship."

"There must be at least *some* nice men who come into your bar!"

"It's not a bar, Mom, it's an event venue."

"Whatever it is, isn't that a possibility?"

Sidonie immediately flashed on Chris, then shoved the thought right off her mental screen. "Never a good idea to get involved with customers. Or employees. So it's tough. You need opportunity and right now I don't have any. But don't worry about me, Mom, really. It'll get sorted out. Now, what exactly is the timeline of this big move?"

They got back to discussing Florida and by the time Sidonie was in her car maneuvering rain-slicked roads back to the city, she made melancholic note that her mother's life was far more exciting at the moment than her own.

FIFTEEN

WITH TROY AND HIS CATALOGUE OF MISERIES REMOVED from the equation, life at The Church glided toward something smoother and less dramatic, allowing productivity—and morale—to soar. There was a frenzy of high-profile events booked, five different celebrity performances, and one unexpectedly viral publicity campaign (with a magazine cover and interviews inclusive of Sidonie and "the new sound manager"). Concurrently, the process of working Chris into the mechanics of the operation was ongoing and remarkably seamless.

He and Jasper immediately fell into a rhythm that was efficient, good humored, and, particularly from Frank's and Sidonie's points of view, refreshingly dependable. Chris's talent was evident from day one, when he worked with Jasper to rehang and recalibrate the sound system to maximize the room's acoustics. The improvement was immediate and Frank, once again, admitted the folly of his complacency with Troy. There were nights when Andrew, the young and capable standby, was required when Chris had no choice but to work a Sound Alchemy gig, but the overall trajectory of his induction was uncomplicated.

Sidonie felt as if the assembled team had coalesced into something they'd never actually had before: a fully functional workforce. Even Al took a liking to Chris, who, unlike most other staff, found the barman's bombast "pretty damn funny," as he remarked to Sidonie. The managerial unburdening that resulted from all this collegiality allowed

Sidonie to participate more effectively with Patsy on the proposed blueprints. Which was good, since Patsy frequently mentioned her desire for more help. Their next pitch was coming up in three weeks.

Sidonie cautiously considered that she might be entering her own new chapter.

It was Thursday morning when Frank stopped by her office, a remarkably tidy space of calendars and band posters, with an unwelcomed announcement. "Hey, Sid, I've got a meeting in Evanston and I wanted to give you the heads-up. Troy's coming by this afternoon to pick up his last check. I should be back in time, but wanted to let you know in the event I'm late."

Sidonie looked up from her computer, brows knitted. "Why did he leave it sitting here for so long? I thought he was broke."

"I guess he—"

"And why didn't we just send it to him? Wouldn't that have been easier for everyone?"

"Slow down, kiddo! I wanted the chance to talk to him in person. As you know, our last call didn't go so well. All I've gotten since then was a text saying he'd be out with a band for a couple of months and would get in touch when he got back. He's back, he got in touch, and he's coming by today. In and out."

"Well, that sucks for me, Frank! I don't want to deal with him. Why didn't you set it up for a time when you *could* be here?"

"Because now, apparently, he does need his check. And relax. I should be back in time, but either way, I left it behind the bar so Al can take care of it. You won't even have to see him."

But she did, it turns out, have to see him. Because at approximately two thirty in the afternoon Troy was standing at her office doorway, leaning on the jamb, check envelope in his pocket and smirk on his face. He looked exactly like he'd been on the road for a couple of months: everything about him was rumpled and reeking of alcohol.

"Hey there, Sid," he drawled. "Long time no see. How ya doin'?"

"Just fine, Troy." She gave him a terse nod. "And you?"

"Better now that I got another gig."

"I'm glad you found something. Hope it goes well." She kept her eyes on the computer screen but felt a low hum of threat in his posture.

"Do you? I kinda doubt that. I don't think you give a fuck how it goes. You don't give a fuck about me at all, never did."

"Troy . . . let's just keep this civil, okay—"

"Always sabotaged me with Frank, always tryin' to make me look bad whenever you could—"

Sidonie's heat finally rose. "Oh, I didn't have to try too hard, buddy. You managed that just fine on your own."

Suddenly he was in the room, the door shoved closed behind him. Her alarm was immediate.

Swaying at the side of her desk, he leaned in with a sneer. "You're a fucking bitch, you know that? I've wanted to say that to your face for a long time. I know it wasn't Frank's idea to fire me."

Her adrenaline pumped, Sidonie got up from the other side of the desk and moved stealthily toward the door, but before she could get there, he lurched in her direction, grabbed her arm, and yanked, hard. He leaned in close, his breath fetid, eyes red-rimmed and hazy.

"It was you who wanted me out, wasn't it? You never liked me, I don't know why. I gave my all to this place, but you had to wiggle that cute little ass, which is probably the only reason you got this job—"

"Take your hands off me, Troy, right now!" she said through clenched teeth.

"You think it's cool to fuck with someone's life? Fuck with someone's job, just cuz he had a bad night or two?" He was wheezing now.

Though he still held tightly, it was clear he was flagging. Sidonie tensed to make another run for the door when it abruptly swung open and Chris charged in. Without a word, he grabbed Troy by the back of the neck, applying just enough pressure to change the dynamics of the situation. His instructions were calm and cold as ice.

"Take your hands off her, Troy."

"Fuck you, man, I—"

Chris squeezed harder, until Troy howled and let go. Sidonie stepped quickly to the corner of the room as Chris shoved his blubbering predecessor out the door and toward the front entrance. By then Al had leapt from behind the bar.

"Troy, man, what are you doing?" He was dumbfounded. "This is not the way to handle things! Have some dignity, man!"

"Fuck you, asshole!" Troy slurred. "You're a joke and everyone knows it." As quickly as Al's face dropped, Troy rolled it back. "Aw, Al, buddy, I'm sorry. I'm just real fucked up right now and that bitch needs some—*ow!*"

Still clamping Troy's neck, Chris maneuvered his charge through the lobby, where Jasper stood with the door open.

"You fucking traitor!" Troy hollered at Jasper. "I should've never—"

A quick shove from Chris and Troy was out the door; he stumbled and almost fell to the sidewalk.

"You're done here, you got that?" Chris's voice was hard as stone. "You know goddamn well why you were fired, so don't come in here blaming the woman who runs the show. I don't know you, you could be a great guy when you're sober, but if I ever see you or hear of you harassing or bothering or, God forbid, laying another hand on her again, I will personally kick your ass so hard you won't sit at a soundboard for a year. You got me?"

Al and Jasper looked at Chris with a mix of shock and admiration.

Troy gave him the finger and shuffled down the sidewalk.

Al yelled out: "Get a cab, buddy. Do not get in your car."

Troy repeated his hand gesture, then turned the corner, out of sight.

SIXTEEN

THE ENSUING NIGHT PROCEEDED AS PLANNED, BUT TROY'S incursion, with its threat and reality show trashiness, provided drama worthy of wild analysis and conversation. Frank was mortified when he heard the news, offering to intervene in some legal way, but Sidonie absolved him of fault, asking only that Troy be officially banned from the club, which he was. Al and Jasper reiterated the story to every employee (and patron) within earshot, and with energy pumped and events still fresh, the place was abuzz.

Chris, however, just went about his work with no further discussion. At one point before the show started, he took a break and walked to Sidonie's office, where he found her on the computer.

She looked up and smiled. "My knight in shining armor. Come in."

He sat down. "You okay? No residual shakes?"

"Some. My arm has a pretty nasty bruise, but I'm okay. That scared me."

"It should. The guy's got a mean streak."

"Thank you for saving me. From what, exactly, I don't know—I don't think Troy would have actually hurt me—but still, you saved me. That's the second time since we met. I'm going to have to start granting wishes or something." She laughed.

"Just did what any sane person would do. I saw him at the bar, saw he was wobbling, so when I noticed your door closed, I figured we had a problem. I'm sorry that happened, Sidonie. No one should have to put up with that kind of bullshit. He might be an okay guy, but he's got some serious stuff to deal with. Good to keep him away."

"We will. He already sent a text profusely apologizing, for what it's worth. I told him to get into a program and get his life straightened out, then blocked his number. Who knows if he'll pull himself together, but he *is* basically a good guy. Just seems to have lost his footing since the divorce."

"No excuse for a man to get physical with a woman."

"No, definitely not. Hopefully he'll figure it out. Just know I'm grateful you stepped in. Thank you."

Chris smiled, stood to leave. "You've now thanked me more than once, and you don't need to again. People do for each other. I was just doin' for you. Maybe someday you'll do for me."

She walked him to the door and was about to say "thank you" again, but stopped just short. She reached out and squeezed his hand. He squeezed back and walked off.

Once more, as if on ridiculous cue, Officer Mike Demopoulos appeared with a drink. "I promise I'm not stalking you! Al suggested I bring this over. Said you could probably use it."

She couldn't help but smile. Al was clearly trying to be sweet, and Mike, with his mopey eyes and goofy grin, was all good-hearted intentions. "Thanks, but I'm not quite ready for cocktails."

"He said you wouldn't be. It's sparkling lemonade. Said that's your early drink."

"He's right." Interesting that Al knew, since she usually poured them herself. She gratefully accepted the offering. "Thanks, Mike. And thank him too."

"Will do. And Sidonie, honestly, if you ever find yourself in a situation like that again, don't hesitate to call me." He handed her his card. "Guys like that sometimes come back, and if he knows where you live or how you get to your car at night, he could be a problem waitin' to happen."

"Thanks, I appreciate it, but I don't think Troy's going to be any further problem. But I'll hang on to your card. Hopefully I'll never need it."

"Well, you *could* always call if you wanted to grab a bite or something." His grin was somewhere between shy and crafty.

"Thanks, but I'm pretty busy these days." She smiled. "But I will hang on to it."

They stood awkwardly for a moment, then Sidonie walked into her office and shut the door.

SEVENTEEN

THE TIME HAD COME WHEN SUMMER AND ITS ONSLAUGHT of weather-related torments dominated every conversation. Chicago heat, as one learned early in Midwestern life, arrived with its own character, a particular weight and density that bore down like an oppressor, rendering one enervated and sticky as a matter of routine. It allowed insufficient air or space or room to move, at least not without raising one's body temperature, which was always, *always*, to be avoided.

Weather, in fact, had been a persistent plaint of Sidonie's adult life. Every summer she fantasized about moving to Maine or someplace where humidity was nonexistent and temperatures remained temperate; every winter she longed for snow-free terrain and the absence of Lake Michigan's tundra winds. And every year she stayed put, reveling when autumn leaves turned or spring renewal left her conveniently amnesic about four-foot drifts or core-melting heat . . . until one of those weather events rolled in again.

The hot one had rolled in. Even with air-conditioning at peak output, sheets kicked to the floor, and a cool washcloth on her forehead, she was in full swelter and incapable of sleep. The curtains were wide open, as they always were, her bedroom high enough off the street to allow privacy, and as she looked toward the sky and noticed it shimmering in the heat rising from below, the sensation of being parboiled was fierce.

She got up and lurched downstairs to the kitchen, grabbed a diet root beer, and enjoyed the sixty seconds it took to quaff, the only sixty seconds she'd enjoyed in the last couple of hours. A broken latch on the glass cabinet that had dangled from its hinge since last week suddenly provoked her attention; she grabbed a screwdriver and remedied its disrepair. Once done, and heated by the activity, she threw herself on the couch to try reading, but the light, ridiculously, felt too much like sun. Exasperated, she clicked it off and leaned back, closing her eyes in a valiant effort to quiet her mind, which allowed the most recent of dramas to swim into focus:

Theo had finally caught up with her. Despite her ex-husband's relentlessness, she'd been able to duck him by simply never answering his calls, but when she picked up the landline in her office that morning, it was his voice on the other end.

"Sidonie, please don't hang up. I know you're avoiding me and I completely understand, but—"

"If you completely understand why are you still calling? I'd think the message was clear."

"It is, and I respect that, but—"

"Not enough to keep your distance."

"Sid . . ."

"What do you want, Theo? You've got me on the phone now. What do you want?"

"I want to talk."

"I don't. What else? Do I owe you money? Do you owe me money? Are you in prison? Is there a death in the family? Do you have a terminal illness? What? I'm very busy."

"Jesus, Sid, I get it! You hate me—"

"I don't hate you. I'm just over you, with nothing left to say."

"*I* have something left to say. It may not change one ounce of what you think of me, but I owe you an amends and I want to make it."

Sidonie's eyes rolled. While she was always supportive when an addict—any addict—reached out for help, Theo's particular brand of roller-coastering rehab over the years had left her largely immune to his amends and apologies. Still, she figured it was only charitable to extend the benefit of the doubt.

"Okay, Theo. That's fine. I accept your amends—"

"I haven't made it yet."

She took a beat, annoyed with the pace of this call. "Fine. Please go ahead and let's get this done."

"I'd like to see you face-to-face. I feel like doing this over the phone is chicken-shit. Can I take you to lunch today? You gotta eat . . ."

Sidonie had the feeling that, in his earnest state, Theo was going to draw this project far beyond what she was willing to endure. Odds were good giving him one hour was her best bet.

"Fine. Meet me at Charlie's at one."

"Can I swing by and pick you up?"

"No. I'll see you there." The last thing she wanted was for those at the club who'd known of her situation with Theo—Al, Jasper, Frank— alerted to his reemergence. Questions and advice would surely follow and there'd been enough of that during the divorce.

LATER, SEATED ACROSS from the only man she'd ever married for the first time in over a year, Sidonie couldn't help but notice that Theo was thinner and looked pale and somehow empty, as if the life force had been sucked out of him. Maybe it was giving up drugs. Maybe he was sick. But whatever it was, he was still the best looking man she knew and, despite no longer loving him, she couldn't help but feel a trace of emotion. She ordered a small salad and gave him the floor.

"You look great, Sid. You must be doing well."

"Thanks. I am. Listen, I don't have much time—"

"This is all it is: I wanted to say that I'm sorry, really sorry, for what I put you through. I was an unbelievable prick, in every way a man can be a prick, and I honestly regret every minute of it. I've been clean and sober for eight months. I go to regular meetings that I'm vigilant about and will continue to be vigilant about, and I'm doing everything in my power to fix everything I broke. You, of course, being the most important."

"You didn't break me, Theo. I'm not something for you to fix." She noticed him check the urge to sigh.

"I know, Sid, I know. I just meant what I broke between us. I want to fix that."

"I don't think that can be fixed."

"No . . . I know. But maybe. . . maybe we could let go of it all and find a different way to be friends."

His sincerity was novel, but still . . . *friends?* "Or maybe we could just get on with making the best of our lives from a distance."

He took a pause as if weighing the option. "If that's the best we can manage."

"I think it is, Theo. But thanks, seriously. I imagine that was hard for you."

"Actually, it wasn't. It's something I've wanted to say for a long time. And I mean it, every word, even if it sounds sort of trite."

"It doesn't."

"Sidonie, you were such a good friend to me, a good wife, and you put so much into our marriage when I didn't. I don't know how to make up for that. I guess I can't. But if there is any way, or anything I can ever do for you, I'm there. If you need anything, want anything, just call. I'm working for a multimedia company in Highland Park. I've got a new condo. I spend my nights going to meetings, my days going to work. That's it. No girlfriends, no partying, no hanging out with the old gang. I'm like a monk now and I plan to keep it that way."

She finally smiled. "You're allowed to have a life."

"I know. I'm just not ready. Anyway, call me if you ever want to talk or grab a cup of coffee. Mostly, just know I'm really sorry. You didn't deserve any of that. You didn't deserve an asshole like me." He stood up. "And now I'm going to leave so you don't feel the need to make conversation. Thanks, Sid. I'm glad things are going well for you."

With that, he put a fifty on the table and walked out.

REHASHING THE EVENT left Sidonie sad and conflicted. His presentation had surprised her. She'd expected more pleading and begging for forgiveness, more histrionics. That was his usual way. What she got was a mature, undefended apology from a man clearly trying to rebuild his life.

Dammit.

Without him to hate, without that comforting wall of rage to lean on, what did she have of her marriage? The heartache of losing the only pregnancy she'd ever had? The ache and embarrassment of their raucous, vile battles, too often fought in public view? Remnants of betrayal and shame? Hating him gave her focus. Now she had nothing but regret.

For some reason pondering Theo led to thoughts of Chris. She sat up, startled. Why did that happen? What did it mean? There was no parity there. Chris was not a man with whom she'd have a relationship. Yet his face popped up, followed by a feeling of . . . what? Some harmonic of desire? Not sexual desire, surely, but what? A desire to connect, a desire for friendship? She didn't know. It was confusing.

She'd thought often of the day he intervened during Troy's assault. It thrilled her, Chris's impulse to defend her, to keep her safe. Likely it was just male conditioning, the response of a good man to a woman in peril, but it happened to *her*, and it had been *him*, and that put something between them. It bonded them.

She could tell he felt it too. She often looked up to find him gazing her way. She felt his concern when rowdy customers got too close for comfort. He always asked if she wanted coffee when he was grabbing a cup, if he could get her a sandwich when the Cuban truck rolled around. Al even teased her one night—"Ooh, I think Chris has a crush on someone!"—but she ignored the comment as she ignored most things Al said.

Certainly she knew that even if she *was* interested, it was completely inappropriate for her to even flirt with the idea of flirting. As good as it might feel, as fun as it might be, it was misguided given her position at the club. Besides, she was (pretty) sure it wasn't about being attracted to *him*. It was about being attracted to his kindness. His calmness. His thoughtfulness. She didn't know many men who led with those traits.

A new thought popped up—what would happen if she called?

How would he be on the phone? Would he be one of those guys who could sit for hours, phone tucked close, rambling from one topic to the next while both parties fought sleep and a sense of intimacy pervaded? Probably not. Given how selective he could be in conversation, it was hard to imagine Chris being a phone chatterer.

She checked the clock: twelve thirty and still hot enough to make sleep impossible. He was working at the club tonight; he'd likely still be there, or, if they'd already wrapped, just leaving and in transit. She picked up her phone, found Chris's number, and texted:

> I know it's late and this is random and probably ridiculous, but if you're still around and as uncomfortable as I am, wanna meet for some lemonade at that coffee shop near my house? It's got epic air-conditioning!!!! 😴

Five minutes; nothing. After ten, she dragged herself upstairs and back to bed.

EIGHTEEN

AS SIDONIE SENT HER TEXT, CHRIS WAS RIDING THE ELEVATOR up to Diante's condo, intent on picking up the three remaining boxes he'd left during the move. It was late, he'd just finished at the club, but he still had a key. He'd texted Diante before heading over and was assured Jordan was out with her girlfriends.

But either he'd misread the text or Diante was misinformed, because when he turned the key and opened the door, Jordan was perched on the couch, looking anything but pleased at his arrival.

"You don't knock?" She got up and sidled to the door. A stunning woman with a face and body most men would find worthy of sacrifice, she generally appeared vexed when Chris was in her presence. He wondered if it was something about him specifically, but also considered it could be her resting expression.

"Sorry, Jordan. I texted Diante. He said you were out."

"And you think you can just come in here any time I'm out?"

"No, but if Diante gives me—"

"Let me just state that, as the person who lives here now, I do not appreciate you walking in like *you're* the person who lives here. You do not live here anymore."

He rarely inspired this level of bitchery in women—except, perhaps, his sister—so it was possible this *was* Jordan's permanent state. God help his buddy.

"I'm well aware of that, Jordan, so my hope is to do what I came here to do and never have to bother you again. Or should I come back another time?"

She huffed deeply. "Just get it over with, whatever you're doing."

As he walked from the foyer, he couldn't help but notice the newly appointed living room. She'd turned the place from a man cave into something *Home & Design* might appreciate.

"Wow! Doesn't even look like the same place. You've got some skills, girl!" He figured flattery might ease her ire. It did, if briefly.

"Thank you. Nice of you to notice. It was a lot of work, especially after you two left it like ass, but I take pride in where I call home. So . . . *why* are you here? I'm surprised Diante even lets you."

"What does that mean?"

"Lets you come over, what with your sabotaging behavior and all."

"What are you talking about?" He honestly had no idea.

"Really? I wasn't going to mention it, but he said you were an ass-hole about leaving. Made a big scene, spilled beer all over his stuff and everything. Said you thought he was stupid for *allowing* me to move in." By now she'd worked back to her previous state of vexation. Quashing the ramp-up was critical.

"Jordan, I love my boy, but that is categorically untrue and if that's what he told you, he and I have very different memories of how it went. Yes, I *accidentally* spilled beer on one of his magazines, and, yes, we *did* discuss his readiness to leap into a committed relationship—"

"We've *been* in a committed relationship, so what was your point?"

"I meant *live-in* relationship. But, hey, turns out he was, you were, it's all good, and I wish you both the best."

"Uh-huh." She looked unconvinced.

Chris was overcome by annoyance and exhaustion. He turned toward the bank of closets near the kitchen. "Listen, I left some boxes here, so I'm just going to grab those and get on out. It's been a long day."

She sashayed over to the closet, flung the doors open, and stood watching as he pulled out three large boxes.

"This will take a couple of trips, Jordan."

"Then you better get going. It's past my bedtime."

With his unwieldy cargo and the slow elevator, it took a good fifteen minutes going between the floor and parking levels twice. As he picked up the last box, sweat dripping down his back, he turned to say goodbye. Jordan stuck out her hand, palm up.

"Really? A low-five?" Chris laughed, incredulous.

"No, loser, the key. You won't be needing it anymore."

Right then, right there, Chris was stunned to realize he felt the *tick*. Standing with a black woman, a sister, he felt the *tick*, loud and clear. He took a long breath in, a slower one out, with Jordan staring at him as if he were a madman. Before she could retort, he set the box down, pulled the key off his ring, slapped it to her palm, picked the box up again, and walked out. She slammed the door closed behind him.

When he reached the elevator, in a flash of improbable timing, the door pinged and Diante stepped out. "Chris! My man! Glad I caught you. You got everything you need?"

"Why are you making trouble between me and your girlfriend?"

"What happened?" Diante looked genuinely concerned.

"First of all, you said she was out."

"Ah, she must have called it early." Diante held the elevator door as Chris got the box situated. "Sorry, man. She does not like you."

"And why is that?"

"She . . . well . . ." Diante shifted his position. "She thinks you're 'romantically dysfunctional'—her words, not mine. Says you can't keep a relationship together so you'd rather I stay single so you've got someone to hang with. I know, that's some crazy shit."

"I've kept relationships together." Chris felt oddly defensive.

"Yeah, but you gotta admit, it's been a while. But hey, whatever, that's none of our business—and I told her that, but she won't let it go. Thinks you're not *for* her."

"Not *for* her? What the fuck does that even mean? But maybe it's understandable, since you told her I was 'an asshole about leaving,' dumped beer all over your stuff—"

"She took that out of context." Then he paused. "But beer *was* spilled . . ." He gave Chris a wink.

Chris remained unamused. "Look, I won't be coming around again, believe me, but in the meantime, do me a favor and don't trash-talk me to your girlfriend. Got it?"

"I got it, I got it." Diante's chagrin was clear. "Sorry, man. It was just one of those nights when she was pitching a fit and I thought if she saw how much I wanted her here, so much that I'd even go against my best boy's judgment, she'd ease up on me."

"So you threw me under the bus because you're too much of a pussy to handle your own woman?"

"Naw, it's not like that, it was . . . well, yeah, might be a *little* like that." He grinned.

Chris pressed the down button.

"Sorry, man, really." Diante blocked the door from closing. "We had a rough start and I don't know why I went there. Was feeling evil, I guess. I'll fix it with her."

"Do, don't, I don't care what Jordan thinks. I just want *you* to be straight about me, okay?"

"I'm straight, for real. We good?" Diante reached out for a fist bump.

Chris didn't return the gesture. "I'll let you know later. Just go deal with that mad woman of yours."

Diante grinned. "She is crazy, but, ooh, even you gotta admit, *so* fine—"

The elevator door slid closed as Chris stared at him, shaking his head.

NINETEEN

WITH THE STOP AT DIANTE'S, CHRIS DIDN'T GET DOWN TO his mother's until two thirty. A glance at his phone alerted him of Sidonie's missed message, which left a sting of disappointment. It was too late now for anything but getting boxes stashed and himself to bed.

He opened the garage door as quietly as he could, but the grate of rusty joints echoed in the still of the hour. He stacked the boxes next to his old Jeep Cherokee, leaving just enough room for his mother's car between his and his sister's belongings. Carefully pulling the door shut upon exit, the unavoidable squeak was followed by the glare of the back porch light popping on. Vanessa stuck her head out the door.

"What's with all the racket?" She looked ornery.

Chris had managed to skirt around his sister in the time he'd been at the house. Occasional bumps in the hallway, passing hellos and goodbyes as he came or she went, but long conversations on topics that triggered contention were assiduously avoided, and very little social time ensued. This moment, however, seemed inescapable.

"Did I wake you up?"

"Yes, you did!"

Chris trudged up the steps. "Sorry. Guess that could have waited till morning." He brushed past her into the kitchen. She closed and locked the door.

"Nah, you didn't wake me up. I was up. I can't sleep and my room is a furnace. Damn air conditioner is pathetic."

"It *is* a steamer tonight." Chris stood at the refrigerator, sweat rolling down his cheeks. Pulled out a soda, drained it before sitting down at the breakfast nook. He noticed her dripping glass of iced tea, the bottle of brandy, and a very full ashtray. "You're smoking again? In the house?" Delores enforced a very strict no-smoking policy.

Vanessa plopped across from him. "Nope." She lit one up, waving smoke through the cracked window. "It just looks that way." She gave him a sardonic grin and inhaled so deeply Chris expected asphyxia to follow. Instead, she exhaled with ease and poured a large shot of brandy into her tea, downing it in a hearty gulp.

"Livin' the dream, huh, sis?"

"Oh, yeah . . . me and Ma, we girls like to party all the time." Her laugh was bitter.

Chris studied his sister, pondering her journey to this grim moment. Vanessa had always been a pugilist, a scrapper, never one to back down from a fight or refuse a necessary stand, and the price paid had been harsh. In her early years, like most young girls, she spent time in tight circles of friends reveling in fashion and music and the giggling pursuit of boys, but by college she'd shed what she called her "cultural baby fat" to become a bona fide activist, joining every social justice and human rights club on campus. An outspoken leader, she'd found the niche that drove her professional aptitudes from there. Meeting and falling in love with Hermes was almost an anomaly, tender departure from "the work," as she framed her focus. But once beyond early romance and true maternal devotion, peace was harder to find. The struggle had taken its toll: thinner than usual, her face lined and weary, she was a portrait of discomfiture and defeat.

Chris felt guilty for not making more time to connect. He reached out and squeezed her hand. "Things still pretty rough?"

"You could say that."

"Is it just the situation with Hermes?"

"That's the foundation. I hate being away from my kids." Tears sprang but she shook her head fiercely to stanch the flow. "We'll figure it out."

"How are they taking it?" Her daughter was six; her son, eight.

They were good kids who were very attached to their mother. Chris imagined this was traumatic for them all.

"They're confused. Angry. Don't know why any of it is happening."

"Do you?" It was a strange question, one he regretted the second it left his lips.

"What the hell does that mean? Of course I do! I don't make decisions that impact my kids on a whim."

"Sorry, Ness, that didn't come out right. What I mean is: are you seeing this as a temporary situation, just a break for a while, or are you and Hermes really calling it quits?"

She slumped in her chair, looking small and fragile, an image Vanessa rarely conveyed. Her hair, usually pulled tightly from her face, hung in knotted tendrils as if she couldn't find the energy to attend their mess. She wore an old nightgown likely found in a bedroom drawer, and her face, slick with perspiration, looked as if it had endured hours of tears.

"I don't know," was all she could muster.

"Do you want to talk about it?"

"Not tonight."

"Okay."

"A boy was shot." The abrupt non sequitur startled him.

"What boy?"

"His mother, Cheryl, comes to the shelter. She's one of my cases. Has a rough situation with a live-in boyfriend, but she loves her kid . . . she *really* loves her kid." Her voice choked. "And today her kid got his head blown off."

Vanessa's job encompassed ongoing involvement with a battered woman's shelter in one of the rougher areas south of Hyde Park. It was heartbreaking work with a disappointing ratio of wins and losses.

"I'm sorry. What happened?"

"Just out with some friends at Harsh Park—you know the one up in Kenwood? Same place that girl from Obama's inauguration got shot? Damn if those motherfuckers didn't get Cheryl's boy too!"

"Which motherfuckers? Do they know?" This recurring story, the death of black children, came far too often and was always a gut punch for Chris, who'd spent time playing in many of those same parks as a kid.

"Just some bangers shootin' it up like it was the wild fuckin' west. Three kids were hit but only her boy didn't make it." Vanessa couldn't stop her tears now. "I'm tired, Chris, so damn sick and tired. So yes, I get upset, I get stressed, and it's hard to let it all go when I get home, hard to enjoy the little things like Hermes wants me to. He says my anger is impacting the kids, and you know what I say? *Good*. It *should* impact the kids! They *should* know what's going on in this world, in this city, amongst their less fortunate brothers and sisters. We have a *black son*! That boy has got to know what's out there for him—his life literally depends on it! But the man just hums to himself and says we should focus on the positive and teach them to be good people, as if that's a suit of armor."

As she stopped to take another deep inhale of her cigarette, Chris grabbed the opening.

"But, Ness, I gotta throw in for the guy here. I know, because I've talked to him about it—he's laser focused on teaching your kids how to deal with the world. He's not brushing it off. I think you know that."

"I do. I know." Her voice softened. "And I want that for them too: to be positive and happy . . . but mostly I want them *alive*! I don't *want* to be the bitch railing on about safety and danger all the time. But then I think of that little boy, not much older than our own son, lying in the dirt next to a filthy trash can, his precious head all torn up, his mother screaming his name, and I . . . I . . ." She broke, raw and anguished.

Chris got up to put his arms around her and she held him close, soaking his shirt with her tears.

TWENTY

THE NEXT MORNING DAWNED WITH NO CLIMATIC RELIEF, torpid air forcing every fan in the Hawkins house to do what it could to aid the wheezing, failing air conditioner.

"Ma, we gotta get that repair guy over today. It's nuts in here." Chris, scrambling eggs at the stove, was already dripping.

"I know, I know. I wanted to put it off until my vacation, but this is unbearable. I'll give him a call this morning." Delores was busy getting coffee started.

"Well, it is a fifty-year-old air conditioner." Vanessa walked in looking as bruised as the night had left her. She plunked to a seat at the table. "I think you've gotten your money's worth."

"Good morning, daughter." Delores bent down and kissed the top of Vanessa's head.

"It is morning, that's true." Vanessa patted her mother's cheek. She turned to Chris. "Thank you, brother, for listening last night. I appreciated it."

Delores smiled softly. Chris brought the pan over from the stove to distribute eggs amongst their three plates. "Glad I could help."

"You did. And I have another favor to ask."

A beat. "Okay."

"My BLM group is sponsoring a rally in the park this Friday night, a celebration of this little boy's life and whatever call-to-action speakers we can bring to the stage. We're looking to grab some news coverage, so we're trying to get as much media out there as possible.

The whole thing's growing as the day goes by. I've already had ten phone calls this morning. We've got a stage setup promised, but the guy who was going to do sound just bailed. I know how busy you are, I know it's only a couple of days' notice, but this is real important to me. I need you to come and help us out." She looked at him with pleading eyes and the whiff of expectation.

He stepped back to the stove, trying not to feel manipulated. "Ness, I wish I could, but I've got Melissa Etheridge at the club that night, on top of two big Alchemy gigs to oversee. I'm already spinning more plates than I can handle, so I can't take it on. I'm sorry."

Delores poured coffee for all three, her face set in neutral repose. She was familiar with her children's trigger points and knew this conversation was likely headed nowhere good.

Vanessa shifted in her seat. "Okay . . . you're busy, we're all busy, everybody's busy, but sometimes you have to step up and put your busy life on hold for a minute. Do something important and essential for the sake of a dead child, for the sake of your community, for the sake of the entire fucking welfare of humanity."

"Vanessa." Delores warned. "That will do."

"I know you hate that language, Mother, but sometimes a point needs to be punctuated."

"You can punctuate without vulgarity."

Vanessa glared like a petulant teen. "So, you have no problem letting him off the hook to always focus on what's best for him, never thinking about the greater good or how he might contribute to something outside himself? Is that right, Mother?"

Delores stiffened, but before she could say a word, Chris slammed the frying pan on the stove, startling everyone. He turned to Vanessa with a hard glare.

"See, this is what you do, Vanessa! You take all the goodwill we manage to scrape up between us, and you spin it and twist it and bash the shit out of it however and whenever it suits you, which is usually when the causes of your life don't jibe with mine. And I get it! *I get it, sister*! What you do is important. I support it, as I support you, and if and when I can help, I'm there. But right now I've got all I can handle, all I can do, and that's a lot. A damn lot, sister! I'm on my own path, fighting my own battles for *my* life—yes, *my* life—because my life is as important as yours, as Ma's, as your battered women, as the kids dying in the park. I'm a black man who's built his own business, who employs other black men who need jobs, which allows them to support their families and help keep our community strong and healthy. That, right there, is *my* contribution. It may not be as noble as yours, but it's what I can do, it's what I *am* doing, and I'll be goddamned if I let you make me feel small for doing it!"

He grabbed his bag, bent to give his mother a kiss, and left, slamming the wooden screen door hard behind him.

TWENTY-ONE

CLEANING CREWS MOPPED THE FLOORS THROUGHOUT THE club, a weekly event that kept cleanliness high but did little to blunt the classic scent of beer and alcohol residue endemic to bars the world over. Al claimed it was his "favorite perfume," made all the more pungent by summer heat, but Frank remained less enamored, doing everything he could to rid this particular bar of its redolence. At the moment that meant tables, chairs, and barstools were scattered everywhere, with yellow Wet Floor sandwich signs strategically placed.

Chris came through from the employee parking lot, still churned from his clash with Vanessa, and found himself annoyed by the clutter, dodging through the obstacle course on his way to Sidonie's office. Patsy was seated at the desk when he walked in.

"Well, hi there! I'm Patsy, Sid's partner in crime. If you're looking for her, sit down. She'll be back in a minute."

He sat, wondering who this ebullient woman—with the short red pigtails and odd jacket—was. "I'm Chris, the sound manager."

"Oh, yes, I've heard so much about you! Nice to finally meet you, Chris."

"And you." He thought of asking what she'd heard about him but decided to move on. "What's the crime the two of you are partners in?"

"She hasn't mentioned it to you?" Patsy's eyebrows rose.

"I'm not sure. Depends on the crime."

"That girl is so tight-lipped! I guess she doesn't want Frank to get all twitchy." She leaned in and lowered her voice. "Sid and I have been working on some plans. She hasn't said anything to you?"

"She mentioned something about a club, was a little cryptic about it. I haven't heard too much beyond that."

"That's so like Sid! Anyway, I'm the chef, she's the brains. She tends to be cynical and all 'we'll see,' so I'm also the cheerleader. We're meeting with potential new investors soon, which is why I'm here getting a check for the blueprints we're having sketched out."

"Wow . . . you've already got a place?" He found himself modulating his voice in accord with hers.

"An *idea* of a place. So these will be an idea of how we'd put it together if we actually got the place." She giggled.

"That's exciting. I didn't realize it was that far along. Sounds like she could be striking out on her own soon." Which surprised him. She seemed so dedicated to The Church.

"Who knows? But it's been a dream since college, so we better get going if we want to launch before we're too feeble to run the damn thing." She laughed.

The idea of their launch left him oddly deflated. "What's the timetable?"

"No idea. It's hard to get any place started in Chicago. Competition is fierce and success ratios are deadly. Investors get skittish. We've been close before but nothing panned out. Hopefully this time will be different."

"I wish you luck. I know what it's like starting your own business." Chris stood up. "Well, I've got to get going, so just tell her I'll check in later. Nice to meet you, Patsy."

"Likewise." She waggled her fingers.

Just as he walked out and pulled the door shut behind him, Sidonie came from the kitchen. "Hey you, paying me a visit?" she asked playfully.

"I was. Wanted to say I was sorry I missed your text last night."

"No, no, please." She laughed, embarrassed. "Forget I ever sent that. I think I was out of my mind with the heat. I shouldn't have bothered you so late."

"I was actually out, over at Diante's getting the last of my stuff, and by the time I checked my phone it *was* too late. I would have loved to have met you."

His smile threatened to trigger a blush she wouldn't be able to hide.

"Well, maybe next time. Hopefully the heat will break and I'll actually be able to sleep."

"I just met your partner in crime in there. You mentioned your project, but I didn't realize things were so far along."

Sidonie glanced around to see what personnel might be nearby. The place was largely empty. "It's all very under the radar around here. Frank has some vague idea, but I don't talk about it much. It's been a long slog and I don't want him getting prematurely worried about me leaving. And, honestly, some days I'm not all that enthused. Others, like lately, I get excited again. I guess having new investors interested has that effect! Anyway, I'll share more of the details when we can talk privately. You never know, it might actually happen one day."

She smiled with an expression Chris hadn't seen before: Lightness. Optimism. It suited her.

"I hope so. Anyway, thanks for thinking of me last night."

"Are you okay?" she asked.

"What do you mean?"

"I don't know . . . you seem a little down."

"Nah, just life. I'll check in with you after the show, okay?"

As he walked off toward the stage area, Sidonie made note of how much she looked forward to him doing that on a nightly basis.

TWENTY-TWO

DESPITE PREDICTIONS OF SHIFTING TEMPERATURES AND cooler lake breezes, disappointment reigned as night made no significant improvement over sweltering day. Sidonie sat in her vintage Audi in the parking lot, sweating and irate, making her third attempt to get the engine started. The alternator light kept popping on, indication that lack of timely automotive maintenance had finally played its karmic hand.

She'd been at the club all day, she was bone-tired, and she did not want to wait for a tow. She got out and stomped back inside.

Chris stepped out of the men's room just as she walked in. "I thought you left."

"My car won't start. Do you have jumper cables?"

"In the van. But I'm driving my Jeep tonight. Sorry."

"No problem. I'll check with Al." She walked to the bar; after a brief exchange, she came back, shoulders slumped. "He doesn't have any either. Ugh."

"I can give you a ride home," Chris offered. "If you have a way back in the morning, you can call Triple A then. Or I can grab my cables and take care of it when I get in tomorrow, probably around two."

"Yeah? That would be great. I can always get a Lyft in the morning."

"As long as you don't mind the Jeep. I just pulled it out of storage, so it's filthy, and currently filled with sound equipment."

"If it runs, we're good." She laughed.

~

AS THEY MADE their way through traffic, a blessed breeze picked up; the mood was comfortable, easy. He tuned the radio to his favorite jazz station, and they both moved in rhythm to the music, smiling at each other from time to time. When he made the turn onto Clark from Lincoln, rejecting the more direct route via Lake Shore Drive, she was pleased; it suggested he was looking to maximize their time together.

She leaned back and relaxed, her eyes gazing out the open window. Making their way past Wrigley Field, which, luckily, was dark tonight, the view was quintessential Chicago: lights, color, the palpable sense of energy. It was a panorama Sidonie never tired of. As much as she dreamed of places with less congestion and easier weather, this city, with its deep history and unique Midwestern urbanity, held her heart.

Chris stuck his arm out the window as if to gauge the air temperature. "Sorry about the air-conditioning. I'm still trying to decide if I should fix this beater or break down and get a new one."

"I'm fine," she remarked gamely, her face agleam with perspiration. "It's still better than sitting in the parking lot waiting for Triple A!"

"I heard cooler temps might be coming in."

"Wishful thinking," she said, laughing. "But let's hope you're right. I'm so done with this heat."

"You and me both." He sighed and grew quiet again.

She looked over. "Are you okay? You seemed stressed earlier and I wondered how things were going with balancing your work situation?"

He liked that she asked. "The first few weeks were a little rough, but the new guys are all good so we're getting it worked out."

"I'm glad. I wouldn't want our arrangement making things too hard on you. Is Andrew doing okay?" Andrew had often been needed when Troy was busy imploding; these days he shadowed Chris like a puppy.

"He's a good kid. Eager to learn, very focused. I think he wants to take on more—"

Woot, woot, woot!

The staccato blast of a police siren signaled the presence of a squad car behind them, its strobe swirling in chaotic blue.

Sidonie turned back to look. "Is that for us?"

Chris glanced in the rearview mirror. His jaw clenched. *Tick, tick.* He steered toward the shoulder, hoping they would fly by. They didn't, pulling right behind.

"Goddammit . . ." he said under his breath. He reached into the glove box to grab his registration and insurance card.

After what felt like an interminable wait, two white officers slowly approached, one on each side of the vehicle. Hands on guns, flashlights were angled first on Chris's face, then Sidonie's, alternately scanning the interior of the car.

"License and registration, please," the driver's side officer barked at Chris.

Chris handed both documents through the window. "What's the problem, officer?" *Tick, tick . . .*

Without response, the officer walked back to the patrol car while the other remained stationed at the passenger side, his flashlight holding them both in its beam. Sidonie felt anxious but since this was clearly some kind of mistake, she presumed it would conclude quickly. Chris kept his mind blank, his focus forward, breathing in and out.

The first officer reapproached and handed back the paperwork while giving Chris a fixed stare. "Do you know why I stopped you?"

"No."

"Looks like you've got an obstructed rear view with all that equipment stacked up in your vehicle."

"Actually, it's purposely packed so I can see fine—"

"What is all that stuff?"

"Sound equipment."

"Did you steal it?"

Tick, tick. "No. It's mine. Bought and paid for."

"Do you have the receipts?"

"With me . . . in the car? No."

"Where are you going with all this . . . sound equipment?"

Sidonie finally sat forward, glaring at the questioner. "What is the problem, officer?"

The officer abruptly leaned in. "If I want to hear from you, ma'am, I'll ask. Until then, sit back and keep your mouth shut!" he snapped.

Before she could react, Chris gave her a fierce look: *don't say another word.*

The officer stepped back from the driver's side door. "Get out of the car, sir."

Tick, tick, tick.

Chris opened the door slowly and stepped out. Sidonie shook her head in helpless frustration as the officer spun Chris around and slammed him spread-eagled against the side of the Jeep.

The second officer held his flashlight on Sidonie's face; she kept her eyes down.

After Chris was frisked, roughly, the officer snapped, "Open the back of the vehicle."

"It's locked. The keys are in the car."

"Then get the keys."

Chris walked to the door and carefully reached in; both officers were taut with attention, hands poised on their guns. Sidonie remained frozen in her seat. Chris took the keys and moved slowly to the back of the Jeep.

The second officer held his gaze on Sidonie as he shined his flashlight on the glove box. "You got a pipe in there?"

She looked at him incredulously—*why on earth would there be a pipe in the glove box?*—her first thought being a sink pipe. Then it struck her. He meant crack pipe. *Dear God* ... "No, absolutely not!" She suddenly hoped that was true.

"Open it."

She wondered if this was allowed, but when she turned to look at Chris, he was occupied with his own interaction. She opened the glove box; the officer reached in and rifled around. Nothing but a small first aid kit, some old CDs, and a flashlight.

"Close it."

She responded like a trained dog, the knot in her stomach grown exponential to her rage.

With the back hatch now opened, the first officer kept Chris in his sights while he ferreted through the speakers and cable bags inside. "And whose equipment is all this?"

"Again, mine." Chris's throat was tight, his mind blank. *Breathe, stay contained.*

"You must be rich, to have all this equipment . . . though not many rich assholes would drive a piece of shit like this. Are you sure you didn't lift this stuff from a club or the back of somebody's garage?"

"I'm sure." His mouth was so dry he could barely swallow.

"Why do you have all this? Seems like a lot more than your average boom box or ghetto blaster or whatever you people are monkeying around with these days."

Tick, tick, tick. "I'm a sound engineer." His voice was flat, no affect, nothing to trigger response.

"Is that right? I didn't think guys like you worked that end of the business. Aren't you usually the ones out front playing the blues or doing that Snoop Doggy Dog shit?"

Tick, tick, tick.

Sidonie's eyes filled with tears, overwhelmed.

At Chris's silence, the officer continued: "Okay, so you're not a hip-hopper. Good for you. Maybe you got better taste than the rest of them. Where is it you do this sound engineering?"

"At The Church. I'm the sound manager there. The woman in the car is my boss. I'm taking her home because her car broke down. I own two vans for my company, Sound Alchemy, but they're both out on private jobs, which is why I'm using my personal vehicle. It's been in storage, which is why it's dirty at the moment."

"Okay, okay, we're gettin' the whole life story here!" He turned to his partner and chortled. He stepped around Chris and walked to the passenger side, leaned in toward Sidonie. "Now, you seem like a nice girl. If you can corroborate Lionel Richie's story here, you'll both be on your way."

His partner again shone the light in her face. "This guy works for you at The Church?"

"Yes." She kept her eyes fixed forward.

A pause.

"All right then!" the first officer declared. "We're good to go! Now take your boss straight home, Lionel, and no funny stuff. We don't want any sexual harassment calls coming in later . . . you know how those 'me too' gals can be. Have a lovely rest of your evening."

They sauntered back to the squad car and pulled slowly out and away.

TWENTY-THREE

IT WASN'T UNTIL CHRIS WAS PARKED IN FRONT OF SIDONIE'S house that either spoke. As she leaned against the door, still shaking, he struggled to quell the rage that had swept in during the encounter. The corner streetlamp flooded the interior of the Jeep, making them both appear as wan and jaundiced as they felt.

"Sidonie, damn . . . I am so sorry . . . I—"

"Don't. Don't dare apologize," she said firmly. "That was *so* not on you."

"But I'm used to that shit. You're not."

Which twisted her, that reality; that he was used to it. She wanted to comfort him. "Would you like to come up for a while? I could make you a cup of tea or something to eat."

"You don't have to do that."

"I want to. I want to end this horrible evening with something nice."

So he did. For the first time, he came up to her house. Sidonie made tea, toast, and a nice spinach and mushroom omelet. They sat in the living room—he, on the couch; she, on the rug at the side of the scrubby coffee table—and ate without conversation, finding familiar comfort in their silence.

Finished, Chris leaned back, hands on his stomach. "So good, thank you. And you say Patsy's the chef?"

Sidonie laughed. "If you thought that was good, she'd slay you. A regular culinary wizard."

"Nice way to feel about your partner." He looked around. "I like your place. It's . . . tasteful."

She had to smile, flashing on Patsy's withering critique of her barren quarters. "Interesting way to put it. I keep meaning to do more, but never get around to it."

"Hey, I'm bunking in my childhood bedroom at thirty-four." He laughed.

"But that's temporary. Has to lessen the sting."

"Yeah, I just need to carve out some time to find a place."

"Then I'm sorry we've made your schedule so demanding. I'm sure it would be easier if you didn't have to drive down to Hyde Park every night. That's a slog."

"But I do get home-cooked meals," he said, grinning. "As long as my sister's not around too much, it's a peaceful little break."

"Tell me about your sister. Why are you guys so at odds . . . or whatever it is that happens?"

Chris thought back to the melee of the morning, which now seemed days ago. Vanessa sent a text apologizing for "having my latest meltdown at your expense," and, as always, Chris let her off the hook. But the cycle was repetitive, making the gaps between them larger each go-around.

"Vanessa's a force of nature. That's a trite phrase, but with her it's true. She's fierce, with a big heart, a *huge* heart, but sometimes her 'full-body immersion in the sea of empathy,' as my brother-in-law puts it, is tough on us mere mortals. But she's always been that way. Passionate, committed, but defensive, so defensive—and really easy to set off. Maybe it's being the youngest—and a girl—in a family of two boys. Maybe it's that both my parents had a sort of 'live and let live' philosophy she bumped up against, but there's something in her DNA. Built for battle."

"You said she has two kids. Has that softened her any?"

"Some. She has her moments. She can laugh and enjoy herself with them. She's a good mom. It's more that everything with her is BIG. Everything is all-in. My dad used to say, 'Pick your battles,' but *everything* is a battle with her, whether it's BLM stuff or the third-grade bake sale. I get tired of it, personally. I think Hermes does too, which is probably why she's at the house these days."

"Hermes is her husband, right? The studio guy?"

"Yes."

"And he's not like that?"

"No." Chris smiled thinking about his brother-in-law. "Hermes is the mellowest person I know. When he and Vanessa got together, I hoped some of his mellow might rub off on her, but I think the opposite happened—her fierce burned him out."

"That's too bad. It sounds like you like him."

"I do. Lots of reasons why. He kind of reminds me of my dad."

"Does he? What's your dad like?"

Chris sat up and drained the last of his tea. "My dad died a few years back. He and my older brother, Jefferson, were killed in a car accident not long after I graduated from college."

Sidonie's responsive shock was both because the gravity of his statement conflicted with the matter-of-fact way in which he said it, and because she'd never known anyone who'd suffered such a profound tragedy. "God . . . Chris . . . I am so sorry. How devastating, especially at that particular moment of your life."

His face clouded, as it always did when he thought of them. "Pretty much changed me from there on."

"How could it not?"

"Yeah . . ." He sat in stillness for a moment. "Made me more serious. Like it was all on me to do right by the family—the only man left, that sort of thing. I lost some of my humor, my ability to enjoy life. I wish I could downplay it, but it was brutal. Still is."

"You can't downplay something like that. It's as shattering as it gets."

"I idolized my brother. He was five years older, literally my best friend. He was in med school at the time, really smart. I always wanted to impress him, to be like him—hell, that old Jeep was his. It's the only reason I keep it around. And my dad was . . . well, he was just a good guy. A tough guy, for sure. A hard worker, completely honest about the bullshit of life, but always said he felt lucky for everything he had, especially all of us."

"What did he do?" she asked gently.

"He was a landscaper. He and my mom met when they were both on scholarship at the University of Chicago working their way through school. He was originally an assistant to the groundskeeper, then took some courses in landscape design and found his calling. He took over the department when his boss retired and ended up being there the rest of his life. He loved the job, loved working near my mom, and we kids got tuition benefits, so it was a good deal all around. He also liked keeping us close, said it made him less afraid about us being out in the world."

Sidonie felt the weight of his memory with its tentacled arms of grief. She was struck by the fact that she could say nothing as moving or loving about her own father, who was alive, up the road, and hadn't shown interest in her in years. "He sounds pretty special."

"He was. He was that strong father figure who demanded we be strong, but taught us how to find our equilibrium too. Said being a black man in America meant knowing when to pause, when to protect yourself, when to hold ground, and when to kick ass. But he always said to breathe first. I have to remind myself of that pretty much every day. Like tonight."

"Yeah . . . lots of breathing tonight." She got up to pour more hot water in his cup.

His eyes followed her. "Have you ever lost anyone?"

"Not like you. Three of my grandparents are gone, but that's not the same. I guess the closest I got was losing my baby."

"Damn, Sidonie, I didn't know you lost a child!"

"It was a pregnancy. I was five months along, everything was fine, then one day I started bleeding and didn't stop until I wasn't pregnant anymore. It was about a year before my divorce."

"That had to be tough."

"It was. For a long time. It was a little girl." She sat back down on the carpet, somber. "But the truth was, I was conflicted about being pregnant. I'd just started building the event business at the club and was really busy, really pushing myself, and things with Theo were already dysfunctional. I wasn't convinced bringing a baby into that mix was a good idea. But things slowly evolved; I started getting all happy about it, then, boom, she was gone. Theo acted devastated, but I didn't buy it. I think it was just an excuse for him to get high. That was pretty much the beginning of the end for us." She looked at him with a woeful smile. "And that's my sad story."

"We all get our sorrows, as my mom says. Hopefully you can try again someday—I mean, if you wanted to and had the right situation." Awkward, he got up and stretched.

But she was touched. "Maybe . . . we'll see. Life is too hard to predict. I don't even try anymore."

"Ain't that the truth?" He sat back down on the couch, restless, though not sure why. He was comfortable being there—in her house, with her—but a certain tension had descended.

She could feel the chemical shifts and changes, too, subtle and nuanced, poignant, in a way. She felt tenderness for him, protectiveness, which was something she'd never felt for a man before. It was unsettling.

"So what was that about tonight, with the cops?" she asked. "Just harassment?"

"Basically. They saw a black guy in a dirty old Jeep filled with equipment and decided to be assholes. Maybe something to shake up a dull night. Who knows?"

"They can just do that, for no reason?" Her face conveyed skepticism.

Chris looked at her sharply. His impulse was to be frank. On the other hand, easy conversation had its appeal. He opted for middle ground.

"It happens, Sidonie. Most of the time I let it roll off, don't give it too much energy, other times I want to push my fist through a wall, like you said. Maybe even through some motherfucker's face." He smiled grimly. "That's when I feel Vanessa boiling up in me."

She remained pensive. The events of the night had been a regretful revelation. "I don't know how you deal with it. That drunk at the coffee shop was bad enough, but tonight I felt like I was going to explode, sitting there, not moving, not responding, while they acted like bullies with guns. If I felt like that, how did *you* stay so calm?"

"Practice. Lots of practice. I stay calm because they *are* bullies with guns and they can do whatever they want, whenever they want, in a system designed to protect them. I stay calm because I want to stay alive."

"Well, that's a pretty shitty way to feel about the police, isn't it? Being scared of the people who are supposed to protect you?"

Again he looked at her, trying to assess the depth of her naïveté. "Of course it is, Sidonie. But it's a fact of life for men like me."

"Black men?"

"Yes, men of color. Women of color. I'm not saying all cops are like that, but too many of them are. And *I'm* the only one who can protect me, protect my body, protect my life. You learn that fast and early if you don't want to become another statistic."

"I understand, but—"

"You can't understand."

"I'm just saying if that happened to me all the time, I don't think I *could* keep my cool. I'm saying I admire that about you. I've never been stopped for anything but speeding or making a wrong turn—"

"You're a pretty white blonde woman driving a nice car," he remarked dryly.

She wasn't sure how to translate the retort. "I realize that, obviously. I am aware of what goes on out there—how can anyone *not* be? —but I guess I haven't been paying enough attention, because I honestly thought things were . . . I don't know . . . better these days. At least in this part of town."

He cocked his head. "'*This* part of town'?"

She caught the sensitivity breach. "I just mean a part of town that's less crime-ridden, more affluent, more—"

"White?"

Sidonie turned to him sharply. "No! I don't mean that. I mean . . . well, maybe it is more white, but what I mean is, it's an area with lots of open-minded people: artists, liberals, progressives . . ." She stopped, realizing the inefficacy of her explanation. "I can't really address it, can I? It's not my world. I *don't* experience what you do."

"You can't, Sidonie." He got up to put his dishes in the sink.

"There are different rules for white and black America, no matter what part of town you're in or who you are. You may know that intellectually, but your side doesn't get how that translates in real life on our side of the divide. You caught a glimpse of that tonight."

She suddenly felt petulant. "Well, that's pathetic. Shouldn't we be past all that by now?"

He came back to the living room and sat next to her on the floor. "You keep saying things like that, and, I don't mean to insult you, but you sound so naïve. Of course we should! But we're not. Not even close. And I gotta face the world that is. *You* gotta face the world that is. My sister fights to *change* the world that is."

She flopped back on the carpet, staring up at the ceiling, talked out and exhausted. He lay down inches from her, their hands almost touching, both suddenly aware of proximity. In that moment, whatever ease had been between them evaporated, replaced by something jarring and keen. A need, a pull. She was confused; he was curious. They were so close there was heat, and decisions had to be made, right then, one way or another.

A million contradictory thoughts rolled through her mind: *What's happening right now? This is a bad idea ... isn't it? But we could both use some tenderness after the night we've had. He is so sweet but all wrong for me, for so many reasons. But when he looks at me, I feel ... This could jeopardize my job. I've never known a man like him. Do I really want to get into "the complications of all that"? I want him to touch me.*

His thoughts rattled in parallel confusion: *This is crazy. What am I thinking? This could jeopardize the job. Complicating my life right now is not a smart move. She's so beautiful. I want some warmth after the night we've had. Is it the best idea to get involved with a white woman ... and my boss? I don't have time to be responsible for a relationship and this can't be a booty call. I just want to touch her.*

She turned on her side and his body adjusted to face her, leaning in so close, so close, until contact was unavoidable. Their lips pressed and, from there, everything was sensation—mouths opened, tongues collided; saliva and softness and warmth surrendered to appetite, igniting an inescapable, head-rattling, breath-stealing, reason-rejecting tsunami of need that ... crashed ... slowly ... over ... them.

She gasped as he pulled her to him, caressing the length of her body as if he needed to know every inch of the terrain. They broke their kiss only long enough to smile, to whisper each other's names, to return to heat and wetness until all walls tumbled and there was no going back.

His fingers traced her cheek, her lips, her throat, trailing down to find an opening to skin. Warm and probing, he caressed her breasts, her nipples, her stomach, her hips, until his fingers were inside and sensation left her breathless. She kept pace, reveling in the smoothness of his skin, the contours of his chest, the curve of his back. She pressed into his hardness as if she couldn't get close enough, immersing herself in his smell and warmth. They struggled out of clothes, unwilling to let go, taking each other in with the pure pleasure of visceral and sexual discovery. When he spread her legs and enveloped her body, entering her as their eyes met, he smiled, she smiled, and they were swept away.

TWENTY-FOUR

HOURS HAD PASSED; IT WAS HARD TO KNOW HOW MANY.

They lay together in her bed, wrapped in sheets and each other, feeling the high of new and remarkable sex. She'd rejected the moon tonight, pulling the shades closed in a nod to privacy, and in the darkened room they were entwined in the intimacy of post-coital conversation.

"Is this crazy?" she asked softly, running her hand down his cheek, enjoying the feel of his stubble, his skin, the persistence of his touch in response.

"It feels nothing but great to me."

"Yes, but crazy because, well, first of all, you're younger—"

"By one year. Please, woman!" He laughed.

"And you're my employee."

"Is that how you see it?"

"Of course not, but I'm thinking Frank might."

"Is Frank in this bed?"

"No, but he is our boss."

"Does he have to know?"

She paused to think about that. "Not right now, no." She felt an approaching hint of regret. "Do you see this as just a one-off? A little fun between workmates, something we'll do once in a while and no one needs to know?"

"I don't do one-offs, but I do think it's too new for either of us to know what it is or isn't. Don't you?"

She sat up and pulled the sheet around her. "Yes. Actually." She began caressing his hair, noting its texture, the tightness of its curls. He reached up, took her hand, and kissed it. She cocked her head.

He smiled. "Don't you know never to touch a black man's hair?"

She slipped her hand from his. "Are you serious?"

He grabbed it back. "No. But it would be for some guys. Diante would snap your wrist."

"Why?"

"Lots of reasons. For him it's vanity. He takes so long to get his hair just right he doesn't want anyone messin' with it, not even his woman. But it's a cultural thing too. There's a weird curiosity with some white people about what black hair feels like, like you're a specimen for their examination. My mom never liked it when white people touched my head. I didn't understand when I was little, but when I got older, she explained how patronizing, even fetishizing it could be."

"Really? People pat kids' heads all the time. I used to get my head patted, and I didn't think anything of it."

"There's a different spin with black kids."

Sidonie again wondered how much of their disparate worlds would need to be clarified along racial dividers. More than realized, she was discovering. "How so?"

"Okay . . . so, there was this white woman in my mom's office when I was a kid, a nice lady from the suburbs, and she'd say things like, 'Delores, your son is just the cutest little black boy' and actually rub my head, saying it was 'for good luck.' She didn't mean to be ignorant, she just was, and my mother had to tell her, 'Please do not touch my child's head,' which was always an awkward moment."

"But that *is* creepy. Rubbing your head for good luck? I'd feel just like your mother."

"But I actually liked being good luck for someone!" He laughed. "Of course, later on those kinds of things hurt. This white kid in my middle school used to get me in a headlock and rub my hair, calling me 'Brillo pad.' Got all his buddies yelling 'Brillo pad' whenever they'd see me in the hall. That's when my dad taught me about breathing."

"What do you mean by that exactly, 'breathing'? You said something about it earlier."

"Yeah, it was a thing with him. He read a book at some point about defusing anger, said it helped him develop a coping strategy for when shit got real. He'd breathe in and out, real slow, over and over, whenever he felt the 'tick,' he called it, that hit of adrenaline that kicks in when someone's acting a fool. He said he knew if he didn't find a way to calm himself down, he'd either end up in jail or dead. It worked for him and what worked for him, he'd teach his kids."

"Did his technique work for you guys?"

"I don't know about my brother, and surely my sister has little use for anything that self-disciplined. But I use it—I *have* to use it—pretty much every day."

Sidonie peered into his face as he spoke. "It makes me sad that you have to use your father's coping mechanism that often." A pause, then she added with a wan smile, "I promise I won't touch your hair."

He looked at her intensely, then laughed out loud—a big, hearty, tension-breaking laugh. He grabbed her hand, placed it atop his head, and rubbed hard. "Touch it, Sidonie, mess it up. I want you to. I want you to touch any part of me you want. Any part, any time . . ."

He rolled over and met her sad smile with his lips, blanketing her body with his to masterfully change the focus of their conversation.

TWENTY-FIVE

IT WAS NOT AN ORDINARY DAY.

It could pretend to be. It tried. The sun rose in the east. Blue jays squawked their usual morning greetings. Lyft drivers shuffled down below, and the coffee pot dinged at the exact prescribed moment. Still, it took only seconds to realize this was not, in fact, an ordinary day ...

THE MORNING AFTER her first night, in a very long time, of ardent sex, profound conversation, and erotically charged sleep, Sidonie sat at the kitchen counter sipping coffee, roiled in a strange brew of anxiety, regret, and elation. Before she could discern which emotion led the day, her sleep-bedraggled bed partner stumbled into the kitchen.

Having never experienced Chris in such an intimate moment—the classic morning-after encounter—she sat back to fully take it in:

Chris Hawkins. Standing at her counter pouring coffee. His hair a disheveled mess of puffs and curls, his eyes sleep-bloated and blurry, his face stubbly with morning beard. Clad in his jeans, his T-shirt slung over his shoulder, Sidonie realized he was better looking than she'd previously thought. Maybe it was the afterglow. While he couldn't claim Theo's model features, his body was incomparable, his face open and kind, and everything he did with that face and body felt like warm honey. Chris Hawkins ... *here.* How strange and marvelous life could be.

"Good morning," she said, smiling.

"Good morning."

He leaned in and kissed her, his breath scented with toothpaste and coffee. "This is nice." He looked around, having his own leaps of awareness. Morning in Sidonie Frame's townhouse. Coffee in her kitchen. Sidonie Frame. The woman who'd been climbing around his head for months was now here with sparkling eyes, the whiff of shampoo, and every inch remembered. Amazing.

"Would you like breakfast?" she asked. "I think I have some eggs, I know I have bread for toast, maybe a little yogurt?"

"I've got to hit it pretty quick, so coffee will do just fine. Would you like me to drop you at the club early, or do you want to take a Lyft over later? I'm planning to pick up the jumper cables sometime this afternoon."

She'd actually forgotten about her inoperable car sitting in The Church parking lot. "Ugh, that's right. Why don't you do what you have to do and I'll head over later? We can get the car jumped then and hopefully that's all it'll need."

He pulled the T-shirt over his head and patted his hair down as best he could. "I also have to stop by my mom's to pick up some clothes. Does midafternoon work?"

"Perfect. I'll plan to see you about two."

"Make it three. That should give me enough time."

Logistics set, he slipped his bag over his shoulder and stood there, smiling. "Amazing night. Didn't think we could rescue it after our encounter with local law enforcement, but I'd say we did a damn fine job."

She slid off the stool and leaned into his chest, wrapping her arms around his waist. "I'd say we did too." She looked up at him. "And I hope it doesn't make things awkward at the club."

"It won't. We'll keep it private, keep our distance, no problem."

"That sounds very professional. We are nothing if not pros."

Chris cocked his head. "You realize that's just at the club, right? Here? You're all mine." He grabbed her and kissed her like the man he'd been the night before.

TWENTY-SIX

FROM THERE DAYS AND WEEKS UNFOLDED IN THE BLOOM of lust, and the hustle of life and its many assignments: car repairs (Sidonie and Chris), charity events (all staff), pitch meetings (Patsy and Sidonie), celebrity performances (all staff), house packing with Marian (Sidonie and Karen), sibling interactions (Sidonie/Karen, Chris/Vanessa), and, most notably (and specific to Sidonie and Chris), prodigious amounts of sex.

Sex became their occupation.

Raucous, relentless, slam-up-against-the-wall sex, enough to fill coffers left empty by years of denial, neglect, heartache, and isolation. Enough to remind them of what it felt to be ravenous and desired. Enough to rub them raw and rip open new sensations, both physical and emotional.

It was as if they'd just discovered the act and found they couldn't exhaust it—usually at her house, once in her office between sets (the door was locked), twice on the stage after everyone left, four times in the little cubby behind the sound booth, and half a time in her car when they were taking advantage of a thunderstorm that inconveniently broke midway. They were reckless and adventurous as neither had been, in what they did, where they did it, and how often. It was transformative, the drug of choice—urgent, imperative, exhilarating.

But while openly besotted in the bubble of their private domain, they were soldiers of secrecy in the nuts-and-bolts world of real life. No one at work had a clue, their families were unaware, and as her townhouse became their haven, Chris rarely found his way down to his mother's. Reluctant to reveal the reason for his absence, excuses piled up and ran thin—how often could he logically blame working late? After long enough, it was time for truth, authenticity, and the drive to Hyde Park.

TWENTY-SEVEN

THE KITCHEN HADN'T CHANGED A WHIT SINCE JOHN AND Delores Hawkins bought their home many decades earlier. In spite of Vanessa's push during high school to "bring it into the modern world," the gold and brown diamond linoleum, walnut cabinets with their worn brass handles, and rustic breakfast nook and benches remained exactly as they'd been. Given Delores's impeccable housekeeping, and despite the activities of three raucous children over a lifetime of growing up, all had endured admirably.

Chris loved everything about this room; it never failed to inspire nostalgia and a deep sense of comfort. And today it was the place where he sat with his mother sharing confessionals and coffee as the sun shot through the beveled panes of the kitchen window.

"Is it serious?" Delores had listened to the generalized Sidonie story without comment, and was now intent on defining parameters. Chris couldn't tell if the question was hopeful or just curious.

"I don't know yet. We spent a fair amount of time together as friends before the romance started, so I feel safe in saying it's got foundation to it. But where it's headed? I'm not sure."

"But you're spending every night with her. That seems fairly serious."

"Ma, I know you think—"

"Sweetheart, I understand passion. I'm not criticizing you. I'm just saying it's been a very long time since you've had that kind of person— or passion— in your life. I'm happy for you, wondering if it signifies something meaningful. I've never known you to be a player."

Chris grinned at his mother's use of the term, grateful for her lack of judgment. "No, I've never been much of a player. You're right about that."

"Then tell me more about her. She must be very special."

"She is. She's smart, she's tough. She's got this deep, soulful thing about her, which I love. She tends to be intense and very direct. She's been through her fair share in life, so she knows what she wants and she's been successful in getting it."

"What does she do?"

He took a pause. "She's the head manager at The Church. She's actually the person who hired me."

Delores turned abruptly. "Goodness, is that wise, getting involved with your boss? That seems ripe for potential problems. Is she older?"

Chris laughed. "There isn't some kind of power dynamic going on, Ma. She's not even a year older, and there's a very casual chain of command there. We're being discreet and professional, so I don't expect there to be a problem."

"Sometimes what you least expect can trip you up. It just seems to me there are enough women in the world who are *not* your boss, that—"

"Believe me, this was not something we set out to do. But it's not easy finding people out 'in the world,' as you put it, particularly when you spend most of your time at work. And sometimes the perfect person just happens to be the one who's most inconvenient."

Delores gave him a measured look, as if assessing his candor. "All right. I'll keep an open mind." She got up and started pulling food from the refrigerator. "You're a grown man. I trust you to know what you want and how to handle it. I just hope you don't sabotage your situation there, especially after working so hard to find balance in your work life."

"If anything, enjoying my life more helps with that balance."

Delores finally smiled, her shoulders relaxing. "Then I'm glad, sweetheart. You deserve a little love. What's her name?"

"Sidonie."

"Oh, what a pretty name! So unusual."

"It's French. Her mother apparently has some French in her."

Delores took a quiet breath. "And she's . . . a white girl?"

"Yes."

She finished cutting the sandwich she'd made, put a few carrots on the plate, set it in front of Chris, and sat down. He watched her intently, wondering what comment would follow.

"I can't remember the last time you dated a white girl."

"It's been a while. Do you have a problem with that?"

Delores's eyes flashed. "No, Christopher, you know me better than that. Your father and I taught you to be your own man, to choose and judge people based on who they are, not their heritage or ethnicity. I'd be lying if I didn't say I *do* think life is easier when you stay within your community—there's no explaining, no defending, no translating this or that, either to the person or those who might be judging her. But ultimately it's about quality and character. If you tell me she's a person of quality and character—"

"She is."

"Then I look forward to meeting her."

"Let me see how our schedules go in the next couple of weeks, and we'll figure something out."

"Wonderful. So, I guess I shouldn't expect you around here much?" She suppressed a wicked grin.

"For now," he said, catching her expression with a smile. "We'll see how things develop."

"How what things develop?" Vanessa was suddenly at the doorway of the kitchen, still in her business suit.

"Sweetheart! I didn't even hear you come in! Sit down, join us. Would you like a sandwich?" Delores immediately got up and started puttering.

"No, thanks, I just had lunch. Came home for a short nap before I have to head out again."

Chris noticed the dark circles were evermore etched in his sister's face. Her expression of curiosity was the most vibrant thing about her at the moment.

"So what things are developing?" Vanessa repeated. "Tell me. I need some good gossip."

"No gossip, just work stuff." Chris's reply was matter-of-fact.

"Bullshit, motherfucker!"

"Vanessa!" No matter how predictably crass her daughter could be, Delores always reacted; it was almost a routine at this point. "Comport yourself with some dignity, daughter."

"Sorry, sorry!" But her eyes stayed trained on Chris. "You haven't been home in weeks, you look like you've been taking vitamins, and you're actually wearing something besides jeans and a black T-shirt—"

"The T-shirt is actually sort of a work uniform—"

"Don't play me for a fool, brother. You're getting *laid!*" she squealed triumphantly.

Delores threw up her hands.

"Sorry, Mom. But am I right? Am I? Oh, happy day! Chrissie's got a girlfriend. Chrissie's got a girlfriend." She grinned from ear to ear, hopping around like a mad twelve-year-old.

Chris couldn't help but laugh. "You are such an idiot. Yes! I'm seeing somebody."

"I knew it! Tell me about her."

"She's . . . great, it's too new to talk about, but I'm having a good time. We'll see where it goes. There, are you happy?"

Vanessa walked up and threw her arms around him. "Yes. I'm happy. Happy for you. I hope it works out, I really do. Then you'll be one of the few people I know who actually has something that's working out." She went back to the door and picked up her bag and coat. "If it lasts long enough, I'd like to meet this woman who's revived your soul. But right now I'm going to sleep because *my* soul is dead and I'm literally beat to shit."

"Vanessa . . . child." Delores just shook her head as Vanessa grinned acerbically and straggled down the hall, her jacket trailing behind her.

Chris grabbed his bag and a duffle full of clothes, then leaned in to give his mother a kiss. "I'm heading out too, Ma."

She walked him to the door. "Please keep me posted so I know when to expect you next." She paused. "And you know your sister's going to ask me about everything. I'd appreciate if you were the one to share certain salient details with her. I don't want to be caught in the middle of any noise." She gave him a telling look.

"I will, Ma. But she actually smiled. She gave me a hug. I'd like us to have that brief moment of her being happy—happy for me—before we get to her wince, or whatever she'll throw at me for betraying the race. Hopefully things will last long enough for us to get there."

Delores nodded. "I hope so too. Now go on, drive safe, and never forget I love you."

"I won't. I love you too." He bounced down the stairs, got in his car, and headed back to where his heart wanted to be.

TWENTY-EIGHT

AFTER TWO MORE WEEKS OF DISCRETION, IT BECAME officially strange having something so fully occupy her thoughts and life yet remain a secret from everyone she knew. When Chris revealed that he'd finally spoken to his mother, Sidonie realized she, too, wanted to bring the good news to someone close. Work people were still off limits, but when plans were made for her and Karen to drive up to their mother's for more house packing, Sidonie grabbed the opportunity. Two birds, one stone; fell swoop, git 'er done. Take whatever they gave in one inclusive afternoon.

"The sound guy? The guy you hired back in March? Really?" Incredulity would be the first of Karen's responses.

"Yes, Chris Hawkins. And he's not just a sound guy. He's actually the manager of the sound department, so we're pretty much on equal footing."

Karen rolled her eyes and laughed. "Okay, if that works for you."

Marian was less in the loop. "I don't know anything about a sound guy. Can you start from the beginning?"

So she did. As they wrapped china and Marian's beloved silver-plated flatware, Sidonie told them of the immediate connection she and Chris felt upon meeting. She talked about how he saved the day when Troy disappeared, how he later saved her when Troy returned. She discussed the success of his business, his exceptional skill at his craft, his admirable work ethic, and his ability to make meaningful conversation. She explained it all and glowed throughout.

"He sounds like quite the prize, darling!" Marian beamed. It had been a long time since she'd seen her younger daughter so happy. "I can't wait to meet him. I hope we can arrange that before Steve and I leave."

"I hope so too, Mom. What's the ETA on that?"

Karen jumped in. "Escrow here closes in two weeks, and the condo Steve found in Orlando is a foreclosure, so they can probably grab it anytime."

"Which means . . . ?"

"They could be hitting the road in two weeks."

Marian's smile was giddy. Sidonie feigned a pout. "Wow. So soon!"

"Mom, take it easy with your glee." Karen grinned. "Your baby daughter might start crying."

"I just can't believe you're really leaving us!" Sidonie wasn't necessarily kidding.

"Oh, stop! I'm not leaving you." Marian laughed. "And you're big girls now—you don't need me around day in, day out. Florida is not that far and, besides, you're both so busy it's not like I see a lot of you anyway. I'll probably see more of you down there!" Which was quite possibly true.

"And you can finally take us to Disney World!" Karen squealed. "How we got through childhood without that rite of passage is beyond me."

"Put it on the list." Marian winked, giving Sidonie a playful push.

Karen turned to her sister. "But let's get back to you. We're not done hearing about Mr. Wonderful."

Sidonie blushed. "What else do you want to know?"

"Is he fun? Does he make you laugh?" Karen always asked those questions, likely because her own husband bore neither of those traits.

"He's not funny in a laugh-your-ass-off kind of way, but he's witty. He makes clever observations. I'd say he enjoys the satire of life, so we spend a good amount of time laughing. And yes, he's fun . . . in all the right ways." She couldn't help the lascivious grin that followed.

"Aaaggh . . ." Karen threw a pillow at her. "We don't want to hear about all that stuff, do we, Mom?"

"Is that what she meant?" Marian said, clueless.

Karen continued. "But what about the really shallow part: what's he look like? Is he hot? Tall, handsome, short, fat? I know they can't all look like your asshole ex-hottie, but I hope you at least get some pretty with the perfection."

An image of Chris sprang to Sidonie's mind—his smile, slanted and, oh, so sexy; his supple arms, his long legs wrapped around her. She thought of his soft lips and warm skin—

"Hello!!" Karen clapped her hands in front of Sidonie's face. "Either snap out of it or let us in. It's gettin' lonely out here."

Sidonie laughed. "Sorry, I was just thinking about how best to describe him."

"No selfies yet?" Karen queried.

"I'm not fourteen."

"Then you're old school, as my daughter would say. Even Mom takes selfies."

"Karen, let your sister speak," Marian admonished.

"Fine. Speak, sister, speak."

"Okay . . . he's tall, he's well built, he's got an amazing face—big eyes, open expression, always interested in what's around him. He's kind of quiet and more observational than out there, if you know what I mean. He tends to be a casual dresser. He's close to his mother—"

"I like him already!" Marian smiled.

"And he's black."

A beat.

Karen: "Wow."

Marian: "Oh."

Sidonie looked at them with a twinge of panic. "Please tell me that's not going to be an issue. We are too deep in the twenty-first century for that kind of nonsense and I really can't fathom anyone having—"

"Relax!" Karen smiled. "I think it's utterly fascinating. It actually raises my esteem of you greatly."

"That's almost as bad. Why is that?"

"I always figured you for a status quo type—"

"Really?" Sidonie cocked her head. "That's oddly insulting."

"I just mean since college you've never done anything particularly controversial, anything that might raise some ire, even if the ire was idiotic. That you've fallen for a man regardless of potential cultural pricklies speaks well of your character." Karen sat down, gazing at her sister with admiration. "I mean it. It's a compliment."

"I guess that's good, but honestly, his blackness has nothing to do with it. There's no sociopolitical statement going on. I just like him and he happens to be black."

"But, honey, you never had a Negro boyfriend before," Marian remarked, her brow almost comically furrowed.

"Did you honestly just say 'Negro boyfriend'?" Karen snapped. Sidonie felt her face flush.

"Well, what are they calling themselves these days? Who can keep up?" Marian appeared flustered.

"They call themselves black, Mother, or African American," Karen retorted. "But I suspect you actually know that. And have you conveniently forgotten Sid's college boyfriend, George? He was black, remember?"

"I never thought of him as a *boyfriend*. You two were just hanging out."

"We dated for over six months," Sidonie interjected dryly.

"Well, I guess I had no idea that was something that appealed to you, Sidonie."

"Mom, what is happening to you?" Karen yelped. "Seriously! Do you hear yourself?"

"What did I say now?"

"'Something that appealed to you'?"

"And what does that even mean?" Sidonie chimed in concert with her sister. "It's not about his *blackness*. That's not the appeal. The appeal is *him*, just him. I'd like him regardless of what color he was."

Karen got up and hugged her sister. "Ignore her. *I'm* happy for you, sis. He sounds like an amazing guy and the fact that he has a good heart, that he protects you and makes you feel loved, that's all that matters. I look forward to meeting him."

The statement was welcomed. Karen could be a tough audience and if she'd reacted badly, Sidonie was sure her head would have exploded.

Marian, on the other hand, remained peevish, biting her thumbnail and staring off silently.

"Mom, what? If you have something to say, just say it and we'll move on," Sidonie said.

"I don't have anything specific to say."

"Then why do you look like you have indigestion?"

"Oh, stop being so dramatic! I'm just concerned. Every day I watch what's going on out there and I worry about you being part of all that."

"Part of all what?"

"The Black Lives Matter craziness, all the shootings and the gangs. I want you nowhere near that, but if you're going to spend time with a black man, that's probably impossible. It seems very dangerous to me, so I worry."

Karen and Sidonie exchanged exasperated looks.

"Mom, he's a respected businessman living a completely normal life, so I'm not in any more danger with him than I was with Theo. Who, by the way, did more damage to my psyche than most men could manage, regardless of color. So I suggest you turn off Fox News and spend a little more time out in the real world where all kinds of people interact daily without incident."

Annoyance crossed Marian's face. "You can stop being condescending, Sidonie, I am well aware of that. But there isn't much sense in courting trouble either."

The comment triggered a flash of the dreaded police stop, but before Sidonie could decide how to respond, Karen stepped back in.

"Jesus, Mother, you act like Sid's out on the front lines throwing rocks at police or consorting with the Gangster Disciples. She's just dating a guy who happens to be black. I don't remember you being so clichéd about all this stuff. Tell me she's kidding about Fox News."

Marian's face turned red and she stood up, rustling around the living room in a huff. "I think I've had about enough of you two and your lectures. Maybe you should skedaddle so you don't get caught in rush hour."

Sidonie was stunned at the direction this had taken. She walked over to Marian and took her hands, peering into her mother's clenched face. "Mom, Mom, let's not turn this into something it doesn't need to be, please. I get your concern. There is a lot of crazy stuff going on in the world, but none of it has anything to do with me. You just have to have faith that neither Chris nor I will be getting ourselves into that kind of trouble, okay?" She meant it. She certainly hoped it.

Marian patted her daughter's hand. "I'm sorry. I'm probably being silly, but I worry about you."

"I understand, Mom, but let's get past it, okay? Chris will come with me when we finish packing next week, and we can take you and Steve out for dinner. Maybe Karen, Josh, and Sarah can join us, and we'll make it a big 'meet Chris, bon voyage' event."

"You don't have to go to all that trouble." Marian went back to fussing with the stacked boxes. "I'll just take a train into the city one night before we leave and we can meet in the Loop somewhere." The emphasis—the Steve-lessness of it—did not go unnoticed.

"Is there some reason you don't want us *all* to gather?" Karen queried with a frown. "Because we'd actually like to say goodbye to Steve too. Sid's idea is perfect."

Marian pursed her lips tightly. "I feel like you two are ganging up on me and I don't appreciate it."

Sidonie was authentically confused. "Mom, I don't understand what's going on right now. You're being very weird and it's hard not to interpret it in a way I don't love."

There was a tense pause; no one said anything for a good ten seconds. Finally Marian blurted: "Steve would have a problem with you dating a black man."

Karen's jaw dropped. Literally. "Are you fucking kidding me, Mom?"

Marian looked up sharply, ready to either admonish her daughter or attempt to defend her indefensible position. She went for the latter.

"I'm not saying it's the way *I* feel, but he's a man with his own mind. Getting together would be too uncomfortable and I wouldn't want to push it on him. It's not that he hates black people. He just thinks we should stick to our own races when it comes to relationships, so it would be awkward for us all to get together."

Sidonie was nonplussed; Karen, not so much. "So the two of you actually sit around discussing the topic of not mixing races? Just chirpy dinner conversation analyzing interracial shenanigans?"

"No! We don't sit around talking about it."

"Then what, Mom? What? How has his hideous point of view become known to you? Did you catch him screaming along with some bigot on TV? Ranting when a black athlete showed up at the Super Bowl with his white wife? Or did it just come up before saying good-night, like, 'Oh, sweetheart, in case I forget to mention it, I think Negroes and Caucasians should never mix, just muddies up the works'? What?"

Marian was shaking at this point. Sidonie had a pang of sympathy for her, but was powerless to stop her sister. She was also curious to see where the prodding led.

Marian snapped back. "You can stop it right now, Karen Marie! I will not sit here and be bullied by my own daughter! I'm just trying to be honest and I won't be attacked for it."

"I'm not attacking you—"

"I know you probably think about all those defendants you worked with way back when, all those black people you thought were being treated so unfairly, and maybe you *are* more admirable than everyone else when it comes to this stuff—"

"Oh no, Mom—it's got nothing to do with that. I'm not more admirable than *anyone* else on this stuff. I got out. I got overwhelmed and disillusioned, and walked away. There's *nothing* admirable about me on that front. But I'm not the point. The point is you . . . and how you're so sure Steve would be uncomfortable around Sid and her new boyfriend. Since it affects us all, I think it's a fair question."

"Because he's talked about it," she offered reluctantly. "He sees things on the news, or reads something in the paper, and he talks about it. He knows I don't agree with him, but since it's never been an issue in our lives, it didn't seem like a big deal. I guess it will be now." She sank into a nearby chair.

Karen walked to the kitchen, opened a cabinet, took out a bottle of scotch, and poured herself a shot. Looked at Sidonie, who shook her head. Karen threw one back, returned to the living room, and sat down next to her mother.

"Mom, that you're involved with a racist is very disturbing—"

"He's *not* a racist—don't even try that on me! He has black friends, he works with black people—"

"Please don't play stupid. You're too smart for that. You want to be honest? Let's be honest. You've accepted this guy, flaws and all, and one of his flaws happens to be that he's a racist. If you're okay with that, so be it. But now Steve's racism becomes a family issue, and *that* I have a problem with."

Sidonie felt slightly nauseous. "Look, you guys, I—"

"I don't know what you want me to say, Karen!" Marian threw up her arms in frustration. "Steve's a good man. He's not a perfect man. But he's the man I'm with now and, you're right: I've accepted him, flaws and all. I can't change him, but I'm not going to end the relationship just because we don't agree on this one little thing."

"Seems like more than one little thing to me—"

"I said *I'd* love to meet Chris, and I would! I'll meet you all downtown and we'll have a nice time together. If Steve's not a part of that, so what? He doesn't need to be involved with every single thing that goes on in this family. It doesn't have to affect *us*. It affects me and him, and I can handle that. You're making me feel—"

"Enough!" Sidonie hollered. This was not at all what she expected and at this point she wanted nothing more than to head home. She looked at her beleaguered mother and angry sister and just shook her head. "We're not going to solve this tonight. Maybe we're never going to solve it. Mom, I love you, I hope you and Steve have a long, happy life together, and I hope Florida is everything you dreamed, but for now I'm going to keep my relationship to myself."

"Honey, I don't want you to feel that way! I want to—"

"It doesn't matter what you want me to feel or what you want, Mom. My relationship is precious to me, Chris is precious to me, and I have no intention of ever making him feel unwelcome in any way related to this family. Explaining why the man you're moving to Florida with will not be joining us for dinner would make him feel unwelcome, and I won't put him through that. Period. End of story. Invitation is off the table."

Karen was now standing at the door, purse over her shoulder, keys in her hand. Marian looked at her, panicked.

"I don't want you two leaving before we settle this," she said tearfully. "I won't be able to sleep if we don't." Karen was unmoved. Sidonie softened.

"We'll leave it for tonight and think more about it over the next few days. We can't stuff it back in the box, but we'll try to figure it out at some point." Sidonie went over and hugged her sagging mother. "I'll call you later in the week and we'll talk about when to finish the packing, okay?"

"All right, sweetheart."

Karen blew a kiss from the porch and headed down the stairs. Before Sidonie stepped out, Marian murmured: "Forgive me, sweetheart. I guess I'm not as strong as you."

Sidonie gave her a sad smile, knowing those words were true and they changed the way she felt about her mother.

TWENTY-NINE

KAREN RANTED ALL THE WAY BACK TO THE CITY. IF SIDONIE had been less tired, she might have participated, but as it was, she was happy to cede the soapbox to her sister, who was riled and in rare form. It wasn't until Willis Tower came into distant view that Karen finally depleted herself, concluding the ride in silence.

When they pulled in front of the townhouse, she double-parked and flipped on the hazards. "Gosh, that was a fun night! Let's do it again real soon, m'kay?" Before Sidonie could respond, Karen looked up toward the second floor of the townhouse. "Is he here?"

Sidonie peered up; the light was on. "I think so. He had an early night."

"He has a key already?" Karen grinned.

"Yeah. It was just easier."

"I'd ask to come up and meet him, but I think we're both too exhausted, yeah?"

"Yeah. But thank you. Thanks for standing up for me . . . for him. It meant a lot." Suddenly she was crying.

"Oh, sissy, I'm so sorry our mother loves a flaming racist." Karen tilted her head with a goofy grin. "But look at it this way: at least the asshole isn't moving her to Mississippi and fitting her with a set of pointy white sheets. That would be worse, right?"

"God, you're horrible!"

Karen patted her knee. "Go be with your guy. He really does sound like a gem. We'll figure Mom out later. Or maybe we won't. But whatever happens, you got me."

She couldn't have said anything better.

≈

FINDING CHRIS AT the dining room table as she walked in, Sidonie was hit with a wave of *home*. He looked up with a radiant smile, lit with the pleasure of seeing her, and she was cleansed of the day.

Without a word, she took his hand and led him upstairs to the bedroom, where assuagement was found in Gato Barbieri on Pandora, good wine on the bed stand, and warm hands banishing all that was cold.

"I love you," he whispered, sweetly altering the day's most indelible feature.

"I love you, too . . ."

THIRTY

THEY MADE BREAKFAST, SMILED AND TOUCHED IN PASSING, but neither referenced the words uttered the night before. Until they did.

"Did you mean what you said last night?" she asked.

He looked at her, surprised. "Of course." He smiled. "Did you?"

"Of course." She smiled back.

"Good."

He poured coffee for them both.

She sat quietly for a moment, then: "Do you want to move in?"

He looked up, startled. "You mean officially? I'm here almost every night anyway."

"Yes, officially. With drawers and hangers, a toothbrush in the glass, your own crappy food in the fridge."

"I don't have crappy food."

"String cheese and Jell-O cups are not gourmet."

"I'm a simple man."

"Do you want to move in?"

"You're serious?"

"I am."

"Are you sure you're ready for that?"

"I wouldn't have asked otherwise. Do you ask because *you're* not ready for that?"

"No. I just want to be sure you are."

"I'm sure. I like knowing you're here when I come home. I look forward to you walking in the door. I like waking up to you next to me. I want you here . . . if you want to be here."

He crossed the room and enveloped her in a deep, resonating kiss. She was breathless by the time he let go.

"I want to be here. Let's make it official." He poured two glasses of orange juice, handed her one, and offered a toast. "We are now bound by the power of love, orange juice, and string cheese. Amen."

THIRTY-ONE

HUSTLING DOWN THE STAIRS TO THE GARAGE, THEY DEBATED whose car and which route, and just as the door rolled open and Chris stepped out to the driveway patio, a perky young woman in a neon orange track suit, platinum hair high in a flouncy ponytail, emerged from the garage next door.

"Sidonie!" she squealed with a wide toothy grin. "My God, girl, where have you been? I haven't seen you in ages!"

"Hey, Alice!" They hugged warmly. "I've been around, but the club's been nuts and so are my hours. How are you doing?"

"I'm fabulous, but Mark is going completely crazy. He did get the job at Skidmore. Remember that architectural firm I texted you about a couple of months ago?"

"Yeah . . . wow! That's a big deal, right?"

"It is, it's fabulous, but it's *such* a steep learning curve. Lots of dramatic whining." She laughed. "But otherwise, everything's pretty much the same." She glanced at Chris.

"Oh, sorry, Alice, this is Chris Hawkins. Chris, this is Alice Rosen. She and her hubby, Mark, live next door and have been my pals for ages." She turned back to Alice. "Chris is the sound manager at the club."

Alice and Chris shook hands. "Fabulous! Nice to meet you, Chris!"

"The same."

"Chris is going to be moving in over the next couple of weeks," Sidonie interjected with a smile, "so you'll be seeing him around a lot more."

Alice looked him over with heightened interest. "Fabulous! Let's plan a dinner or something when you guys get settled. It's been too long since we've done that—like, what, over a year? And I know Mark is dying to have a Scrabble rematch. He's convinced you cheated last time!" She stopped with an awkward laugh, "last time" clearly having involved a certain ex-husband.

Sidonie slid over the conversational bump without a hitch: "Mark was always a sore loser, but let's have at it. I bet Chris is better at Scrabble than Theo could ever hope to be." She turned to Chris, who smiled and took the prompt.

"I haven't played since I was thirteen, but at the time I was quite the wordsmith. Count me in."

Sidonie leaned into him appreciatively. "Great . . . so you're on, Rosen. We'll get in touch when we're more organized. Tell Mark to get out his dictionary!"

"Fabulous! Well, listen—oh God, there she is." Her voice suddenly dropped to a whisper.

Both Sidonie and Chris turned as the other neighbor, the "cranky old shrew" as Sidonie had initially described her, stepped out to her deck above. Alice looked away immediately as the older woman glanced in their direction. Sidonie gave a terse nod; the woman nodded back, shook two small rugs from the balcony, then turned and went inside.

"Ugh," Alice continued, "I can't even stand to look at her!"

"Now, be nice. It's better than getting into a brawl."

"Do you know how many times I've fantasized about just that, punching the shit out of that bitch?" She laughed. "But, yes, I'll be nice. She's not worth the trouble. All right, gotta get my run in. Great to meet you, Chris. Enjoy the neighborhood and I'll see you around!"

"You got it." He smiled as she trotted off, ponytail wagging, her skintight suit literally glowing in the midday sun. Chris watched for a moment, realizing he'd have never imagined, in any scenario, having a neighbor with quite the perkiness of this quintessentially blonde white woman. He smiled as he got in the Jeep.

Sidonie noticed. "What?"

"That's the nice neighbor?"

"That's the one."

"She's cute. Likes the word *fabulous*."

"She does." Sidonie laughed. "She runs a very trendy Chicago tour company, so her enthusiasm is a commodity. She and Mark are actually great. We used to spend a lot of time together, but after the divorce . . . I don't know . . . and then the club got busier. Anyway, it'll be fun for you guys to get to know each other."

"I look forward to it. What's the story with the other neighbor? Obviously there's some bad blood there." He pulled into traffic.

"Yeah, Sandra. We all pretty much avoid her. She lives alone, generally unfriendly, mostly keeps to herself unless she's stirring up trouble. I'm just grateful I never had a dog to contend with. Mark and Alice had this little yapper about two years ago, and it got really ugly between all of them for a while. Animal Control, mediations, fines, the whole thing. I stayed out of it, but wasn't too unhappy when they finally shipped it off to Mark's brother's up north. It *was* pretty noisy. But Sandra was hideous about it all."

"I'll look forward to avoiding her too."

Sidonie smiled. "Yes, wise. But let's definitely take Alice up on the invitation. I think you'll like them."

"We will. We'll do all that stuff, just like the real couple we are."

They grinned at each other. A dashboard light pinged.

"Damn." Chris sighed.

"What's that?" Sidonie asked.

Chris tapped on the dash screen but the light persisted. "My radiator's going. I still can't decide whether to overhaul this thing or bite the bullet and get something new."

"You could use something prettier. And cleaner," she added slyly.

"It *is* pretty rough." He laughed. "Even my brother would probably agree it's time to let it go . . ."

She reached over and squeezed his hand. "Probably."

"Let's make a date to go look at something new on one of our days off."

"A car date—how romantic!"

"I know how to treat my women," he growled.

She smiled. "You do. You really do." She leaned back to look out the window. Their chosen Lake Shore Drive route, usually easy at this time of day, was hampered by street construction that repeatedly held them at full stops. She fell into silence, long enough that he finally looked over.

"Everything okay?"

"Just thinking about yesterday. My mom . . . the whole mess."

"Tell me what happened. You were pretty quiet when you got home."

Sidonie detailed the unfortunate circumstances of the previous afternoon, with its revelation that her mother would be making her relationship with Chris an awkward family issue for the foreseeable future. "Which is the last thing I expected."

"She never gave a hint of anything like that before?"

"Not really. She isn't the most socially evolved person in the world, and even though she pretended to forget my black boyfriend in college, it didn't seem to be a problem at the time."

"You never mentioned a black boyfriend before."

She looked at him sharply. "What does that mean?"

Her tone surprised him. "It means you never mentioned it, that's all." He frowned in response. "What did you think it meant?"

"Sorry." She blushed, chagrined. "I'm being oversensitive. It just bugged me that she framed it like it was some sort of proclivity that *appealed* to me, dating black men . . . jungle fever and all that."

"Is it?"

She turned with her mouth agape only to catch his mischievous grin. She slapped his arm with real feeling. "That's not funny, Chris!"

"It kind of is. I mean, come on! You date one black guy in college and your Mom's concerned it's a *thing*? That's kind of funny."

"Yeah, hilarious. Her boyfriend's a hoot too."

"What's his story?"

"I don't know. I haven't spent that much time with him, just seemed like a normal Midwestern dude. Not terribly sophisticated, but generally decent. Finding out he's a Fox News segregationist is disturbing." She looked over to gauge his reaction. "Does all this give you one of your ticks?"

"Once removed, maybe. It makes me feel bad for you. It's your family—you want their support. But people do what they're gonna do, that's a fact. Just let me know how you want to play it."

"I don't know yet. She's leaving soon, so I'll have to figure something out. But I'm sorry. It shames me to have to apologize for my family."

"It's not your shame to bear. I'll be dealing with something similar with my sister."

Sidonie was taken aback. "Really? But you said you dated white girls before."

"Twice, briefly, and both times Vanessa let me know how disappointed she was."

"In what, exactly? Something as simple as Steve's equation, that races shouldn't mix or . . . what?"

"Some version of that, but less personal, more political. When it comes to black men with white women, my sister goes to the reality that black women have been denigrated throughout history while white women have been idealized. So there's a sense of betrayal when a brother chooses a white woman over a sister. When it's *her* brother? All the worse. Like it or not, agree with it or not, that's where Vanessa lives."

"I shall be sufficiently terrified to meet her."

"We'll take it slowly," he said, smiling.

They rode in silence for a moment. Then she looked over at him.

"How do you feel about all that?"

"Her view?"

"Yeah."

"I understand it, but I won't live my life limited by history. To me that's just another form of slavery. Part of my freedom is being able to love who I choose. Who I fall in love *with*. I don't fetishize white women, but I won't reject love if it happens to be with one either. She sees it differently."

Sidonie had no opposing angle to offer. No argument, no debate.

Again, she was struck by the gap in their experience, the complexities that affected him that she'd never given thought to beyond history class or observations of contemporary culture. It was jarring.

Chris looked over, concerned. "What's going on over there?"

"It's just . . . I don't know . . . all this. It's new. I've never had to think much about it before. Race didn't affect me. I know you've had to think about it your whole life, but it's an education for me."

"Maybe that's a good thing."

"Or maybe just sad."

"How so?"

"That both of us leapt in without really thinking about the racial angle."

"I always think about the racial angle—"

"What I mean is, we got involved with just *us*. Just who we are as people, a man and a woman who feel something for each other. Now we're dealing with Steve and Vanessa, and race and black history, and police looking for pipes in the glove box, and it's all so strange and invasive."

"This is the gig, Sidonie," he said, not unsympathetically. "And hopefully this is as bad as it gets."

She looked at him with alarm. "What does that mean?"

"Just that I hope this is the worst we have to deal with: cranky family members and occasional police stops. I can live with that. Can you?"

They'd arrived at The Church. He'd pulled into the employee parking lot and turned to her, waiting for an answer.

"Yes, I can live with that," she said somberly.

"Good. Then I'll find time over the next week to get my things over to your place—"

"*Our* place."

"*Our* place. I might even pick up some necessary essentials, like, say, a better TV and a wider selection of string cheese and Jell-O cups." He grinned. "And let's be sure to talk about my contribution to the overhead. If I'm living there, I'm part of the payment formula, okay? Mortgage, utilities, whatever."

She liked that he offered. "You're a noble man."

"I am very noble. And hopefully worth the trouble."

She reached out and caressed his cheek. "No trouble, Chris. But yes, worth it. Every bit." She meant it. "Okay, I'm heading in." She hopped out of the Jeep.

"I'll follow in a few." They were still working the secrecy angle.

Just as Sidonie turned toward the door, Al came out with trash bins in hand. He stopped and looked at them both. His expression—wheels of curiosity spinning like mad—compelled her to squelch a grin.

THIRTY-TWO

"HEY, KIDDO, I JUST GOT A CALL FROM LOUISE BARTON OVER at ALZ and they want to add fifteen people. Is that possible at this point?" Frank, more frazzled than usual, grabbed Sidonie the second she walked in the door. The Alzheimer's Association was throwing their annual benefit this coming weekend and last-minute additions were wrenching the works.

"Fifteen? Are you kidding me? That's . . . I don't know. I'm guessing that puts us over occupancy and the last thing anyone wants is a visit from the Fire Department."

"That's what I told her. She's apologetic, says she knows it's way past the head count deadline, but apparently the add-ons are big hitters. She's hoping we can accommodate them."

Sidonie shook her head, annoyed. "Let me look at the layout and see where we are." She started toward her office.

"Hey, before you go, can we talk a minute?"

She turned, surprised. "Sure. What's up?"

"Let's go sit in my office."

Sidonie felt a wave of reminiscent dread, the feeling that descended with every directive to the principal's office. They walked into his well-ordered space—walls covered with event posters, framed citations and awards, family pictures and neatly arranged stacks of folders—and as she sat in the chair across from his desk, he shut the door, further piquing her concern.

"You're making me nervous. Am I about to get detention?"

Frank laughed. "Sorry, I'm not trying to be mysterious, I just want to keep this private. Al's probably out there right now with a highball glass to the door."

She laughed, almost picturing it.

"So, kiddo, this is a personal question, which is not usually in my playbook, but I think it's time I asked. Is there something going on between you and Chris Hawkins?"

Boom. Like a cannon. Sidonie had been convinced of their success in hiding the situation; clearly she'd miscalculated.

"Yes. To put it bluntly."

"Okay. On a personal level, it's none of my business. On a professional level, I'm concerned about potential conflicts."

"I understand, Frank, but let me lay out my thoughts, if you will."

"Please." He sat back, not unfriendly, but certainly contained.

"The fact is, I've been here for many years, in various positions with various titles, and I have never gotten involved with anyone on the job. So this is an anomaly, as you know. I thought about the appropriateness of it all, given my position, and while it's never ideal to get involved with staff, Chris *is* in a management position, which puts us generally on par in terms of chain-of-command . . . along with Al, which of course, always seems ridiculous."

They both grinned.

"I also took into account that Chris is a very private and respectful person, someone who understands required decorum, and I have faith in both his discretion and his ability to compartmentalize his personal life and the job."

Frank appeared to suppress a smile. "Was that a prepared speech?"

"No. Did it sound like one?"

"Pretty much."

"Well, I have given it some thought. I was actually planning to talk to you about it. I didn't know when for sure, but he's moving in over the next week, so I figured you deserved to know at this point."

"Wow . . . that seems pretty quick. Unless you've been dating for longer than I realized."

"It's been several months. We spent a lot of time getting to know each other, and then things changed. Does that create a problem for you . . . for us?"

"Sidonie, I know you've had a rough go these last couple of years, and it hasn't been easy, recovering from all that. No one wants you to be happy more than me, and while I have to be honest in saying I wouldn't necessarily have picked Chris as an option for you—"

"Why? Why do you say that?" She felt immediately wary.

"I don't know. Maybe because I knew Theo and have some idea of the kind of guys you go for."

"Good-looking drug-addicted asshole cheaters?"

He sat back, thrown by her abruptness. "Sidonie, come on. I think you know what I mean."

"I don't know what you mean," she said defensively.

"I like Chris. I don't know him all that well, but the contact we've had has always been cordial. He seems like a bright kid who's done very well for himself—"

"You realize he's not even a year younger than me."

"I'm just saying he's got a young thing about him. Maybe it's the way he puts himself together, maybe it's his personality, I don't know. It's not a criticism, it's just an observation. Look, he's built an amazing business all by himself and I've got nothing but respect for that. He stepped in here and took over like a master. He's made friends of the entire staff; he's got a great work ethic. What's not to like?"

"Then what's the problem?" She could feel something akin to her mother's response lurking somewhere behind his controlled demeanor.

"I'm not saying there is a problem. I just don't know him personally. Which means I don't know enough about what attracted you to have an opinion about it. I just wanted to discuss how this relates to the club."

"Bottom line, Frank, if you trust me, then trust us to keep our personal relationship from overlapping here at the club."

"I trust you implicitly, you know that. If you tell me that will be the case, I trust that as well."

"Good. Beyond that, trust that I know what I'm doing with Chris. I get that you don't know him. I hope you'll get to know him better as time goes on. He's one of the kindest, most openhearted people I've ever met, and the way he looks at the world is . . . I don't know—it's different from anyone I've ever known before. It pushes me to be better, maybe even a more compassionate person. I think that's a good thing. And he's made me happier than anyone has in a really long time."

Frank sat up. "Then that's all that matters."

"No detention?"

"No detention. Get going. And let's plan to get back to Louise as quickly as possible."

"Will do."

She felt relief, but suspicion lingered. Hopefully that would dissipate over time. Stepping into the hallway, she was surprised—or maybe not—to see Al heading quickly toward the bar. She half expected to see a highball glass in his hand. He turned and winked at her, a walking cliché.

She marched right up to him. "Okay, lurker, say what you're going to say and let's get this over with."

"I barely heard anything as I walked past." He grinned.

She rolled her eyes. As she turned toward her office, he called out: "Hey, Frame!"

"What?"

"In all seriousness, I like the guy. Even if my buddy Mike is gonna be disappointed."

She walked back to the bar, leaning in with ferocity. "Goddammit, Al, can you just once not act like a dick?" Her snap got his attention. "My private life is not a game for your entertainment. The last thing I need is some moony-eyed cop giving me a hard time. Whatever you think you heard, fine. But I'll ask, as a fellow manager and, hopefully, a halfway decent human being, that you keep it to yourself. Do you think you could possibly do that?"

"Jesus, take a frickin' chill pill! Of course I can do that. I'm not an idiot. And I mean it, I like the guy."

She shot him a fierce look, trying to assess his sincerity. He grinned . . . like an idiot.

"Thanks." She had to laugh. "He is a pretty great guy."

THIRTY-THREE

DIANTE STOOD AT THE DOOR OF THE TOWNHOUSE, WINE in hand and an affable smile on his face. He handed the bottle to Sidonie with the flourish of celebration.

"Chris said you liked California reds, so this here is a 2012 Napa Valley Cabernet Sauvignon that I'm told gets ninety-one points in the ratings."

She laughed and accepted it graciously. "That's very sweet, Diante, and I'm so happy to meet you! With all our crazy schedules, it's been hard getting together, but I've looked forward to finally connecting. Chris talks about you all the time."

"He's my boy, that's for sure. We've spent some hardcore time together over the years, tearing up this town from one end to the other."

"Can you come in for a while? Chris should be home soon. He just called from the club."

"I would, but I am literally on my way to a company shindig. Had this bottle in the car for long enough that I wanted to swing by, hoping someone would be home so I could drop it off. Sort of a housewarming thing, a toast to you guys in your new living situation."

"Thank you," she replied, genuinely touched. "We will enjoy it in your honor."

He looked around, then back at her with a warm smile. "I can see why he likes it here. Nice neighborhood, nice woman. He's a changed man since you guys hooked up. It's been a long time since I've seen him so happy."

She blushed. "Well . . . it's mutual."

"Nothing better than true love—me and my lady can attest to that. Listen, I gotta bounce, so just tell him we'll hit each other up later. Oh, and I'd love for you and Jordan to meet. She was real happy to hear Chris settled into something solid. Maybe the four of us can work a night out together soon."

"I'd like that."

"Great, I'll talk to him about it. Enjoy the wine, and really nice to meet you, Sidonie!"

As he swept down the stairs with a wave, she made note of his genuine warmth. It was a good reaction out of the many her relationship with Chris had inspired. In fact, as much as it had been strange when no one knew, reactions had become litmus tests as more were let in on the secret.

Chris's friends and colleagues, by and large, were either completely lackadaisical ("Cool . . . good luck, man."), or moderately to extremely impressed ("Wow . . . she runs The Church?"). And though Chris's decision to start moving his things from Hyde Park to Andersonville disappointed his mother, she never failed to mention how much she looked forward to meeting Sidonie. Vanessa was still uninformed of the particulars and had been too immersed in her own drama to care much anyway. That chapter had yet to be written.

On Sidonie's side, everyone at the club was thrilled, with endless questions and curiosities. Jasper, the undisputed conduit of their meeting, took particular pride-of-ownership. As promised, Al kept the news within staff circles, though he wisely circumvented further entreaties from Officer Mike (which Sidonie appreciated). There'd been a delay in Marian and Steve's Florida departure (the foreclosed property fell through), so the resolution of that awkward sidebar was on hold for the time being. Patsy—out of town on extended family business—had yet to receive her personal debrief, and Karen remained a staunch supporter, eager to meet the man in the middle. All felt to be unfolding as well as could be expected.

Then came the call.

It was Wednesday afternoon, about two o'clock. Chris was not expected in that night. The only scheduled event was spoken word, which Andrew was handling on his own, and since Sound Alchemy was also dark, Chris was taking the rare free time to get settled at the house.

When her phone rang, Sidonie, expecting it to be Chris, was surprised to see "Alice Rosen" pop up on caller ID.

"Hey, Alice! What's going—"

"Sidonie, you need to get home, right now!" The panic in Alice's voice triggered an immediate chill up Sidonie's back.

"What's going on? What's all that noise?" A melee of some kind was audible in the background, the sounds of men yelling and the high-pitched screech of a female voice.

"It's a clusterfuck here. I'm recording it so you can see what's going on—"

"*What's* going on? You're scaring me!"

"The police are here! I heard all this noise out back and didn't know what the hell was happening, so I came out to the patio and there were cops everywhere, guns pointed at Chris, all sorts of craziness. He was on the back stairway going up with a TV box—I guess he bought you guys a new TV—and Sandra, that fucking bitch . . ." Alice cut out.

"*What?*"

"Sorry, I was just trying to see around the corner. Anyway, I guess she saw him going up and down the stairs with boxes, thought he was robbing you or some bullshit, and called the police."

Sidonie felt a spasm of rage. In her home. In *his* home. *Fucking hell, was there no sanctuary from this shit?*

"Sidonie, are you still there?" Alice was panting.

"I'm here, I'm here," she answered, rushing to her office. "What's happening now?"

"Sandra's still carrying on about how she'd never seen him before and how she figured he was up to no good—"

"*Goddammit!* She's a fucking liar! Can you say something to the cops—tell them you know who he is?" Frantic, she grabbed her purse and ran past the bar toward the parking lot door, eliciting a perplexed look from Al as she flew by.

"I did, but they're ignoring me. They yelled at him to drop the TV, so he tried to set it on the step, but it just rolled down and smashed at the bottom. I kept screaming, 'He lives here, he's my neighbor's boyfriend,' but they completely ignored me."

Sidonie careened out of the parking lot. "I'm in my car, Alice. I'll be there in twenty minutes if traffic isn't too nuts. Can you tell them that?"

"I'll try. They don't seem too interested in what I have to say. I'm hiding at the moment."

Tears gathered as Sidonie sped down a tangled street faster than was probably wise. "What's happening now? Tell me what's happening now, Alice!"

"They told him to step down to the bottom of the stairs, hands above his head, and all of them had their guns pointed at him. There was so much yelling I was terrified they were going to shoot him. Sandra kept carrying on about him robbing you, and I kept saying he wasn't, but then they just slammed him down to the ground and were all over him. God, I'm so furious! They got his license out and this one cop checked it, asked me his name, asked me your name." Alice was crying now. "God, Sidonie, this is awful."

"Are you still recording?" She could barely breathe.

"As much as I can. One of them told me to shut up and stop interfering. That kind of freaked me out. So I'm standing back by the garbage bins and recording from here. They said they're going to interview me at some point, so I'll say all the right things, I promise."

"I know you will." Traffic bogged down as she made a left turn. "Dammit. Listen, Alice, I'm not far, but traffic's getting worse and I'm afraid my phone is about to die." She thrashed around the glove box. "I can't find my charger. Okay, if I lose you, just tell them I'm on my way." Sidonie was stunned by her own driving, half expecting to plow down a hapless pedestrian or sideswipe a car in the next lane.

"I will, Sid. Get here as fast as you can."

Just as Alice uttered those words, a series of mechanical screeches erupted as the car in front of Sidonie swerved wildly to the left, attempting but unable to avoid rear-ending the truck it was tailing. The impact was concussive, followed by the clamor of brakes all around. Sidonie slammed to a stop, luckily averting contact. Dust swirled as the redolent odor of overheated brake pads filled the air. Traffic ground to a complete standstill, and, moments later, her phone died.

THIRTY-FOUR

THE LIVING ROOM WAS DARK, COOLED BY THE EVENING breeze that had mercifully rolled in off the lake. The street below was quiet for this time of night, and a general sense of calm pervaded. Calm after the storm.

Chris sat in the chair closest to the window, staring out, blank and expressionless, his mind oddly fixated on the roster for the upcoming week, a busy one for both the club and Sound Alchemy. A large Sony box encasing the demolished TV lay on the floor at his feet —he couldn't remember why he hadn't left it in the garbage bin—and the beer he nursed had warmed in the time since the police left. After Sandra slunk back to her townhouse, Alice attended to him with great concern—and longer than his exhaustion preferred—yet Sidonie, still, was not home or answering her phone.

A truck raced by bleating its horn, startling Chris from circular thinking. He gingerly touched the side of his head that had earlier made contact with the concrete patio. It ached badly, he couldn't seem to slow his heart rate, and the adrenaline that washed through every corpuscle of his body refused to recede. The result was a kind of feverish stew that came with nausea, dizziness, and the unavoidable punch of humiliation.

Had there been an overall ratcheting up of police interactions lately? Or was proximity to this new woman in his life—a white woman with no reality of the racial paradigm of profiling—making it seem so? He'd been stopped by police before—frequently and for equally groundless reasons—but the gaps in between had been longer and the sense of true danger less imminent. Now the pervasive sense was one of onslaught.

He'd always kept his greater focus on the day-to-day building and bolstering of his life, trying to keep a safe distance from the ubiquity of racial chaos and the political demands of resistance. It wasn't that he lacked cultural pride; it was that he took life as it came, and his life came largely as peaceful, supported by strong family ties, viable opportunities, and tangible success. Yet lately he felt unprotected by that success, by his intelligence and civic diplomacy, by his choice to live an ethical life, avoiding controversial behaviors. There seemed no buffer now, no differentiation. As if he'd been reduced to nothing more than a generic black man in Chicago, with all the attendant baggage of that assignation.

He sat up stiffly, his head throbbing, and felt like he might throw up. Deep breathing was getting him nowhere tonight. He leaned forward, put his head in his hands, hoping the lightheadedness would pass. It did, finally. Just as he was about to attempt rising from the chair, he heard rushed footsteps coming up from the garage and the door burst open to a breathless Sidonie.

She took in the mood and immediately adjusted her emotional state, for which he was grateful. He was certain he couldn't handle her needs at the moment. She set her bag down, focused on containing herself, went to the kitchen, and poured two glasses of water. She came out to the living room, set the glasses on the coffee table, went to Chris, and gently put her arms around him. He leaned into her as she caressed his tousled hair, picking bits of leaves and debris from the knots. Finally he pulled away, guiding her to the chair across from him.

"Sit down ... it's okay ... I'm okay."

She sat peering at him as if trying to see through skin and bones to assess the damage, flooded with questions, concerns, apologies, sorrows. Finding no words to articulate any of what she was feeling, she went for the mundane. "I got caught up in someone's fender bender. It was a mess. Everyone was stuck for almost an hour. I couldn't call because my phone died."

"I wondered what happened. Don't you have a charger in your car?"

"I must have left it in my gym bag."

A long pause followed. She got on her knees in front of him and gently took his face in her hands, silently demanding eye contact. He met her stare.

"What?"

"Tell me what you're feeling. Please."

"Sore. Sick."

"Chris . . . I'm so sorry. I don't even know what to say. Here I welcome you into my home, my neighborhood, and this . . . this insane thing happens. I want to fix it but I don't know how."

"You can't fix it and it's not your fault. Your neighbor—Sandra—really seemed to think I was robbing your place. Maybe you can't fault her for that."

But Sidonie could. They'd all made eye contact the day Chris and Alice met. She knew Sandra had seen Chris walking in and out of her place several times; looks had been exchanged, glances noticed. Her neighbor *knew* he was a part of her life, yet *still* had the effrontery to pretend otherwise. Sidonie's rage was commensurate with the damage inflicted on the man she loved.

But she kept those thoughts to herself. She didn't want to further inflame what was already raw. She would find a moment with Sandra . . . and soon. For now she wanted only to comfort Chris.

"Is there anything I can do, anything I can offer?"

He shook his head. "I just need to calm down. My adrenaline is doing a number on me. Do you think you could make me a piece of dry toast?"

"Of course." Sidonie went to the kitchen, pulled out the bread, and plugged in the toaster.

"I'm grateful for Alice," Chris said from across the room. "Glad we'd already met, that she was there. I hope you'll tell her that for me."

"Definitely."

"The cops weren't too thrilled about her recording everything, but she is one fierce chick. Kept insisting she was filming for everyone's protection, very adamant about spelling out that she knew you, knew who I was. She even suggested they escort me to the door and make me unlock it, which they finally did. I guess when they realized I actually had a key, they had nothing to stand on. Anyway, I want to do something nice for her as a thank-you—maybe take her and her husband to dinner or something."

That struck Sidonie. After unwarranted and violent police mishandling, his first thought was a thank-you dinner. "Yes, we'll do that. I'll certainly let her know how much *I* appreciated her intervention. I can't imagine what would have happened if she hadn't been here."

"You'd be bailing me out of jail right now instead of making me toast." He looked over to the kitchen. "In fact, Sidonie, forget the toast. I can't eat right now. I think I'll just take a shower and lie down. We can talk more tomorrow. Will you be around?"

"I'm supposed to meet my sister for lunch, we moved it to Thursday, but I can—"

"No, no, go ahead, I've got stuff to do anyway. We'll just plan on talking when we both get home, okay?" He got up, aching and dizzy.

She went to him and put her arms around him again. "Would you like some company? Maybe a light massage would make you feel better."

He smiled, but his eyes were somber. "A nice offer . . . but I'll have to take a rain check." He turned and made his painful way up the stairs.

THIRTY-FIVE

WHILE CHRIS FITFULLY SLEPT, AND TOO EARLY FOR HER own repose, Sidonie made two critical nighttime visits.

Her first was next door. To the good neighbors. She found Alice and husband, Mark, watching a movie in their living room, "trying to distract ourselves from the craziness of the day," as Alice put it. There were hugs, tears, expressed gratitude, and a cringeworthy viewing of the video (a copy of which was forwarded to Sidonie's phone). Loose plans were made to get together for dinner, more hugs and tears, then Sidonie left them to their evening.

Her next stop was equally emotional but significantly less friendly. The bad neighbor. Sandra.

It was late enough that Sidonie expected no response to her sharp and repeated rapping, but the light finally popped on, the peephole was engaged, and the door cautiously cracked. Sandra, either feeling or feigning terror, didn't open it wide enough to suggest entrance, nor did Sidonie attempt to make one.

"Look, Sidonie, I don't know what you think happened today, but—"

"Sandra, stop."

"Seriously, I had *no* idea who that was and I thought—"

"*Stop!* I mean it. Just stop. Don't even try to bullshit me."

"Listen, I was only trying to—"

"No, *you* listen! I have tried to keep things pleasant between us. When you were cold and unfriendly, I didn't take it personally. When you were rude and obnoxious to my ex-husband, I let it go. When you were mean-spirited during the dog situation with Alice and Mark, I kept my distance. But when you do something so hateful and ugly to a man who could have been arrested or even fucking *killed*, I will *not* keep my opinions to myself."

"I didn't know who he was! I honestly thought—"

"Don't you *dare* use the word *honestly* with me! There's not a thing about this that was honest. But let me ask, are you just a stupid busybody or an actual, bona fide racist?"

"Now, wait just a minute. I will not allow you—"

"Because I *know* you'd seen Chris here before. You *knew* he and I were spending time together. I've seen you standing at your window looking at us when we were coming up the stairs together. I saw you look at him in the parking area when we were talking to Alice a couple of weeks ago. You were in your front yard when he picked me up the other night—*I saw you look at him.* So don't even try to pretend you didn't know he was a friend of mine, because that's a boldfaced lie. You're lying to me right now, just like you lied to the police, which must be some kind of crime. I don't know why you did it, but I suspect when you saw the chance to fuck with a black man and get away with it, you went for it."

"That is not true! I'm telling you, I never fully saw his face when he was coming down with the TV, so I thought—"

"He wasn't coming *down*, Sandra, he was going *up*. Because he's moving in with me. That was his gift to me, to the house, a new TV . . . which is now smashed to pieces because of you. Your small-minded, presumptuous, ugly racist self caused an incredibly kind and honorable man to be treated like a criminal in his own backyard. So how about this—"

Sandra recoiled as if physically fearful of Sidonie's next move.

"Don't you dare shut that door, Sandra. We are going to resolve this right here and now."

"What does that mean?" She was actually trembling.

"Very simple. You are going to reimburse the cost of the TV and any potential medical expenses Chris may incur from being slammed to the ground by the police. I will get you an invoice for the TV, and should there be doctor bills, I will get you those as well. You will pay immediately and in cash. If you do not agree to pay for those items, I will hire my sister—who is a kickass lawyer—to sue you for harassment, assault, false police report, and anything else I can get you on. Additionally, don't *ever* come near me or my family and friends again. If you do, I will take out a restraining order against you. But pay those bills, stay in your area and as far away from mine as possible, and we should have no problem peacefully co-existing. You got that?"

Sandra pulled her cardigan tight, jaw set, eyes livid. "Are you done?"

Sidonie just glared and walked away as Sandra's door slammed behind her.

THIRTY-SIX

Shaky video focuses on Chris standing halfway up the outdoor staircase leading to the second-floor deck of the townhouse. He is holding a large Sony TV box. Sidonie's neighbor, Sandra, in a sagging cardigan and sweatpants, stands at the second-floor deck of the adjacent townhouse to the left, phone in hand; very agitated as events unfold. The mood is tense, volatile.

Off-camera male voice, abrupt: "Just put the TV down, sir, and move slowly to the patio."

"Okay," Chris responds, "but I'm afraid it'll fall—".

"Drop the TV," second off-camera male voice shouts, "and put your hands up!"

"Oh my God," Alice mumbles off-camera.

Bam, bam, bam ...

The TV box tumbles down the stairs and crushes to the patio. The sound of glass shattering.

Alice's voice gasps.

Chris, face clenched, taking visibly deep breaths, raises his hands and edges slowly down the stairs, stepping carefully around the box splayed across the bottom step. The camera follows his descent, capturing a cadre of six police officers positioned around the patio, guns drawn and pointed at Chris.

Officer shouts: "Get down on the ground!"

Chris moves to comply; second officer holsters his gun, grabs Chris by the shoulders, and slams him to the ground. The side of Chris's head hits the pavement, hard.

"Fuck," Alice's voice, quietly.

~

SIDONIE YANKED THE headphones from her ears. Seated at her desk in the darkened bedroom, the air cool and still in the late hour, she felt her outrage surge in waves that were impossible to quell. Just as a sob attempted to make its way from her throat, his voice murmured from the other side of the room. "Do you really want to deal with all this?"

Startled, she got up and walked to the bed. The clock read three thirty. "Why are you awake?" she whispered.

"I slept for a while. Why are you awake?"

"I was watching Alice's video." She climbed in and rolled to face him. "They could have killed you." The catch in her voice threatened to release a torrent. "In our own backyard. They looked like they could've killed you."

"Yeah." He pulled her close. "Which is why I asked if you really want to deal with all this."

"No. I don't. I want all this to stop. I want all this to have never happened. I want all this to never happen again." She stroked the clenched lines between his eyebrows. "Can you promise me that?"

"I wish I could."

"I wish you could too. So I'll *have* to deal with all this, because you're my guy and whatever comes with you is mine to deal with as well. At least it won't happen here again."

"How's that?"

"I paid Sandra a visit."

He laughed out loud. "You sound so gangsta! I can just picture you walking over there with a baseball bat."

"If I had one, I might've."

"How did you handle Sandra?"

"Very firmly. Set some ground rules, some boundaries—"

"Bet she loved that."

"Thrilled. I told her she was going to pay for a new TV and any doctor's bills you may have—"

"I won't need a doctor."

"Hopefully not, but we'll see. I made it very clear that she needs to take care of that and then stay as far away from us as possible. She got it. And since she's the only one around here who's ever caused any trouble, we should be good."

He couldn't decide if she was gullible or optimistic. "One small step for mankind, I guess."

"We take 'em where we can get 'em."

He shifted to caress her face, looking into her eyes with concern. "What I don't want is racial fatigue to set in. I've seen it happen and it's a bitch. I think that's what my sister and her husband are going through, and they're both black. I don't want all these issues—your mom's boyfriend, or my sister, or the cops, or whatever—to suck the energy out of this relationship. We're all about love and happiness. Is that still possible?"

"Of course it is. I'll meet Vanessa and your mom, you'll meet my family—well, most of them—and after that, we'll focus on good things —like new chairs and new paint and loads of love and happiness."

"You may be naïve—"

"I'm not naïve—"

"But I like the way you think." He relaxed in her arms.

"In fact, why don't you stop by the farmers' market later . . . I'll be there with Karen around noon. You don't have to stay long, just grab a cup of coffee or something. I know she'd love to meet you."

Pain suddenly shot through his head and he was hit by weariness. "I can't think about that just yet . . . but maybe. Let me see how I feel and where my schedule goes. Leave the address and I'll text you when I know what I'm doing."

"Okay." She ran her fingers gently over his lips. "Do you want to make love? It might relax you."

"Ah, Sid." He kissed her forehead. "I do, but my head is killing me."

"Okay. But let me know if there's anything I can do for you."

"Just love me . . . just keep loving me."

"That's easy."

She curled around him and within minutes he was asleep.

She, however, could find no such solace. She lay thinking about his question: if she wanted to deal with all this—"the complications" her father had so presciently posited years ago. She wondered if what he'd been concerned about was in any way resemblant to what she was actually facing in the here and now.

It was strange to think of her father in the context of current life, a life so detached from the one in which he had any involvement. He was irrelevant to her now. Sad, since he'd been so dutiful early on, when he was enamored of his perky wife and two little girls, convinced the American dream could be found in beige, suburban contentment and the role he played as "father." It was when he became disabused of that notion, mollifying his angst with meaningless affairs, that he dropped the façade. Sidonie was old enough to be devastated by his paternal abdication; later she saw him as nothing more than a distant, inconsequential figure.

Which made the memory of him now all the more off-putting. As she lay in bed next to the battered man she loved, the erstwhile question her father asked and she now had to answer echoed with cruel reverberation.

THIRTY-SEVEN

SIDONIE ARRIVED AT THE FARMERS' MARKET HER USUAL thirty minutes early to enjoy her first latte of the day. She gazed over the burgeoning crowd, feeling oddly upbeat; perplexing, given yesterday's events. Maybe it was that Chris woke up acceptably fit, scrapes and bruises notwithstanding. Maybe it was the browbeating she'd given Sandra the night before, an empowering exercise, she hoped, in thwarting further ill will. Whatever it was, Sidonie welcomed the emotional boost, reveling in the warmth of a perfectly bright and balmy day.

A text pinged. Expecting Chris, she was surprised to see it was from her mother, to both her and Karen.

> Have some amazing news! Know you two are getting together
> for lunch, so I'll call in a few minutes! Xo Mom

Intriguing.

Sidonie and her mother had had little conversation since the packing debacle of weeks earlier. Excuses were made—the scramble of selling her place, issues related to their Florida housing options, the ever-fluid date of departure—distracting from any honest attempt to gather or even talk about it further. Sidonie hoped the imminent call might offer progress on that front; she was convinced she needed at least one parent invested in her life.

Karen approached with a large burrito and Diet Snapple. "I can't believe that new Mexican place! Yum-my! Did you get Mom's text?" She plopped to the table and dove in without pause.

"Yeah. What do you think her big news is?"

"I have no idea. She texted this morning about some paperwork, and when I mentioned we were getting together, she said she wanted to talk to us both."

"Maybe she and Steve eloped."

"Please. She'll make a brouhaha out of that in every way possible. *I'm* worried she's backing out, and can't fathom what that would mean. The condo is in escrow, there's no room at either of our places—"

"Unimaginable to even consider—"

"Seriously! So her not leaving at this point would come with a whole shebang of bullshit. Let's hope she just wants to talk about what size cabana they should get or if gluten really does cause dementia."

"By the way, there's the slightest chance Chris might stop by."

"Where? Here?"

"Yeah. He's doing some running around today, but since he doesn't have a gig tonight, I invited him join us—thought you guys could finally meet."

"Oh, wonderful, I'd love that!"

"I haven't heard from him yet, but—"

Karen's phone rang. "It's Mom." She took a slug of Snapple and picked up the phone. "Hey, Mom, you've got us both here. Sid's right across from me. I'll put you on speaker." She placed the phone in the center of the table and hit the speaker button.

"—and it was too hard to figure out anyway."

"Mom, we didn't get any of that. Start over."

"Can you both hear me?"

"Yes, Mom," Sidonie chimed in. "What's your news?"

"Are you sitting down?"

Karen rolled her eyes. "We're at a table eating lunch, so, yes, we're sitting down. Fire away."

"I'm in Florida!"

The two girls looked at each other, flummoxed.

"You're actually *in* Florida? Like you've *moved* to Florida?" Karen queried, mystified.

"Yes. Isn't that something?"

"'Something' is one way to put it. When did that happen, Mom? I thought you were waiting for Steve to decide on a place."

"He wanted my input, said we'd both be sittin' on the front porch so Lord knows I'd have to like what he picked. It seemed silly to wait and I was raring to go, so off I went. I'm a Florida gal now!" She was positively giddy; her daughters less so.

"Where's all your stuff?" Sidonie asked.

"Steve had it shipped down. His stuff too. We're staying in a really nice residential hotel and everything's in storage until we close on the place we chose—"

"Wait, so you've actually picked a place?" Karen shook her head, floored.

"Yes, and it's just darling. You girls are going to love it when you get here. It's got a small backyard, but it's part of a bigger complex with a pond and a swimming pool—"

"When were you going to tell us you'd left the state?" The edge in Karen's voice was unvarnished. "You do remember you have a granddaughter who might've liked saying goodbye, right?"

"Sweetie, it's not like I moved to Mars! I'll be back up at some point in the next couple of months, and we'll get you all down here once we're settled in. There's a big guest room where we'll have two double beds. We're even going to put bunks in the basement level. Steve's got a whole passel of—"

"I'm real happy for you, Mom, but leaving without saying goodbye to your family, your granddaughter, is just bad form." Karen crumpled her burrito in its foil wrap, appetite gone. "I appreciate that you wanted to get started on your new adventure, but considering our last conversation, your stealth exit is a little suspect."

"Oh, for God's sake, Karen, this isn't something I planned weeks in advance and didn't tell you! Steve just came up with the idea and I decided to go with it. There were no intentions, or whatever it is you're trying to imply. I'll call Sarah tonight and I'm sure we'll have a great time talking about Disney World and when she can visit. As for the two of you, I'd love for you to come down as soon as you can."

"A vacation to Florida is not on my schedule, Mom. I think you know that," Sidonie countered.

"Nor mine," Karen echoed. "And let's get real, Mother. Sidonie's in a new relationship with a man you pretty much announced your boyfriend would have problems with, so ignore the elephant all you want, but how's a vacation down there gonna fly?"

"Let's please not get into all that again! Isn't it possible for my two girls to spend some quality time with their mother without *any* of the men around? How about that? We could have a girls' weekend, just the three of us. I'll show you my new town and ..."

By now Sidonie had checked out of the conversation, jaw clenched to control words she would surely regret if they escaped. After the trauma of yesterday, she was particularly unappreciative of "the dialogue of smaller minds," as Karen once described their mother's tendency toward banal chatter, disappointed that she was solidifying her place in that demographic.

"... and we'll do some of that great shopping Florida is known for—"

"That's not going to happen, Mom," Sidonie finally asserted. "I'm incredibly busy at work, and in the beginning stages of a very important relationship, so we'll just have to leave it at that. Listen, I've gotta get going—"

Karen gave her a *do you really?* look, to which Sidonie shook her head. "Me too, Mom. Have fun getting the place locked down, let me know if you need any papers looked at, and enjoy the, uh ... well, just enjoy it all." Her voice was flat, noncommittal; Marian was oblivious.

"Thank you, sweetheart. I will give Sarah a call and we'll catch up later. Bye-bye." And she was gone.

Karen was dumfounded. "Unfuckingreal. She's so damn afraid to rile her alt-right boyfriend she's absconded like a thief in the night. Damn, sister, look what you've gone and done with your 'Negro boyfriend' and all. Shattered the entire family dynamic." Her tone was bitter as she looked at Sidonie with authentic chagrin. "I'm so sorry. She's a coward. A coward living with a racist. Quite the couple. I'm not sure when she lost her spine, but it must have been somewhere between ignoring Daddy's affairs and meeting this regressive redneck."

Sidonie's text alert beeped. "What timing. Chris is on his—" Before she could finish the sentence, there he was. Watching as he loped across the plaza in his jeans and black T-shirt, his eyes bright and smile warm, she felt a surge of emotion. "Hey, you!" she called out.

He was upon her in a swooping hug. "Hey you, yourself! I managed to reroute my day. I hear the coffee here is real good." He turned to Karen. "And you must be the big sister."

Karen pushed her chair back, stood up, and grabbed him in a hug. "I am so glad to meet you, Chris. You've made my sister very happy, which makes me happy, *and* I hear you're a technical wizard. I'm not sure any combo gets better for her these days." They laughed in that awkward-pleasant "just meeting" way, and he joined them at the table.

After coffee and food were procured, they launched into standard introductory chatter. Chris and Sidonie had earlier decided not to mention the police encounter of the previous day, so excuses were made about his facial scrapes and bruises, keeping the conversation breezy. By the time Karen got through her second Diet Snapple, watches were being checked; Chris was the first to stand.

"I have to get going, got a couple of microphones to get out to my Shure guy before he closes." He leaned down and gave Sidonie a warm, meaningful kiss, then reached over to squeeze Karen's hand with a smile. "Great to finally get together, Karen. I look forward to meeting the rest of your family when we can. Take care, ladies."

He was off. Both women watched as he traversed the busy plaza and made his way down the street. Karen turned to Sidonie with a pleased grin.

"Oh, I like him. I like him a lot."

"Yeah?" Sidonie hadn't realized how important her sister's approval was, but after their mother's strange dismissal, it was a much-needed balm.

"He's everything you said: warm, uniquely handsome, present, interested. That he's talented and successful in business is just a bonus. Excellent job, little sister, excellent job!"

Sidonie couldn't remember a time when she loved her sister more.

THIRTY-EIGHT

"IS NO ONE INTO THIS ANYMORE?" SIDONIE LAUNCHED without preamble.

Patsy looked at her as if she'd blurted heresy, but the fact was, twice in two months pitch meetings had been cancelled by the investors, with a third only "penciled" in, and yet neither of them seemed all that bothered.

"Is that a serious question? I don't think that's it—wait, do you?" That Patsy asked was itself telling.

They'd agreed to meet to discuss strategy, and were now seated in Patsy's River West catering kitchen, a spit-shiny monument to the gourmet culinary arts currently bereft of kitchen staff. Coffee and fresh cookies were set on the long baker's table where they huddled with notes and folders.

"I just sense evaporating momentum," Sidonie replied.

"Whose?"

"Everyone's? Mine?" So caught up in everything from her mother's exodus to her progressively more demanding role at the club, mixed with the incessant pull of her budding relationship with Chris, Sidonie realized how infrequently, lately, she'd thought about this enterprise that had held her attention for the past many years.

And with Patsy largely absent from the conversation—and the city —over the last couple of months, caught up in a dire family emergency involving an alcoholic brother, a third DUI, and a smashed storefront somewhere in her hometown of Urbana, her designated role as project cheerleader had been significantly blunted.

"Yes, it's been slow, but evaporation?" Patsy was either feigning surprise at Sidonie's take, or she truly was.

"It seems to me that neither of us is as excited as we used to be. You've been gone a lot, I'm crazy busy," Sidonie continued. "And it's too hard to keep this going on the basis of distraction. Or apathy. Or whatever it is we're feeling."

"Okay, I admit I've had all the bullshit in Urbana to deal with, which makes it harder for me to stay on top of things, but apathy is not applicable. I *will* get back in touch with these guys, and I *will* find out what's up with them. I promised I'd take this role on and I will get us back on track, Sid."

"If you think that's realistic. I think we might need to reevaluate our strategy."

"Tell me what that means."

"The all-eggs-in-one-basket thing could be working against us. Maybe we need to cast a wider net, get the word out more. See if we can stir up other investor interest. It might shake things up a bit."

"Or send these guys straight for the door. They were very clear about *not* wanting to get into a bidding war that ratchets up the numbers. They want first rights."

"Say the guys who cancelled our last two meetings."

"I know, but there are many nuances to this group and this level of investment. When I talk to them this week—and I will talk to them —I'll reiterate that our deadline leaves no further wiggle room. I do agree with that."

"Okay . . . if that's the best we can do. Just keep me posted."

"Of course!"

"How's your brother doing?"

"He's a fucking asshole. Seriously. He put three people in the hospital and *still* acts like he's the victim. I don't know why I spend so much time down there fending off disaster. Somehow I've become the family spokesperson."

"You're fearless and you've got a big mouth." Sidonie laughed. "Makes you perfect for the job."

"Did I tell you my mother ended up in the hospital too?"

"No! What happened?"

"Nothing . . . other than hysteria, panic, dehydration, more hysteria, blood pressure—you know the drill. She's enabled this idiot his entire life and, I swear, the two of them deserve each other."

"You're so harsh."

"I am. But they deserve it."

"Well, I'm sorry you have to deal with all this stuff."

"But I don't, do I? I could just leave them to their madness and watch the house burn down."

"You're too good a spokesperson for that." Sidonie looked around the empty kitchen stacked with shiny chrome bowls, endless utensils, and pots of every shape and size. It always amazed her how much equipment was required by a proper catering kitchen. "Quiet today . . . has it been slow lately?" As a sought-after chef who called her own shots, Patsy's freelance status allowed for contingencies like recurring monthlong visits to dysfunctional families.

"It's only quiet because I gave everyone the day off. Actually I'm busier than I'd like to be. But that's good. I need to keep busy—keeps me from getting too involved in Jerry-Springerland down south. How about you? What's the latest?"

Sidonie had not yet told Patsy about her relationship with Chris, much less his moving into the townhouse. Which was strange, considering how long it had been and how close they were. Part of it was the distraction of Patsy's long absences and the lack of meaningful time together over the last several months; part of it was some intangible hesitation Sidonie couldn't identify. But there was no rationale she could conjure up for putting it off any longer.

"Actually, I've got some big news."

Patsy looked up with wide eyes. "Oh my God—you and Theo are back together!"

The snap in Sidonie's neck was almost painful. "*What?*! No . . . ugh . . . no! Why would you say that?"

"I just thought . . . since he's been calling so much."

"No. Never. He's in AA and just wanted to make an amends apology."

"Well, that was nice, wasn't it?" She never stopped trying.

Sidonie rolled her eyes. "Anyway . . . no. But I do have news on the love front. Chris Hawkins and I have started seeing each other, and he moved into my place a few weeks ago."

There was a beat of silence as Patsy frowned, trying to put together who Chris Hawkins was. Then: "The *sound* guy? That tall, scrubby-looking black dude I met in your office? Are you kidding me?"

And there it was—why Sidonie had hesitated in telling her old friend about her new relationship. Wrong tone, wrong emphasis; wrong words.

"No," she said in a measured voice. "I'm not kidding you. And your descriptive phrasing doesn't quite capture him or what he means to me, so tread lightly, girlfriend, please."

Patsy looked at her, incredulous. "Wait, are you serious?"

"About which part? The guy or the way you just framed the guy?"

"Sorry, but I'm just a little stunned. I had no idea, *zero* idea, he'd be someone you'd even consider, much less move into your home. I mean, he seems like a nice enough guy, and I know you were thrilled he took the job, but come on! Aren't you *fantastically* out of his league?"

The next beat of silence was even more burdened.

"Let's see . . . you don't know the guy, you've spent all of five minutes talking to him, and though you *do* know—because I told you—that he's built and runs his own very successful company and is incredibly talented as the sound manager of The Church, one of the most prestigious venues in the city of Chicago, you've somehow come up with the equation that I'm out of his league. Care to explain that?"

Patsy was now fussing with items on the table, straightening various papers and folders, sweeping up cookie crumbs. "I don't know why I said that. You're right, I don't know him."

"That's right. You don't."

But Patsy continued fluttering. Sidonie sat back in her chair, silent and sullen. The pause was much too long to be anything but baiting.

Patsy finally cracked. "Okay, Sid, you can sit there and act all indignant because I didn't immediately clap my hands, but why would I have ever expected you to pick a guy like that? Let's not forget, I've *known* all the guys you've picked, and, say what you will, he's quite the departure."

"How so, exactly?" Sidonie was quietly seething.

"He may be nice enough, and good at business or whatever it is, but come on, what's the pull? Seriously. He's not that good-looking, he dresses like Mark Zuckerberg, and I know you're going to take this *all* the wrong way—but he's *black*! Yes, yes, I know you dabbled briefly in college, but really, what do you know about black culture, black guys? What, are you going to start hanging out on the south side, stocking the fridge with fried chicken and watermelon? Listen to hip-hop, discuss whose lives matter, and debate diversity at the Oscars?"

Sidonie was on her feet. "What the fuck is wrong with you?" She was stunned that her best friend just trumped the obtuseness of her mother.

"I know, I know, I'm a bigot, you're so open-minded, blah, blah, blah—"

From there, Sidonie wasn't clear how much of Patsy's diatribe she absorbed. Somewhere after "watermelon" and "fried chicken" a loud *whooshing* sound descended that only grew as the jabbering continued, blocking out words in lieu of metastasizing anxiety.

"—but I'm actually *not* a bigot. I feel for their issues and have nothing against anyone. I'm just trying to make a point here," Patsy prattled on. "I've known you a long time, and I suspect there's something else going on. Like, some self-esteem issues wrapped up in all this."

"What?" Sidonie had now completely lost the thematic arc.

"Let's honestly look at the trajectory of things: you were married to one of the best looking men in the city, you were part of a social circle of Chicago movers and shakers, all while running the hottest club around. Then you suffered a miscarriage, the asshole dumped you for a hot babe, you crashed like the fucking Hindenburg, and after a year of crying about what a loser you are, you're suddenly *living* with some nebulous black employee who could use a stylist. Maybe you think that's the best you can do, that's all you deserve, and, hey, if that's true, part of me admires that. There's way too much emphasis on looks and money and status anyway, so if you honestly *don't* care about those things, kudos to you, girlfriend! But I think you need to look at it for a minute. I get that you're lonely, Sid. Maybe you're desperate, but I'm finding it hard to believe *this* is the guy you want to invest the next chunk of your life in."

Sidonie watched her friend's arms flailing, the occasional wag of a finger, the intense expressions and articulating lips, but conscious awareness had stepped aside in the rush of disassociation.

She and Patsy had been friends for so many years it never dawned on her that they did not share some very basic and essential life philosophies. They rarely discussed privilege or race, and had, in the mutual self-absorption of career building, relationships, and family wrangling, largely avoided sociopolitical issues that swirled not only around the world and country, but specifically the city in which they lived. Their lives had not been particularly controversial, their experiences not exceptionally diverse, and the extent of their generalized empathy and compassion stuck largely close to home.

And while she resisted the idea that Patsy was a bona fide bigot, a person who, like her mother's boyfriend, would find interracial relationships inherently problematic, she could not deny that the perspectives conveyed in this heated, incendiary lecture suggested otherwise. She also suspected that if Chris dressed like Theo and looked more like Idris Elba, they'd be having a different conversation. The mix of elitism and racism was potent.

She could see Patsy's mouth still moving, but the *whooshing* had only gotten louder; her heart beat faster, her stomach clenched tighter. She picked up her bag, turned toward the door, and, without a look back, raced from the room as fast as she possibly could.

THIRTY-NINE

Patsy Gilmore info@patsygilmore.com
Sidonie Frame sidonieframe@thechurch.com
...My bad behavior

Sid—

I know you're furious with me right now and you have every right to be. I am so SO sorry! I don't know what else to say except I'M SORRY. You surprised me with your news, but I should have waited and taken more time to think about my reaction before blurting out all that crazy shit. I know I hurt you and that wasn't my intention, honestly.

I think you've known me long enough to know I am NOT a racist. I don't know why I spewed out all those horrible clichés—I think part of it was me trying to be subversively funny, another part was being the devil's advocate, and the worst part was me being incredibly stupid and insensitive. It was defenseless and in poor taste and I'm sickened by my own behavior. Really, I am. I've been crying for hours and I think I will be until we talk.

Can we write it off to my being exhausted from my fucked-up family situation? It probably really does have something to do with it. I've left a couple of messages on your phone and since you haven't called back, I guess you're still too angry to talk to me. But when you can, please call. PLEASE.

I hope you'll forgive me. And I hope you'll give me another chance to talk to you about Chris. If you love him enough to invite him into your life and your home, I should trust you enough to know he must be someone very special. I'm an asshole for going anywhere else with this.

I'm sorry . . . . . . 😣

xxoo
P

— — —

Sidonie Frame sidonieframe@thechurch.com
Patsy Gilmore info@patsygilmore.com
Re: . . . My bad behavior

Patsy:

You're right. I don't want to talk to you.

You're also right that Chris is someone very special. And not just to me. He's special to everyone who knows him. He's also someone who has shown integrity and grace in situations that you or I would probably find unendurable. So to hear you reduce him to sickening racist tropes was unforgivable.

Maybe you aren't a racist, maybe you are. I don't know. We've never had our sensibilities tested on the topic, at least not in front of each other. But the fact that you went there, whatever the reasons, whatever the rationale, is something I think YOU really need to look at.

I could rebut every single thing you threw in my face, but I don't even want to give it the energy. But please be assured: my self-esteem is deeply intact and I feel honored—HONORED—that a man of Chris's heart and soul loves me.

I can't predict the future, but I want to take a break from you right now. I'm not trying to be punitive, I just don't want to talk about this with you at the moment. I don't want to hear your perspective. What that means beyond that, I don't know. I'm still reeling.

If you get another meeting scheduled with the investors, let me know and we'll sort that out then.

For now, deal with your life, I'll deal with mine, and we'll see where we are later on down the line.

S.

FORTY

FOR THE FIRST TIME IN HIS LIFE, CHRIS WAS KNEE-DEEP IN the process of renovating a living space and discovered both talent and enthusiasm for the activity. Sidonie's townhouse had architecturally impressive bones—varied levels, exposed brick, high ceilings, and dramatically set windows—and given her own design abdication, Chris, once ensconced, had carte blanche to explore his inner *Fixer Upper*.

Something about the assignment grounded him, made him feel like he was creating *home*. He'd rarely experienced that sensation as an adult; he'd always been more of a temporary resident, a roommate, someone who came and went but was never invested. Even in his last relationship he'd kept a suitcase under the bed. Sidonie's invitation into this warm, appealing place, and his subsequent involvement and creativity, seemed to seal the deal: they were making a life here together. It felt profound to him.

Sandra had slipped an envelope in the mailbox weeks earlier with little over half the cash demanded for the shattered TV. Discussion ensued about whether raising further ruckus was merited, but Chris convinced Sidonie it wasn't worth the contact or the stress chemicals; he took care of purchasing a new one, along with a variety of wall hangings (largely photographic), two living room chairs, a vintage mid-century coffee table, and a rather dramatic bookcase. Whenever Sidonie returned home after he'd had a block of time to devote to the project, she'd gleefully applaud the color and character he was bringing to her previously spartan quarters. He appreciated the encouragement and continued.

On this particular Thursday, with Sidonie off to a client meeting with Frank and nothing on his own schedule until noon, he was painting a bedroom wall, just one wall, a deep shade of burnt sienna, when his phone rang. He was prepared to ignore it until he saw his mother's name. She didn't typically call during the day, so he quickly wiped his hands and picked up.

"Hey, Ma, everything okay?"

"Not really, Christopher. You have now been in this relationship for long enough that it could hardly be considered new, and I have yet to meet this woman of yours. Don't you think that's a problem?"

Chris suppressed a smile. "It's just about timing and schedules, Ma. It has nothing to do with either of us not wanting to come down."

"Is that so? I believe I'm only fourteen miles south of Andersonville. Is that too far for you these days?"

He grinned. "Of course not, I just—"

"Have you met her mother?"

"No, I haven't." He was relieved he could answer honestly, even if the attendant reasons were convoluted. "Between juggling Alchemy gigs and my responsibilities at The Church, I've hardly met anyone from her life outside of work. So consider yourself in good company."

"Humph. We need to remedy that. I want the two of you to come to dinner this weekend, and do *not* tell me you can't find the time. You can find the time."

"I promise I will sit down with Sidonie tonight and see what she's got coming up. The problem is we both work weekends—"

"Didn't you say you were closed on Monday? I'm perfectly capable of making dinner on a Monday."

"Okay, okay." Chris laughed. "I surrender. Unless she's got something going this Monday, we'll be down. What time and what do you want us to bring?"

"Six o'clock and just yourselves. I've been stockpiling for weeks."

As he went back to painting, he realized he hadn't asked if Vanessa would be joining them. He couldn't decide if knowing or not knowing was the better approach.

FORTY-ONE

SOME FRAMES WERE ORNATE, OTHER WERE SIMPLE AND plain. Black-and-white photos, color and sepia. One picture after the next capturing faces, smiles, celebrations—family. A lifetime of events and moments memorialized in these frames.

Sidonie walked slowly down the hall, gazing at each photograph hung carefully in an eclectic, appealing pattern. She soaked in the images of Chris's past. His father—tall, broad-shouldered, always with a smile. His brother—slender and studious, brows furrowed under dark horn-rimmed glasses. There was Chris—from cherubic, to gap-toothed, to gangly, to now. Vanessa was all fierce eyes and wiry limbs, her poses brimming with energy. And of course, Delores, the matriarch of the family: beautiful, buxom, meticulously dressed; delight in her family exuding from every picture.

It was a mesmerizing collection, with its myriad glimpses into the life Chris had led, the beloved family that surrounded him, including the two no longer there. It felt sacred, this wall, and she viewed it with commensurate reverence.

"Quite the crew, aren't they?" Delores stood in the hallway gazing at one of the photos, misty-eyed. "I never get tired of looking at these. They're a testament to all that is most dear to me." She glanced at the portrait across from Sidonie. "Chris was a little doll, wasn't he?"

"He was. He still is. It's so great the way you put this together, Delores, like a collage. It inspires me to do something similar at my . . . at our house."

"Thank you! I think it's a nice way to display any collection of photographs, but when it's family, it all becomes so precious. I try to add at least one new picture of Chris and Vanessa every year, but it gets harder as they get busier and we don't gather as much. Plus, I'm running out of wall space!" She laughed.

"Maybe we can take some pictures tonight. I'll want to memorialize it, too. It's a big night for me, finally meeting you."

"As for me. I knew you had to be someone special. Chris has always been picky about who he spends his time with. And it's been so long since he's had anyone in his life I started worrying he'd end up a confirmed old bachelor! Watching him glow every time he speaks about you has done my heart good. I'm a typical mother, Sidonie. I just want my boy to be happy."

"I hope he is," she responded shyly. "I think he is."

Delores put her arm through hers. "I think he is too. And he's putting dessert together for us to enjoy in the parlor, so why don't we head down there now and find the best seat in front of the fireplace?"

Sidonie loved that this old house had an actual parlor where dessert could be enjoyed, where the chill of autumn allowed for the coziness of a real fire. She was relieved that they'd been able to share an extraordinary meal of rib roast, mashed potatoes, and sautéed green beans without the feared tension of intra-family dissent—Vanessa called early in the evening to alert Delores that work would keep her later than expected.

Now, seated as instructed in the chair closest to the fireplace, Sidonie felt . . . happy: sated with good food, warm spirits, and an overriding sense of well-being. She could hear Chris and his mother laughing in the kitchen, the whirr of an electric beater (there'd been promises of real whipped cream), all lilted by Billie Holiday's singular voice floating softly from the stereo. Sidonie appreciated the fact that she'd be able to share these experiences as often as they could get down here. Chris and his mother were close, Hyde Park was an easy drive during nonpeak hours, which meant enjoyment of this lustrous setting, and the ease and charm of Delores's company, were sure to become a part of their relationship. The thought pleased her, particularly given her own familial deficit.

Suddenly the front door clamored open and, in the rush of cool air that accompanied her entrance, Vanessa stumbled into the foyer. Literally stumbled.

"Oh, fuck me! Goddammit . . ." she growled as keys were dropped, then retrieved and flung onto a table. There was rustling of coats and scarves, then the inevitable approach from around the corner to the parlor, where Sidonie, with dread descending, awaited the moment of contact.

"Sidonie! There you are! I hoped I wouldn't miss you." Tidy in a navy business suit and white blouse, her hair pulled in a tight bun at the nape of her neck, Vanessa presented as the professional she was, but her speech was slurred, her eyes droopy and unfocused, and her movements decidedly wobbly. It was not hard to determine that she'd spent at least some of her previous hours in the company of alcohol. Perhaps even lots of alcohol. Oddly, her cheerful greeting to Sidonie seemed authentic.

"Hello, Vanessa," Sidonie responded, rising from her comfortable seat to extend a hand. "I'm so glad to finally meet you."

"Are you? My husband says I'm not cheerful enough to make anyone glad . . . or something like that." Vanessa chortled, shaking the proffered hand. "No need for ceremony with me, we're all family here." She dropped to a nearby chair and leaned back, eyes closed, her entire being suffused with exhaustion. "I'm sorry I missed dinner. But my husband—well, actually, my soon-to-be-*ex*-husband—served me divorce papers today, at my job, on a really difficult day, so . . ." She faded.

"I'm sorry. That's got to be—"

"He is an unmitigated, unequivocal—as many fucking 'uns' as you can possibly pull out of your ass—*prick!*"

"*Vanessa!*" Delores and Chris, bearing trays of coffee and peach cobbler, walked smack into the assault of Vanessa's vituperation. Delores displayed her disciplinarian side without hesitation. "That is completely unacceptable at any time. It is certainly unacceptable when we have a guest."

"Hey, Ness." Chris put his tray down and walked over to his sister, leaning in to give her a hug. "Smells like you've enjoyed some spirits tonight, little sister. Hope you didn't drive."

"Fuck you. I'm not an idiot, despite what some people think. I did have a drink or many," she responded slyly, "that's true, but there was no enjoying. Everything tasted like piss, but what the fuck, right?"

"Child, you are going to break me!" Delores set a dessert plate down loudly enough to make a point. Vanessa rolled her eyes and turned to her brother.

"But yes, Christopher," Vanessa continued, "I was very responsible; I took a cab home, and since I don't have to work until ten tomorrow, I've got plenty of time to mourn the death of my marriage before heading back out to save other, less fortunate people."

"Well . . . good." Refusing to volley with her, Chris sat next to Sidonie, who, hoping to avert conversational Armageddon, was forkfuls into dessert.

"Oh my God," she exalted, her mouth full. "This might be the best thing I've ever eaten! Did you make it, Delores?"

"I did. A favorite recipe." She beamed. "Vanessa, would you like some cobbler?" There was terseness in the question.

"No, Mother, unless you want to see me vomit it all over your beautiful parlor rug."

Delores could hold back no longer. "Then I suggest you get yourself to your room and begin your recovery process right quick. We are entertaining a guest and I do not appreciate the vulgarity and rudeness you've introduced into our evening."

Chris interrupted. "Actually, Ma, if you still want me to see if I can get your computer unfrozen, we should probably do that now. Sid and I have to get going pretty soon." He queried Sidonie with an *is that okay?* look; she nodded, hesitantly.

Delores rose. "All right, son." With a shot back at Vanessa: "Do you think you can be civil for a few minutes?"

Vanessa sighed like a teenager. "I will do my very best, Mother."

As they, perhaps unwisely, trundled off, Vanessa leaned back on the couch. "I'm sorry. I'm being a bitch."

"I know you're going through a lot right now," Sidonie said cautiously, aware that the portentous mood could explode without warning and bloody them both. For Chris's sake, for Delores's sake, she was determined to keep things in check.

Vanessa sat back up and took a slow sip of coffee, her hands shaking in the effort. "I have no doubt Chris has told you how I feel about him dating a white woman."

And right into the fray.

Sidonie felt the weight of inevitable conflict descend. Her thoughts went immediately to the repair upstairs, hoping it was a quick fix.

"He mentioned it. I'm not quite sure how to respond, but I do know it makes me sad."

Vanessa looked up sharply. "Sad?"

"Yes. Chris loves you, you're his family. It's important to him what you think."

"Chris doesn't give a shit what I think."

"I know he admires you for the things you do, the things you fight for. He's shared a lot of that with me too."

"Uh-huh. Anyway . . ." Vanessa leaned over her mother's cobbler and started picking at it. "Do you have any thoughts about all that?" Her voice was baiting; Sidonie felt both trapped and curious.

"You really want to get into this right now?"

"Why not? We're here, two grown women, sipping coffee and eating cobbler. The moment is now—let's have the conversation."

"I think it might be wiser to wait until we're both clear-headed and know each other a little better."

"Nah! I may be drunk, but I'm not unconscious," Vanessa retorted, eyes flashing. "Look, Sidonie, it's not personal. It's not about judging you because you're white. It has nothing to do with you at all. And you're right—I don't know you—certainly not well enough to know how good or not good you are for my brother. You could be perfect, but that's not the point."

"Feels like exactly the point to me."

"It would, coming from your position of privilege."

Sidonie shook her head; she was being drawn in despite all efforts to stay out. "Ah . . . there it is. That word that presumes so much about me. That presumes I have what I have because it was granted to me somehow, and nothing could be further from the truth. Everything I have I got through my own hard work, and I resent being made to feel otherwise."

Vanessa's face softened. "But I'm not saying that. I have no doubt you've worked really hard for what you have. That's not what privilege means in this context. You should know that by now."

"Then explain the context."

"Okay . . ." Vanessa stood with a slight teeter. Glancing toward the staircase as if to assess how much time she had, she launched with the didacticism of a professor. "*Privilege* is walking into any situation armed with the confidence of your perceived majority, the blank slate of your whiteness and its status as the cultural norm. It's your whiteness exempting you from suspicion, from limit, from microaggressions and implicit bias, from being followed around department stores, or getting profiled by the police or the court system. *Privilege* is what allows you to get a loan, or rent an apartment, expect proper medical care without any thought to your race. It's about your race not being a reason *for* anything, whether shoving you into a category or impacting an outcome. *Privilege* is living without the color of your skin being the first thing people see, think, know, or judge about you." She turned to Sidonie, almost apologetic. "Can you understand that?"

While Vanessa was talking, Sidonie flashed on the encounters she'd already experienced with Chris and couldn't avoid her own epiphanous view of exactly what Vanessa referenced. "I can."

Taken aback, Vanessa dropped to her chair. "Really?" she asked sincerely.

"To the extent I can. Being with Chris, seeing certain responses and reactions he gets, things I never noticed or imagined before, yeah . . . it's been enlightening. It's made me pay more attention."

"Good. You need to be enlightened. Your whole race needs to be enlightened."

"I'm sure that's true, but what does it have to do with me and Chris?"

"It doesn't directly. The problem is tangential. There's a long, painful history to this . . . centuries of oppression mixed with the cultural aggrandizement of whiteness, that thing we *couldn't* be. White women, white beauty, white value—it all got put on a pedestal while our people were brutalized as ugly and inhuman. Black men were hung for even *looking* at a white woman, yet some in my community actually try to look white, as white as they can. Can you believe that?"

"No, it's really—"

"Our men and women suffered this history together, *transcended* this history together, but that idealization still leads some of my brothers to want what they couldn't have. So instead of choosing black women to build our communities and create family, they want the freedom of personal choice—the freedom to be with white women. Which to many of us feels like repudiation." Vanessa leaned back and closed her eyes as if the exercise of articulation had depleted her.

Sidonie felt gutted. "So you see Chris's involvement with me as a repudiation of his race? Our little personal relationship bears the burden of that much weight?"

"In a personal sense, no. In a cultural sense, yes. I don't think he chose you to betray his race, but I don't think my brother gives a shit *what* his choices mean."

Sidonie could hear shuffling upstairs, chairs scraping, the movement of feet; her anxiety silently begged Chris to wrap it up and find his way back down. "Or maybe he sees true freedom as having the right to make any choice desired, without obligation to race. Isn't that the purest, most basic form of freedom?"

"Is it? Then, tell me, why don't all my people get to make any choice desired? Why are they still dying in larger numbers at the hands of police, incarcerated in larger numbers? Why are they struggling in an economy that doesn't give a fuck about pulling them out of poverty? Is it right for one person to exercise his freedom when so many don't have theirs?"

"So Chris should sacrifice his personal life for the cause of—"

"Shouldn't he? I am. Even my own husband, a proud black man, thinks I'm too strident, too fixated on these issues, so much so that he's divorcing me. How about *that* sacrifice? But my own brother shouldn't play his part?"

Sidonie, perilously close to losing her cool, stood in defensive posture. "Maybe he *is* playing his part and it's just a different part than you think he should play. Maybe we're all doing the best we can to move society in a more progressive direction—"

Vanessa started slow clapping with a sardonic smile. "And now you want a pat on the back for doing the best you can? A cookie for *not* being a racist? For being a nice white girl who's so colorblind she'll even date a black man?"

Sidonie finally snapped, leaning toward Vanessa with barely contained anger. "If you think my being with Chris has anything at all to do with showing how *not* racist I am, then you don't know him any better than you know me. But actually, I think we're done here." She walked to the staircase and called up: "Chris! We need to get going please!"

Vanessa's expression conveyed discomfort at the potential of her mother and brother intervening in this tête-à-tête, but she was all in and couldn't stop. "Look, if the truth hurts your feelings, then maybe you need thicker skin. It's not my job to *not* offend you. It's your job— it's all our jobs—to change the damn narrative. That's all I'm saying."

Sidonie actually slammed her foot down. "That's not all you're saying, but there's nothing more I *will* say tonight. I love your brother, he loves me. That's separate from the very real issues of racial politics in America. This isn't about racial politics—it's about two people who love each other. Period."

Vanessa stood, wearing her exhaustion like a pall. "Okay, I throw in the towel. I could apologize, but . . . this is my life. I'm worn out. I don't have the energy to make this easy for you, to make it any less harsh. Our reality *is* harsh, and we're fighting it from every angle. If you really want to get 'woke,' to be a true ally, a worthy accomplice in this movement, I would welcome you. As for you and my brother . . . I . . . I think I'm going to throw up . . ."

Before Sidonie could react to the remark, she realized Vanessa meant it literally. Just as Chris and Delores descended from upstairs and walked into the parlor, Vanessa raced to the kitchen and vomited into the sink.

FORTY-TWO

THE EVENING LOST ITS ABILITY TO BE ANY MORE THAN A mixed bag after Vanessa's diatribe. Delores struggled to assure Sidonie that her daughter "really could be a lovely person," even if, as Chris interjected, one lacking manners, decorum, and the ability to hold her liquor, but all efforts to bring what had been a fine event to a more positive conclusion faltered. Still, Sidonie couldn't deny the larger impact of Delores's warm welcome and the thoughtful, engaging conversation that had woven throughout the night. Plus, as she made mention to her chagrined hostess, the cobbler was transformative.

Chris, however, was incensed. "Fuck Vanessa!" he railed on the drive back to Andersonville. "I swear to God, she's like that asshole kid who'll say anything just to get a rise out of her parents."

Sidonie's impulse was to defuse the situation. "But it's not like I didn't expect it. Actually, after everything you've told me about her, I was afraid she'd roll in with a flamethrower. I think I got off pretty easy."

"She needs to keep her shit to her damn self. I might even have more respect for your mother—if nothing else she understands the conflict and doesn't try to shove everyone's face in it."

"Let's not get carried away. My mother is less about understanding and more about cowardice. At least Vanessa has no fear of speaking her mind. There's something courageous about that. And, come on, she'd been drinking because she *did* get served today, so you've got to give her at least a little break."

THE ALCHEMY OF NOISE | 173

"Yeah, sure." He was not swayed.

"Plus, and I say this honestly, she made some really valid points. I'm hoping after we get to know each other a little, she'll see me as more than just a nice white girl who stole her brother." She playfully leaned in to kiss his cheek, but Chris couldn't let it go.

"It's disrespectful to you, it's disrespectful to my mother, and it's really disrespectful to me. I'm gonna have to change some things up before we go down there again."

"Like what, demand Vanessa not be there?"

"Maybe! Or at least demand that she keep her mouth shut, or maybe remember the good manners our mother taught us."

"Chris, I understand and that's fine, but I think we need to rise above rather than play into her divisiveness."

"Fuck rising above." He said it so vehemently Sidonie had to suppress a smile. When he glanced over and caught her expression, they burst into laughter.

Sidonie, determined to end on a good note, added: "And, really, the rest of the night was so wonderful. Your mom couldn't have been nicer. I really enjoyed the whole thing—the dinner, the conversation, the cobbler . . . oh, my God, the cobbler."

"You really had a moment with that cobbler, didn't you?"

"My mother's big dessert is Entenmann's and boxed ice cream—"

Woot, woot! The blue lights of a patrol car flashed behind them as they took Fifty-Third Street toward Lake Shore Drive, the siren bursts loud and jarring.

Tick. Tick. Tick.

The rush of adrenaline—sudden, familiar, dreaded—hit Chris like a rock. He took a deep breath, then another, as he carefully set his right turn signal to move into the slow lane.

Sidonie's heart went from normal to pounding so fast she unconsciously reached for her wrist, convinced the count was precipitous. A sensation of terror swept over her, fear that, this time, something life altering really could happen. Something painful, something deadly.

Tick. Tick. Tick.

Breathe in. Breathe out.

Chris kept his hands on the steering wheel and slowly, carefully, edged as close to the guardrail as he could.

He looked at Sidonie. "Please don't say a word, okay?"

"I won't," she responded, her mouth dry.

Tick, tick, tick.

In a roar of acceleration, and just as Chris leaned across to reach for the glove box, the patrol car flew past in a flurry of dust and debris, tearing down the road in pursuit of whoever it was they were after.

FORTY-THREE

THE "FRAME/HAWKINS URBAN RENEWAL PROJECT," AS CHRIS jokingly called his renovation effort, was complete: he'd added a striking sectional to fill out the living room; the multicolored palettes of each room perked the general ambiance, and lights and artwork were set to highlight the high ceilings and gallery-like walls. Sidonie was delighted. The townhouse had never been so smart and stylish, and she was overcome by the urge to celebrate.

"We'll crack champagne bottles and raise a glass to feng shui!" She laughed.

"Okay. And when would we do that?" Chris countered, glancing over the calendar on his phone.

It was a relevant question; there wasn't much give in either of their schedules. It was that time of year—kids back in school, the holidays approaching—when the business of entertaining hit high gear and The Church kept them both extraordinarily busy. Sound Alchemy, riding on the wave of Chris's expanding reputation, was booked enough that more hires had been necessary, along with discussion of an additional van. They had yet to arrange the discussed dinner with Mark and Alice; Diante's invitation to join him and Jordan for a night out had been put off; Sidonie skipped a few Karen lunches; and there'd yet been a return to Hyde Park. They were busy.

"Let's do it on a Monday when we're all off," Sidonie suggested. "We'll just set a date and whoever can get here, gets here. Come on, we need to show this place off *and* we need a little fun!"

Chris, pleased that his contribution had so elevated her mood, finally acquiesced. "Fine. What Monday?"

"How about the Monday before Halloween? We'll make it a theme."

"I'm not wearing a costume," he groused.

"You'll feel left out when everyone else does. And everyone else will."

"I'm comfortable being an outlier." He grinned.

"We'll just see . . ." She marked the date on the kitchen white-board. "There! That gives us three weeks. I'll manage the invitations, you wrangle the menu. And now I'm heading out for a walk," she said, twirling a scarf around her neck. "The trees are starting to turn, and if there's any perk to living in the Midwest, it's autumn leaves. Wanna come?"

"I do, but I can't. I've got a meeting with the team over at Univer-Soul Circus, and since I'll be in the neighborhood, I'm stopping by my mom's. Oh, hey, I'm looking at some SUVs over the next few days and if you've got time I'd like you to come along."

"So let's make that car date."

"Which gets us back to schedules—what time do you have this week?"

"After today it's nuts for me, but maybe next Monday? Tuesday? Pretty open either day, though I do have my Karen lunch on Tuesday and I can't miss another one. Oh, and Monday I have a hair appointment, but I think it's later—"

"Okay, okay." He laughed. "We'll reconvene over the weekend. But I have to make a decision real quick—the Jeep is definitely on its last legs." He leaned in and kissed her. "I'm putting *car date* on the calendar for next Monday."

SIDONIE STEPPED OUTSIDE to be wrapped in crisp afternoon air and the iconic, nostalgic sensation of Midwestern autumn. Early Halloween decorations sprouted here and there, and the trees were melding into shades of orange, yellow, and red, their fallen leaves crunching in cadence with passing footsteps. Fireplaces set to ward off the encroaching cold sent smoke wafting from chimneys, dusting the scene with musky, memorable fragrance, and the golds and off-whites of windows lit early on these shorter days made for a luminous setting. As much as she loved spring, this time of year was Sidonie's favorite, aided by her childlike anticipation of the holidays to come.

She sauntered down the sidewalk, swinging her bag with teenage sass, a bounce in every step, as her thoughts turned toward the upward trajectory of her life. The rough spots had been smoothed, the ones remaining had diminished in their impact. Vanessa had sent a group email—to Chris, Sidonie, and Delores—apologizing for her drunken rant. The apology was accepted (with "boundaries to come," according to Chris), and Sidonie hoped a future one-on-one would help traverse the chasm that lay between them. Her mother continued to pretend all was well on that front—which was fine with Sidonie, who found Marian's graceless rationale for avoiding meaningful conversation to be transparent. The only negative was that, after the investors for the restaurant ultimately pulled out (claiming "costs not in sync with our current goals and resources"), there'd been no further action on the project, likely a result of her and Patsy's continuing estrangement.

But Sidonie didn't care. She didn't want to care. She didn't want to think, talk, listen, or explain. She wanted only to *feel*. The holistic embrace of Chris's love, the nerve-tingling experience of his sex, the overwhelming pull of his desire. She wanted to believe, for as long as was possible, that life was meant to be lovely, that she, even *she*, could expect and demand encompassing joy. It had been too rare for too long, and now that she had it she was greedy as a child, unwilling to set it down or share it with the unappreciative.

Patsy, however, was operating on a decidedly different agenda. Her calls, texts, and emails pleading her case, referencing their long friendship, even, at times, berating the intransigence of the situation, were relentless. Annoying. Guilt inducing. Sidonie refused to engage. She rejected the distraction, the demand for her attention. She wanted Patsy to disappear for a while, long enough to dull the sting of her transgression. Some disagreements needed time to season; this was one of those.

Her phone vibrated. Karen.

"You cannot believe how gorgeous it is in my neighborhood," Sidonie exclaimed. "I'm actually taking a walk for absolutely no reason other than to revel in it all!"

"Hey, Sid." It was not Karen. As if magically conjured, Patsy was on the other end.

"Wow. Is Karen lying in a pool of blood somewhere?"

"I had to get creative. We met on business and I grabbed her phone when she stepped out to the bathroom."

"That's invasive."

"These are desperate times."

"Is it impossible for you to take a cue?"

"I took the cue. I'm now trying to change the script."

"If I wanted this conversation, I would have returned one of your other billion calls. Stalking does not improve rapport."

"Fuck rapport. I'd just like some nod to the years we've put into this friendship. I think I deserve at least that."

A beat.

"Possibly." Sidonie's lack of enthusiasm was palpable. Patsy was undeterred.

"Can we meet and talk, Sid? Please. If you still hate me afterward, then we'll call it a day."

Another beat.

"Fine," Sidonie acquiesced.

"You wanna come by the kitchen?"

"No. Someplace neutral."

Patsy sighed. "Really?"

Sidonie didn't budge. "If you want to do this, meet me at the Star-bucks near the club in an hour."

"Fine. Enjoy your leaves."

FORTY-FOUR

Camera is focused on three police officers, faces terse, guns pointed at Chris, who sits cross-legged on the ground, sweating, forehead scraped and bleeding, head bowed, chest moving up and down with agitated breaths.

"Why don't you take him upstairs and unlock the damn door with his key?" Alice's exasperated voice calls from behind the camera. "That should prove he lives here!"

A fourth officer moves into frame, stares directly at the camera. "Ma'am, I cannot emphasize enough how you need to step back and shut up." He fixes her with a heated expression. He turns to Chris. "Do you have keys to this house?"

Chris turns toward the camera, eyes grimaced in pain, and nods. As he reaches his hands slowly toward his pocket, another police officer yells from off camera:

"Move your hands away from your pocket! Now! Now!!"

Two guns are pointed within inches of Chris's head as another officer swoops in to grab the hand reaching into his pocket.

The video pauses—

Patsy leaned back in the chair, Sidonie's phone in her hand, visibly shaken. "I can't watch any more of this."

Sidonie took a sip from her latte, affecting an almost detached air. Nothing about Patsy's reaction softened her, her face set and hard. "Exactly. And guess what triggered that madness?"

"Don't make me guess."

"Words. Someone's words. The words of a hateful neighbor who decided there was something to be gained from calling the police and accusing Chris of vandalism. Her words caused him to be terrorized and humiliated in a situation where one wrong move could've gotten him killed. Words can be damn powerful, can't they?"

Patsy squirmed in her chair. "I get it, Sid, I do . . ." Her eyes welled up. "And I'm sorry, I'm so sorry. Poor Chris. I can't even imagine what he went through. Motherfucking cops. Motherfucking Sandra."

"Yes. Motherfucking Sandra." Sidonie looked away, sensing there was no way to get past what she felt. Which was nothing. In this moment she felt nothing for her old friend. Nothing but the feeling that Patsy was no longer an integral, essential part of her life. And even that reality was met with emptiness. Which was strange, really.

Patsy watched the subtle, shifting expressions on Sidonie's face, and could feel the opportunity for mercy slipping away. "Sid."

Sidonie looked back, eyes flat.

"I know you well enough to know where you've gone with this," Patsy said. "I know the door is almost completely shut and I'm on the outside. And I get it. I do. I don't blame you. But when I think about what you just showed me, think about what goes on out in the world, then think about what I said, I want to puke. I mean it. I'm not kissing your ass, I'm not pandering. I want to puke out of pure shame." She stopped to dab a napkin to her eyes.

Sidonie remained unmoved.

"I've thought a lot about what I said, Sid, and, for the most part, I got nothin'. It was indefensible and unforgiveable. But I want you—I *need* you—to forgive me anyway. So I've tried to figure out *why* I said it, what part of me, consciously or unconsciously, went for those particular words."

Patsy was having a hard time getting her current words out. Tears streamed down her face and she had to stop to take a slug from her water bottle. Sidonie kept silent, both women ignoring the occasional glances from nearby customers.

"I hate to get all 'family of origin' on you," Patsy continued. "I know how trite that sounds, but it really is the foundation for all this.

The way my dad used language—it was couched in humor, sure, but later I realized it was just outright racist. At the time it never struck us kids as anything but funny. So when he'd call our black garbage man 'a trash coon,' or see black families picnicking and say things like, 'Let's go steal some of their fried chicken and watermelon,' we thought it was a riot." She blew her nose again. "And I went right for that bullshit cliché, didn't I?"

Sidonie looked away, but Patsy peered at her so directly a response was unavoidable. She looked back and said dryly: "Yes, you did."

"Which makes *me* a cliché. But even my mom had that sort of careless, casual racist streak. She had church friends who were black, not close friends, but people she associated with, and she'd talk about them like they were idiots, lower class. She had this one friend, Sadie, a mixed-race woman, and she'd say things like, 'That half nigger wouldn't know her head from a hole in the ground.' She passed it off like it was folksy, salty, and it rolled right off me when I was little. But I guess it stuck somewhere in my emotional DNA. We *were* a family with a rusty pickup in the backyard, so that should tell you all you need to know about us."

"Funny, you've never referenced any of that before, in all the years I've known you."

"Because it makes me sound like white trash. It's fucking embarrassing."

"Plus there's no statute of limitations on blaming parents for our bullshit, right?"

Patsy sighed, taking the hit. "I get it, Sid, I get it. It's all on me. But I really am trying to figure out why *any* part of me went there, and beyond emotional heritage, the only other thing I come up with is this: I was hurt that you didn't tell me you were seeing this guy until *after* he'd already moved in. That was unreal to me, and it made me realize how far out of sync we'd gotten. It hurt me. It made me feel rejected, so I lashed out . . . in as ugly a way as I could. I honestly think if Chris were Asian or Swedish I would've snarked about exceptional math skills or the hideous fish balls his people like. It wasn't his ethnicity, truly. It was about striking out at you for excluding me. Does that make sense? I mean, I know it's offensive and pathetic, but does it make any sense?"

Sidonie took a pause. "In an offensive, pathetic way."

"Well, that's a start." Patsy smiled wanly.

"But it's not a defense," Sidonie rejoined, not willing to lighten the load. "Because I wasn't excluding you. I didn't tell anyone for a long time because I wasn't sure how even *I* felt about it. Dating someone like Chris *was* a departure for me. Not just his race, but his background, his focus, everything. And you're right: he doesn't have Theo's good looks, or the wardrobe, the car, the lifestyle—any of those trappings. And I'm ashamed that part of me was initially hesitant because of those reasons. So in some ways I'm just as shallow as you."

"Sid, I—"

"But the more I got to know him, the more I found him to be this incredible man, so beautifully different from men I'd known before— his take on the world and what he's had to deal with. So, yes, some of what makes him incredible *is* his being black. He's had to learn things, overcome things that no white man would ever have to confront. And that, at least in his case, has given him a deep sense of himself and what's important. I don't know if you can possibly understand that."

"I think I can—"

"But I didn't think you would. And given the way you responded, I wasn't wrong. So I kept quiet for as long as I could without going underground. With you being out of town so much, you were just the last one on the list."

"I should've have stayed in better touch—"

"It wouldn't have mattered. Because I had a suspicion—I don't even know why—that you'd do exactly what you did."

"I am so sorry . . ."

"And I really want you to know this about me: I'm not overcompensating for losing Theo. I'm not desperate or lacking self-esteem. I've just had the rare chance to get to know a guy I might have overlooked if we hadn't been thrown together. And when I took that opportunity . . . lucky me. I discovered a really spectacular person, someone I feel so fortunate to have found. And, Patsy, you don't have to like him—I don't need you to like him. I don't *care* if you like him. Though I can't think of any reason why you wouldn't. But whatever you do feel, get beyond his race, or his looks, or his T-shirts. Judge him as you would any person: with an open mind."

Patsy reached out and grabbed Sidonie's hand. "I will, I promise. My mind has been opened. I'm rejecting my racist ancestry and embracing the higher self I briefly abandoned." She looked into Sidonie's face beseechingly. "Will you forgive me?"

Sidonie squeezed Patsy's hand, then pulled away. "I can intellectualize forgiving you, but right now I just feel empty. It's not about punishing you. It's that there are some big themes wrapped up in this for me, and right now I can't *feel* forgiveness enough to extend it. So I have no choice but to take whatever time I need to get there. Thank you for explaining things from your end. It does help me put your thinking into perspective. But I can only offer détente at this point. We'll see where that leads us."

Patsy visibly slumped, but gave her friend a mournful smile. "I guess that will have to do. And I'll take it . . . with hope that I can redeem myself in your eyes one of these days soon. I miss you, Sid."

Sidonie reached out and squeezed Patsy's hand again, then rose and walked away, eyes welling.

FORTY-FIVE

"CHECK, CHECK, CHECK, ONE-TWO, ONE-TWO, ONE-TWO."
Ruben Yazmin, lead singer of Ragged Road, the opening act for the
big blues extravaganza set for the next two nights, leaned into the mi-
crophone for a final test, simultaneously strumming his guitar in
rhythm. Jasper and Andrew hustled to make minor adjustments while
Chris fine-tuned from the booth. They'd already run a short set, and
as the sound check drew to a close, Andrew looked up to see Sidonie
glance at her watch and motion them into the bar area.

"Hey, you guys," he called out to Jasper and Chris. "Sidonie wants
to get the meeting started. Are we about wrapped?"

Ruben gave a thumbs-up as band members unstrapped instru-
ments and climbed out from behind drums and keyboard stacks.
"Sounds good to me, gents. Thanks, Chris. Appreciate the extra reverb
on the vocals. You know I like 'em wet! Just make sure the monitors
are kicking and we're all good."

"They'll be there," Chris confirmed. "Go get some dinner and we'll
see you guys back here at seven."

As the band trundled out the employee entrance, Chris, Jasper,
and Andrew jumped from the stage and made their way to the bar.

IT WAS RARE The Church held mandatory staff meetings on a
Thursday afternoon before opening hours, but Saturday's scheduled
event was as high-profile as the club had hosted, and Frank and
Sidonie wanted to ensure that every element was in order, from entertainment and staff, to supplies, service, and menus. Ten Tables,

one of the largest food bank organizations in Chicago, was holding their annual celebration and fundraiser at The Church for the first time. The guest list included the mayor, several state representatives (from both parties), and a substantial roster of Chicago billionaires. This was a hard-won account for Sidonie, one she'd worked over a year to secure, so the stakes—and expectations—were high.

Gathered in the bar area were the wait and hosting staff, all kitchen personnel, Al and the bar crew, Chris, Jasper, Andrew, even the extra sound techs hired from Sound Alchemy for the event. Frank and Sidonie perched on stools at the bar, going over each bullet point on their lists, taking questions, and giving detailed instructions along the way. After forty-five minutes, and as they were about to conclude, Sidonie stood up.

"Okay, thanks, everybody, I think that's it. All the bands tonight and tomorrow are phenomenal, we're expecting a big crowd both nights, and Saturday is going to be spectacular. Let's have a great weekend. And listen, before you scatter, one more thing." She looked across the room at Chris and smiled. "Chris and I are throwing a party."

Smiles and cheers inspired her laughing response.

"I know, I know, hell or something froze, right? Anyway, we've— or rather, *he's*—refurbished our place—not sure you all knew he was HGTV material—and it looks amazing. Which seemed to warrant some celebration. So we'd love you all to come by for a soiree."

"When?" shouted Jasper from the back of the room. "You know my social calendar is pretty packed, gotta get this penned in right quick!" The group laughed, poor Jasper infamous for never having reason to leave the club.

"With you specifically in mind, Jasper, we looked at our schedules, and since all of us are off on Mondays, we've set it for the Monday before Halloween. That'll give everyone a chance to get creative with party finery. Hope you can all be there because I really want to celebrate. There's lots of good stuff going on right now—the club is doing so well and you guys really are the best team we've ever had—so it feels like a perfect time to party. Everybody up for it?"

Whoops and hollers.

"Great! I'll send out evites by the weekend, all the deets will be in there. Now get to work!"

As everyone hustled off, Chris approached, bag on his shoulder.

"Are you leaving?" she asked, surprised.

"Yeah. I've gotta get my guys over to an Alchemy gig, but I'll be back in about an hour. By the way, I'm set to stop by the Jeep dealership on Western and Peterson Monday morning, around eight thirty. Are you in?"

"My hair appointment isn't until one, so yes. Fun! We'll finally have our car date!"

He leaned in with a kiss. "We're so *out* now, aren't we?"

She grinned coyly. "We are. Positively coupled."

"Mmmm . . . I like the way you say that." The look he gave her sent tremors to her midsection. "Later, sweetheart." His kiss held long enough that she laughed as she toppled off her tiptoes.

As he headed out, Al sidled up behind her and leaned in.

"What are you doing?" she asked, swatting him away.

"I've got a question for you, kind of private." He looked slightly embarrassed.

"Fine, but stop breathing down my neck, will ya. What? What question?"

"First of all, I'll definitely be at your party, but I wanted to check about bringing a date."

"*That's* your private question?"

"No, I just—"

She laughed. "You're such a geek, Al! Of course bring a date. I'd love to meet any woman willing to be seen with you in public." She slugged his arm. Things had gotten easier between them since he'd made a point of pulling Chris into the fold.

"Cool, cool. Listen, the other question . . ."

"Quick, cause I gotta get going."

"Would it be okay if Mike was included?"

"Mike Demopoulos? Officer Mike? The cop that sits at the bar and occasionally brings me drinks? The Mike you've been trying to foist on me for over a year?"

"Yeah, him."

She looked at Al like he was not an intelligent being. "Why would I want a cop with a crush to come to the party I'm hosting with my relatively new boyfriend?"

"I know, sounds weird, but I'm actually trying to be a nice guy here. Turns out he's been seeing this girl and she dumped him the other day. He and I have kinda become friends—you know, gone out for burgers a few times after I've gotten off work—and he's poured his heart out to me. So I was just thinkin', since he's so lonely and down on himself right now, I bet he'd really appreciate being included. He's around here enough that he knows a lot of the staff, so it wouldn't be weird. And hey, you never know, he might hit it off with someone just by gettin' outside the club. What do you say?"

"Wow . . . who knew you were such a yenta? Fine, I'll send him an invitation."

"You have his email?"

"Yeah, he gave me his card a while back."

"Awesome. Thanks, Frame. You rock." He attempted a fist pound, but she just rolled her eyes; there was only so much bro-dom she could handle.

With Al back behind the bar, Sidonie took a look around the room and suddenly realized, for the very first time, that every one of the floor staff was white, with the exception of one waitress who was half-Chinese. The bar staff was white, the hostess team was white; other than Chris (and the occasional Sound Alchemy temps), the sound team was white, and, while the kitchen staff was largely His- panic, not a one was black. That was odd, she thought. How had it escaped her attention all this time? Whether she wanted them to or not, Vanessa's words echoed. What *was* she doing to change the nar- rative?

Frank rushed up, dressed for the outdoors. "Okay, kiddo, I'm off to my meeting. You've got everything under control here?"

"We're good. Hey, Frank, have you ever noticed how white our staff is?"

He stopped, glanced around. "No, can't say I have." He turned back to Sidonie with a cock of his head. "Is this a real problem or are you parroting someone else's concerns?"

That rankled. "What a weird thing to say! Have I lost my ability to have a new thought, or speak my own mind on diversity issues because I now have a black boyfriend?"

Frank twitched. "Sorry . . . perhaps a poor choice of words." He looked around again. "No, not much diversity in here, you're right. But you're the one who hires the staff. If it's important to you, broaden your outreach. It's a good point." He patted her on the back and swept off.

Sidonie took a deep breath. She couldn't decide if Frank was being condescending, patronizing, insensitive, or all the above. Once again Vanessa's words resonated: she might just need to toughen up.

FORTY-SIX

BY THE TIME THEY GOT HOME THURSDAY NIGHT, LEAVING Andrew to wrap up the last two bands, the temperature had dropped considerably. With wind portending a coming storm, they had reason to light the first fire of the season. Sidonie huddled over her computer, designing the invitations for the party, fully absorbed and enjoying the task, but Chris was restless. He wanted to walk, but it was late enough that optics had to be considered; he had become more cautious about such things lately. He paced until she finally glanced up.

"What?"

"Nothing."

"Okay." She went back to the computer.

Shaking his arms at his side, he sighed loudly.

"Okay, now you're making me crazy," she remarked.

"I'm just restless for some reason. Think I'll get out and walk for a while."

She looked at the clock. "This late?"

"It's not that late."

"It's almost midnight."

He felt her concern; he understood it, but he refused to capitulate. "It's eleven forty-five, Sid. People are still out. I've been locked up in a sound booth all day, haven't had a chance to exercise all week, and I need some air, some motion."

"Then I'll come with you," she said, pushing back her chair. "It would be better."

"You don't have to. I know you want to get the invitations done."

She looked back at the computer. "I do need to get them finished . . ."

"I won't be long. I just want to clear my head."

"Okay."

He grabbed his hoodie from a coat rack near the door.

"Really? You're wearing *that*?" The question was sharp.

"It's cold," he remarked, not getting her point. Then he got her point. "Seriously? Would it be okay if it were earlier? If you were with me? If I kept the hood down? Or should I grab my sport coat and tie?"

"Yes, yes, yes, and no—a light-colored sweater or your jean jacket will do."

"I think you're being a little—"

She leapt from the chair, yanked the hoodie from his hands, flung it on the foyer table, and pulled his jean jacket from a nearby hook. "Here! Wear this! It has no fear factor, no hood. It's just a fucking jacket!"

He was stunned by her vehemence. "Okay, Sid, Jesus. It's not that big a deal."

"Isn't it?" She was dead serious. "You're a black man walking on a residential street in a predominantly white middle-class neighborhood at almost midnight on a weeknight, so you are *not* wearing a fucking hoodie with its blaring 'come harass me, Chicago PD' fashion statement. It sucks, I agree, but please do not make it any easier for them and harder for you, okay? Would you do that for me?" Her expression made clear there was honest panic behind the request.

He put the jean jacket on and went to her, pulling her to him. "Okay. I get it. No hoodies at night. I can do that."

She burrowed her face in his chest. "I'm sorry. I'm probably being neurotic, but I get scared for you. I feel like you're a walking target."

"I feel that way too sometimes. So I'll change my jacket, Sid, but I won't crawl in a box. I won't be fearful. That's not me. That *can't* be me." He kissed her. "And now I'm going for a short walk before the rain hits. I won't be long. Go get our evites done." He shoved her toward the computer with a smile.

She sat down at her desk. "Text me if you're going to be later than a few minutes, okay?"

"I won't be, but I will." He opened the door. "Back in a few."

~

TAKING LONG STRIDES down sidewalks unburdened by daytime foot traffic and the noise of passing cars was as head clearing as Chris had hoped. Clouds tumbled above as if ready to unload their deluge, and the wind, cool enough to chafe, was bracing.

He remembered the first night he walked down this particular sidewalk with Sidonie. It seemed like both yesterday and years ago. Strange how time could effortlessly bounce from near to far with so much unfolding in the moments and spaces between.

Chris thought about Sidonie's offer to accompany him tonight, her clear consideration that her presence would offer some buffer, some protection; make him less conspicuous to anyone who might find him so. It was an absurd equation, the idea that he'd need a small white woman to keep him safer out in the world. How ironic. How imbecilic. How probably true, at least in this neighborhood.

The phone buzzed. His immediate thought was that Sidonie was overthinking his departure, so he was surprised to see Diante's name. "Hey, D!"

"Wassup, my man?" Diante had clearly been partying. "I'm just leaving a work thing, not ready to pack it in yet. Thought I'd see if you wanted to meet for a drink. We haven't hung in a while. I can swing by your place if it's easier."

"Ah, thanks, I would, but I'm up real early tomorrow. Another time?"

"Cool, cool." There was a pause.

"Something wrong?"

"Nah, just goin' through some shit with Jordan . . . don't really dig the idea of walking into that buzzsaw just yet."

Chris crossed the street to head back to the townhouse. "What's going on? I've got a minute."

"Just, you know, she . . . I dunno. She was all into this living together thing, excited about bringing her stuff in, hanging pictures, acted like she was real pumped about it. Now she's like, 'I'm bored.' Says she hates her job, says it's beneath her—"

"What does she do again?"

"Receptionist at a dental office. No big thing, sure, but it ain't scrubbin' floors at the bus station either!"

"No, but maybe she—"

"When she's home, all she does is watch TV, and not that I expect her to cook every night, but *never*? I cook more than she does! The rest of the time she's either hanging with her friends, moping behind a magazine, or trying to get me to party with her. It's wearing me down, man. It's really wearing me down."

"Have you talked to her about it?"

"Yeah, but you know how she is. I keep telling her if she's not happy with her job to figure out what she wants to do and go get it. I even tried brainstorming with her one night, but she just sat there flipping through a magazine. Fucking crazy, man! And the thing is, I hang with all these fine sisters at work who could not be more opposite and it's got me thinkin'. They're driven, you know? Really focused on building something for themselves, and, to be honest, it's making me see Jordan in a different light. She's just . . . I dunno . . . just young, I guess. Just young."

"Come on, D, it's not like you didn't know that."

"I know, I know . . . that's on me."

"Are you messin' around with any of those fine sisters at work?"

"NO. Hell, no! Not that it hasn't crossed my mind. There's this one, Jackie—drop dead, man, crazy smart. We sit at lunch talking about markets and high current income funds and she knows her shit so good it drives me crazy. And sure, if I was free, I'd definitely be makin' a move, but I do love Jordan and I am tryin' to make it work. But here I am, hustling you to come out with me 'cause I don't wanna go home. That ain't a good sign."

"Maybe you're just romantically dysfunctional," Chris said dryly.

"Hah—I see what you did there!" Diante laughed. "You could be right, man."

Chris noticed a couple—white, middle-aged, well dressed—approaching from the opposite direction. He felt more vulnerable on the phone, yet their body language suggested they were wary of him. The woman stealthily grabbed the man's hand as they approached, their pace quickening as they veered away from him. *Tick.* He made a point of smiling as they passed. They smiled back. Everyone moved on safely. Nightlife on the streets of Chicago.

"Hey, you still there?" Diante asked.

"I'm here, I'm here."

"How are things goin' on your end?"

"Good, real good. We're throwing a party in a few weeks. You'll be getting an invitation."

"Cool, man. I'll definitely come by. Don't know about Jordan . . . you know her."

"She still hatin' on me?"

"Yeah. She's convinced you're trying to push me away from her. It's like she's on a loop. I think it just gives her reasons to keep fightin' with me . . . I dunno. Fuck! Anyway, what about Sidonie?"

"What about her?"

"Is she cool? I mean, obviously she's cool, but you know—is she cool with you, cool with her life, has a plan, has stuff she wants to do? Or is she waiting around for you to come home and make her happy?"

Chris laughed. "You seriously need to spend time with her if you have to ask that question! She's one of the most driven people I know. Kicks ass at the club, and that ain't no small thing. Plus she's putting the pieces together for her own place. She squeezes me in where she can."

"For real?"

"Nah . . . we've got a good thing going, a good rhythm."

"Then you are one lucky brother, brother."

When he got home minutes later, Sidonie was still at the computer. She looked up and smiled, and it struck him just how right Diante was.

FORTY-SEVEN

A MAJOR KERFUFFLE WAS BREWING AT TABLE #1. THOUGH guests were not yet being seated, Mona Perez, aide to the mayor, waved a place card in Sidonie's direction with marked urgency. Mona was tasked with ensuring that the mayor's public appearances proceeded smoothly, and it seemed having a certain city councilman at Table #1 was *not* smooth. Despite the fact that all seating arrangements had been approved only two days earlier, this particular fellow had piqued the ire of the mayor within the last twenty-four hours and was to be banished.

Like the pro she was, and with nary a blink, Sidonie, decked in a smartly cut Jones of New York tux, her hair swirled in some fabulous do that got all the men smiling, exchanged the offending card with some lucky attendee's from Table #13. With a quick smile, concerns were allayed, concluding with Mona at the bar happily sipping a rum daiquiri.

Saturday had rolled in with much fanfare, and everyone and everything at The Church gleamed, ready for the big show. Still, and despite the night's myriad demands and distractions, there was considerable chatter about the invitations that hit their mailboxes earlier that day—Chris and Sidonie's party was shaping up to be the must-attend in-house event of the year.

As the smartly dressed crowd, inclusive of the mayor and his entourage, slowly made their way from the foyer to the bar area, Sidonie buzzed with the slightest edge of anxiety, a result, no doubt, of the inherent pressure of this weighted event. She swept through each room, liaised with each manager, and checked each prep item off her list, calming herself as the approaching hour of production came into tangible form.

She smiled when Frank flew by in a tuxedo. They'd all agreed to gussy up for the evening—even Jasper was wearing black dress pants and a vintage tux jacket—and as each staff member found a moment to model their attire, she again noted the goodwill flowing amongst this team she'd assembled. When Al gave her a thumbs-up from behind the bar, resplendent in a paisley jacket with a big red bowtie, she shook her head, laughing. This was going to be a good night.

She wasn't aware that Chris hadn't checked in until her phone rang and she was stunned to see his name. "Where are you?" she almost yelped. "I didn't even realize you weren't here!"

"Goddamn Jeep! The temp light came on about ten minutes ago and when the gauge shot up, I had no choice but to stop. I'm parked on some random street—don't know which one but it's not far from the club. I'm waiting for the radiator to cool down enough to dump some water in, at least enough to get there."

She looked at her watch with panic. "Chris! It's five twenty. Your whole team is waiting for you!"

"I'm well aware of that, Sidonie. I'm doing the best I can. I should be there in half an hour at the most. All I know is, we are buying me a new car on Monday."

"Okay, fine. Grab a Lyft if you have to but get here as quickly as you can."

"I will. Tell Jasper to pull up all the cues and start refreshing them with the guys, okay?"

"Just be careful. I want you here in one piece."

"Don't worry. I won't be long."

When the head waitress approached with a request from the kitchen, the distraction pulled Sidonie away from the main floor and her bubbling concern. By the time she wrapped up issues related to proper staging of the appetizer service, and alerted Jasper that the mayor would be speaking from his seat rather than the stage, Chris rushed in from the employee entrance, sweat pouring, navy sport coat over his arm and a harried look on his face.

She grabbed him as he flew past. "Everything okay?"

"Yeah, got it here. Sorry about that. Obviously I let this car thing go on for too long."

"It's all right. We're okay with time. I'm just glad it made it."

"No kidding! Luckily there was a hose where I stopped—just filled it as much as I could and limped over. It will be leaving on the back of a tow truck, I promise you that." He shook his head. "Okay, off to the booth. Let's have a great event and I'll check in with you later." He leaned in for a quick kiss and was off.

That was the last time Sidonie took any particular notice of him until the world turned upside down.

FORTY-EIGHT

BY TEN THIRTY THE HIGHLIGHTS OF THE EVENING HAD concluded, but every room of the club remained packed with celebratory patrons. The scheduled speakers had all been brief and articulate, the auction raised an astounding sum, and the mayor wheedled and cajoled further support from the deep-pocketed corporate leaders in attendance. As he and other elected officials slowly made their grand exit, with much stopping and shaking of hands along the way, and with the senior demographic largely peeled off in early departure, the younger crowd jammed the dance floor as the music got louder and drinks flowed.

Frank walked along with the mayor, working his own charm offensive as he moved from table to table making new friends, and the floor staff was playful and relaxed now that the major service portion of the night had concluded. Al and his team were slammed behind the bar, but he was in full-performance mode and enjoying every minute of it. He had just finished placing a gimlet in front of Sidonie, who sat with Mona Perez discussing the timely arrival of the mayor's limousine, when Jasper bolted up.

"Sid." He leaned in to whisper. "You need to come with me."

With one look at his ashen face, she turned to Mona. "Mona, the head valet just texted that the limo is being retrieved. Could you give me a moment and I'll walk with you to the foyer?" Mona, distracted by the fresh daiquiri Al placed in front of her, nodded.

Sidonie swung back to Jasper. "What is going on? I'm trying to—"

"Just come with me." He grabbed her arm and pulled her through the clotted crowd toward the employee entrance. There, incongruously and alarmingly, two uniformed police officers stood inside the door, faces fixed and inscrutable in the dim exit light. Sidonie felt an immediate clutch of trepidation.

"Officers, can I help you? We're planning to escort the mayor out the *front* entrance—"

The shorter of the two spoke. "We've got a situation outside and need to verify if anyone here knows a tall, black man wearing a navy jacket who claims he's an employee."

As if jabbed by an electric prod, Sidonie bolted past the two officers, leaving Jasper to stumble through confirmation of Chris's identity.

Bursting through the doors, she entered an alternate universe that came at her like frantic jump cuts from a hand-held camera: a cacophony of noise and lights, the squall of voices; surging bodies emanating an acrid mix of threat and rage. At least five patrol cars were jammed into the back parking lot, seemingly from every angle, with lights flashing and the occasional burst of sirens. A crowd of about twenty people, mostly white with a few faces-of-color mixed in, undulated on the sidewalks and adjacent street, craning through the fence, some hollering invectives, others holding up phone cameras. All that was missing were the pitchforks. The focal point of their wrath was initially unclear to Sidonie, who tried frantically to grasp the situation in the midst of pandemonium. When someone shouted, "That's him, that's the guy!" she spun around like a madwoman.

There, in the swirling, violent center of mayhem, on his knees and surrounded by a cadre of police officers, was Chris, his face glistening with sweat, blood streaming from his mouth and nose. His jacket was ripped and dirtied; a brawny blond cop behind him had his fist curled in Chris's hair, pulling his head back in a constraining hold.

In that split second, Sidonie's psyche shattered into a million different pieces, taking with it all rational thought. "What are you doing?!" she screamed, thrusting herself into the melee. Faces turned her way, offering no response. She shoved toward Chris, hips and elbows of the burgeoning crowd jutting her this way and that, while repeating her howling question: "What the hell are you doing? He works here!"

Chris appeared to hear her over the din. He turned blindly in her direction, bellowing: "Sidonie! Tell them, tell them I—" Before he could make eye contact, he was slammed to the ground, one cop planting a knee on his back while the others converged, guns drawn, night sticks making violent contact. The crowd surged, one voice after another rising in a Greek chorus of taunts:

"Kick his ass!" brayed a man in a Lynyrd Skynyrd hat.

A small woman, incongruously wrapped in a bathrobe, screeched, "That's the bastard. I seen him, I seen him a few times!"

"Keep your filth out of our neighborhood, you piece of shit!" another woman echoed.

A black man, his phone camera focused through the slats of the fence, hollered in counterpoint, "What are you gonna do, shoot him? You gonna fucking shoot him? I'm filming, you motherfuckers, I'm filming you!"

In the stutter-stop unraveling of this horrific moment, Sidonie's eyes darted from their twisted faces to Chris being manhandled by the police, and she could not fathom the level of vitriol. What happened? They couldn't possibly mean Chris, could they? What were they yelling about; what was going on; what did they think he'd done?

As she got within feet of the storm's eye, repeating her futile protestations to stop—stop beating him, stop hurting him, stop mistaking him—she suddenly felt herself yanked backward. A burly female officer had grabbed her arms from behind, and was rousting her in the opposite direction so quickly Sidonie almost tripped over the rustling feet in her path. She was shoved against the brick exterior wall of the building, her face scraping the rough-hewn surface as the officer slapped on a pair of handcuffs.

"What are you doing?" Sidonie cried out. "I'm the manager here. That man is my employee. I was just trying to—"

"Ma'am, you can explain all that down at the station. Right now you're interfering with police business." The officer pulled her toward the patrol car closest to the side street, and as she was shoved into the back seat, Sidonie could hear Chris's voice keening her name from the bowels of bedlam.

Senses scrambled, disorientation complete, she glanced despondently out the window . . . to see Frank, about two hundred feet away near the front entrance to the club, standing with the mayor at the valet station, his back angled as if to block notice of what was happening around the corner. As the cruiser pulled out of the lot to make a left, thankfully away from the club, Frank turned slightly and, for a brief moment, caught Sidonie's eye. Neither registered emotion. He shifted quickly toward the mayor, taking his elbow to usher him away from the madness and closer to the parked limo, where Mona stood holding the car door open.

Sidonie could only close her eyes as the police car sped away in the opposite direction.

FORTY-NINE

IT HAD BEEN A SIMPLE MATTER. HE NEEDED WATER FOR the Jeep. Just enough to get it to the club. There was no time for Triple A, a Lyft might take too long, and there was a hose right there. Not tucked under a bush, not attached to a reel, but stretched down the narrow sidewalk between two houses, almost to the public walk.

He considered knocking on the door of the house to which it was attached, but there were no lights on, and no one appeared home. Since he couldn't imagine anyone begrudging him a quart or two of water in a situation that demanded urgent response, he decided to help himself. He walked up and turned on the spigot; stretching the hose the final few feet to his car, he carefully filled the sputtering radiator, still warmer than advised for such an emergency fix. When done, he rolled up the hose and neatly deposited it near the spigot.

As he turned to walk back to the Jeep, he glanced left toward the window of the adjacent house. He caught the flutter of lace curtains, the glint of a female profile. He reflexively smiled but there was no eye contact, no other movement, so no thought followed the moment. He got in the Jeep, started it, and carefully moved on, pulling behind the club into the employees' parking lot about twenty minutes after his call to Sidonie.

FIFTY

EVERY LITTLE SWALLOW, EVERY CHICKADEE, EVERY LITTLE bird in the tall oak tree—

The patrol car took a sharp right and Sidonie, unable to keep balanced with her hands cuffed behind her, tilted hard into the door, her head knocking the window.

"You okay back there?" asked the passenger side officer, his pale face strobed by the passing streetlights. She didn't respond.

Handcuffed in the back of a police car at eleven ten on a Saturday night was a happenstance Sidonie could not have anticipated in any real or imagined version of her life. The cuffs hurt, her face hurt, her heart hurt, and she was queasy, both from the movement of the car and the gut-wrenching turn of the unfathomable evening.

The wise old owl, the big black crow—

She'd been hustled to the cruiser without a moment to alert anyone inside, leaving her churned about the concerns this would surely stoke. The look on Frank's face as he watched her being hauled off in a police car was both inscrutable and damning, and it made her nauseous just thinking about it.

More critically, she had no idea what was happening with Chris— where he was, what condition he was in, why he'd been beaten and likely arrested . . . or possibly worse. She had no idea why he'd been out in the parking lot in the first place; she hadn't noticed him leave the club at any point during the evening. The aberrance of the entire situation was so absurd it triggered dissociative thinking that left her inexplicably ear-worming "Rockin' Robin," over and over.

Flappin' their wings singin' "go bird, go," rockin' robin ...

She hadn't said a word to either officer since she'd been shoved in the car, so after about fifteen minutes of maneuvering through traffic, the passenger side cop looked back again.

"What's going on back there? You're awfully quiet."

Pretty little raven at the bird bandstand ...

"So tell me," he persisted, "what's a nice white girl like you doing with a fucked-up nigger like that?"

Taught him how to do the bop and it was grand ...

The driver, who appeared Hispanic, looked over at his partner. "Hey, come on, take it easy. She's probably just in over her head. The pretty girls, I dunno, they can get anybody, but they go for the thugs. You gotta feel bad for her."

They started going steady and bless my soul ...

"Is that right, sweetheart? You're slummin' for a little street flavor?" The passenger side cop smirked over his shoulder.

He out-bopped the buzzard and the oriole ...

The driver glanced at her through the rearview mirror, his tone dropping as if to affect gravitas. "Seriously though, you gotta know he's a bad guy, your fella. We've been looking for him for a long time, so you're lucky we caught up with him when we did. He's done some real bad shit, and he could be dangerous for a girl like you."

Blow rockin' robin 'cause we're really gonna rock tonight ...

When he realized she wasn't going to engage, he shook his head and let silence take over.

By the time they pulled into the station, Sidonie had been through the song more times than she could count and her queasiness had grown to full-blown nausea. They ushered her from the car up a small flight of steps, into a dank, narrow hallway adjacent to the reception area where they handcuffed her to a bench. Both transporting officers walked off behind the counter, disappearing without a word.

And there she sat for the next two hours, without intervention, without information, cold, terrified, and sick. She threw up twice into a trashcan fortuitously placed to her left. No one in the vicinity appeared to notice.

FIFTY-ONE

LIMPING, HIS ARM HELD PROTECTIVELY ACROSS HIS midsection, Chris was led into an empty holding cell. He suspected, given the searing pain in his side, that he had at least one broken rib, maybe two, and possibly a ruptured muscle in his back. Both made breathing an excruciating event. He also knew his wrist and arm were badly injured, he had two loose teeth, and was likely suffering a concussion, judging from the dizziness and head pain he felt. His face was swollen and sticky with blood, making the term *beaten to a pulp* never more accurate.

It was difficult, in his current state, to string things together, but as he sat there waiting for whatever was next, he went through the timeline, struggling to make sense of how he got here.

What happened exactly? How did this go down? *Assemble the details, man.* Okay, back at that house. Didn't think much about the woman behind the curtain. That might have been a mistake. Was she the one who followed him? Pointed him out? He'd had the slightest sense of disquiet when he finished up with the hose. Was he worried about using a stranger's property? Being on a private lawn? When he pulled away from the curb, he thought he saw someone (a man? a woman?) exit from the house next door and get into a parked car. He brushed it off, deciding it was just someone getting on with their night. But when he pulled into the employees' lot, he noticed a car fly past and remembered thinking: *Was that the same car from in front of that house?* He hung back for a few minutes, waiting to see if the car swung around again. When it didn't, he figured he was being paranoid and headed in.

Later, after they'd shut down the PA and turned things over to the DJ, there it was again: that sense of foreboding. Couldn't shake it. He made the excuse to Jasper—"Left my phone in the car, gonna dash out and grab it"—expecting to walk out and see nothing, nothing but the employees' parked cars and the limos lined up at the valet station around the corner. But he needed to get out there, needed to confirm his paranoia was off the mark.

But that wasn't what happened. He stepped through the door to find foreboding come to life. A phalanx of police officers was huddled around cars pulled into the lot in every direction, and as soon as he walked through the door, a loud "that's him!" bellowed from a heavy-set woman hovering near the officers, setting the melee in motion.

What happened then? It was such an insane, explosive series of moments it was hard to reconstruct it in any kind of cogent sequence. He remembered his reflexive impulse was to turn toward the door, to get help, to alert Sidonie or Jasper, to protect himself. But when he angled in that direction, and before his feet could even move, he was hit by the force of three officers. They grabbed him by his arms and pulled him back, hard, while others circled with guns drawn. It was in that moment—cold, dark, and terrifying—that he realized, *I might die tonight.*

The thought made him sad. Made him think of Sidonie. Of his mother. About the really beautiful paint job he'd finished just a few weeks ago in the bedroom. That was an odd non sequitur.

It was so damn noisy; he remembered that. The dissonance of barked commands, overlapping and colliding from every direction. He kept pulling toward the door, kept repeating, "*I work here,* I need to tell my boss what's happening!" but he couldn't break free, and he knew if he did they would shoot him.

He was also in panic mode, survival mode, and a strange rigidity set in that made compliance almost impossible. His body stiffened as he instinctively angled toward the door, and that translated as resistance. They wanted him down on the ground, but he feared if he went down he might never get up. A nightstick slammed across his back so hard he dropped to his knees, subsequent blows smashing against his jaw. The pain was explosive, like nothing he'd ever felt before. He raised his arm to defend himself, and the stick came down on his wrist and arm, inflicting jolts so severe he thought he might pass out. There was so much going on, with so much accompanying noise and commotion, he lost awareness of the onslaught's direction, stymying his ability to fend off the knees and fists making contact.

It was then that he caught sight of Sidonie struggling toward him, which struck him with both hope and horror. Once again, the narrative of his life was dragging her into battle, and there was shame in that. The hope he felt, however slim, faded quickly as the evolving furor offered her no chance to save him. He couldn't see all that happened, but he watched with helplessness as Sidonie was pulled away. In that moment, he succumbed to the reality that he'd probably be beaten to death, and gave in, collapsed.

Which possibly saved him, because once fully down, they ultimately stopped beating him. There was some relief, then, in being carted off. Secured inside the transporting vehicle, he transitioned from panic to a state of holistic numbness, which offered a degree of dissociative calm.

Now, locked in a holding cell that reeked of sweat and urine, he could only sit in agonized silence and wait. It didn't take long before the blond cop who'd been at the scene opened the cell door and swaggered in. His expression was a combination of arrogance and gratification, as if he found some part of the unfolding events to be pleasing.

Chris squinted through his swollen, battered eyes and said not a word. He tried to breathe without moving a muscle. It was impossible.

"Well, buddy," the cop said, "it's been a long night and we're gonna have to get down to business. I'm Officer O'Malley, and whatever you think has happened or will happen, I'm about to be your best friend."

Chris said nothing, his eyes fixed coldly on the man in front of him. *Tick, tick, tick ...*

"I know you've been running your game for a long time. You got all those fancy north side people you work for suckered real good. You got that nice white girl of yours convinced you're a good guy, but you and I both know the truth, don't we?"

Tick.

"You can sit there with that stone cold look on your face if you want, but wouldn't you rather get it off your chest, be a man and own your shit?" O'Malley sat down on the bench, leaning in with faux concern. "Listen, I gotta be honest with you: it might be good if you came clean to me before the rest of 'em get a hold of you. We've been working this case for a long time, a *damn* long time, so there are some seriously pissed-off cops out there ready to slice and dice. Me? I'm a little more understanding, a little more Zen. I wanna give you a shot at redemption."

Tick, tick ...

O'Malley stood. "Okay, if you think silence is your best bet, so be it." He rolled up the sleeves of his shirt and flexed his arms, thick and muscled. "Your choice, buddy. I'm cool either way. But you gotta know I work out every day of my life just to have an occasional night like this—"

Tick ... tick ... TICK—

Chris knew as soon as contact was made that another rib gave way.

FIFTY-TWO

SIDONIE, HEAD ON HER CHEST, WAS LOST IN DISTURBED SLEEP when a female officer startled her awake by unlocking her handcuffs. Freed from the bench, she rubbed her wrists, raw and swollen, and wiped her crusted mouth. The officer nodded with a seemingly sympathetic, "You're free to go," and as Sidonie glanced up, she was stunned to see Mike Demopoulos, Officer Mike, approaching from the desk, as disorienting a sight as every other aspect of this event.

He was in street clothes, his face a mask of concern. He turned to the officer and said quietly, "Thanks, Sheila. I owe you one." She nodded and headed back down the hall toward the desk. Without a word, Mike took Sidonie's arm and gently led her out the door. The wind was cutting and she shivered as he helped her down the steps.

Once in his car—a Cadillac Escalade, not his police cruiser—Sidonie did her best to keep emotions in check, but within minutes she burst into tears. Mike drove in silence as she sobbed so hard he feared he should pull over to see if something needed to be done, some first aid administered. Finally she wore herself out and looked over at him, confused and grateful.

"I don't know what just happened, but thank you."

"I had a favor to pull. Police interference is a bullshit charge, especially under those circumstances. You didn't need to get caught up in all that."

"So I'm not arrested?"

"Well, you were arrested but they didn't charge you."

"Thank you. I don't know what to say."

Mike looked unsettled himself, as if he couldn't quite reconcile his role in the metastasizing drama. "Sidonie, I gotta be honest with you: Chris is in some pretty deep shit here. It's not minor. He's charged with criminal trespassing, resisting arrest, and peeking, no small beans right there, but they're also looking at him for a few other things."

"What does that mean?"

He glanced over, took a beat, then looked away. "They got his fingerprints in a rape case."

If the world could have tilted any further off its axis, this moment made the push. Sidonie leaned forward, her head dropped to her lap.

Mike drove in silence. While she remained wordless and immobile, he continued: "There's been a rash of break-ins in that neighborhood over the last year, so people have gotten real on edge, real vigilant about it all. Then about six months ago a young girl, I think she was about thirteen, was raped in the basement of a brownstone not far from where Chris stopped his car, and . . . well, they said they found his fingerprints on the windows of that basement."

"No!" Sidonie's scream was so loud Mike panicked and finally pulled over.

"I know this is real upsetting, but fingerprints don't lie—"

"But police do! They do, Mike." Her words tumbled out as if she couldn't hold them any longer. "I know you're a cop, I know you're a good person, and maybe you're different from the bad ones, but they can be assholes who profile and abuse and falsely accuse a black man without the blink of an eye. I've seen it, I've experienced it, I know. And I'm sorry to say that to you—because you just rescued me—so if you want to let me out right now, that's fine. But I will not sit here and let you tell me that the man I love, the man I live with, the man I've known long enough to know his heart and soul, is a *rapist*! That is *insane!*"

Mike, his own discomfort severe, motioned for her to quiet down —as if anyone on the street at two o'clock in the morning cared a whit about the commotion in his car. "Sidonie, I'm not gonna try to defend the whole department, and I'm not trying to convince you of anything. I've always thought of Chris as a good guy. But if they have fingerprints from a crime scene that incriminate him, you can't just look away and call it profiling. He'll need to get a good lawyer and play this by the book, or life could get real ugly, real fast. I don't want that for either of you."

"What's going to happen to him right now? How do I get him out of there?"

"He'll be booked, there'll be a bond hearing, and, depending on what he's ultimately charged with, his bail will be set. I'm assuming he'll make a call to get that taken care of. Hopefully he'll be out by later today, but if they do run with the rape charge, things could get complicated."

"So he hasn't been charged with the rape?"

"Apparently not yet. Not sure what the deal is there, but these guys have been on this case for a long time and they're motivated. Anything could happen."

Sidonie looked out the window with a thousand-mile stare, so exhausted she couldn't put anything into cohesive form.

"Do you want me to take you home?" Mike asked carefully.

"No, my keys and everything are at the club . . . I need to get my car. Can we call and see if anyone's there? I won't be able to get in if it's closed."

"Frank and Al are there. Said they'd wait until I brought you back."

FIFTY-THREE

FRANK WAS THE LAST PERSON SIDONIE WANTED TO SEE. She wanted to go home, scrub away the stench of her unfortunate circumstances, and sleep until she could start making calls.

After repeating her appreciation to Mike for his intervention, she climbed out of his car and knocked on the employee entrance. Mike pulled away with a quick wave when he saw Al crack the door.

As she stepped into the empty club, Al grabbed her in a clumsy hug that held long enough to convey true consolation. "Jasper wanted me to tell you he was gonna wait, but Andrew's windshield got smashed up in all the bullshit, so he needed a ride home. Said he'd call you tomorrow."

"I know, thanks. He texted me."

Al assessed the abraded side of her face. "That looks pretty rough."

"Feels pretty rough. I'll soak it in peroxide when I get home."

"Damn, Frame . . ."

He led her to the bar as if she might break, gentleness she found touching. Frank sat on a stool nursing a port, looking miserable. He, too, gave her a hug, though his was a tidier affair. Sidonie could feel the tension between them and it riled her.

Al whipped together a gimlet without even asking, and, after draining it, Sidonie ran down the whole tawdry tale, leaving out, for the moment, the doomsday fingerprint theory. While Frank held a pensive pose, Al exploded in righteous, appreciated indignation.

"That is fucking nuts! Chris is one of the best guys I know. I can't believe they'd charge him with some pansy-assed bullshit like peeking and trespassing!"

"I know, and thank you, Al. The problem is, he did walk into the yard to use the hose, so if they want, they *can* make a case for trespassing. The peeking thing is utter fabrication."

"Unfortunately," Frank countered, "his being in the yard could give a jury reason to believe he *was* peeking, so he needs to get a really good lawyer." Sidonie knew he was right, but something about Frank's tone rankled. Right now she wanted him to be less practical and more infuriated.

"I agree, Frank, and as soon as I'm able to talk to him, we'll start figuring that out. My sister knows a lot of good people. His sister probably does too. Between all of us we'll get him set up."

"Sidonie, if there's anything I can do to help, let me know, okay?" Al interjected.

She smiled, noting his atypical, and endearing, use of her first name. "Just sending Mike down was a huge favor. If you hadn't, I'd probably still be cuffed to that bench, or I'd be booked. He saved the day, so thanks."

"No problem. I told you he was a good guy."

"You did. And he is one of the good ones. I need to believe there are some."

Frank bristled and Sidonie noticed.

"Frank, is there something you want to say to me?" The edge in her voice was undisguised. "I feel like you're sitting there with judgment seeping out all over the place and if we need to hash something out, let's do it now, okay?"

"It's not judgment, Sidonie, but as someone who's worked with and knows a lot of honest, courageous men and women in the police force, it annoys me when you use such a broad brush in your condemnation."

"That's what you think is the salient point here? My condemning the cops?"

"Look, I understand you've got issues with them now that you're involved with certain racial demographics, but—"

"Wait, what? 'Involved with certain racial demographics'? What does that even mean? Why don't you quit with the jargon, Frank, and say what you want to say?"

He turned to her squarely. "Okay, kiddo, I will. I'm going to say this now and I hope we can get past it and onto what needs handling, both in your personal life and here at the club."

"Fine. Have at it."

"First of all, one of the reasons I don't like in-house relationships is their potential to impact the club in ways very particular to in-house relationships. As this one has. I've now had a night where I had to duck and hustle the goddamn mayor into his limo so he wouldn't see my top managers being hauled off by the police, with both of them now wrapped up in legal issues, my sound manager likely unavailable for who knows how long. And while I have empathy for the plight of the black man in America, I'm concerned that *your* concern is contributing to a sort of reverse racism scenario, where you think *everything's* about race . . . when sometimes it just isn't. I love you, kiddo, and I care about what happens to you, but I don't want to see you get caught up in someone else's problems. And because I love this club and the people who work here, I also don't want to see those problems impact our operation. There. That's it in a nutshell." He leaned back. Done.

Sidonie was too tired to be outraged. There were far worse things to be outraged about than Frank's decidedly offensive disapproval, and she needed to pace herself. "I get it, Frank. From an objective, professional point of view, I get it. And I'm truly sorry about the mayor—"

"Luckily there was enough hoopla going on out front that he didn't notice the circus in the back."

"I'm grateful for that." And she was; after all the work she'd put in, it would have been a humiliating denouement if he had. "But what's really important to me is that you understand that none of this was our fault. Neither Chris nor I deserved what happened. If you can't see that, we've got way more than club logistics to deal with."

"I'm not saying anyone *deserved* anything—"

"Secondly, if something happened to someone you loved, your wife, your kids, I'd expect it to impact you and maybe even spill over into your work. That's human, that's real. I'll do my best to limit that, but I don't want to be judged for it either. As for reverse racism, *that's* just complete bullshit. You might not even realize how bullshit it is. And because you haven't experienced or witnessed any of the things Chris has—or even I have in the short time we've been together—I don't honestly think you can speak on that topic at all. But please be assured that I haven't magically lost my ability to discern and differentiate. You've trusted me for a long time, Frank. Don't stop when I need your support the most, okay?"

Frank stood up, grabbed his keys, and tapped the bar a couple of times. "Okay. Deal. Will you be in later today?"

She was taken aback by his abrupt shift. "I don't know what's happening with Chris, so I'll have to see. Jasper texted earlier and said he can run things. He also said Andrew is booked to do sound—it's just an acoustic set—so Chris probably won't be back until Wednesday at the earliest. I'll keep you posted on my end."

Frank squeezed her shoulder as he turned to leave. "By the way, the event was spectacular. You did an amazing job. I'm only sorry it ended the way it did. Go home. Get some sleep. We'll get it sorted out."

As Frank exited, Al gave Sidonie a somber smile and another gimlet. She was grateful for both.

FIFTY-FOUR

BY ONE O'CLOCK THAT AFTERNOON, CHRIS HAD BEEN bailed out by his mother and sister, and taken to the emergency room at Rush University Medical Center, well south of Andersonville. He wanted to go to a hospital closer to home, but Vanessa had insisted: the defense attorney she'd hired, Philip K. Lewis, worked near Rush, making it convenient for him to stop by on short notice to photograph and document Chris's injuries for the brutality lawsuit she was already discussing. Chris was too overwhelmed to put up a fight, so they were now ensconced at Rush, waiting for his various treatments to conclude.

While all this unfolded, Sidonie had no idea where he was or what, exactly, was happening, and her repeated texts and calls to him, Delores, and Vanessa had all gone unanswered, which left her in a slurry of anxiety. She was just about to contact Karen to see what she might advise when Delores finally rang with an update.

"The doctor says it would be better if he was admitted. He's in a lot of pain and they're worried about latent concussion effects. But Chris is adamant about getting out of here. The truth is, there's not much they can do except ease his pain and wait for bones and muscles to heal, so they don't have much leverage to talk him out of it."

"Do you want me to try? I might have some influence on him."

"I'm sure you would, sweetheart, and Vanessa would probably appreciate that. She thinks it would be better for a brutality suit if Chris spent some time in the hospital, but, of course, the minute she mentioned that he got furious. I'm afraid if you talk to him now he'll feel like we're ganging up on him. Like it or not, he's in charge of his own care and he wants out."

"Okay, but let me know if you change your mind. I think it'd be better if he stayed there too." She was in her car and pulling out of the garage.

"Also, Sidonie, I'm going to suggest he come down to the house for a while. I'm not trying to circumvent you, but I know how busy you are at the club, and he'll need substantial hands-on care for at least the first week or so. It seems like it might be the best solution for now."

Between Vanessa securing an attorney and Delores's desire to get him to Hyde Park, familial wagons were circling in ways that set off alarms of exclusion. Sidonie felt the immediate impulse to stake her claim.

"I understand your thinking, but I can be as flexible with my schedule as needed. Plus, I think he'd be more comfortable at home than back in temporary quarters, don't you?"

Delores was suddenly crying. "Oh, I don't know much right now, sweetheart, but knowing Chris, he's going to make the decision regardless of what any of us thinks. Let me see what happens and I'll call you back."

Sidonie continued toward the hospital with dread leading the way. She wanted to talk to Karen, wanted both her sisterly support and legal expertise, but didn't relish opening the floodgates of concern and inquiry until she had more information.

She felt ghastly. Facial contact with a brick wall had left her scraped and swollen; the right side of her face was slick with cortisone cream and strategic dabs of concealer. Her stomach was empty and awash in acid. There was a major headache to contend with, panic about what lie ahead, and, most painfully, grief and concern about what was happening with and to the man she loved. It was astonishing how much *bad* could exist in one single moment.

Then she thought about what Chris was going through and immediately felt pathetic.

Her phone buzzed again. It was Chris. She burst into immediate tears somewhere between seeing his name and answering, though she did everything possible to rein them in. "Chris . . ." was all she could get out as she pulled over to the curb.

"Hey, Sid." He sounded as battered as he was. "Are you coming to get me?"

Relief flooded. "Yes. Your mom thought you might want to spend the next few days at her place so—"

"I'm coming home. I should be ready when you get here."

By the time Sidonie arrived at the hospital, an exhausted Delores had left in a cab. Vanessa, who looked exactly like a woman who'd been up all night, stood stoic and soldierly. She greeted Sidonie at the entrance of the waiting room, prickling with efficiency.

"Here's his attorney's card. Philip K. Lewis. He's the best I know. He's worked with lots of my clients, specializes in brutality and profiling cases. He's already been here and taken the photographs we'll need, but you'll obviously have to talk to him as soon as possible. He'll want to hear your side of the story while it's fresh." She was all business, detailed and detached; clearly this kind of scenario was not new to her as a professional. As a sister, odds were good it was leaving a mark.

"Thank you for jumping on this so quickly, Vanessa. I was planning to call my sister. She's worked with a lot of great of defense attorneys over the years and—"

"It's handled. She doesn't need to worry about it."

"I'm just saying there are options if need be."

"There won't be a need." The look she gave Sidonie shut down further discussion. "As for his injuries, they're not life-threatening, but they're substantial, meaning I'm not sure how quickly he can get back to work—all of that will go toward the brutality case—but for now you'll need to replace him at your club. I'll discuss with him how he wants to handle Sound Alchemy."

It was clear Sidonie was being hip-checked from the equation, but she suspected Vanessa had not yet conferred with Chris on any of this. "I understand how you see it, but Chris and I will discuss together how

218 | LORRAINE DEVON WILKE

he wants to proceed in either case. Obviously, beyond getting him healed, the priority is handling the criminal charges, so I'd like to be brought up-to-speed on what the police actually have and don't have. I assume they talked to you about the fingerprints?"

Vanessa's head snapped in her direction. "What fingerprints?"

Immediate regret. Clearly Mike had told her something that hadn't been communicated to the family, or maybe even yet attached to the case. Her backtrack was swift and clumsy. "I'm not really sure. One of them was blabbering about fingerprints and other cases, but if they didn't say anything to you, I assume it was just a scare tactic."

"Those motherfuckers. Okay, we'll see what they pull out of their trick bag as things develop. I'd suggest you get your own attorney in case they try to get you to incriminate him in any way. That's probably something you could talk to your sister about."

The implication chafed. "Vanessa, let me be very clear," Sidonie said, seething. "There is absolutely no way I would *ever* incriminate Chris, nor do I have anything that *could* incriminate Chris, so take that concern right off the table."

Vanessa cut her a look. "Fine. You just best be prepared for how manipulative cops can be when they set their sights on a black defendant. Odds are good this will be a very different battle than anything you're used to."

"I'm not used to any kind of legal problems, so this is all new to me."

"Well, you are the lucky one." Vanessa turned and walked down the hall.

FIFTY-FIVE

SIDONIE REMAINED IN THE WAITING ROOM, IRATE AND jumpy. She'd been informed that Chris was going through the discharge procedure with his sister's help, leaving her annoyed that Vanessa had commandeered that task as well. Still, the woman's efficiency was impressive, and given how exhausted and disoriented she felt, Sidonie couldn't deny some grudging appreciation.

The external door of the ward hissed opened and a tall, dark-skinned, exceedingly well-dressed man swept in. Sidonie instinctively knew this was Hermes, Vanessa's soon-to-be—or perhaps already—ex-husband. He looked around, focused and concerned, then turned to Sidonie with marked curiosity.

Cocking his head: "Sidonie?"

"Yes. Are you Hermes?"

"I am!" In a surprising move, he swept her into a hug so intense she almost burst into tears of gratitude. "I'm so sorry that you ... that Chris ... that all of us have to deal with this insanity. Unbelievable."

After extricating herself, and with little knowledge of how this man operated in life beyond this momentary encounter, she was most struck by the contrast between him and Vanessa. It was not hard to imagine them clashing over issues large and small. "It's horrible. Chris is battered, the charges are ludicrous, it's just ... horrible."

He made note of her face. "You look a little battered yourself. Are you okay?"

He was the first person on Chris's side of the family to express any concern for her, and it, too, almost set her to tears. She willed herself to hold it together, deciding no one involved knew her well enough to endure her sobbing. "I'll be fine. I'm just scared about what all this means for Chris."

"Clearly it's a case of mistaken identity that needs to get sorted out. Ness has the best lawyer in that arena all set up—"

"Yes, she gave me his card."

"And she'll be on top of the legal stuff every step of the way. He couldn't have a better advocate, that much I know. And he'll have the rest of us, especially you, for the love and moral support stuff . . . that will definitely be needed."

Already she loved this man. She could see why Chris loved him; he was all heart. "Thank you, Hermes. I appreciate you framing it that way. Right now I just want to get him home and comfortable, from there . . . we'll see."

"That's actually why I'm here. Vanessa said he'll need some help navigating, so I'm providing the muscle. He's going back to your place?"

"Yes. That's what he said he wanted," she added almost defensively.

"Of course. There's no place like home, especially after you've had your ass kicked."

She looked him, smiling. "You are just so . . . great. Chris has had nothing but accolades for you, and now I see why."

He smiled warmly. "Right back atcha."

They heard the bark of a woman's voice as Vanessa rounded the corner at the other end of the hallway. When her eyes lit on Hermes, her face spun through a kaleidoscope of emotions so stealthily that most observers would have missed the flicker of softening. Sidonie didn't. It was touching.

Vanessa reset her face and approached in her usual no-nonsense mode, pushing Chris toward them in the requisite discharge wheelchair. "All right, we're wrapped here. Sidonie, if you could grab these papers under my arm. They're care instructions. I'd suggest you go down now and pull your car up to the patient departure area. Hermes, you can help from there."

Before Sidonie responded to her assignment, she took the moment to connect with Chris, who she was seeing for the first time since she'd been dragged off in a police car. His swollen, bandaged face was shocking, making her attempt at composure a struggle. His wrist and forearm were both in soft casts, there were cuts and contusions everywhere, and it was clear he was in pain. He looked up at her with a doleful, lopsided smile.

"It's okay, Sid, I'm okay."

A sob finally escaped her lips and she bent in front of the chair, wrapping her arms around him in a gentle, tentative embrace. "I was so scared. I didn't know what they would do to you," she whispered in his ear.

"I know. I didn't either. But I'm okay. How about you?" He gingerly leaned his head against hers.

"I'm okay. Better now, seeing you."

Vanessa cleared her throat, a cue to move the party along, and as they stepped through the doors toward the elevator, Chris reached out with his uninjured arm and took Sidonie's hand.

FIFTY-SIX

ALICE AND MARK FROM NEXT DOOR, WHO'D ARRANGED TO
be at Sidonie's to supervise delivery of the medical lift chair, were in
the kitchen getting coffee made and snacks put out as Sidonie bound
up the stairs from the garage. Shaking off the chill of the raw October
afternoon, she quickly cleared the path of small tables and magazine
baskets, anything that would make Chris's progress more difficult.
Vanessa swooped up and past her, positioning herself to help the ma-
neuver in any way she could.

The process of getting Chris up the stairs to the main floor made
Sidonie wish she lived in a ranch home. The multilevel design that
once seemed so artful and clever now loomed as an obstacle course.
Even the hallways felt too sharp and narrow, the stairs too tight, with
hardwood floors too slick and slippery. As she watched Chris make
his slow, painful way, Sidonie kept reaching out helplessly, as if to
avert threat of further injury.

Beyond wrist, arm, facial, and head injuries, it turned out Chris
had three broken ribs, a torn latissimus dorsi in the left back area, and
a severe hip contusion, all of which made navigation a challenge.
Hermes half carried him up, stopping to lean against the wall and
bannister as needed to catch his breath and get stabilized. The lift
chair had been set up in the first-floor guestroom, alleviating need for
further ascension. Until he could comfortably lie flat, that room
would be his refuge.

Once Chris was safely ensconced, and the chair set to the desired recline for sleep, Hermes and Vanessa moved out to the kitchen. Sidonie stayed behind, arranging water, meds, and various snacks at his side table, carefully tucking the blanket around his legs.

"Are you comfortable?" she asked.

"As much as I can be."

"Can I get you anything else?"

"I think you've got it covered."

"Do you want to talk about it, or ask any questions about anything? Of course you don't have to—"

"I need to sleep," he said bluntly. When she pulled away ever-so-slightly, he glanced up, chagrined. "Sorry. I'm . . . just fried."

"It's okay, I understand." She kissed him on the forehead, his mouth too wounded for contact.

After she slipped out, closing the door behind her, he lay staring up at the ceiling, trying to organize the swarming internal chatter. Whether it was the painkillers or the pounding in his head, the task was beyond his abilities. His only prevailing thought was: "This is not my life. This is not *her* life." But apparently it was.

Too much to take in, he drifted off to sleep.

WHEN SIDONIE ENTERED the kitchen, she noticed Hermes and Vanessa out on the deck with the sliding glass door closed, engaged in what appeared to be a serious conversation. Alice and Mark were still sorting through the various food items they'd brought over. There was a frozen Costco lasagna, roast chicken, several platters of sandwiches, and an enormous bag of spinach. Sidonie slumped to the counter and shook her head. "I appreciate you guys doing all this. I won't have to cook for a week."

"That's the idea, Sid. You've got enough going on." Alice smiled dolefully.

Mark grabbed his coat, then handed Alice hers. "We're going to give you guys some privacy now. Just holler if you need anything else. We're right next door . . . anything you need."

"You two are the best. Getting that chair in here was a lifesaver. I don't know how long it'll be before he can manage a bed, so thank you. For everything."

"We're just real sorry you're going through this," Mark said. "Have you talked to your sister yet, gotten her take on everything?"

"She knows the broad strokes. I'll talk more with her later."

"Just take care of yourselves," Alice said. "The rest will work itself out, I have faith."

Sidonie was grateful for Alice's faith; she was currently bereft of any.

Shortly after their quiet departure, the heated conversation on the balcony abruptly stopped and the sliding glass door opened. Hermes came in from the deck. His face, tucked behind a thick scarf, was clouded and tired. "Okay, Sidonie, I'm heading out. You've got my number, text me with yours. I'll want to stay up on things, so don't hesitate to call anytime."

"It was so nice to finally meet you, Hermes, even under these hideous circumstances. Thank you for helping out. We couldn't have gotten him up here without you."

He once again pulled her into a sturdy hug. She liked that about him, his tactileness. She liked him in general, hoped he'd stay in her life regardless of what happened between him and Vanessa.

After he left, she expected Vanessa to follow suit. It was chilly outside and the sun had almost set, but she remained on the deck long enough that Sidonie pulled on her coat and slid the door open. Even in the shadows of gathering night, she could see Vanessa had been crying. Sidonie slipped into the chair next to her and said nothing. They sat that way for a good ten minutes, both huddled against the cold, until Vanessa finally spoke:

"I want to hate him but I can't. I love him more than anyone I know and can't bear to think of life without him." Silent tears streamed down her face.

Sidonie knew she was in tender, fragile territory. Vanessa's vulnerability was an ephemeral thing; saying the right words was critical. Or at least not saying the wrong ones.

"Is there hope . . . even a bit? Enough to keep trying?"

"I don't know. It doesn't feel like it."

She didn't snap; she didn't brush her away. Sidonie took the small victory as Vanessa, unexpectedly, continued:

"He seems set in his belief that we're too far apart to find any way back." She wiped her eyes and took a sip of wine, hand trembling as she lifted the glass. "The thing is, I'd *like* to see the world the way he does, with his sense of optimism, but that's not the world I see. What *I* see is the worst of life—kids getting shot, women abused, and my brother, one of the most honorable men on earth, beaten like a dog. Hermes tells me I can't bring my anger home, that I have children and need to nurture their hope and joy, and he's right. I want to be that person. I try so hard to be that person! Then I walk away from those sweet faces into the raging world and anger grabs me up." She stared straight ahead, her eyes glassy with sorrow. "And so . . . I lose him. I lose my husband to that rage. And that makes the world's agonies all the more tragic to me." She sobbed quietly.

Sidonie could think of nothing to say. Nothing that didn't sound patronizing, that wouldn't be feeble and petty next to the depth of Vanessa's anguish. The only thing she could do was reach over and take her hand, hold it tight and hope the empathy she felt would stream from her heart, through her hand, to offer at least some comfort and solidarity to the woman she touched. Vanessa wept and held on tight.

FIFTY-SEVEN

CHRIS, AWAKENED FROM FITFUL SLEEP BY THE MURMUR of voices in the foyer, heard the click of the front door and the silence that followed, relieved. He'd hoped no one would feel a need to check on him one more time; to offer bromides about healing quickly or overcoming obstacles. He wanted none of it. He wanted to freely indulge in the anger and affliction he felt.

His attempt to move his body in the lift chair was thwarted when he dropped the remote twice before finding the necessary leverage to sit up. The pain emanating from his midsection and back made him yelp. He'd never broken a rib before, much less three, and would not have believed, prior to this event, how agonizing it would be. But it was, in fact, just one of the aching parts that screamed at him as he lay inert and overwhelmed.

This was a tipping point; of that there was no doubt. The moment when the equanimity and patience taught by his father, the acceptance and decorum passed on by his mother, ebbed and evaporated to be replaced by his rage, his sense of injustice. The sweaty realization that he would get a pass for *nothing*—not the blackness of his skin, the quirks of his nature, the innocent turn of his head; not even the choice of woman he loved—broke him. He would pay full price for it all and there would be no rules to protect him, no predictions of when it might strike, or certainly how it might end.

Police, lawyers, trials, threats of incarceration, the loss of all he'd created. It loomed, it harangued—it terrified him. It made him want to cry.

When she slipped in after tentatively cracking the door, wanting to see if he was up and in need, Sidonie saw his tears, something she'd never witnessed before, and they frightened her. She needed him to be strong so she could believe they'd get through this, mostly because she couldn't hold that belief on her own.

She sat on the bed across from him. "Are you in pain?"

"Yes."

"Can I get you anything?"

"No. I've taken everything I can. I'm just waiting for it to kick in. I ate some yogurt. That's all I can handle."

They sat in silence. He wiped his eyes with his good hand.

"Do you want to talk about it?" she finally asked.

He looked at her. "You know whatever they said I did, I didn't do?"

"Of course. What I don't know is why they beat the crap out of you." Her eyes flashed.

"They said I was resisting."

"Were you?"

"No. I was just trying to get to you."

Which put another crack in her heart.

A wave of exhaustion rolled over him. "I'm too tired to talk about it right now. I just wanted to be sure you knew I didn't do anything but put water in my car."

Her eyes teared up. "I know."

"Good. Then hopefully I can sleep. We'll break it down when I feel better, okay?"

"Okay," she said helplessly . . . because all she wanted to do was talk and talk and talk until she understood what had just happened to them.

FIFTY-EIGHT

SIDONIE LAY IN THEIR ARTFULLY DECORATED BEDROOM upstairs, her phone close in case Chris texted or called from below, feeling hollow and isolated. The distance between them was one floor and a few feet, yet it felt like a chasm, one she feared would only gape wider in days to come.

Just as she was drifting off, her phone buzzed. She jerked to a seated position, certain it was Chris and he was in pain, or emotionally distraught, or in need of something urgent. In a strange moment of conflicted emotion, she saw Patsy's name. Despite her continued moratorium on their friendship, despite her stoic belief that they needed to keep their distance, the thing she felt most in this moment was the urge to talk to her oldest friend.

She picked up. "Hey."

"Sid. My God. I just talked to Karen. I know it's late, I know you don't want to talk to me, but I had to call. I figured if I was overstepping, you'd just ignore me."

Sidonie began quietly sobbing. "They hurt him so bad, Pats. He can hardly move. They beat the living shit out of him . . ."

"Oh, Sid." Patsy's voice was almost a whisper. "I can't imagine how you feel, how he feels. I am so sorry. I don't know what else to say. It's awful. I just want you to know I'm here, if you need me for anything. I mean it. You might not want my help, but I'm here."

"Thanks. I appreciate it."

"*Is* there anything I can do?"

"I don't think so. At least not right now. It's all so . . . I dunno. I don't know what it is yet."

"Just remember you're not alone. You have Karen, you have me. I'm sure you have Chris's family. We'll—you'll get through it."

"Will we?"

"Yes! I promise."

"You don't know what you're talking about."

"I don't, that's true." Patsy sighed. "But I actually believe it. And I'm gonna go now. I know you've had a rough twenty-four hours. I just wanted to reach out, Sid, and tell you that I love you and I'm here anytime you need me, okay?"

"Thanks, Patsy. It means a lot that you called."

It did. On this particular day, it did.

FIFTY-NINE

THE NEXT FOUR DAYS CAME WITH A BUZZ OF ACTIVITY that perversely mimicked the process of event production: there were intersecting calls and texts, various meetings with a rotating list of participants, furtive discussions, passionate arguments, and a prevailing sense that everyone involved felt they knew best, cared most, and had primary investment in the outcome.

Chris focused on managing Sound Alchemy from a laptop set up near his lift chair. He hobbled around as instructed by the doctor, but had yet to tackle the stairs. Sidonie arranged for his unavoidable replacement at the club: Andrew and Jasper would do the smaller gigs coming up, with two of Chris's Alchemy team coming in during the larger events. Frank operated on the assumption that Chris would be out for two weeks.

Hermes stayed in regular touch with Sidonie, a bright spot she anticipated. He brought food over twice, delivered handmade get well cards from Chris's niece and nephew, and in general maintained his role as the family optimist. Diante came bearing bags of Chris's favorite takeout, none of which was eaten but all of which was appreciated. On the other end of the spectrum, Vanessa stayed fierce and focused on gleaning whatever information was available from the police, handling all ongoing conversations with the defense attorney, Philip K. Lewis, while pulling together funds to pay his not inconsiderable retainer. Sidonie insisted on contributing, something Chris and Vanessa initially resisted until an impassioned speech about love and commitment won her a seat at the table.

Somewhere in the stew of need and anxiety, Vanessa and Sidonie entered a new phase of their relationship. After the night on the deck, when vulnerabilities had been too revealed to pretend otherwise, they were almost forced to find a tentative foundation for what might later become a friendship. It was too soon to tell at this point, but for now walls had been breached and connections made. Anyone in the family circle who noticed was pleased.

Sidonie reluctantly went back to work Friday afternoon. The "we're unfortunately cancelling the party" notices had been emailed the night before. Everyone uniformly sent regards and regrets, decorously avoiding questions, but Sidonie could feel their palpable curiosity as she made her way to the office.

When she checked in with Jasper, his distress was evident, translating into monosyllabic conversation. "Hey, Jasper, Chris said all the cues for the weekend are programmed, but he does want to talk to you about tomorrow night. He's hoping you'll give him a call sometime today."

"Okay."

"Did Andrew do okay running the shows this week?"

"Yep."

"And you've got the contact info for the Alchemy crew?"

"Yep."

"Jasper."

"Yep."

"What's going on? Just the Chris thing, or are you upset about something else?"

Jasper looked up as if he'd been hit. "Isn't the Chris thing enough? And your thing? How do you think I feel, leading you into that clusterfuck?"

She was stunned to see his hands shaking. "You must know that wasn't your fault!"

"I've never seen anything like it in my life. On TV, sure, in movies, but this was real life, man. My life. Your life. Chris's life. It made me sick." He finally looked at her. "How are you doing? Your face looks like shit."

She had to suppress a smile. "I'm okay. Chris is going to take a while, though."

He shook his head. "All I can say, Sid, is I hope you kick their asses. Right to the fucking curb. Get that lawyer to sue them for everything they've got. Chris did not deserve that, no way, no how." Jasper's fervor was cleansing.

"Thank you, I agree," she responded. "But right now the focus is on getting this trial moved ahead so he can exonerate himself. After that, I have a feeling his sister will look forward to going all scorched earth on their asses." She had to grin, picturing tiny Vanessa taking on the whole of the Chicago police department.

Frank approached the stage area, a raft of Fed Ex envelopes in his hand. "Sidonie, can we sit down and go over these contracts? I want to get the calendar updated."

She squeezed Jasper's arm as she stepped off the stage and followed Frank to his office.

His pace seemed purposefully brisk, and, as he got situated at his desk, he avoided eye contact, making clear that remnants of his annoyance remained.

"So, Frank . . . am I being hypervigilant or do we need another conversation about this before we get down to work?"

He sighed and finally looked at her. "Sidonie, I'm not going to lie: this situation is a problem. I'm sorry Chris has got some injuries to deal with, but his being out for two weeks is no small thing at this particular time of year and with the roster we have coming in. I just hope *you* can keep your focus on the job during all this."

His bluntness was skin scraping. "I'm sorry you're having a problem with the inconvenience of it all, but those injuries he's dealing with, as you put it—which are significant and brutal, by the way—are the result of serious police overreaction. I know you hate to hear that, but it's the truth."

He shifted in his seat. "Is it possible, though, that there's a lack of objectivity in the way you continue to characterize it?"

"I don't know, Frank." She was seething but struggled to contain herself. "If there is, it's probably because it's hard to be objective under these particular circumstances. But which characterization, specifically, are you referring to? Where I tell you the man I love and have lived with for the past seven months is *not* a criminal but was still beaten to the point that he can barely move? Where I mention that I *know* whoever these people think they saw breaking into their garages is *not* the man who's done an amazing job improving the status of your club? The part where I assure you that, despite his significant injuries, Chris has every single event staffed and cued, with Jasper and Andrew set to manage everything as needed? In fact, the worst thing that's happened in relation to your club is that I had to cancel our party, which, it turns out, was something the staff was really looking forward to. So which part, Frank?" Her eyes were blazing.

His posture softened. "I get it. It's been horrific for everyone involved, especially you and Chris, but the legal issues put me in a bind. We've hosted events for the police department every year for the past decade, we have one on the books for March, and I don't relish the prospect of an adversarial situation with you two spilling into the club, with trials and lawsuits and bad publicity. It doesn't reflect well. That's all I'll say. But I have to trust that you'll keep it as far from here as you can, and we'll go from there. Is that cool?"

She shifted in her seat. "It's cool, Frank. It's cool."

It wasn't cool, but she didn't want to talk about it with him any longer. She picked up the contract envelopes and proceeded as if everything was . . . cool.

SIXTY

PHILIP K. LEWIS WAS A SHORT, STOCKY, BESPECTACLED black man wearing a brown suit that was too tight to be buttoned at the middle and too short to be worn with beige socks. Despite his sartorial failings, he was known as a brilliant attorney and powerful advocate for victims of overzealous prosecution and police brutality, both of which, Vanessa assured him, factored into this case. She'd known him since college, relying often on his expertise with both her social work cases and those funneled through the BLM chapter with which she was affiliated. She trusted him implicitly, enough to defend her own brother.

Though she'd met privately with Philip at the hospital when he came to photograph Chris's injuries, this was the first official discussion between the two men, one arranged by Vanessa at a time that conflicted for Sidonie, despite it being held at their home. Vanessa claimed this was not intentional. Chris promised she'd be kept informed. Sidonie was irked but chose to believe them both.

"Let's get right to it, Chris," Philip intoned briskly. "The arraignment is next Friday, so let's take this time to prepare, okay?"

Chris nodded. Vanessa took out a notepad as Philip began.

"The case is built on eyewitness testimony only, at least at this point. Records show that where your car broke down is an area that's suffered a rash of break-ins and robberies over the last year, and the Neighborhood Watch there is one that's been active since the Cabrini-Green days. The woman who saw you use the hose and followed you to the club not only positively identified you the night of your arrest, but later ID'd your picture as the perpetrator of at least one break-in. A second witness, a man—another neighborhood resident who claims to be unacquainted with the first woman—also pointed to your picture as someone seen peeking in windows that were later broken into."

Chris shook his head, exasperated. "How is that possible? I've never been on that street before in my life."

"Not even just walking or driving by?"

"I have no memory of ever being on that street before that day."

"Okay, let's leave that for the moment. The bigger problem we have was conveyed to me today by the prosecutor." He took a pause.

Vanessa looked up, alarmed. "What?"

"About six months ago, about a block away from where your Jeep broke down, a teenaged girl was sexually assaulted, raped, in the laundry room of the apartment building where she lives with her family. They never caught the guy. She said he was black, and they say they have fingerprints. They're implying they're Chris's."

Boom. It was on the table.

"Are you fucking kidding me?" Chris recoiled like a bullet had struck.

"*Implying?*" Vanessa almost screeched. "What possible legal precedent involves the *implication* of evidence?"

"Vanessa, I understand your outrage. My guess is they're floating it in hopes of shaking the trees, police strategy meant to—"

"Oh my God!" She looked as if a light had gone off. "Sidonie said something about fingerprints!"

Chris, stunned, turned to her. "What are you talking about?"

"Sunday, at the hospital. She said something about a cop mentioning fingerprints when they had her at the police station. She brushed it off, but clearly this is what she was referring to."

Chris, who'd purposely avoided discussing the case at home, was now confused about what Sidonie did or didn't know. "Even if I had been in that neighborhood before, which I'm pretty sure I haven't, the only things I touched were the water hose and the spigot. That's it. Unless they're talking about that, they're talking shit."

"It's all talk at this point," Philip rejoined, "so let's not get too wrapped up in what it means yet. My guess is they have nothing, but when we get to the arraignment, they'll have to produce the charging documents and whatever evidence they do have. We'll have a clearer picture of what we're dealing with then."

"What exactly happens at this arraignment?" Chris queried, feeling the weight of his new legal burden.

"For a misdemeanor case like this it should be brief. The prosecutor is Brad Reisman, a decent guy, generally fair, not overly aggressive. He'll present the charges and the range of penalties for each charge. You'll make your plea—not guilty—and we'll be given a trial date. I expect the entire process, including the trial, to be on a fast track, particularly since, as we discussed at the hospital, we're opting for a bench trial. We're getting into the holidays, the charges are relatively minor, based on only eyewitness testimony, and you have no prior record. It's Chicago and they have much bigger fish to fry, so they're always looking to clear the smaller stuff as quickly as possible."

Chris's face bore a sheen of sweat. Vanessa glanced over.

"Are you okay?" she asked.

"No. I feel like I'm being railroaded. All I did was put water in my car and suddenly I'm in this insanity with no way out." He knew he sounded peevish, but lacked the energy to change his tone.

"Certainly there's a way out, Chris," Philip asserted. "But, yes, these steps are unavoidable—that's the frustrating part."

"And how is it that I'm even being looked at for all this? Something *so* far from who I am I . . . I don't even have words for it? Explain that to me!" He slammed his fist on the table.

Philip's voice softened. "Chris, let's try to—"

"Sorry, man," Chris cut him off, chagrined. "But I'm freaking out."

"No apologies necessary, this is tough stuff. And, yes, given that it's he says, she says, on top of CPD's history with black defendants, there's reason for concern. Let's get through the arraignment and sort it out from there. As for the fingerprints, I'm pretty convinced it's a ruse, but we'll know soon enough. Can you hold on till then?"

"I have no choice," Chris replied morosely.

"Here's the time and place of the arraignment." Philip slid a print-out in front of Chris. "Be on time, wear a suit, be humble, but be confident. We'll be in and out."

SIXTY-ONE

"YOU DIDN'T THINK TELLING ME ABOUT THE FINGERPRINTS was necessary?" Chris yelled from the living room. "Maybe I would have liked knowing about that before my attorney dropped it on me!"

Sidonie was in the downstairs bathroom getting ready to meet her sister across town, and Chris's insistence on going over this one point at this particular moment was not only slowing her progress, but triggering her increasingly aggrieved state of mind. She stomped out, eyes aflame.

"What did you want me to do, Chris, wake you up from a drug-hazed, pain-addled state to tell you that Mike from the club *heard* something about some fingerprints and that was all I knew? Why would I have done that? When no one mentioned it to you or Vanessa after you made bail, I figured it was just some stupid trick meant to freak me out. Which it did. So the last thing I wanted, considering the state you were in, was to freak *you* out! I was thinking about *you!*"

"Fine. But in the future, if you hear anything, see anything, read *anything* that has to do with my case, fill me in, okay? And since your police buddy hangs out at the bar, maybe you could get the inside scoop on the latest bullshit they're trying to pin on me. That'd be good." As much as he wanted to storm from the room or drop angrily to the couch, his still-aching body preempted dramatics. All he could do was carefully lower himself into the living room chair he'd hand-picked about a hundred years ago when trivial things like decorating a house and living a normal, unencumbered life seemed possible.

Sidonie tried not to roll her eyes. While sympathetic to his belea-guered state, her patience was being daily tested. She briefly considered cancelling her plans, but one glance at his smoldering countenance dissuaded her. She pulled on her coat and looked around for her keys, eager, frankly, to get out of the house.

"I won't be late. Call if you want me to pick anything up on my way home."

"I'm fine. Say hi to Karen. And . . . sorry for being an asshole."

She looked at him and sighed. "You're not being an asshole. Okay, you *are* being an asshole, but I understand." She grinned; he grinned back . . . just slightly.

FORTY-FIVE MINUTES later, Sidonie lay on the deck chaise on Karen's patio, alone and wrapped tightly against the cold, sipping a cup of decaf green tea. She wished it were warm enough to stay exiled out here for the rest of time. To sleep out here. Live out here. Build a little cabin and eat berries and nuts and banish the grid. Away from it all.

Her niece, Sarah, was entertaining friends, and though her brother-in-law Josh was keeping them corralled so she and Karen could talk privately, the thump-thump-thump of hip-hop booming from inside was loud and completely at odds with her mood. Karen's entrance from the house came replete with a bowl of chips, salsa, and choreog-raphy of a certain groove factor.

"Get down, get back up again," Sidonie joked feebly from her chair on the dark side of the patio.

Karen set the snacks down and joined her sister on the adjacent lounge. Munching loudly enough to elicit a frown from Sidonie, Karen waited for the conversation to start. When it didn't, she looked over pointedly.

"If we're not going to talk about this, let's go inside and watch a bad movie. It's cold out here."

"I'm *living* a bad movie." Sidonie sighed.

"Aw, sissy, I get it, I do. It's ridiculous and frightening. I understand. Which is why I want to talk about it a little, get you prepped for whatever might happen."

"What does that mean: 'whatever might happen'? Is there something else that might happen that isn't already happening?"

"I'm just saying you're probably going to get pulled into at least one interview with the police, and that's something I thought we should go over."

Sidonie bolted upright, put her cup down, and looked at her sister with panicked eyes. "Seriously? I'll have to go down to that hideous police station? I swear, I'll throw up if I ever have to walk through the doors of that hellhole again."

"I don't know. They may come to you. I called Philip Lewis—that's Chris's attorney—"

"Wait, how did you get that information?"

"I still have friends on that side of the law and I made a few calls. I actually know Philip. He's a really good guy and knows his stuff, particularly in that arena."

"I know. I had to meet with him the other day—"

"He mentioned that, said it went well."

"Really? How does an interview with your boyfriend's defense attorney about a crime he didn't commit 'go well'?"

"He just said you were direct and clear. Thought you'd make a credible witness if need be."

"God, I hope there's no 'need be.' Why did you want to talk to him?"

"To see how he thought they might come at you."

"And?"

"He thinks basically the same thing I do: they'll try to shake you up, get you to admit to something you saw Chris do, or heard him talk about. Anything that might help their case."

"Which I know nothing about."

"*You* know that—they don't. Get inside their mindset, Sid: they're looking at Chris as a criminal, which means they're looking at you as the criminal's girlfriend—someone who likely knows things and is withholding them on his behalf. Of course they have no sense of who the two of you really are. They're operating on profiles and standard procedures that have worked enough times that they're go-to."

"So what do I do?"

"Tell the truth. Say exactly what you know. No more, no less. Try not to stress about it too much. They're fishing, that's all. Don't let them get to you. You've got nothing to hide, nothing to lie about, and you're not charged with anything. Be confident of that and answer whatever they ask truthfully. You can't lose with that strategy."

Sidonie lay back down on the chaise, arms flopped to her sides in frustration. "How is this my life? Really. How is this what I'm dealing with?"

Karen was quiet for a moment. "I know ... but think about Chris. Think about what Vanessa deals with every day. This *is* life for a lot of people. I wish we could write it off as an anomaly—it *is* for you. For Chris, not so much. It's the tragedy of our times. It's why Vanessa's group exists. It's why we're having this conversation."

"I know ..." Sidonie said quietly, shamed by her petulance.

"I'm not trying to make you feel bad—you get to protest this as much as anyone. It's just important, I think, especially given who you're involved with, to keep it in perspective."

"Mom!" A lanky teenaged girl with an active pout and too much makeup careened through the patio doors. "The Internet is out again and we're *right* in the middle of a game! This is getting ridiculous! When are we getting better wireless? What, are we poor or some-thing?" She looked over. "Oh, hi, Aunt Sid. What are you guys doing out here? It's freezing!"

"Hey, Sarah ... just patio chatting with your mom."

"And we don't need interruptions from loud, snotty teenagers. Go talk to your father," Karen ordered. "If nothing else, unplug the router, wait a few minutes, then plug it back in—that always works. Now, take your entitled ass outta here and leave us alone."

Sarah stuck her tongue out and dashed back inside.

"First world problems." Karen rolled her eyes. "I remind myself daily that she really is more than that, but there are times ..."

"She's fine. She's a teenager. With you as her mom, she won't avoid growing a social conscience."

"I appreciate your optimism, but sometimes I wonder. Listen, I'm going inside where there's heat. Maybe you should go home, at least attempt normalcy. Do what you can to distract each other. This will get handled and life will get back to something you recognize, I promise."

"I'll hold you to that." Sidonie sighed as she climbed out of the chaise, thinking, for the first time, that her sister might not know what she was talking about.

SIXTY-TWO

CHRIS SAT HUNCHED AT A TABLE IN THE COURTHOUSE cafeteria, sullen and uncomfortable. With most parts of his body still thrumming in pain, he was grateful to have made it from the parking lot through security, up to the courtroom and later back down, largely without assistance. Now enervated, he nursed a club soda while waiting for Philip to return from a "quick meeting with the prosecutor." He took the moment to scrutinize his cacophonous location:

With the ponderous Cook County jail just next door, and weaponized security personnel at every turn, this was a place that insinuated guilt. It was weighty and sweat inducing, with din and activity reminiscent of a busy airport, where every kind of human being, wearing every kind of uniform, attitude, demeanor, or expression, swirled in gradations of anxiety. Strange to realize that most of them, many of them, were dealing with situations as life-altering as his own, making them reluctant confederates in a club to which he had no desire for membership.

The arraignment was over. He'd pleaded not guilty to two Class A misdemeanor charges of resisting a police officer and criminal trespass to residence, and one Class B misdemeanor of window peeking. Their request for a bench trial was filed, and the trial was set for December eighteenth. Philip said the date was "excellent," a nod to the scheduling complexities of the holiday season, as well as a desire on the part of the court to clear the docket of smaller cases. He wasn't as crazy about the judge, the Honorable Howard Gutchison, but insisted he'd be fair.

Chris had gotten so dizzy during the proceedings that he had to sit at one point when he should have been standing, and now hoped the club soda would offer some remedy. So far it hadn't. Philip finally rushed in with his requisite briefcase and air of professorial efficiency, motioning to Chris that he was going to grab a cup of coffee, clearly at home in this beehive setting. Joining Chris at the table, he jumped right in.

"Okay, I just talked to Reisman and they're willing to put a deal on the table."

"Is that good?"

"It gives us options."

"What's the deal?"

"Know that I plan to spend more time going over their discovery, but in glancing through what they gave us today, it's flimsy. Still seems to come down to eyewitness testimony. They do have a third witness who identified your picture, but she knows the initial witness, so I'm not sure how much additional leverage that offers them."

"Nothing about the supposed fingerprints?"

"No, but Reisman insists they're continuing to investigate that case in connection with ours, so it remains the unknown element. There's some reason they're maintaining that stance, which worries me a bit. We can't presume it won't come up later."

Chris felt a wave of panic wash over him. "But if there really were fingerprints, and the fingerprints were mine, don't you think there'd be additional charges *already*?"

"I do, but I also know how tricky this stuff can get. We can't discount it completely. They're obviously still dangling it in hopes of scaring you into admitting something useful in the charges already filed, a common tactic."

"They can just lie?"

"Actually, yes. If it helps get a confession."

"That's insane."

"It's the system we're in. But let's put that aside for now and focus on the charges we do have. Reisman reiterated that the Neighborhood Watch in the affected area has been so persistent they've actually become a nuisance, and frankly, the department wants them off their back. They're eager to tie this case up so they can assuage the group and get them out the door. Which is where the deal comes in."

"What's the deal?"

"It has some negatives but I'm obligated to put it out there and you can decide how you want to proceed."

"What's the deal?" Chris asked for the third time.

"A no contest plea to trespassing and window peeking, they drop the resisting charge, two years' probation, a fine of fifteen hundred dollars combined on both charges, and no jail time. Now, no contest pleas are relatively rare in this state, and the court doesn't have to accept them, but it is a legally available option, and the advantages to you—"

"Why would I ever take that deal?" Chris cut him off. "How does it offer *any* advantage to me? I've already pleaded not guilty. Why would I now admit to something I didn't do?"

"First off, with no contest you're only admitting to the *facts* of the case, not guilt itself. That's an important distinction. As I said, the prosecutor really wants to wrap this up before the holidays. What he gets with this deal is at least the no contest on two charges—the case is done, the neighbors are mollified. What you get is no jail time, one big charge dropped, reduced fines, *and* you're protected from these same charges being used in any civil proceedings that might come up later. Beyond no jail time, that's a big carrot."

"But what possible civil proceedings would come up?" Chris challenged.

"This is a case where witnesses claim you not only destroyed their property—breaking doors and windows, stealing items—but you terrorized the neighborhood, creating a climate of fear and panic over a lengthy period of time. You do not want these charges used against you if the parties involved come after you for property damage, invasion of privacy, emotional distress, pain and suffering ..."

"Fuck me ..." Chris looked away, stunned by the metastasizing scenario.

"And let me reiterate what was pointed out to you at the arraignment: resisting and criminal trespass are Class A misdemeanors that come with a maximum of three hundred and sixty-four days jail time and up to twenty-five hundred dollars in fines. Window peeking is a Class B, with half the fees and time, but it all adds up to a lot. The plea they're offering cuts those fines by half and, more importantly, takes jail completely off the table. That's critical."

Chris absorbed his words for a moment, then shook his head in frustration. "But I have no record, they have no evidence. I'm a business owner who employs members of my community, and I have lots of people who'd give me great character references. Isn't it possible I could walk away from this either way?" The edge of desperation in his voice was shrill enough that even he heard it. Before Philip could answer, Chris stood up and limped to the food counter, purchased a banana, then hobbled back to the table. After a couple of bites, he drank more water. He still felt queasy.

Philip looked at his watch. "Chris, I have to—"

"I won't admit to something I didn't do. It's just not in me to do that. With window peeking, I'd basically be saying I'm a pervert. How could that possibly be good for me?"

"As I said, no contest is not an admission of guilt—"

"Then what's the goddamn point?"

Philip took a beat. He had a preliminary hearing in a half hour, and while Chris's petulance was understandable, it was also time to crystallize the issues. "Chris, listen to me. I know all this sounds intolerable and inexplicable right now, especially looking at it from your point of view. But it's my job to protect you and make sure you have the best possible defense with the best possible outcome, and I believe you should think long and hard about this plea offer."

Chris leaned in. "So it's your perspective that I don't stand a chance?"

"That's not my perspective. But I'm not going to bullshit you either. This is the real world, this is the Chicago court system, and you are a black man accused of sustained criminal activity against a cadre of white people. On top of that, the judge in your case sometimes likes to 'make a point,' as he puts it. Make someone an example. Will he decide to do that with you? Decide you need a lesson about staying out of other people's yards, about scaring nice white ladies, or taking quick peeks in their windows? Maybe. Maybe not. Maybe he'll look at the flimsy evidence and throw the whole thing out. We don't know."

"So it's pretty much lose-lose either way?" Chris said morosely.

"No, you have options. If you take their offer, you walk away, you do some probation, and you protect yourself civilly. If you don't take the plea and stick with not guilty, you may be acquitted and walk away free and clear, or you may go to jail for a year, *and* lose your ass later in civil court."

Chris leaned back, rubbed his eyes hard.

Philip looked at him, not unsympathetically. "Think about it, talk to your girlfriend, talk to Vanessa, to your mother. We've got until the trial to make the decision. Now, I must go." He stood, patting down his irreparably wrinkled suit.

Chris rose slowly from the table. "Sorry I'm being so uptight—"

"It's a lot to take in."

Chris reached out. "Thank you, Philip. Everything about this sucks, but I trust your opinion and will give it some thought."

Philip somberly shook his hand. "Good, thank you. I hope you can enjoy the holiday season even with all that's going on. Cold as it is, I do love this time of year!"

As Philip hustled through the room and out the door, Chris was struck by the fact that he hadn't even realized it *was* the holiday season.

SIXTY-THREE

WHEN SIDONIE ARRIVED HOME LATER THAT NIGHT, SHE went immediately to the guestroom where Chris was ensconced in the lift chair dressed in sweats, a half-eaten bag of tortilla chips on his lap, and the TV tuned to an incredibly loud British car show.

"Chris!"

His head jerked up, startled. "Hey! I didn't hear you come in."

"How could you? I'm surprised the screen hasn't cracked." She took the remote from his hand and lowered the volume, then sat on the edge of the bed with something approaching a pout. "Where were you this morning when I left for work? And why didn't you answer my texts?"

He had responded to her texts, but had purposely left out answers to "where are you?" "Sorry I left without saying goodbye. I had an early appointment and didn't want to wake you."

"An appointment that required a suit? I saw it hanging in the bathroom last night. I don't think I've ever seen you in a full-blown suit, which means this was either a breakfast wedding I wasn't invited to, or something to do with the case." There was a twinge; she continued to feel like an outsider in the proceedings.

Frankly, he hadn't wanted to tell her. He wanted to get through the arraignment without a lot of hoopla, without triggering predictable fears and frustrations. He knew the drip-drip-drip of the case was eroding their joy-and-happiness quotient, and he felt protective of that status. It was hard explaining that to her, particularly when there was ongoing competitiveness between the familial parties involved.

"The arraignment was this morning. Philip said it would be quick and it was. I was literally in the courtroom for fifteen minutes. No one was there but me and Philip. It was not worth your time to come down."

She examined his face, trying to find clues in his expression. Nothing. Finally she just asked. "How did it go?"

"As expected. I pleaded not guilty. The prosecutor seems okay, the judge is hard to read, but Philip says he's usually a fair guy. The trial is set for December eighteenth. There was no discussion of fingerprints, and Philip said that with just eyewitness testimony, I stand a good chance."

"That's . . . good, yes?" Something felt off, but she couldn't identify it.

"Yeah, I guess." His attention went back to the TV. He had no intention of divulging the plea deal at this point.

"Well, great then. Let go to dinner. Let's do something normal. Remember when we used to do things like go to dinner and act like a couple?" She sounded like a sad wife.

"I do." He sighed deeply, "but I'm not in the mood to get dressed up and be around people."

"We'll go someplace sloppy and dark. You can stay in your sweats. I'll put on mine in solidarity." She turned and ran up to the bedroom to do just that, yelling behind her, "You can't call tortilla chips dinner and I'm hungry."

He groaned, but raised the chair until he was on his feet. "I will do this for you under heavy protest. But what you see is what you get, messy hair and all. I'm not changing a thing."

She came back to the room in blue sweatpants and an oversized cable knit, grinning. "There. Now we both look like slobs." He rolled his eyes but couldn't help laughing.

～

DINNER WAS AN exercise in forced gaiety, with the sharing of a "naughty" martini, as Sidonie so anachronistically put it, and the perusal of a porn rag left behind at the cash register. They laughed louder than was necessary, indulged in burgers and fries like they used to, and pretended everything was just fine. Normal. At one point Chris leaned in to kiss her, reminding them both of just how lacking intimacy had been of late.

When it was time to leave, Sidonie helped Chris into his wrinkled jean jacket and gingerly wrapped her arm through his. They made their way slowly down the sidewalk toward the car, and just as she made laughing comment that they could be mistaken for an old homeless couple, they heard a chirpy "Sid?" from behind.

They turned. There was Theo with what might have been the most beautiful woman in the world. Chris and Sidonie stopped and stared. The two people in front of them were absolutely stunning. With their perfectly constructed outfits of lush scarves and faux fur, skin aglow, and poses of casual insouciance, one might assume a catalogue shoot was underway. Clearly life had improved for Theo since the amends of so many months ago.

"Wow, Theo . . . hey . . . long time!" Sidonie said with strained enthusiasm.

"Yeah," he replied warmly, pulling away from the beautiful woman to offer Sidonie a hug, made clumsy by the fact that Chris still had his arm around her. "How are you? It's been a while."

"Doing . . . great. We just came from dinner over . . . there." She weakly indicated the down-market burger joint they'd just exited, feeling as unimpressive as she possibly could. In fact, if more divergent contrast could be drawn between two couples, it would be hard to imagine.

"Looks like a good old greasy spoon. Haven't been there—we don't eat meat—but maybe we'll check out their other items sometime, right, babe?" He turned toward his exquisite partner, who nodded gleefully.

"If they have the good French fries, I'm all over it!" She smiled with a mouth full of perfect teeth. She had an accent: something Eastern European? "I live on the French fries. Did you ever try them with gravy?" She looked like a woman who hadn't consumed a French fry since puberty, much less with gravy.

"Um . . . no, can't say I have," Sidonie responded.

Theo leapt to introductions. "This is Anika. Anika, my ex-wife and current good friend, Sidonie Frame."

Sidonie oddly appreciated the qualifier. Anika reached over to shake her hand, gushing:

"Oh, I've heard so much things about you, Sidonie, and, trust me, it's been all so good. Theo tells to me you were a saint to him, and he was a shit! All I know is, you make him better for me, so, believe me, I appreciate it. Thank you so much!"

Everything about her declaration was bizarre. Sidonie didn't have a response other than to smile and turn to Chris, who, she realized, had been silent throughout.

"And this is Chris. He's the . . . sound manager at The Church," she said with the slightest tweak in her voice.

Though Chris subtly cocked his head at the description, the other two were oblivious. Handshakes, smiles, and various inanities were exchanged. It became clear things were officially uncomfortable when the stunning couple started sidestepping gingerly down the sidewalk. The sloppy couple just stood there being sloppy. Giddy goodbyes were offered, some "maybe we should all get together" nonsense, then they were gone.

Chris immediately turned to Sidonie, incredulous. "'He's the sound manager at The Church'? You couldn't just say, 'He's my boyfriend'?"

She blushed, but went for deflection. "Really, Chris? You're hurt because I didn't get personal enough about my personal life with my incredibly shallow ex-husband and his new arm candy?"

"Maybe not *hurt*, but damn curious. Were you too embarrassed to introduce a grungy, criminally charged, meat-eating Negro in sweats as your boyfriend?"

"Chris!" she snapped, honestly angry. "That's ridiculous. In fact, it's offensive!"

"I was kidding—"

"No, you weren't! You meant it. There is *nothing* about you that embarrasses me. Theo may be pretty—hell, he made me feel like a bridge troll half the time and I was his wife—but you are *so* far beyond him, in every imaginable way, that you could be covered in filth and wrapped in garbage bags and I'd still rather have my arms around you!"

He took a pause, then grabbed her hand and pulled her slowly into the parking lot. "Not exactly poetry, but I'll take it." They affectionately, gently, bumped shoulders and got on with the mechanics of getting his battered body into the car.

But he was partially right: she *had* been embarrassed. Not because he was black, not because he wasn't as good-looking, not even because he was dealing with a criminal case she wouldn't have mentioned under any circumstances. It was because, for some insipid reason, she wanted Theo to know, to really *see*, that she'd traded up. And without the superficial trappings he most innately understood, he probably didn't.

It shouldn't matter. It didn't matter. But, dammit, she wished they'd looked better.

SIXTY-FOUR

A SIMPLE SOLUTION. A REPRIEVE. NO THREAT, NO TRIAL, NO panic or fear of outcome. Walk away and hope never to revisit. Fulfill obligations, sign required papers, then go quietly back to life with no further disruptions. It made sense. He owned his own business, so no concerns about criminal records creating obstacles against future employment, against hoped-for advancements and promotions. It was expeditious and predictable. The other option was not.

But still.

No contest might not be an admission of guilt, but, as Philip K. Lewis made clear, it confirmed the facts of the case. And there were no *facts* in this case. There were only miscalculations. Misremembered circumstances. There were presumptions, guessing, faulty identifications and implications. There was the revolting, mortifying accusation of standing at someone's window peeking inside with lascivious and voyeuristic intent.

It made him sick to even be seen in that light. To allow that specific charge to be affixed to his name was unacceptable. No future expungement or sealing would erase that stink.

Still.

A year in jail? *A year?*

Lying in bed next to Sidonie's warmth, thinking of iron doors and threatening inmates, clangorous locks and overlit cafeterias with bad food and arcane in-house politics, he knew he would not survive a year in jail. Particularly for the crime of standing at someone's window and peeking inside with lascivious or voyeuristic intent . . . which he did not do. Would never do.

The dangling rape case triggered a tsunami of dread; he could not even ponder the consequences if they moved forward with that.

A plea would possibly knock that off the table too. A plea would keep him from jail, would keep guilt from impacting civil proceedings. A plea would make real the facts of the case that he was a trespasser. *A peeker.*

Still.

SIXTY-FIVE

THERE WAS A KNOCK AT THE DOOR. WHICH WAS ODD. NO one knocked at the door. They either texted from feet away or rang the bell. No one knocked.

Detectives from the Chicago Police Department knocked.

"Miss Frame? Sidonie Frame?" The male component of the two-person team standing at the landing took the lead. "I'm Detective Joseph Lieu, this is Detective Marjorie Nunzi." He was an unremark-able-looking midsize Asian fellow bearing a pleasant, unthreatening expression, likely arranged for the purpose of disarming witnesses. His female counterpart was an even smaller human, possibly not even five feet tall, with short, spiky blonde hair and the air of someone who liked being seen as sassy. Sidonie perversely wondered if they'd been paired because of their height, the Tweedledum and Tweedledee of the department.

"Yes. I'm Sidonie Frame."

"We're investigating the Chris Hawkins case and would like to go over a few things with you, just to verify some items we're wondering about. We understand you and Mr. Hawkins live here together?"

"Yes."

"Could we come in? We only need a few minutes—"

"Actually, Mr. Hawkins is here at the moment, in the first-floor guest bedroom recovering from the broken bones and various other injuries inflicted the night he was mistakenly identified and your guys beat the living crap out of him." Her gaze was defiant. She wasn't sure this was the best way to go—she could hear Karen snapping to calm down and just answer their questions—but this was the first opportunity she'd had to make salient points to anyone from the police department, and she was compelled. "I don't want to disturb him. Or have him wake up to find police in our living room."

Detective Nunzi came up a step; she was still a head shorter than Sidonie. "We understand. Is there somewhere in the neighborhood we could sit and talk, maybe grab a cup of coffee? If not, we'd be happy to get you to and from the station."

That had the intended effect. They were shortly seated at a small table in Sidonie's least favorite coffee shop near Clark, tucked in the grubby section where patrons huddled with endless refills meant to justify table squatting. Sidonie purposely ordered nothing, intent on making clear this was not a visit. The two detectives stirred coffee.

Detective Lieu led again. "Basically, we're just trying to get an idea of what you might know related to the night and case in question. There seems to be some confusion about what actually happened, but since positive IDs have been made, we'd like to know what you believe happened."

"It's not about what I *believe* happened. It's about what *did* happen."

"Okay, what did happen . . . from your point of view?" Detective Nunzi asked, eyes attentive.

"Chris is the head manager of the sound department at The Church. We had a very big event that night—the mayor and other city and state leaders were there." She wanted that point known. "Chris was late getting to the club because his car, his Jeep, which has been having cooling problems, overheated on the street where he stopped. He called me at exactly five twenty—I know, because I looked at my watch when he called—and told me what was happening. He said there was a hose nearby that he would use. He got to the club about twenty minutes later."

"Do you know if he—"

"No, wait—he didn't tell me about the hose in that conversation. I think he mentioned that later." Dammit. Now she sounded like she was hedging.

Nunzi made some notes. "Okay, so he didn't mention seeing the hose until a later conversation?"

"That's right. I think he mentioned it when he first came into the club after he handled the problem. Sorry. I just want to be exact about everything."

Lieu looked up with a smile. "That's fine. We appreciate your clarity. So, do you know if Chris had ever been on that street before?"

"I don't know, but it's not that far from the club, so it's possible it was a route he'd driven in the past."

"But not walked?"

"What?"

"Do you know if he ever walked on that street before?"

Sidonie was struck by an unnerving thought. Chris's penchant for wandering around neighborhoods "enjoying the passing vignettes of life" was innocent and poetic in proper context. When faced with a charge of peeking, undeniable suspicion could be ascribed to the activity.

Nunzi noted Sidonie's pause. "Did you think of something?"

"No . . . no. I was just trying to remember if he ever mentioned walking on that street. And he didn't."

"He didn't mention it or he didn't walk on that street?"

"He didn't mention it."

"Would he normally tell you all the streets he might have walked on?"

"He is someone who enjoys walking, but no. Unless he saw something remarkable, or had a reason to tell me he was on a specific street —like what happened when his car broke down—probably not. Not any more than I would . . . or you would."

"Okay." Lieu nodded as if Sidonie was making perfect sense. "Does Chris ever go out at night without telling you where he's going or what he's doing?"

"Not really. We work together most nights, so we usually come and go together."

"He never goes out to visit friends, or have dinner with his family, or just leave the house without telling you where he's going? Circumstances where you might not know what he's doing before or after he goes somewhere?"

She shook her head, confused. This sounded like word salad meant to trip her up. "I don't know what you're implying—"

"We're not implying anything, Sidonie," Nunzi chimed in. "We're just trying to determine if it's possible that Chris might have been out on certain nights when you didn't know his whereabouts every minute of his time away."

"I'm still confused, but let me say that I always knew where he was going if he was going out, which was rare. But I certainly wasn't tracking him in some weird way to know where he was every second of the night."

"So it's possible he could have, say, spent time in a certain neighborhood, engaged in certain activities on certain dates, and you wouldn't necessarily have known."

"Look, I get what you're trying to do and it's not going to work."

"What are we trying to do?" Lieu asked.

"You're trying to get me to contribute to this bullshit scenario where Chris is a voyeur or a peeker or whatever idiotic things he's been accused of, and I'm not going to do that, because I know he isn't. His car broke down. He grabbed a hose near the curb and used it. Maybe he shouldn't have done that, maybe he shouldn't have stepped into a private yard to turn the water on, but most people wouldn't have a problem with someone doing that. The people accusing him are either profiling him as some nefarious black man in the neighborhood, or they're just confused."

"Does the fact that three different witnesses pointed to his picture and said, 'That's the guy' have any impact on your thinking?"

"No. People mistakenly identify other people all the time. Google it. Eyewitness testimony is predictably unreliable. And it may be a cliché, but white people still tend to think all blacks look alike."

"That may be true," Lieu countered, "but what if we told you we have fingerprints?"

And there it was: the dreaded fingerprint dangle.

"Right." Sidonie was purposefully dismissive. "You're not the first cop to mention that."

"What other cop mentioned it?"

Sidonie realized it might not be wise bringing Mike Demopoulos into this. She didn't know *why* that might be, but it somehow felt politic to avoid his further involvement. "That's not relevant. What's relevant is that you're pretending you have Chris's fingerprints and—"

"We're not pretending. We do have fingerprints from the location where more than peeking occurred. A thirteen-year-old girl was raped." Lieu didn't look so pleasant now.

Sidonie wanted to continue her charade of imperviousness, but the hardness of his face, the cut of his words terrified her. "Okay. I'll bite. Whose are they?"

There was a pause. "Chris Hawkins's." Brittle, cold.

Before she could respond, and as the dreaded, familiar *whoosh* of disassociation crept in, Nunzi leaned in with another tack. Sympathy. Commiseration. Understanding.

"Look, Sidonie, I know this is a lot to deal with. You think you know this guy, you live with him, you probably love him. But you would not be the first woman to be fooled by a clever sociopath. There are lots of men who seem like the greatest guys in the world, but they've got a darkness inside that makes them capable of things you could not imagine—men whose wives and girlfriends were absolutely convinced they were incredible husbands, incredible fathers, yet they were guilty of rape, murder . . . horrible crimes. The mind is a strange thing, and you can't let yourself be fooled into ignoring what's really going on."

Sidonie steadied herself, then looked up at them both. "Are either of you married?"

Lieu and Nunzi glanced at each other. She answered, "He's married. I live with someone. Why?"

"You know how you *know* that person? How you've shared enough life to know who they are? You've seen them in their smallest moments, their most intimate, subtle circumstances, and you have a sense of them? You listen and watch and exchange enough life that you have a gut knowledge that says *this* is a person to marry, *this* is a person to live with. Well, just like you, Detective Lieu, know your spouse, and you, Detective Nunzi, know your partner—well enough to know who they are, who they *really* are—I know Chris. And he's not a rapist. He's not a peeker. He is one of the best men I've ever known, and whatever you think you have on him, you don't. You're either lying or mistaken. You don't have your peeker and you don't have your rapist. So I suggest you keep looking, because *that* guy is still out there." She stood up. "I have nothing more to add, so am I free to leave?"

Nunzi closed her notepad. "I get it, Sidonie. I get what you're saying. And I appreciate that you believe what you're saying. But do me a favor: keep your mind open. If you see anything, hear anything, if you think of anything that might change the dynamics of this case, give us a call. You may be surprised by what you remember later on, or what you might find as things reveal themselves. I get your point, but I hope you get ours."

Sidonie had no response. She almost ran out the door.

SIXTY-SIX

THERE WAS A BRAND-NEW JEEP CHEROKEE, BLACK WITH tinted windows, parked in the garage when Sidonie got home. Its unannounced presence was startling; it didn't seem possible Chris could've wrangled this event in the short hours she'd spent wandering the Lincoln Park Zoo after her police interview.

"What happened to our car date? I thought we were doing this together!" she wailed like a disappointed child.

"A lot's happened since we made that plan, Sid, and I needed to get some wheels. You were gone when I got up, so Hermes came over and we just, quick, got it done, no big deal."

"But it is a big deal! We aren't exactly doing much together these days and, silly as it was, I was looking forward to it." Not exactly true —car shopping wasn't high on her list—but it made the point.

"Then I'm sorry. I didn't think it would matter. I have to get over to the police impound yard, so I wanted to get this done."

"What's happening with the old Jeep?"

"The guy told me they ripped it apart looking for evidence, which didn't exist, so I'm welcome to come pick it up. Solid of them, right? Especially since they're charging me for every day it's been there. It's nothing but salvage at this point, so Victory Towing is hauling it away for scrap, but I need to grab a few things out of the back, some cords and stuff."

"Do you want me to go with you?"

He looked at her, conflicted. "Sid . . . I just want to fly over there and get it done, okay?"

"Okay." Her response was listless. She turned toward the stairway. "I'm going to change for the gym."

"Oh, I figured that's where you were."

"No . . . " She wasn't sure if telling him about the interview was wise, then decided there was no way around it. "I was being interviewed by two detectives on the case."

"Really? When were you going to tell me that?"

"As soon as we had a minute. You were still sleeping when they came by, so I dragged them to that hideous café down the street. It was all pretty basic stuff."

"Was it Lieu and Nunzi?"

That was unexpected. "How did you know that?"

"They interviewed me too."

In the never-ending list of surprises with this case, Sidonie felt herself bouncing between concern and real annoyance on a regular basis. "When?"

Chris stooped over carefully to tie his shoes, nonchalance affected. "The other day—you were at that meeting in Schaumburg. I got called in. Philip went with me. It was routine, according to him, and they asked all the same stuff they did the first time: 'Did you ever look in people's windows on that street? Did you break into any houses on that street? Have you ever been on that street before?' They rattled off some dates when these things supposedly happened, and I gave them all the same answers I gave before: 'No, no, and no.'"

"So when were you going to tell me about *that*?"

"I figured we'd talk about it the next time we discussed the case together . . . which I guess is when you were planning to tell me about *your* interview." He gave her a sly grin, trying his best to turn the mood. It worked . . . marginally.

"I guess so." She sighed. "But, please, can we promise to be more vigilant about sharing what's going on? I feel like things are so crazy right now we need to stay in better sync."

"Okay. We'll spend some time together later, get caught up with each other, maybe watch some Netflix."

She agreed, but knew they wouldn't. He didn't stay up late these days, wasn't interested in anything on TV, and repeatedly commented that he didn't feel like talking. He remained in the lift chair—said getting up from a flat position still hurt his ribs too much—so there wasn't even the comfort of a shared bed. Right now all they had was coping. Enduring. Waiting. Dreading.

After he left, she called her sister to report on the interview. Karen's professional opinion was that Sidonie had done pretty well (her petulant attitude with the cops left out of the debrief), but when she hung up, Sidonie was hit with an emotional hangover. A feeling of doom, of something not being quite right.

What was it? What particular thought was niggling at her brain, stirring this unsettled feeling? She followed the thread back to where it started: the detectives' reaction when she mentioned the walks. Chris's walks. That's what was sticking. Not just the fact that it piqued their attention, but that it piqued hers as well.

She thought back to the first night they'd spent time together, when he talked about his love of walking and observing life in the process. She'd found the predilection charming, but the regular appeal of those walks, and the fact that he seemed to enjoy them alone, now rippled like a red flag.

She hated her reaction.

Because those walks were innocent. They were endearing. A quirk, nothing more. Nothing.

Goddammit. They'd gotten to her. The detectives had fucking gotten to her. Chipped away at her conviction. She had to make sure that stopped right here and now. The walks meant nothing. *Nothing.*

SIXTY-SEVEN

CHRIS WAS BACK AT THE CHURCH. MAINTAINING THE pretense that everything was fine—on his part and everyone else's—took herculean effort and was ultimately a charade. The staff was careful and solicitous. Frank patted him on the shoulder at least twice a day. Al checked repeatedly if he needed anything, Jasper was concerned that Chris might shatter in the volume, while Sidonie forced herself to stay out of the performance room all together. Heroic attempts were made by everyone to frame his return as "getting back on track." But it wasn't. He wasn't. They weren't. Nothing was.

For him it was like being back at the scene of the crime. He lost count of how many times he glanced at the parking lot door, half expecting gun-toting cops to burst through at any moment. His body still ached and his ever-present headache ate up whatever energy he had within the first couple of hours. The satisfaction he typically derived from designing sound cues and organizing unique stage setups was gone, and though he was determined to act "as if" for his own sake, he was fairly certain Sidonie could see through the façade.

She, meanwhile, focused on convincing herself that the usual minutia of the job was productive, essential to those whose show or event was of utmost importance to them. She tried to hold creeping cynicism at bay, but when clients called to make sure the appetizer salsa was cilantro-free, or the dressing rooms had the appropriate mineral water, it was all she could do to keep from beating the phone to pieces.

Still, there was some comfort in being there together, doing their jobs, checking in with each other, making an effort to retrieve normalcy. That was the goal. Normal.

Thanksgiving came and went, and since they each had familial obligations, they went their separate ways. Sidonie spent the day with Karen and family, inclusive of an uncomfortable FaceTime chat with Marian and Steve down in Florida (who'd been given no information about Chris's situation), in which Steve remarked that "if I get any tanner, I might get deported!" No one listening, not even Marian, found the comment humorous.

Chris, meanwhile, went to Hyde Park to celebrate with his family, which, given Vanessa and Hermes's continued separation, was dominated by the strained scenario of their children demanding that "Mommy and Daddy sit next to each other!" They did, but tensions were high, Chris had little appetite, and Delores, though disappointed in the overall ambiance of the night, insisted there was still much to be grateful for.

The week after the holiday brought another round of forced routine and exhausting pretense. There were no updates on the case; no confirmation on the fingerprints; no further interviews. And while Chris lost hours of sleep each night rolling it through his mind, he still hadn't discussed the plea deal with Sidonie. With Christmas moving quickly to the fore, and work demands requiring dogged attention, the plan was to proceed as if nothing hung over their heads.

Yuletide decorations went up at the club.

Chris gave it his best shot, *had* given it his best shot, but on that particular Wednesday, after supervising the procurement of ornaments from the storage space for a waitstaff giddy with holiday spirit, he walked into Sidonie's office, sat in the chair across from her, and changed their lives once again.

"I can't do it. I'm sorry, Sid. I just can't. I've made sure I'm covered for the next four weeks, which will hopefully be enough time for you to find a replacement, but I'm giving my notice as of today. I can't work here anymore."

She'd gotten so accustomed to life spitting unpredictability at her that the gut punch of this was almost ... predictable.

"Okay." She felt like a bomb had been dropped but wanted to say the most useful things she could before it exploded. "I know this is hard, Chris, but I'm wondering if—"

"Sid, it's not a negotiation," he said, gently enough to convey his real regret. "It's the culmination of time and thought, resulting in the conviction that it's not working. My heart's not in it, and if my heart's not in it, I'm not the best person for the job. I love everyone here, it's been a great experience, but I've only got so much I can deal with right now, and I can't deal with this. I can't be here. I just can't. I'm sorry. I hope you understand." He stood up.

"I'll try, but is there no way for me to talk you out of this?" The desperation in her voice echoed what she was feeling. It seemed like she'd been losing him, step by step, since the night of the arrest, and not having him here, at the club, driving back and forth, having common issues to share, to debate and discuss, felt like the death knell of another chapter of their life together. She feared if many more little deaths occurred the whole thing would lose its bone and muscle and end up in a heap on the floor. "I don't want you to leave."

"It's not that I *want* to leave. It's that I have to. If you don't understand right now, I hope you will later." He turned toward the door. "Do you want me to talk to Frank?"

"No. I'll tell him."

"Okay. I've got Andrew set up for tonight, and, like I said, the next four weeks are fully covered. There's nothing for you to worry about." He paused uncomfortably at the door. "Okay then . . . I'll see you at home."

"I won't be late."

Frank had left by the time she went in to talk to him, which was a relief. There was a pall of failure to this information, specifically in regards to Frank. She hoped she'd feel differently when the time came tomorrow.

Before she left for home, a text came in from Patsy:

Sid, I'm not sure you're up for giving this your focus, but have a hot prospect. A women's investing club is looking to finance women-owned businesses. That'd be us. They love our business plan and want to meet to talk ideas. Let me know if you want me to pursue this, and if so, let's find a time to talk. Hope you're doing better . . . been thinking about you. P.

It was good news. Progress. And she felt not one ounce of enthusiasm.

SIXTY-EIGHT

HE WAS LYING IN THEIR BED WHEN SHE GOT HOME, THE first time he'd been there since the event. She took it as a good sign. She climbed in next to him and gently put her arm across his waist. He pulled her close.

"I'm glad you're home," he said, almost as if it had not been expected.

"Me, too. Frank left early so I just slipped out." She pressed her face into his neck. "I miss you, Chris. I miss . . . this."

"Me too."

"Let's make love," she whispered.

He leaned over to kiss her forehead. "I can't yet," he replied softly. "There isn't a position that wouldn't hurt."

"I'll get on top. You won't have to do anything. I'll do all the work. You can think of it as physical therapy," she teased.

He smiled sadly. "Sounds good but even that would hurt. I'm sorry . . . I want to. I'm just not there yet."

Undeterred, she trailed her hand down his leg, back up his hips, over his taut stomach, his chest. Her touch was soft and light, hoping to dispense, if not pleasure, at least a little comfort. He cued her continuance by breathing more deeply, closing his eyes and leaning his head back, allowing her caress to stir something in him beyond ache. When her hand trailed back down, his sharp intake of air told her that, despite his caution, she could still sway him with the power of her touch.

Emboldened, she gently opened his zipper and pulled down his jeans, a task made easier by the weight he'd lost during recovery. When he lay naked and open to her, she took a moment to gaze at his body, realizing how successfully outside forces had kept them from intimacy. Tears sprang to her eyes, a rush of loss and longing, and she kissed his stomach with the whisper of her lips. "Now just be still . . ."

When she took him in her mouth and drew his thoughts and feelings to that point of sensation, she felt as if she were giving him a gift, the gift of forgetting and remembering, both desperately needed to shift the trajectory of their journey. She could feel the gratitude in his response.

After the brief but meaningful encounter, Chris leaned over and kissed her. "Thank you . . . that was unexpected and really nice. I owe you one. I owe you many."

He took a long, thoughtful beat, then carefully got out of bed. He pulled on his jeans, and turned to her. "I have something to talk about with you. Let's go downstairs."

Immediately anxious, she put herself together quickly and followed him to the kitchen. He poured them both a glass of wine. She sat on the stool, waiting, as adrenaline slowly pumped.

"The date of the trial is coming up, the eighteenth, just a couple of weeks away."

"It's terrifies me to think about, but I'm glad we can get it over with in time to enjoy Christmas."

"Or not."

"What do you mean?"

"I mean we have no way of knowing how the trial will go. I could end up getting convicted, that's a real possibility, so—"

"Wait—did something happen with the fingerprints?" Her heart immediately started pounding.

"No. Philip still thinks it's a ploy, but I'd sure like to hear that from them. He says no news is good news on that front."

She shook her head; there was something confusing about this fingerprint issue. "But how can this keep coming up? If they have nothing, how are they allowed to dangle it like a sword over our heads? Aren't there rules about these things?"

"He said they can lie, they can twist things, they can say anything they want to try to get a confession. Beyond that, I don't know." He slumped to a stool, weary as he always was at this time of night. "But here's the thing I haven't shared with you yet: they offered me a plea deal."

She sat up, alert. "Really? When did that happen?"

"After the arraignment. I didn't tell you because I wanted to think about it on my own before we discussed it."

"Okay ... that's fine." It wasn't. "What's the deal?"

"I plead no contest to criminal trespassing and window peeking, the resisting charge is dropped, I get two years' probation, fifteen hundred dollars in fines, and no jail time—that's the main thing."

She shot up from the stool. "*That's* the deal? They want you to *admit* to something you didn't do? Why would you do that? What am I missing?"

"See, this is why I waited to tell you!" That her initial reaction mimicked his own was not lost on him. "It's not *admitting* guilt—it's not admitting anything. Philips says it just confirms the facts of the case, but no guilt. It also prevents the charges from being used against me in any possible civil lawsuits, say, if someone in the neighborhood decided to sue me for supposed damages. Anyway, we have to respond to the plea offer at the trial, so I have to decide."

"You cannot seriously be considering it. Tell me you're not considering it."

"I'm considering it."

"*Why?* You said yourself the fingerprints are bullshit, so what else do they have? Eyewitness testimony, that's all. Not very convincing. How could you possibly be okay with having *peeking* on your record? Something that makes you sound like a skeezy perv who jerks off looking in people's windows? No! I won't let you do that to yourself. My God, Chris, wouldn't it be better to stand up and say, 'I did *not* do this thing,' and take your chances—your very good chances—of acquittal? They have *nothing. Nothing* ... come on!"

Bam! Chris slammed his good hand down on the counter so hard a water glass hopped in response. His eyes burned in her direction, his face taut with his own anger and confusion. Startled by his uncharac-teristic vehemence, she retreated to the living room and dropped to the couch. He followed her.

"I'm sorry, Sid, but you have *no* idea what I'm dealing with here! I cannot, I will not, survive jail. What you're missing, and what Philip made very clear, is that incarceration *is* a real possibility. It doesn't matter what they have or don't have. They have white people who pointed at me, who pointed at my picture, and said, 'That's him!' And that's all they need. Do you understand? That's all they need to throw me in jail for a year—a fucking year! And I will not survive jail. Really get that, Sidonie. I will *not* survive jail." His face was so intense it hurt her to look at him.

He moved slowly to the staircase and went up.

Her entire body was shaking, but she sipped her wine, trying to calm herself. He needed her to be calmer; she knew that. *She* needed her to be calmer.

She was suddenly struck by a deeply undesirable thought and dashed upstairs, finding exactly what she feared: his bags were on the bed and he was putting things in them.

"What are you doing?" she asked frantically.

"I'm going to my mom's for a while. I'm sorry, Sid. It's not a statement about us. It's not a statement about anything. I just need to separate myself right now. I need to think without worrying about anyone else, especially you."

Regardless of how desperately she wanted to hold back tears, they resisted all efforts and came pouring down. She sat on the bed, suppli-cating, pleading. "Chris . . . please don't. Please don't go, don't leave me here alone." She was aware of how pathetic she sounded. It didn't matter; if she could've grabbed him by the ankles to hold him there, she would have.

"I'm not leaving you, Sidonie. I'm just stepping away. We'll talk every day. I'll keep you posted on what's happening with the case. Until you find someone to replace me at the club, I'll be around for consul-tations, whatever you need. I'm not going anywhere. I'm just taking some time for myself. I need that. You have to give me that."

She knew she did. But it left her as bereft and abandoned as she could possibly feel, and despite his assurances, she had an aching premonition he would not be back.

SIXTY-NINE

FRANK LISTENED AS SIDONIE UPDATED HIM ON THE STATUS of various club issues. She saved for last the news that Chris had given notice, dreading his reaction. But as she spoke, he just nodded and mumbled "uh-huh" as needed. It wasn't until she was done that he registered his annoyance.

"Well, that's a big problem," he said tersely. "Particularly with our holiday events, which are many."

"As I said, he's got them all completely cued and staffed, so it's covered."

"Okay, kiddo, I'll leave it in your capable hands. I can't say I'm surprised, given the circumstances, but I'm disappointed things turned out this way. You'll have to get on the search ASAP. I like Andrew, but he's young and I'm not sure he's ready to handle the job."

"I agree. I've already put out feelers."

"Good girl." He took a long breath. "Okay . . . new chapter. We'll get it sorted out. I hope things go well for Chris, I really do. He's a good guy. And hopefully this will help keep distractions to a minimum for you." He stood up and walked out.

She hated him in that moment.

An hour later she went to the bar for a lemonade sparkler and was jarred to see Mike Demopoulos back in his usual seat. She hadn't seen him since the night of the arrest. Al had alluded to him staying away in deference to Sidonie's potential discomfort, something she appreciated, because, frankly, seeing him now stirred deeply uncomfortable feelings.

Still, ignoring him would be graceless. She waved. "Hey, Mike, haven't seen you in a while."

Al set down her lemonade and quietly asked, "You all right?" She nodded.

"Yeah, hey Sidonie," Mike responded. "Guess I've been busy. Not as much time for my usual barhopping." He laughed awkwardly. "How are things going with you?"

"Not great, actually. Chris's trial is coming up, so that's been really stressful." She ambled over, Al watching like a hawk. "I don't know if you knew, but the cops who arrested him beat the living crap out of him, broken bones, torn muscles, the whole brutality playbook." She could see him squirm, but didn't care. "On top of that, they charged him with all sorts of bullshit he's now got to defend. All because he stopped to put water in his car. Gotta say, I know you guys are out there to serve and protect, but some of the gang seem a little too swift with the street justice, you know what I mean?"

Al shot Sidonie a *what the fuck are you doing?* look, but she ignored him.

Mike started tapping a toothpick nervously on the bar. "I'm sorry that happened. But I don't know the details, so I'm sure you can understand if—"

"Oh, I understand—I understand that what they're doing to Chris is pretty heinous."

"Sidonie, I'm completely out of the loop on this." He put some money on the bar. "But I heard he got ID'd by two or three different witnesses, so something's going on there."

Her face flushed at his logic, but she rebutted: "Yes, but the unreliability of eyewitnesses is well-documented, particularly when it's white witnesses pointing the finger at black men, so there's that."

"Like I said, it's not my case, so I can't really be of much help." His unease was palpable.

Sidonie realized she was being overly aggressive and briefly pulled back. "But also, Mike, I did want to say how much I appreciated you stepping up for me that night, I really did. It was a very decent thing to do. And I was hoping if you knew anything more about the fingerprints you mentioned, you'd fill me in. They brought it up to Chris's attorney, and the cops interviewing me threw it out like it was a real thing. But since nobody seems to be able to produce them, I'm wondering if you heard anything else."

Mike took a last slug of his beer and twisted on his stool to leave. "I haven't. I'm sure Chris's lawyer will get all that worked out. Sometimes you just gotta trust the system to do its job and not let paranoia drive you too crazy."

"Paranoia?" That hit like a dart. "What does *that* mean?"

Mike sighed and stood up, keys in hand, literally trapped by Sidonie between two barstools. "Maybe that wasn't the best way to put it. I'm just tryin' to say that not everything comes down to race."

"Who said it did?" And she was off again. "But, you know, sometimes it actually does!"

His body language was about fleeing the scene, but his face proclaimed a modicum of professional indignation. "And sometimes bad guys who commit crimes just happen to be black. So even if the people identifying them are white, it's not always about those people being racist."

Al, still hovering, began frantically wiping down the bar.

"Wow," Sidonie said, seething. "So you see Chris as a bad guy who happens to be black?"

"Jesus, no, I'm just—I'm not talking about Chris specifically! Look, I like you, I like Chris, but I gotta defend my department too, because I don't think you get the full picture. I know lots of cops who come to the force completely unbiased, totally unprejudiced, ready to treat everyone on equal terms. But when you're a cop in Chicago, you deal with black crime on a regular basis, day in and day out. It's hard and it's ugly and it can change you. It can *make* you a racist."

"Oh, please! Nothing can *make* you a racist. You either are or you aren't!"

"You can think that, but I've seen it happen. Even good guys can get worn down. I'm not sayin' it's right, but it happens. I can't speak to your specific case, and, like I said, Chris is a good guy, so I'm not sayin' he did anything, or they got it right, or even that the cops were perfect in how they handled it. I just think Chris would have a better chance if he got past the whole black thing and dealt with it straight out."

"The *black thing?*"

By now Mike had edged his way to the lobby, Sidonie trailing like a stalker. He was not the kind of guy who enjoyed conflict and Sidonie's rage felt assaultive. "So I guess I said another wrong thing. Look, we're not gonna solve this, you and me, and I really gotta get going."

"Do you know what the cop said to me in the car on the way to the police station?"

"I don't know—"

"'What's a nice white girl like you doing with a fucked-up nigger like that?' That's what he said. Not something a person forgets. So, things like 'get past his black thing' and 'paranoia'? I don't know . . . you tell me, Mike."

Al had come from behind the bar into the lobby, hoping to thwart further combat. Mike was halfway out the door. "I'm real sorry that happened. That's not cool. But he doesn't speak for the whole department any more than I can. But I gotta get going, so . . ."

Desperate to make his escape, he lurched out. The door closed slowly in his wake, taking with it all incoming sunshine to leave them in the lobby's gloom.

Sidonie dropped to a nearby chair, drained.

Al shook his head. "What the hell, Frame? You just went postal on the only cop in Chicago who likes you."

"You don't think I have a point?"

"You got lots of 'em, but why piss off the one guy who actually helped you?" He yanked her up and practically dragged her to the bar. "Sit here while I make you a gimlet. Maybe think about better ways to win friends." As he pulled bottles from the tray, he mumbled, "Dammit, now I gotta find me a new policeman to hang with."

SEVENTY

Sidonie Frame sidonieframe@thechurch.com
Mike Demopoulos offmike204@yahoo.com
. . . apologies

Dear Mike:

I promise this will not be a verbal assault. I just thought I'd take advantage of having your email address to send a much-needed apology.

I'm really sorry for going off on you the other day. You didn't deserve that. You've been nothing but nice to me, especially on a night that will go down as the worst of my life. I was, am, and will always be grateful for that. You are one of the good guys, truly.

My only rationale for losing it, I guess, is that this experience with Chris has been brutal, especially for him. Since he and I have been together, I've witnessed just a hint of what it's like being a black man in this city, and it's been a very unhappy eye-opener.

I understand your comments from the "blue side," but I have a feeling that you, as a white man *and* a cop, don't have much awareness of the other side. Chris's side. That's probably true for most white people . . . we can't know what we don't experience. The closest we can get is living next to it. Proximity is illuminating. It's been illuminating for me.

I haven't shared with you all the other encounters Chris has endured just since I've known him, but suffice it to say, it's been shocking. It's changed my view of the world, and, unfortunately, my view of the police. I know lots of good people exist in that world, but lots of bad people do too. I don't know the ratio, but as one of the good ones, Mike, I hope everything you do every day keeps you on the side of right.

So that's my defense. And my apology. I promise you can come back to the bar and I will NOT harass you . . . besides, Al tells me he's got a taser under the counter in case I get ornery again! :(☹

Sidonie

— — —

Mike Demopoulos offmike204@yahoo.com
Sidonie Frame sidonieframe@thechurch.com
Re: . . . apologies

Dear Sidonie,

Thanks for your email. I appreciated it. I do my best to understand things from your side and from Chris's side, and I wish it were different. I wish everyone on the force was one of the good guys, like you said. Most of them are. I really believe that and hope you can too someday. But I know what you experienced was real, so I won't try to downplay it. There definitely are some bad apples.

I really do hope things work out for the best for you and Chris. You're both good people, I honestly believe that. Again, thanks for your apology.

Sincerely,

Mike

P.S. I probably will take you up on your invitation to come back to The Church. It is my favorite bar!

SEVENTY-ONE

DELORES'S WORKPLACE HAD CHANGED LITTLE IN THE YEARS since Chris's first visit. He'd been five or so when his father brought him, Jefferson, and Vanessa to the Christmas party she organized that year for her coworkers in the Administration Office. Even as a young child, he could see she was beloved and in charge, a combination that inspired his filial admiration. They watched in quiet awe as she sashayed amongst the many guests, tossing off one-liners and refilling drinks like the "hostess with the mostest," as his father called her, and Chris concluded that she was the most amazing woman in the world.

Sitting now in the visitor's chair of her colorful office, with its abundance of Christmas flair, broad windows overlooking the main quad, and every inch of wall space covered with commendations and awards, Chris felt, once again, like the little boy in awe of his mother.

"Good morning, son." Delores swept in and didn't bother to sit before grabbing her coat, purse, knit scarf, and the rubber boots necessary to traverse the slush now carpeting roads and walkways. She took Chris's arm as they quickly exited, waving their goodbyes without allowing time for inconvenient chatter ("What's happening with you these days, Chris?" and so forth). Once outside, she pulled on her boots and guided Chris down a busy sidewalk to her favorite Mediterranean restaurant.

With her mint tea steeping and hummus appetizer set, she didn't waste time getting to the heart of the matter. "Have you broken up with Sidonie?"

"No. I just can't carry anyone right now."

"What does that mean?"

"It means I've got a lot to figure out. This plea deal is no small decision."

"No, it's not."

"And I need to make it without feedback from anyone, especially someone who can't honestly understand the stakes."

"Because she's white."

"I hate to put it that way, but yeah."

"She's white, so she can't possibly understand the risks you face, the biases you're pushing against, the odds that might sway you to take this deal. She can't fathom any reason why you would, and she'd think you're an idiot if you did, is that it?"

He couldn't tell if she was baiting or agreeing with him. "Well . . . yes."

"Hmm."

"What?"

"Do you think *I*, as your mother and a black woman, have any clearer sense of what you should do with this plea offer? Do you think I am any more certain of which choice is the right one?"

"I don't know, Ma, I just—"

"I have no idea what you should do. I'm as outraged and furious as you are, as Vanessa is, as Sidonic is. But I have no idea what the right choice is. Even *I*, a woman of the community who's seen it all—who watched my husband being treated as less than the spectacular man he was, who watched my sons harassed by police, bullied at school, and threatened by gangbangers, who watches my daughter destroy her marriage and lose her sweetness because she can't shake the rage she feels—even *I* don't know what you should do. How can she?"

"I know, Ma, I know."

"Do you?"

He dropped his head. "No. I don't know anything right now."

"Christopher, look at me."

He did.

"Why have you left Sidonie?"

He looked out the window as ebullient college students rushed by in packs of two and three—black, brown, white, Asian; couples arm-in-arm; happy, young, and hopeful—and pondered his mother's question. "Because I need detachment. Not just from her. I need to move away from whatever it was we were creating, a life that, right now, doesn't feel real, doesn't feel like it's mine. It feels like someone else's, someone who's no longer there. A guy who could shake things off, who could follow Dad's example of how to cope. I can't cope anymore. I can't. And she doesn't understand that."

"Oh, I have a feeling you're selling her short."

"Maybe. Maybe I'll figure that out when all this is over. But right now I don't want to have to consider her. I don't want her opinions and fears to impact what I have to decide. It's my life in the crosshairs, not hers."

"That's right, son, it is. So take your time to figure out what you need to. But remember this: life is not a solitary endeavor. We are each obliged to find our way between dark and light, anger and love. If you lose sight of that, you'll end up as lonely and heartbroken as your sister. I don't want that for you any more than I do for her."

DARK AND LIGHT. Anger and love. Was it really so binary, so archetypal, he wondered. Was it possible his mother missed the nuances, lived her life in more boldly defined spaces where conflict could be reduced to either/ors? Maybe at this point of her life, older and less engaged in the cultural zeitgeist that seemed to explode and attack daily, she simply didn't get it.

Or maybe she was right. Maybe it *was* that simple.

Lying on his childhood bed later that night, Chris knew time had run out. Philip K. Lewis had texted earlier that evening; they were days from trial, and the chasm opening beneath his feet demanded he choose one side or the other. He hoped that, whichever way he leapt, he'd land on solid ground.

SEVENTY-TWO

HE WAS TAKING THE PLEA. DESPITE ARGUMENTS TO THE contrary, Chris's consuming fear of conviction outweighed the burden of a humiliating record, of fines and probation. His family grimly accepted the decision, but Sidonie was inconsolable. Her call to Karen was so distraught that within an hour her big sister was on the porch with a bottle of tequila and a large box of Kleenex.

Their conversation led to discussion of their parents and the sad reality that neither mother nor father was relevant enough to be included in this critical event. How strange, Sidonie thought, particularly looking at the circle-of-wagons the Hawkins family made. That her mother was too self-absorbed to even inquire about her life, and likely, if she knew, would offer a tart, "I told you so," was alone cause for weeping. It was only after Karen pulled up the recent ballroom dancing photos their father had posted on his Facebook page that Sidonie laughed hard enough to stop crying. Yet even with three shots down and bitter humor shared, the theme of the night remained somber.

"He's not a coward," Karen asserted. "He's a realist who understands the playing field he's on. This is a bench trial, meaning there's no jury—a judge will decide Chris's fate. Judges can be mercurial, and when your life is in their hands, mercurial is not a trait you want to gamble with. A bad mood, an unfortunate experience on another case, just a hardline attitude, and a judge can swing from logic and compassion to something else altogether. Do you really want Chris depending on one person—a person who doesn't know him, who's basing his opinion on the opinions of others who don't know him, all of whom may have biases and prejudices—to be the *one person* deciding if he spends the next year of his life in jail? I wouldn't. Not in a million fucking years. And I surely wouldn't if I were a black man."

Karen was unvarnished when reviewing, organizing, and making clear the theses and theories of her arguments, which made her a good lawyer. It also made her a reality check for her sister. Though Sidonie continued to bemoan the situation, in her heart of hearts she knew Karen's logic was unassailable. Alone in bed that night, missing Chris and heartbroken that he'd been forced to make this decision, she finally accepted why he had.

SEVENTY-THREE

THE MORNING OF THE TRIAL DAWNED WITH FREEZING drizzle and a cover of thick, dark clouds, appropriate ambiance for the solemnity of the day. Chris had called the night before to let Sidonie know she wasn't obligated to attend, serving only to further damage her feelings and force a declaration of, "I will be there." Karen insisted on accompanying her, certain a solid shoulder would be useful.

Lining the hallway between the doors of the courtrooms were benches occupied by anxious, chattering people. Seated on one, in orderly fashion and dressed as if going to church, were Delores, Vanessa, and Hermes. When Karen and Sidonie entered from the elevator, all three stood, introductions were made, and warm, commiserating embraces were exchanged. Sidonie made particular eye contact with Vanessa. While the usual terseness was there, she thought she saw a quick smile, though it might have been wishful thinking.

They were the last case scheduled before lunch, which left them waiting long enough to rattle nerves and raise anticipation. When the door finally opened and the preceding party filed out, they were ushered in without ceremony. Their assigned room was a small, unremarkable space populated by a court reporter, a clerk, the bailiff, and one or two random people who sat hunched over their phones. Perhaps it was all the trial movies and TV shows she'd seen, but Sidonie was surprised by how empty and prosaic it appeared. Vanessa, however, took it all in stride, instructing everyone into seats behind the defense table.

The prosecutor, Brad Reisman, sat alone on his side of the courtroom. Nattily dressed, with a neat comb-over and trim goatee, he appeared frustrated and distracted, turning often to check the door, making frantic notes, occasionally texting from his phone. His face shone with perspiration.

Philip K. Lewis, on the other hand, was a study in composure. Neatly set at the defense side, he was in an uncharacteristically well-tailored blue suit, exuding repose: calm, prepared, and ready to get this done. Chris was seated next to him, attired, as assigned, in a sharply creased suit, courtesy of Delores. Sidonie noted that he looked weary, but still so handsome and dignified. She felt a flush of love and sadness just looking at him. He turned and caught her eye; meager smiles were exchanged. Before she could mouth any words of encouragement, he looked away. She adjusted in her seat and focused in front of her. After an excruciating ten minutes of waiting, Sidonie was shaking so badly Karen reached over and squeezed her hand.

Vanessa rotated to peruse the room; when Sidonie noticed, her eyes followed. It was impossible to miss that no one was seated behind or anywhere near the prosecutor. He looked so harried Sidonie flashed on the White Rabbit from *Alice in Wonderland* sputtering about "the Queen of Hearts!". When his cellphone buzzed, the conversation that ensued, impossible to hear from across the room, appeared to rattle him further.

The bailiff, an imposing man with a smooth pate and booming voice, suddenly intoned, "All rise," snapping the proceedings into existence. As everyone complied, he announced, "The Honorable Howard Gutchison presiding." The court reporter straightened up as Judge Gutchinson strode imperiously to his bench.

Sidonie's heart jumped. With his steely expression devoid of any particular warmth, he presented as someone not to be trifled with. Yet after the bailiff announced the case, and the judge asked if the prosecutor was ready to proceed, Brad Reisman rushed to the bench with a clear case of concern, launching into a fiercely whispered discussion. Moments in, the judge motioned Philip to join them. Chris looked back at his family and shrugged, unclear of what was going on.

Vanessa shook her head and leaned into Hermes's shoulder.

When he reached up to pat her cheek, Sidonie was immediately alert to this tender exchange. Had they reconciled? Delores caught the moment too; she turned to Sidonie and the smile she offered seemed confirmation. This elicited a glint of happiness that helped offset the churn Sidonie was experiencing.

Chris stared straight ahead, rubbing his hands repeatedly on his thighs to keep them dry, working hard to calm his roiling agitation. As the judge and lawyers continued to argue his fate, he closed his eyes in an attempt to get grounded in this unfathomable moment. He was drawn to thoughts of his father and brother Jefferson; wondering what they'd have done in similar circumstances, if they'd have understood the decision he made or, conversely, would think him a coward for making it. He hoped he wouldn't judge himself too harshly when all was said and done. Overwhelmed by the irrevocability of events, he dropped his chin to his chest.

"So, let's get all these details straight for the sake of everyone who did bother to show up today," the judge suddenly barked. Clearly exhausted with the lawyers' whispered exchange, he began addressing them loudly enough to be heard by everyone in the gallery. "Mr. Reisman, your case included scheduled testimony from three eyewitnesses who were supposed to be present at this time, in this courtroom, is that correct?"

Reisman looked miserable. "Yes, Your Honor."

"Yet, as of fifteen minutes ago, one witness recanted in a phone text, claiming she's no longer sure the defendant is the 'right guy,' as she put it, because she just saw another black guy who looks more like the black guy she thinks she saw on the night her garage was vandalized. Do I have that mess about right?"

"Yes. That's . . . right."

"Then, in a twist right out of some crappy legal soap, our other two witnesses, the woman who identified the defendant the night of his arrest, as well as the fellow who was positive he'd seen the defendant on other nights peeking into people's windows, are not here because they're both, inexplicably, in Hawaii. But you didn't know that until they called you just a few minutes ago. Is that correct?"

"Yes, Your Honor." Reisman's face had taken on an alarming shade of red.

"But, tell me, because I'm the nosy sort, why are they in Hawaii instead of here offering testimony about the defendant they claim has been terrorizing their neighborhood for the last year?"

"I don't have all the particulars, Your Honor, but apparently they got the dates mixed up . . . they're on vacation."

There was a barbed pause.

"On vacation?"

"Yes."

"Together?"

"It seems so."

"I see. So let's forget for a moment that they blew off this trial to go surfing or whatever it is they're doing in Hawaii, but how did these two witnesses who claimed to *not* know each other at the time of their interviews end up taking a vacation together?"

"I asked that same question and they said they met at the police station, just started talking, and it went from there."

"Well, good lord, who needs Match.com, right, bailiff?" the judge chortled acerbically. The bailiff nodded as if none of this was unusual. "We've got Chicago PD to stir romance amongst the citizens!"

Philip stepped in: "Your Honor, I—"

"Hold on, Mr. Lewis, I want to be stone-cold sure I've got this right." His voice took a decidedly terser edge. "Because I arranged *my* day to be here for this trial. I rushed my breakfast, didn't get to my daily Sudoku, even paid my gardener to walk the dog, just so I could be here this morning, on time and ready to fulfill my duty. I assume, Mr. Lewis, you did some version of the same?"

"Yes, sir, though I'm—"

"And I have no doubt the defendant is sitting there with a big knot in his stomach, all ready to defend himself in an attempt to keep his life from going off the rails, is that correct, sir?"

Chris looked at Philip, confused about what was happening or how to respond. Philip nodded like an anxious parent.

"Uh, yes, sir," Chris answered. "Yes, Your Honor."

"Of course. And the family and friends I see out there—you must have all made accommodations to be here, yes?"

Again, with a look from Philip, they each assented with "yes" and nods of agreement.

"Yet you, Mr. Reisman, are confirming that the *only* evidence you have in this case is the testimony of your scheduled eyewitnesses, not one of whom has shown us the respect of their attendance."

"Yes, Your Honor, but trust me, I—"

"How can I, when clearly you can't even manage your own case?"

In this sharply defined moment, Brad Reisman embodied a person who'd rather be anywhere—literally *anywhere*—than in front of this judge under these circumstances. "I apologize, Your Honor. I'm as stunned and upset as you are. It was bad enough getting the text, but the call from Hawaii was unprecedented."

"Indeed . . . unprecedented. Yet here we are. While they enjoy luaus and tropical snorkeling, their case is going down the drain." He brusquely gathered his papers into a pile. "Since there appears to be no other evidence and no other salient points to make, I suggest, Mr. Reisman, that you spare us further waste of our time and do the only logical thing you can."

Reisman stood at the prosecutor's table, downcast in defeat. "Yes, Your Honor. I make a motion to dismiss the case of—"

"Motion granted." With the slam of his gavel, the judge rose from his bench and swept out, changing the lives of every person seated in the gallery.

SEVENTY-FOUR

THE SURREALISTIC MOMENT THAT FOLLOWED THE JUDGE'S gavel seemed to recalibrate time into something slower and more poignant, with eyes moving to eyes, arms reaching to arms, bodies colliding with bodies, all choreographed by incredulity. This strange and unanticipated twist was followed by the joyful clamor of reality: the case was over. It had been dismissed. There were no fingerprints, no witnesses, no plea deals. Chris was reprieved, free, unencumbered— vindicated. Emotions flowed from gratitude to disbelief to jubilance in the whiplash of the dramatically adjusted narrative.

While Karen hugged a shaking Sidonie, who was too astounded to cry or offer much verbal response, Philip K. Lewis tucked documents into his briefcase with a subtle, satisfied smile, as Brad Reisman fled the courtroom with nary a look back. The Hawkins family huddled together with laughter and cries of thanksgiving. In the midst of their raw and profound expression, Delores opened the circle where Chris was seated and Sidonie stepped inside, waiting for a signal. When Vanessa gave her a good-natured shove toward Chris and she literally fell into his lap, he laughed and accepted her hug, but, in what she felt was a subtle rebuff, lifted her off more quickly than she'd have expected.

A plan was made to gather at a nearby restaurant to celebrate the unexpected victory, but Karen had to get to a civil proceeding across town and had been Sidonie's chauffeur. Delores, who'd driven up with Chris from Hyde Park, offered to get Sidonie home, as did Hermes, but when Chris didn't push the point, which Sidonie took as another snub (unintentional—or not), she demurred.

As she and Karen clattered down the steps toward the parking lot across the street, Sidonie defended her reticence by sharing her list of perceived rejections. Karen would have none of it. "If you want to get things back on track, little sister, I suggest you put your hypersensitivities aside and leap back in, tout suite."

But Sidonie held firm. It wasn't that she didn't want to go; it was that the strain between her and Chris needed preemptive one-on-one to smooth the edges, and he didn't appear interested in providing any. Which left her sullen. Under the circumstances, it seemed charitable to not inflict that mood on the joyous family.

Just as they were about to enter the parking lot, Chris came loping across the sidewalk. "Sid, are you sure you don't want to join us?" he asked breathlessly. "This is your celebration too, and everyone would like you there."

She noticed he left out the personalization of, "*I'd* like you there." She hated feeling petty in this monumental moment—and she did—but his distance was tangible and she couldn't adjust.

"I have a feeling your mom would enjoy some family time for a bit, so go ahead and do that. We'll have our time to celebrate later." She hoped that was true. She also hoped he'd say something about *her* being family. He didn't.

He looked back at the group. When Vanessa tapped her watch, he turned to Sidonie. "You're probably right. I just don't want you to feel left out."

"I don't." She did. "But I was wondering . . . do you plan on coming home tonight?" She hated asking the question but felt it was inevitable.

He took a longer pause than she would have liked. "I'm not sure. This was such a shock. I think I need a little time to process it. Feels like I'm walking on a cloud and it might not bear my weight, you know? Want to be sure it's real. Philip says it is, but man . . . I did *not* expect that!" His eyes shone.

Hers welled up. Aside from her own melancholy, she could feel nothing but joy for him. "Me neither. A gift from the gods."

"No kidding. Anyway, let me have a few days to wrap things up at my mom's and then we'll get together."

An odd way of putting it. "Get together as in come home?"

"Yeah . . . of course." He kissed her, somewhat perfunctorily. "Thanks for being here, Sid. We've got a lot to celebrate and I look forward to doing that."

"Me too. Have fun and we'll talk later."

She watched as he strode off, a lift in his step she hadn't seen in a long time. As the family headed toward their cars, Hermes gave her a hearty wave before turning to pull Vanessa close. Delores wrapped her arm through Chris's, creating a cozy family picture. Sidonie wanted to run after them shouting, "Wait, I changed my mind. Take me with you. Please take me with you!"

But she didn't.

SEVENTY-FIVE

THREE DAYS LATER CHRIS WAS STILL IN HYDE PARK. Sidonie went through the motions of her life while wondering what her life was beyond the state of waiting for Chris—for him to heal, for him to be adjudicated, for him to come home. The realization that she'd reduced herself to little else struck her as pitiful.

Work had become drudgery. Nothing dramatic, but the air had gone out. This was new. Even during the worst with Theo, escaping to The Church had been a respite, a place to engage and connect away from the angst of her marriage. That it was devoid of such uplift now didn't bode well.

Mostly she was lonely. Besides Karen, who'd once again become her rock, she kept everyone else at a distance. It was all too much and too hard to explain.

Though still there was Patsy, who remained committed to the goal of reengagement.

They hadn't seen each other since their delicate détente. They'd spoken several times in recent weeks, mostly to discuss matters related to the potential new investor, but Patsy was reluctant to invite herself back in and Sidonie wasn't sure she wanted her there. Yet.

She did email the good news of the trial. They traded phone messages, but now Sidonie wanted to talk. She didn't care what it did or didn't mean. She was relieved when Patsy picked up.

"Hey, Sid. What's up?" Her voice was tentative, as it usually was these fragile days.

"I just realized it's almost Christmas and I have nothing on my calendar," Sidonie lamented. "I remember months back thinking how fun this holiday was going to be."

"No word from Chris?"

"Not about coming home."

"Shit. I'm sorry, Sid."

"I guess he'll be spending Christmas at his mom's."

"That sucks. What does it mean, all this staying away?"

"I don't know. Nothing good."

"You think?"

"What else could it be?"

"Maybe he's still dealing with his shell shock and just isn't ready to deal with yours yet."

That seemed astute. "Maybe. I keep hoping that now that he's got a clean slate, he'll get happy again, and decide happiness is best served with me by his side."

"Give him time. At least the trial's over. You guys can put that behind you."

"Absolutely. That's the main thing." Her joy and happiness clearly less main. "What are you doing for Christmas?"

"Not sure. I've been seeing this guy for the last couple of weeks and we talked about some fancy brunch shindig. Not sure I want to get all that civilized, but I'll be damned if I go down to Urbana. Unless *you* want to do something . . ." Patsy said hopefully.

Sidonie reflected on how strange it was that their relationship had reorganized so that Patsy could be dating someone for weeks and have no reason or opportunity to share it with her. Karma.

"I'll probably just go over to Karen's, eat too much catered food. Sarah will sing, Josh will drink. It'll be loads of fun, though not enough to turn down a fancy brunch."

"Probably not." Patsy laughed. "Listen, let's both have a nice Christmas no matter what we do, then we'll ring in the New Year by getting this new deal closed. Chris will come home, and all of us will finally start moving forward with our lives, old acquaintances *please* be forgot!"

Sidonie finally smiled. "Sounds good, especially since there's a few old acquaintances I wouldn't mind excising."

"Frank still being an asshole?"

"Not an asshole. We just see things differently."

"An elegant way of saying 'asshole.' Have you found a new sound guy yet, or are you hoping Chris changes his mind now that he's been freed at last? Wait—was that insensitive?"

Sidonie felt a twitch, but decided on equanimity. "Borderline. We'll let it pass. I have no idea if Chris will change his mind, but I wouldn't bet on it. I'm hoping we can talk about it when he gets home. I haven't found anyone yet, but I do have some interviews set up."

"Oh, speaking of: I wanted to ask if you still have those boxes of photographs I left in your garage a million years ago. Remember those?"

"I do. I assume I still have them. Why?"

"I'm going to use some of those old photos for our pitch presentation. They're all on film so I have to get them scanned. Can I come by and pick them up sometime tomorrow?"

"Sure. Just text first. I'll have to find them."

"Will do. Now go relax, try to find your positive self again, okay?"

"I'll do my very best."

"And Sid?" Patsy paused.

"Yeah?"

"Thanks for calling. I like that you thought of me."

"Me too."

Baby steps.

SEVENTY-SIX

HE STOOD IN THE DRIVEWAY OF HIS MOTHER'S HOME AND peered down the well-lit street. Even with cars passing and a smattering of nighttime pedestrians, it struck him that he was afraid to take the walk he'd set out to take. It was dark out there and people had strange notions. They saw things and thought things; sometimes they got things wrong. Those simple mistakes could change a man's life, *take* a man's life—irretrievably destroy a man's life.

Though he had his own back. He could grasp it and feel it a thing of pulsing possibilities again, freed from the weight of pointed fingers and twisted perceptions about what his face resembled or who he might be. It was his to protect and keep safe; he would never again be so cavalier about it. He was informed now by caution and wariness, by what was and was not necessary.

Walking down this street, at this time, in this moment, was not necessary.

When he came back through the foyer, Vanessa, reading in the living room, looked up. "That was quick."

"Suddenly felt tired."

Her gaze rolled over his face, seeing the lie and knowing why he told it. She'd seen that lie in too many faces. The lie to hide unease, the abdication of free choice. She hoped her brother would recover from its hold sooner than others did.

"Hey, I've got some news," she said, actively shifting the subject.

"Yeah?"

"I'm moving back home. We're going to give it another try." Her smile radiated, making her briery edges melt in the warmth. He couldn't help but mirror it.

"Wow, Ness, that's excellent! I'm so happy for you guys. What happened?"

"You."

"Me?" He sat on the couch. "How so?"

She put her book down. "Watching you deal with everything you were going through . . . made me think about Daddy and Jefferson."

"Yeah, me too." He nodded somberly.

"Then I got thinking about me and Mom . . . Hermes in the mix, feeling how we all click, how our family always takes care of its own. I realized I didn't want to lose that. Didn't want to lose *him*."

"You know how I feel about Hermes."

"I do. But I had to figure out what to do about *me*. I'm not wrong to feel righteous in my anger, to use that anger to push me, to fire me up to do the things I do. But at the end of the day, I do want more than that, more than that anger. I can't lose my kids, and I don't want to lose my husband. I don't know if I can find the balance Mom always talks about, but I've got to try. I've *got* to. So I made the pitch and he threw the doors open. I'm walkin' through 'em, big brother. Wish me luck."

She smiled again and he grabbed her in a bear hug, squeezing so hard she squealed, and they pushed and shoved each other with the silliness they'd often felt as children in this very room. The moment felt nostalgic, rare yet familiar.

When she finally pulled away and got up to leave, she looked back and said: "And by the way, Sidonie is all right."

The poignancy of the statement, at this particular moment, struck him. "Where'd that change of heart come from?"

"Not so much a change of heart, more a change of perspective. I never *didn't* like her. But I don't know . . . watching her struggle with your shit, in so over her damn head but still treading water like a sailor. I liked that. She's tougher than she looks. And there was this one night at her house—Hermes and I got into something, and after he left, she sat with me on the deck. Didn't say much, no judgment, not a lot of bullshit this and that—just kept me company. I liked that too. She's good people, Chris. Made me want to be less judgmental. I still don't think she's right for you, but she's good people."

She was. Yet he was here. At his mother's.

SEVENTY-SEVEN

FOURTEEN MILES NORTH, WRAPPED IN HER WOOL PEACOAT, a scarf tight around her face to ward off the cold, Sidonie brushed snow from the bench across from the opened garage and sat down. She stared upward and thought, as she always did when she tilted toward the sky, about Jovana Stanton and her poetic words. Yet on a night like this, when she felt so alone in the ancient, humbling universe, Professor Stanton's cosmic optimism seemed far away.

Chris wasn't moving back home; she could feel it. Or maybe she was just scared he wasn't. She didn't know. He'd called several times since the trial, four to be exact, chatting each time for fifteen minutes or so. He sounded better—lighter, less coiled—but while she was happy he was finding equilibrium, the sting of his needing distance to do so remained hurtful. He exhibited no urgency to come back to their home . . . or her. She wanted to ask why, but something always stopped her, an innate sense that pushing him would be unwise; that presenting herself as needy would translate as pressure.

Part of her did feel needy. But that wasn't the impelling reason for wanting him home. She wanted him home as anyone would want their partner home. She wanted him home as the woman who loved Chris Hawkins, who'd built a life with Chris Hawkins, who'd survived a trauma with Chris Hawkins would want him home. Because she loved him, she missed him, and, yes, she needed him. Simple and logical, she thought. Though, evidently, not so for him.

Seasonal timing added to her chipping angst. She had hoped they'd celebrate Christmas, her favorite holiday, together, decked in the joy of knowing they'd been unburdened, that everything was open and available to them in the new year to come. She'd imagined kissing him on New Year's Eve, toasting new chapters of their enduring and deepening relationship, healing in the prescription of love and happiness. That no longer seemed inevitable; in fact, it seemed unlikely.

He texted an hour earlier suggesting he'd come by in the morning, pointedly emphasizing it was "just a visit." They'd have breakfast and catch up, he wrote, "see how it feels." She acquiesced, greedy for more but accepting it as a step in the right direction. She hoped he would be warm and open, exhibiting some semblance of his earnest, adoring self. She hoped they'd get past their awkwardness to make love, to find a way back to that intimate place they'd visited so often and found so connective and empowering. She'd be patient, whatever he offered, but she hoped.

The wind took a hard buffet past her, sending shivers that refocused her on the task at hand. She'd come down to look for Patsy's photography boxes. She flipped the light on in the garage to be reminded that a fair amount of space had been co-opted by Chris's sound equipment. "Damn." She sighed. This would make finding two relatively small boxes more of a challenge, but with Chris coming by in the morning, she wanted to get it done.

She pulled out a heavy duffle bag of cords, shoved a large monitor aside, and ferreted through a metal cabinet filled with microphones and stands. Nothing. Patsy's boxes were likely on the higher shelves. She climbed atop a stool, and with some heft, pushed aside a stack of small black Anvil cases, catching a flash of something pink.

Pink?

Incongruous.

She arched up on her tiptoes and reached back to grab the anomalous object.

A pink backpack. A girl's backpack. The checkered material in various shades of pink was adorned with flowers; a small felt owl was clipped to the zipper. It was flattened from being shoved behind the cases, but when she shook it open, she found a stack of spiral binders, a handful of scrunchie hair ties, and a pair of designer sunglasses.

There was identifying information on the notebooks: *Samantha P—Mrs. Bradshaw—8th Gr. Homeroom.*

A cold shudder crept down her back. Why was *this* here?

Sidonie stepped down, the backpack in her hand, and sank to the stool, her mind a babel of competing questions: Why *was* this here? Why was it hidden behind Chris's equipment? Who was Samantha P and why would Chris be in possession of her belongings?

As if an electrical switch flipped on, her body started shaking. Her mouth got so dry she could barely swallow. She stared at the pack and felt dread descend.

There was no explanation that made sense. None. For some reason Chris had taken and kept this pack, *hidden* this pack, a pack belonging to a girl in the 8th Grade class. That would make her . . . thirteen.

Thirteen years old.

The age of the girl who'd been raped in the building where the police claimed they'd found Chris's fingerprints.

A cry of "oh God" escaped her lips before she could stop it. Sidonie was horrified that her mind went *there*, but that's exactly where it went. What should she do? She couldn't put it back; she couldn't pretend she hadn't found it. But the last thing she wanted was to stir up more drama, more turmoil, especially after everything they'd all been through.

She glanced around as if terrified someone might see her, might point a finger and shout, "That's the child's backpack, that's *evidence!*" She stood still long enough to calm the clamor in her head, to allow less hysterical options to take hold. *You don't know what this means. It may mean nothing. Wait until you have more information.*

Yes. That would be her tack. She'd wait to talk to Chris and certainly he'd have a rational explanation. She went upstairs, threw the backpack on the counter, and sat in the living room, trying to calm herself. *What was it Chris always did? Breathe in . . . breathe out . . . breathe in . . . breathe out . . .*

Her eyes popped open. What if she *had* been tricked? What if he *wasn't* who he seemed to be? What if the cops were right when they said she could be mistaken about him?

As much as she'd resisted giving those insinuations a moment of her time, a perverse thought flashed by and snagged: What if he'd just gotten away with something horrible simply because of absent witnesses and unexpected good luck?

It was just a flash, so ephemeral it didn't fully form . . . but long enough to make her gut churn.

She never did find the photography boxes.

SEVENTY-EIGHT

JOGGING UP THE STEPS OF THE TOWNHOUSE, CHRIS FELT the anticipation of hope. Hope that there would be good coffee and scones from A Taste of Heaven; he missed those. Hope that Sidonie would have reconciled with his need to spend time away, and would be open-armed and conciliatory. Hope that she would smile and press her body against his as she welcomed him home. Hope that they would make today a new starting point.

What he didn't anticipate was everything that happened.

He saw the pink backpack the moment he walked through the door. It was propped on the living room chair like an exhibit, with Sidonie seated across from it with eyes swollen, her face a mask of suspicion. He had no idea what narrative he'd just entered, but he could see it was fraught.

"Where did you find that? I forgot all about it."

"You're not going to deny you have it?"

He looked at her, puzzled. "No, why would I? Where was it?"

"In the garage, crammed behind all your stuff, way back in the corner of one of the high shelves. Clearly I wasn't meant to find it, though I don't know why you'd leave it there if that was true." The monotone of her voice was chilling.

"Because it's not true." Intent on getting through this minefield without detonation, he kept his voice modulated. "But I did complete-ly forget about it in the craziness of the last few months. I found it at a bus stop on one of my walks and threw it in the back of the Jeep when

I got home. My plan was to leave it at the club. I called the number, but never heard back, and then I just forgot about it."

"What number?"

"There was some ID card thing, like a luggage tag. It was clipped to the handle. I took it off, had it in my pocket when I got to the club, so I called from there. Talked to some kid, said I'd found the pack. I planned to leave it with Al behind the bar, then everything blew up and I just forgot about it."

"If you called, why didn't anyone come and get it?"

"I don't know. Clearly it wasn't that valuable to them."

"Where is that number now?"

"I have no idea, Sidonie. This was a long time ago and it was not a priority for me, at all, certainly not with everything else going on."

She felt a shift in her mental posture, but was compelled to continue. "Okay, so you called and left a message but somehow the pack ended up in my garage stuffed as far behind a stack of Anvil cases as it could possibly get. Why does that seem strange to me?"

"I don't know . . . there's nothing strange about it. It was in the back of the Jeep. Stuff got thrown on top of it. At some point, I had to clear out the Jeep to haul a bunch of equipment to an Alchemy gig, so I shoved whatever was in there anyplace I could find in the garage. There was room on those top shelves. Obviously I threw the pack up there at the same time. Why am I explaining this like I'm a suspect or something?"

She moved to the kitchen and poured herself a glass of water, roiled in the contradiction of what she was feeling. Clearly he hadn't yet made the connection to what those feelings were . . . or was pretending not to.

Chris observed her with alarm. "What is going on, Sidonie? I'm lost."

"That makes two of us."

"What does that mean? You think I'm lying to you?" His voice ratcheted up. "Why would I lie about this? What possible reason would I have to lie about some kid's backpack?"

She took a pause before responding, and in that moment, as if light suddenly dispelled the murk of this conversation, he was hit with it: the lethal thing she was hinting at.

"Wait, you think this pack belongs to *that* kid? The one from the nonexistent fingerprints? *Are you fucking kidding me, Sidonie?*" His arm swung through the air and the water glass on the counter flew across the kitchen, shattering against the wall.

It was a shocking moment. She'd never seen him display any physical rage, and it scared her, particularly in this freighted circumstance. "Chris, you need to—"

"I need to what? *What,* Sidonie? Accept that my girlfriend—*my fucking girlfriend*—thinks I raped a thirteen-year-old girl and then kept her backpack as—what? A trophy? What kind of monster do you think I am?"

"I don't . . . it was . . ." She stumbled for words she couldn't find, his rage disorienting her.

"If you honestly think any part of me could do that, could *be* that, then everything we had, everything we shared, was utter bullshit. After what I've been through, after what *you've* been through, how can that be where you went with this? How can you not know me well enough to know that could *never* be me?"

The profound and unfathomable weight of that statement hit her.

"But I do know that!" she cried out. Which was true. Because in the illumination of morning, it was insane, really, how utterly implausible the scenario was. But she'd spent an interminable night wallowing in unimaginable imaginings, and it was hard to make the pivot quickly enough. "Chris. Listen. Of course I don't think you raped anyone. I could *never* think that about you! I just found this girl's backpack and it seemed odd that—"

"No! Just stop!" He refused even one second of her equivocation. Too much had transpired, too much had been endured to reconcile her capitulation, however temporary. It was a tipping point.

And she knew it. She'd crossed a line, probably irrevocably. Panicked, she moved toward him. "Chris, I'm sorry. I don't know why any part of me went there. It was just a fleeting, weird, terrified moment when I—"

He held up his hands as if to ward her off. "No. I'm done. I'm done."

His voice had a dreadful stillness to it. Then he turned and slammed his fist into the wall. Once. Twice. She screamed as clots of bloodied plaster splattered across the counter. When, startled by his own impulse, he stopped and turned back to her, the fear in her eyes froze him. Enraged him.

"I'm not going to hit you. I've never hit a woman in my life, but I guess if you thought I could rape a child, you have no idea who I am." The darkness of his expression shook her to the core. He turned and stormed out the front door, slamming it hard behind him.

Sidonie's phone immediately rang. Alice. She didn't want to pick up, but knew there was no choice.

"Sidonie, are you all right? My God, I didn't know what was going on! I heard all this yelling and wanted to be sure you were okay."

"I'm okay. Chris and I had a big fight, but I'm okay. I think we're both just really fried from everything, but it'll be fine. Thanks for checking."

"No problem. And I promise I wasn't being nosy. I just wanted to check in before Sandra called the fucking police."

As the assuaged Alice hung up, Sidonie flashed on the horror of that possibility. The idea of police showing up at her door right now, in this moment, was intolerable. She quickly pulled up Sandra's number and called. It rang and rang; she hung up before it went to voice mail, not caring what Sandra might guess was behind the missed call.

As she took in the plaster and glass strewn everywhere, it struck her that nothing in this house was more shattered than her heart.

SEVENTY-NINE

CHRISTMAS WAS FUNEREAL. THERE WAS A SLEETY BUMPER-to-bumper drive to Karen's, an uninspired gift exchange, followed by an obligatory call to their father—brief, generic, and bereft of real feeling. Thankfully, Marian and Steve were on a Christmas cruise to the Caribbean, though they did send an awkward reggae-themed text and photo.

Since it was just the four of them (Patsy ultimately chose the fancy brunch shindig with the mystery boyfriend), Karen, Josh, Sarah, and Sidonie took a town car to a five-star restaurant downtown, which provided a requisitely festive, delicious, and very expensive Christmas dinner. Table conversation centered largely on Sarah's upcoming spring break trip to upstate New York where she'd be interning at a farm co-op. No one asked about Chris.

After the driver dropped them back at Karen's, Sidonie decided to forego Josh's traditional après-dinner mulled wine. With snow now falling in earnest, and ice making the traversal of streets and sidewalks a challenge, it seemed wise to start the trek home. As Karen walked her carefully to her car, a quick slip almost brought Sidonie to her knees.

"Goddammit!" she snapped. "Have I told you how much I hate winter?"

"Yes," Karen responded dryly. "Every December through March." When she looked over at her sister, she saw authentic angst. "I know Christmas was awful for you, but times will get better, sissy, I promise. Chris will come around."

"I don't think so. I pretty much made sure that won't happen."

Karen frowned. "Why? What did you do?"

Sidonie looked up, squinting to keep the snow from getting past her eyelashes. "I refuse to obliterate whatever semblance of holiday cheer we've managed by getting into all that right now. But I do have a favor to ask—a really big favor, actually." The plaintiveness of her voice stirred Karen's reflexive protectiveness.

"What can I do? Tell me."

"Can you get any information on the fingerprints they brought up during Chris's case? Find out if they actually exist, if they were really connected to a rape case with a thirteen-year-old girl, or if they ever caught anybody . . . even what the girl's name is?"

Karen was taken aback. "Wow. That's some to-do list! And what's this about? The case is over." She suddenly frowned. "Did someone come at you guys with something else?"

"No, no, nothing like that. I just feel like we're—like Chris is—still vulnerable to suspicion if that's not cleared up." The knot of guilt in her stomach turned. "I want to be absolutely sure nothing *could* come at us—ever again." That sounded plausible enough to preempt further explanation. It also deflected from her own shame and anxiety on the topic.

Karen remained unconvinced. "I'm not sure what that means or what could come at you, but, first off, it was sexual assault of a minor, so the girl's name is off limits. Secondly, the justice system is notoriously slow during the holidays, so not sure what can get done before the new year. But I'll check with my pal at the DA's office, see if there are any details she could share."

"Thanks . . . whatever you can do." She smiled wanly, hoping to cover what had now become a chronic state of panic. She looked around at the swirling, billowing snow. "Wow. A white Christmas."

Karen put an arm around her and pulled tight.

EIGHTY

THERE WAS NO WOUND BECAUSE HE WOULDN'T LET HIMSELF bleed. There was no heartache because love and its tender ingredients were buried too deep for access. Chris immersed himself in work, and let that be the needy child of his attention.

Sound Alchemy, once again his sole focus, had sprouted branches of opportunity while he was managing both jobs, and his goal was to take full advantage, to build his company and the protective shield of its success. It felt good, like working a muscle that had atrophied; the demand on his time and energy offered distraction from thoughts of Sidonie.

But still he thought of her, as if his mind refused to cooperate with her banishment. He'd notice someone in passing who reminded him of her. He'd hear a song they'd sung together and sweet memories would flash. He'd lie in his childhood bed and long for her, dream of her touch; imagine her mouth on his, the lushness of her body.

Then he'd remember her face the day she confronted him. The revelation of what she'd allowed herself to believe, even for a moment. It was a betrayal neither of them could transcend, that he knew.

Which meant the plates shifted once again as a new formation of life took hold. A new living situation, new job scenario; the old, familiar sting of loneliness. It was an arduous process, this cyclical realignment, making Jordan's dismissal of him as a romantic dysfunctional seem not all that misguided.

He was onstage at the Kennicott Park field house setting up for a small wedding when Hadi Bashir, one of his best guys who often joined The Church team when additional personnel were needed, approached.

"Hey, Chris, wanted to check with you about something, make sure I wasn't stepping out of line."

"What's up?"

"You know they've been interviewing people over at The Church to replace you, right? It's my understanding you quit the job, they didn't fire you. Is that a fact?"

"Yeah. It was my decision. Why?"

"Cool. I have too much respect to put my name in the mix if they fired you, but if it was your call, and it wouldn't be a problem between us, I was thinking of checking it out. I love this gig, man, but I got a little boy coming and I gotta get a full-time thing, you know what I'm sayin'?"

"Sure, but don't we keep you pretty busy?"

"You do, but not every week, and I think it would be better for my family if I was settled in something regular. We don't live too far from Old Town, so my wife would be real happy if I got located somewhere easy."

"I get it. And hey, it's a good gig, they're a good group of people, so if it's something you want, go for it. I got no problem with that. Thanks for asking."

Hadi grabbed him in a handshake. "Absolutely, man. And I'm not sayin' I'm gonna get it, so don't write me off too soon!" He laughed nervously.

"You got a gig here as long as you want."

Hadi jumped down and crossed the room toward the door. Chris watched him go, thinking it was ironic: feeling jealous of the man looking to take the job, and work for the woman, he'd just forsaken.

EIGHTY-ONE

SOUND PEOPLE IN CHICAGO WERE QUITE THE CONFEDERATION. Almost everyone Sidonie interviewed either knew or had worked for Chris, expressed professional awe of Hermes, or was on a friendship basis with Jasper. Even the women she interviewed came with one or more of those connections and, as with any artistic community, there was a cultish sense of loyalty and camaraderie amongst them. Hiring one was difficult, however, because none stood out quite like Chris.

As she sat in her office mulling the list of candidates, a text came in; Frank wanted to see her in his office. Odd; whenever she got those texts now, her heart sank. She headed over.

"Hey, kiddo, have they got the New Year's decorations down yet?" One of Frank's quirks, which she used to find endearing, was outdated holiday flair.

"Yes, all down, packed away until next year."

"Good girl! What's the latest on the search? Have you locked in on anybody yet?" Frank had reverted to his more congenial self since Chris left, and while relieved to be on his better side, Sidonie resented the reason.

"I have two people coming in for second interviews: Hadi Bashir, who worked here when we needed additional staff, very good, knows the room—"

"One of Chris's guys, right?"

"Yes, one of Chris's guys, and this amazing woman, Natalie Herrera, who ran the boards at Second City for years. Both good, both great choices, and nice to pull in some diversity either way we go."

"That's fine. I have an idea I want to run by you as well, and I need you to keep a very open mind. As ideas go, it's a bit of an outlier."

"Oh, brother." She sat down and sighed deeply. "Does one of your kids want to follow in Daddy's footsteps?" she teased.

"I can't decide if that's an insult or a compliment." He laughed. "And no! But listen, Sid, I've been thinking about this for a while, and it's time we discussed it."

"The lead-up is scaring me."

"Troy."

"What?"

"Troy. He and I have been in conversation over the last couple of months. He's been clean and sober since you last saw him—what's that now, seven, eight months? He's ready to do whatever needs doin' to fix things between the two of you and—"

"No. Absolutely not."

"Okay. What exactly does that mean?"

"Exactly what I said. I will not work with Troy. Ever. I'm glad he's clean and sober, I wish him well, but I won't put the club, or myself, at the mercy of someone who can get stupid and violent and then write it off to his personal problems."

"I get it, I get it—"

"I don't think you do, Frank, or you wouldn't be suggesting it."

He sat back. The shadow that crossed his eyes reminded Sidonie of when they'd discussed Chris. It was portentous and unyielding, and she didn't like its implication.

"Let me remind you, Sidonie, this is a democratic search for a new sound manager, not a fiat from your department. I believe I get some say in this." There was sarcasm in his tone; she noticed it only because he rarely went there.

"First of all," she retorted, "I don't understand why you'd drop this on me now, after I've spent weeks meeting with people and zeroing in on two excellent candidates. If you were just going to overrule me with this idea, why did I bother putting in the time?"

"I'm not overruling anything. I wanted to give it ample consideration before I brought it to you. Do you think *I'd* put the club at risk if I didn't think Troy was ready to come back? I've spent a lot of time discussing the situation with him, laying out the boundaries, and he gets it. He's humbled and ready to start at the bottom to rebuild his position here."

"He doesn't have a position here." The idea that Frank had been discussing this with Troy behind her back infuriated her but she kept that in check for the moment.

"If you can put aside your rancor for two minutes, you might realize this will make things easier for *you*. There's no learning curve. He knows Jasper, he had a decent rapport with the staff, and we can start him off at a lower salary, let him prove himself again, let him work to get back to where he was. Seems win-win to me."

She stood up, suppressing every thought and feeling perched at the edge of her psyche. "I've made clear how I feel, Frank. If this is a top-down decision and I have no say, you let me know. If I do have a say, I will give it the serious thought you're requesting. But I do need to go right now."

"It's certainly not a top-down decision, and I do want your input, so please do me that favor. Let's plan to revisit this and make a decision by the end of the week, okay?"

"Yep."

She fled from the room and found herself in the dusty confines of the little sound office behind the stage. She'd frequently availed herself of its privacy on days when Church life was particularly trying. When Chris was around, it had made a seductive stop for their occasional and passionate rendezvous. Sitting there now, with the door shut and the light dim, she wanted to turn the lock and never come out.

Her life was stuck. In every way.

Efforts to get the latest investor meeting set up had been stymied by holiday schedules, and now Patsy was out of town on some prestigious cooking show in Los Angeles. Karen's attempt to dig up further information on the fingerprints had been fruitless, inspiring the cliché, "It's sometimes best to let sleeping dogs lie," but Sidonie had already decided it was a fool's errand.

And Chris . . . he'd come back to the townhouse when she was at work the Wednesday after their fracas. His left his closet empty and the holes in the wall plastered and sanded. A paint can and brush were left on the counter with a note: "The plaster needs to fully dry. I can either come by later to finish up, or you can do it yourself. Text me and let me know what you'd prefer. CH." The impersonal nature of the note slayed her. Even the air in the house felt different, as if his energy, his life force, had truly left the building. She'd cried most of that night . . . and many thereafter.

Yet here in this musty little room, the floor cluttered with remnants of past events, the worn black walls a testament to years of sweaty men leaving notes and putting out cigarettes, she could find him . . . feel him. The air still held his breath, and, like fossils from another era, each item left behind told of his erstwhile presence: a napkin with "phantom power, channel two" in his handwriting tacked to the board, the dirty coffee cup he always used, an Excel sheet of Sound Alchemy gigs from previous months. She felt like she was peering over a gravesite, and her heart broke for the two millionth time.

Al's voice could be heard in distant conversation with Frank, likely out on the dance floor, and she did not want to exit this cocoon until they were gone. She swirled around in the chair, absently sifting through old magazines and stacks of paper. She pulled open the drawer on her right to find a staple gun, a canister of paper clips, and a baggie of Velcro cord ties. The drawer to the left held a pack of empty manila folders, bent and brown with age—she thought about how someone was going to have to clean up all of this for the next manager. The middle drawer revealed a Miles Davis CD, a pack of Wrigley's Doublemint gum, and—as she shoved aside a stack of random schematic charts—pink.

Incongruous pink.

In a flush of adrenaline, she yanked the papers out, tossed them to the floor, and there, lying at the bottom of the cluttered drawer, caught in the light like a precious artifact, was the pink nametag from the backpack. Same material, same color. She picked it up: "Samantha

P (312) 555-2239." She refused to think, she ignored all questions and emotions, and with the familiar pounding of her heart, pulled out her phone and punched in the numbers.

A woman answered. "Hello?"

"Hi, I'm the manager at a club called The Church and I believe we may have a backpack that belongs to someone at this number."

"Oh, my God!" the woman yelped. "I am so glad you called! My daughter has just been heartbroken about losing her sunglasses . . . they were a gift from her grandmother. When the original guy called, he spoke to my idiot son—and I'm only kidding, I love my son—but my idiot son obviously got the number wrong, because when I called, I got some woman at a senior home. I kept hoping the guy would check back—though, why would he, right?—but I'm *so* glad you did!"

The guy. That would be Chris. Her Chris. He called. Just as he said he had.

"Can you confirm your daughter's name and color of the backpack?"

"Samantha—and it's pink. Are the glasses still in it?"

"They are."

"Oh my God, she's going to be thrilled!"

An arrangement was made: Sidonie would bring the pack to the club and leave it behind the bar; whoever was working when Samantha's family came by would hand it over. Gushing thanks were bestowed, a little girl was predicted to be delighted, and a man's honor . . . a man's honor . . . had been doubted.

Sidonie could not possibly reconcile what she was feeling. She could do nothing but walk out of the booth and go to her office, where she typed a note that was left on Frank's desk:

```
Frank: I'm leaving for the night; it's a slow one so
Jasper can handle things. I wanted to let you know
ASAP that I will not work with Troy. Period. If that
means it's either him or me, that's fine. I think
it's time for me to move on anyway. Sid.
```

EIGHTY-TWO

SHE WENT DIRECTLY HOME, SAT AT HER COMPUTER, TYPED out everything she wanted to say, printed it up, and put it in an envelope. She then got in her car and took the long, fraught drive to Hyde Park, with no idea if Chris was home or would even acknowledge her presence if he was. When Delores answered the door, the surprise on her face conveyed that she was fully aware of the status of things. It stung, but was certainly understandable.

"My goodness, Sidonie! What a nice surprise!"

"I doubt it's really that nice."

"Nonsense. Come in." When Sidonie hesitated, Delores stepped out to the snow-crusted porch to pull her in. "It's cold out there and you do not need to be foolish with me."

It turned out Chris was working for Vanessa—a fundraiser at a local high school—and not expected until later. Sidonie and Delores had the place to themselves.

They settled in the parlor, where they'd sat that first memorable night. A night when amazing peach cobbler had been savored, an inebriated Vanessa castigated her whiteness; when Chris proudly presented her as the woman in his life, and Delores made her feel like family. A night that seemed so long ago as to be a different century.

Sidonie's plan had been to find Chris, give him the letter, and see where his response took them. Now, seated on Delores's sofa, cold, discombobulated, and ashamed, she wasn't sure if what she'd hoped to achieve had any footing in reality. She shook her head as if trying to rearrange her thoughts.

"Sidonie," Delores asked quietly, "what is it?"

With that the tears started. "I'm not sure I know how to lay this out."

"I usually find beginning-to-end is best." Delores smiled gently.

"How much do you know?"

"I think I have it all."

"Even the backpack thing—"

"Yes, dear, all of it."

The burn of humiliation was fierce. "I know how horrible that must seem."

"Yes, horrible, indeed. You lost your faith in someone you love. You began to believe something that could not possibly be true. But I'm aware of how much weight you were bearing. You suffered too, Sidonie, I know that. And the forces pulling at you—the police, the prosecutor, the people in your life who doubted Chris—they created a lot of noise for you to sort through. Should you not have buckled? Stayed strong, believed in your man? Certainly! We should all be so brave and unbowed as to never question what we know, what we feel. But we're human. You're human. And you'd been chipped at for long enough that your emotional immune system was compromised, enough to let doubt creep in. And here we find ourselves."

It was astonishing to Sidonie how one person could take a pile of words and arrange them in ways that turned chaos into cogent, sensible assessment. She'd not been able to formulate that explanation for herself and she knew Delores's take was as close to absolution as she'd likely get.

"Thank you. I don't think I could face myself again without *someone* having that understanding. That it was you means everything to me."

Delores took her hand. "Life is a damn beast, isn't it?"

Sidonie's tearful nod was her answer.

"When my beloved son and husband were taken from me far too early to be acceptable, I railed at God and thought I would never again be able to embrace a good and loving moment. But like I tell Vanessa and Chris, you have to find the balance—it's your obligation as a human being. You get both, good and bad, joy and sorrow. We all do. It's how we handle those polarities, how we adjust and heal and forgive— sometimes even ourselves—that allows life to go on, to have some meaning. And it seems to me that if you got in your car and drove all the way down here in the snow, willing to face whatever came your way, you are ready to go on."

"I think I am . . . I don't know. Do you think he is?"

"That's his to answer, sweetheart. He's angry and he's hurt. And though much of what I've said to you I've also said to him, what he comes to is his journey. Not mine, not yours. Part of yours will be accepting whatever he chooses. You do what you can, yes, but you adjust to reality, whatever it may be. That, Sidonie, is finding the balance."

The concept demanded a level of wisdom and maturity she wasn't sure she had in her toolbox these days. Still, she remained committed to her quest. "I wrote a few thoughts in a letter," she said, pulling the envelope from her purse. "I was hoping to give it to Chris, let him read it on his own, and if he wanted to talk to me after that, we could."

"Sounds like a good plan. Why don't you leave it on his bed?"

As Sidonie rose to go upstairs, Delores added:

"I do want to say one more thing, sweetheart, just so you understand. I want the best for you both, I do, but I don't know if that means you two should be together or if this was just one chapter in your lives. But whatever it is, I respect Chris's process and I won't intervene from here on out. No matter what he decides, I won't try to talk him into anything and I won't represent your perspective. This remains solidly between the two of you. I hope you can understand that."

She did. It made sense. She was on her own with this, as it should be.

Sidonie put the note on his bed, hugged Delores, and set back out to a cold night and the uncertainty of what was next. When she got in the car, she checked her phone: there were two text messages. The first was from Karen:

Wanted to get this to you as quickly as possible. They did and do have fingerprints . . . which belong to a repeat felon named Jelani Thayer, in custody as of yesterday, positively ID'd in the rape case as well as the neighborhood break-ins. Unbelievable, right? My friend shot me a picture and damn if he doesn't actually resemble Chris a little, which might explain a few things! It kind of makes me sick when I think about what happened . . . what could have happened. On the other hand, I hope this news gives you some peace. Call me! xxoo

The second was shorter. And more unexpected:

I said I'd stay out of it, but this seemed important. Fingerprints belong to a Jelani Thayer, a repeat offender collared yesterday. He's been charged with all the stuff they had on Chris. I don't know if this makes you feel better or worse, but I wanted to pass it on since it answers some questions. Mike.

It did. The irony was, all the important questions had already been answered.

EIGHTY-THREE

CHRIS HAD A LATE NIGHT, BUT A SATISFYING COLLABORATION with his sister, a changed woman these days. Though earlier in the week there'd been a brief but intense spat about the brutality lawsuit—she wanted to proceed; he didn't—they'd come to an accord (shelving it until further notice) without bloodshed. Given the tumult in every other corner of his life, it was gratifying to find peace with someone who'd so long been a source of agitation. That she didn't ask him about Sidonie or offer any input on the situation kept things nonconfrontational. Mostly he was happy to see her happy. It made it easier to oblige when she asked for help.

Chris wasn't surprised that his mother had already gone to bed. Though she occasionally stayed up reading until one or two, more recently her lights were out by eleven. He wondered if the tangential stress of his life was wearing her down.

The small lamp in the parlor was on. It was a room rarely used and certainly not by Delores herself, so that was strange. When he went in to turn it off, he noticed two teacups on the table. Interesting. Normally his mother would have tidied up. Since there'd been no mention of expected visitors, it felt like a clue.

He took the cups into the kitchen, and utterly exhausted, stood over the sink eating a well-seasoned drumstick with a side of home-made potato salad. While he thoroughly enjoyed his mother's cooking, one of the perks of being there, he was also aware of how unsettled he felt. Diante texted earlier in the week with the not unexpected news that Jordan had moved out, extending to Chris an invitation to return, but it was time to get his own place. He already had appointments to look at a few lofts in the Brownsville neighborhood.

When he got to his room, he was again surprised: the desk lamp was on. Then he saw it. The letter on his bed. The *Chris* on the envelope was not his mother's handwriting, though he recognized it immediately. He sat and opened the letter; held it for a long moment, then began reading.

Chris . . .

You're right to be angry with me. If someone I loved wasn't able to hold on to their knowledge and belief of who and what I am, I wouldn't want them in my life either.

I never before experienced the world as I have over this last year. I didn't know it existed. In the world I knew, I worked hard, I had family dramas like anyone else, I built a career, married an asshole, lost a pregnancy, got divorced, started a project that excited me, then fell in love with you.

Falling in love with you was the best part of this new world. YOU were the best part of this new world. Your being black was not an issue. It was not a deterrent, a strange fascination, or a reason to reject you. It was just one of the characteristics attached to you, and I fell in love with YOU, the man, the person, the being, the soul.

What I didn't know then is that by falling in love with you I would be stepping from my world into yours. Or maybe, more accurately, straddling both. I didn't know that because I didn't fully realize there were two worlds, two really distinct worlds with different sets of rules, as you said.

It's not that I'm naïve or unaware. I read the papers and watch the news. Events shock me. I'm outraged about people being treated differently, by the statistics and stories that prove that everything about life in this country can be, and too often is, biased and bigoted against people of color, but somehow I thought it was all out there somewhere. Out there impacting gangbangers and hoodlums and street thugs and bad guys and clueless, irresponsible people. I'm ashamed to say I wasn't as aware that everyday people—honest, hard-working, good people living their lives while existing in black skin—were just as vulnerable. That someone like you was just as vulnerable. Loving you and living with you has taught me that . . . and so much more.

But I was unprepared—from the first time the cops stopped us, to the moment I watched Alice's video, to the night I walked out to see you battered and bloody, to being handcuffed to a police bench, to being told you were a rapist and serial criminal—I was unprepared for all that.

And I didn't deal with it as well as I should have. I lost my footing. I overreacted. I felt stupid and helpless. I got scared and confused. I felt abandoned by you sometimes. Dismissed and ignored. It bothered me, but I kept telling myself I wasn't the important one, all that mattered was you and what you were going through. So I did my best to hold my center, to hold on to what I knew, even when people were telling me I was wrong, that you were a bad guy, that I was being duped and manipulated. And even though I knew that wasn't true, sometimes it was confusing. It was always overwhelming.

All that led up to me finding the backpack. After the trial was dismissed, you went home to your family, you didn't come home to me. I was really hurt by that. I said I understood, and on a certain level I did, but it made me feel like I wasn't important to you, that I didn't matter, that everything I'd endured with you and for you had been of little significance. When I found that backpack—a bizarre thing to find and something I hadn't heard anything about—given my turbulent, anguished, diminished state of mind, I admit, it shook me. I couldn't figure it out. As if I were in a fugue state, or some delusional, paranoiac hysteria, fear got the better of me and my mind went toward a sort of weird, disconnected "what if?" I kept batting it away, grabbing on to what I know of you so clearly, but it was like an evil bee and eventually it bit me. It was brief and quickly lost its sting, but yes, it bit me. Which shames me to even think about.

Looking back now, completely outside of that state and clear on the facts, my fear looks completely insane. I look completely insane. I look faithless, traitorous, and disloyal. Did I honestly believe it? NO.

But my mind did go there, ever so briefly. And I am so deeply sorry for that.

If it really is unforgivable, if you feel like you can never trust me again, I understand. All I can tell you is that it was one tortuous night of doubt and disbelief. The rest of the time, which is all the time, I know exactly who you are: you are Chris Hawkins, the best man I know. Whether you give me another chance or not, I promise you I won't ever forget that.

I love you.

Sidonie

He stared at the letter as if trying to decipher nuances behind the words. He could sense his emotions gathering—grief, anger, loss, betrayal, longing—but the walls built against those feelings, solidified in the weeks since he'd last seen her, were thick and impenetrable. He tried, in deference to her clear earnestness, to breach them, but couldn't.

He felt . . . empty.

So he folded the letter, slipped it into its envelope, and dropped it on his desk on the way to the bathroom. When he returned after brushing his teeth, he shut the light, turned off his roiling confusion, and fell asleep.

EIGHTY-FOUR

AFTER TWO DAYS WITHOUT RESPONSE, SIDONIE HAD NO choice but to do as she'd promised Delores: "Accept whatever way he chooses . . . and adjust to the reality." There were tears, but she was so cried out, so exhausted and weary of being weary and exhausted, there was some relief in just letting it go.

She made the requisite calls to Karen and Patsy, omitting details of the backpack, which carried more shame than she was willing to share right now. She explained that the distance between her and Chris had become insurmountable. Which was true enough.

Karen, devastated for her sister, was subdued in her response; sad, empathetic, and thoughtful. She told Sidonie she had no wise words, but would call when some dawned on her. That was worth a grin.

Conversely, Patsy wept with her friend. They had a good, commiserating cry, with Patsy declaring she wouldn't talk about Ned, the brunch fellow, until she felt more certain and Sidonie felt less raw. Sidonie alerted her that she'd need employment, as odds were good she was out of a job. Patsy promised to light a fire under the investors and, in the meantime, offered the option of producing a few high-end catering gigs for good money. Sidonie shuddered, but knew she'd take her up on it. It would be like returning to the galleys.

Frank's only response to her note was a text saying he hoped they could talk about it when she got in on Wednesday, but Jasper confided that Frank had already floated the Troy idea, clearly greasing the rails for his new agenda. Life, it seemed, was determined to transform itself whether she was leading the charge or not.

Her last step was to sweep through the house and restore it as best she could to pre-Chris days. It was too painful otherwise. Pictures came down and chairs were moved, though she so loved the way he painted the walls she knew they'd stay.

By evening's end the only thing left was laundry. She stripped the sheets and when she emptied the basket, found one of Chris's T-shirts. She held it close and breathed in, hoping some vestige of his warm, musky scent remained. Though the softness against her cheek brought his touch to mind, it had been too long for anything else.

She headed down to the garage and loaded the washer, turned off the light, and walked out to her favorite bench. She sat, jacket pulled tight, and stared upward. The cyan of dusk was giving way to inky darkness, the glow of streetlights illuminated the clouds that floated slowly across the sky. It was a beautiful night, not too cold, and the wind's gentle push seemed determined to sweep out the day.

"'I look to my feet to keep from stumbling. I gaze straight ahead to find my way . . .'" A man's voice suddenly wafted from the sidewalk.

Startled, Sidonie sat up. Did she hear that right? Was she imagining things? She looked past the gate and as her eyes adjusted to the dark, she saw . . . him. Standing with his hands in the pockets of his jean jacket, his face drawn but empty of anger. Chris Hawkins.

"'I Tilt Toward the Sky,' remember?" he asked, his eyes meeting hers.

She took a quick breath and held still, afraid he was a mirage that might drift with too much motion. "Yes. Jovana Stanton."

He walked slowly across the yard and sat at the other end of the bench. "I remembered the story you told me that first night. I searched around and found her book, decided I'd memorize the poem you loved just to impress you. Somehow I never got to it."

"Impress me now," she said quietly, her eyes on the sky.

"Not sure I remember it."

"Try."

He paused a moment. Then: "'I look to my feet to keep from stumbling. I gaze straight ahead to find my way. I touch and smell and feel to appraise my surroundings, and hold dear to those whose hearts hold mine. And when I wish to open myself to the wilderness of life, to the connections that join us or tear us apart, I tilt toward the sky, where infinity's cloak sparkles, making exploration an endless wonder.'"

A smile flitted across her face. "Professor Stanton would be impressed."

"And you?"

She turned to him, eyes glistening. "Yes . . . me too."

His hand slid slowly across the weathered wood until their fingers touched. Just touched. Then they leaned back and stared up to the starlit heavens, swirling blue in the big, embracing, connecting universe.

THE END

AUTHOR'S NOTE

Thank you for choosing *The Alchemy of Noise* amongst the many titles available to you. Your readership is deeply valued and I hope you were moved by Chris and Sidonie's story.

Given the subject matter of this book, I wanted to share a little background as to why I felt this specific story was mine to tell, particularly at a time when concerns surrounding "cultural appropriation" and which voices get to tell stories of race are widely debated, and deserving of meaningful conversation.

Earlier in my life I spent six years in an interracial relationship. As educated as I thought I was on the topic of race and bias, and as open-minded and racially progressive as my upbringing had been, it turns out I had only a glimpse of the bigger picture and so very much to learn. Witnessing, tangentially experiencing, and reacting to the "microaggressions," recurring police harassment, and flat-out bigotry my partner dealt with on a day-to-day basis forever changed my worldview on the reality of race in America.

I learned then, before the phrase had even been coined in its more current context, the insensitivity and arrogance of "white privilege." I was forced to acknowledge the racial disparities found in law enforcement and the justice system. I vicariously felt the pain of the "million little cuts" inflicted by ignorant men who'd admonish him to "get over his black thing," terrified women who locked their car doors as he walked past, or friends whose casual racism was brushed off as "just a joke."

Later in my writing career, it struck me that this experience offered not only the seeds of a topical and dramatic story, but brought into the conversation the specific, shared, but disparate perspectives of a mixed-race couple. That seemed a useful point-of-view to explore, particularly when lack of experiential empathy too often leaves participants in the discussion struggling for true understanding. As a longtime contributor to *HuffPost*, I referenced my personal experience in a couple of op-eds on the topic of race, which not only gave me access to a wide audience open to the conversation, but allowed me proximity to dialogue and feedback from both sides of the racial divide. As I began to formulate the narrative of this novel, that education brought the story into the current zeitgeist.

But I'm also aware of, and have occasionally written about, the controversies surrounding white writers including black characters (or any characters outside their own culture) in their literary works, which has sparked a debate about who gets to tell those particular stories; who has true insight to offer; who should talk, who should listen, and how we process information from the side we're not on. Even with the sensitivities surrounding those issues, my gut told me I had a worthy story to tell. *Because* of those sensitivities, I was determined to accomplish that goal as authentically as I could, allowing the unvarnished, sometimes painful, and frequently illuminating viewpoints of each character to be honestly expressed throughout.

From there I created a fictional set of characters, put them in contemporary Chicago (the city of my birth), plotted out their story arc, and gave them many of the challenges and obstacles I'd witnessed and experienced in my long-ago relationship . . . ones that, sadly, still resonate in current times. Adding perspective gleaned from prodigious research, myriad interviews, and essential input from sensitivity readers, *The Alchemy of Noise* came to life with as much humanity, truth, and credibility as I could capture. At its heart it's a love story, if one framed by the provocation of race dynamics in modern day America. I hope you found it both genuine and moving.

I invite you to be in touch with any thoughts you may want to share, and, if you enjoyed the book, I hope you'll help spread the word via social media and by leaving your honest review at the page where you made your purchase. If you'd like to be on my mailing list, either shoot me an email or sign up via my website. Know that your support is deeply appreciated and I thank you in advance for yours.

Lorraine

info@lorrainedevonwilke.com
www.lorrainedevonwilke.com

ACKNOWLEDGMENTS

This being my third novel, I felt like an old hand when I first sat down at the computer to start plotting out the story. There was no fear of the blank page, no lack of confidence that I could craft something with chapters and a beginning, middle, and end, but with this particular story, one I felt a profound obligation to get right, I looked beyond, to a wider community, to ensure that essential goal.

First, always, I must acknowledge my husband, Pete Wilke, my rock like no other. He has been witness and support to my many years of artistic struggles and successes, wins and losses, and nobody knows me, and my devotion to creativity, better. He keeps a roof over our heads, reads my work, listens to my music, attends my plays, hangs my photos, and convinces me there's always reason to carry on, no matter what the obstacles or disappointments. "Tomorrow's another day" is his mantra, and he not only lives by that resilience and optimism, he's imbued it in me. I cannot imagine this journey without him, nor can I find adequate words to thank him for all he is and all he's done for me. I love you, Peter Jay.

To my son, Dillon Wilke, who's grown up since I started my career as a novelist, and launched his own successful career as a civil engineer. A participant in my artistic adventures from the time he was old enough to attend my band gigs, theatrical performances, book readings, and photo ops, this time around he stepped up in a big way, a way I couldn't have anticipated, by financing the entire budget for the marketing and promotion campaign for this book, an astonishingly generous gift. When I asked, incredulous and so deeply touched, "Why would you do that?," he simply said, "I believe in you." Nothing could be more profound for a mother. Or a writer. Thank you, sweetheart. No words can capture my gratitude or what you mean to me.

Certainly I must acknowledge my brother, Tom Amandes, my editor and champion extraordinaire. Not only did he do a masterful job with the developmental edit of my last book, *Hysterical Love*, he devoted countless hours, weeks, even months, to the meticulous, thoughtful, painstaking evolution of *The Alchemy of Noise*. As a talented, accomplished actor, director, and writer himself, he has an unfailing sense of story, narrative development, and character arc, all of which I relied upon in seeking his input and perspective. I counted on him, always, to be unfailingly honest, and he always was; my work is all the better for it. He was also my "Chicago consultant" with this book, helping me identify, specify, and define the places in my birth city that worked for the story, allowing me to infuse the many settings with essential authenticity. Once again, I am grateful beyond words, dear brother.

Regina McRae was essential to the evolution of *The Alchemy of Noise*. An indefatigable BLM activist; award-winning NYC baker and entrepreneur (owner of Grandma's Secrets bakery in Brooklyn); author of *Taking the Cake, Your Ultimate Cake Guide*; and mother, grandmother, and fierce advocate for social justice, she was and continues to be pivotal to my education as an ally. We connected via a piece I wrote for *HuffPost* called, "No, White People Will Never Understand the Black Experience," after which she accepted my invitation to participate in a three-part interview series for *HuffPost* on the topic of racism. Her unvarnished perspective, clarifying insight, and unapologetic candor not only made for a bracing series, it informed much of the background and character elements of this story. She was my most trusted and effective "sensitivity reader," generous and supportive with her time and attention, and I relied on her more than anyone to make sure I got it right. I knew once Regina McRae gave me the thumbs up, I was good to go. Thank you, sis . . . forever grateful.

My own sis, Grace Amandes, must be acknowledged for her indefatigable "location scouting services" offered while I was researching the book. A current native of Chicago, she spent days with me driving through the neighborhoods and locations I'd assigned as the various work and living quarters of my characters, which gave me a visceral, authentic sense of *place*, so important for a book grounded in an iconic city. Thank you, Grace, for your time and involvement; so much appreciated.

There are various readers who jumped into the process at different points of the book's evolution, all of whom contributed greatly to its development: Pamela May, Susan Morgenstern, Barbara Tyler, Nancy Locke Capers, Patricia Royce, and Debra Sanders, in particular. Early readers are gold, and every single one of you gave me invaluable and important feedback . . . thank you.

I also want to acknowledge my publisher, Brooke Warner, president of She Writes Press, who came along at the exact right moment in my life. Not only was I delighted to have someone of her expertise and perspective interested in my work—particularly after my many years as a self-published author—I was and am impressed and inspired by her passion and vision, her mission statement of fearless and creative innovation. I am thrilled to be part of the SWP community and honored by her faith in my own creative vision.

Thanks to *all* the team at SWP, especially my project manager, Samantha Strom, and the publicity and marketing team at Book-Sparks/SparkPoint Studio, particularly President & CEO, Crystal Patriarche, and Senior Publicist, Tabitha Bailey, who enthusiastically ushered this book into the public forum. Additionally I want to thank the network of other SWP authors who have been so universally supportive along this literary journey.

A special thanks to Julie Metz for her stunning cover, which beautifully captures the setting and sensibilities of the story; additional thanks to Stacey Aaronson for the artful interior design of the book.

The life of a writer demands an undeniably cloistered existence, at least during the process of writing, so friends become all the more precious in reminding one that life exists beyond the page. My close personal circle has been an intense, valued network since my early days in Los Angeles (with some before; some more recent), and their unconditional support, reliable affection, great humor, and deep, historical importance in my life is both essential and impossible to overstate. They include Tina Romanus, Joyce DiVito Jackson, Nancy & Hedges Capers, Patricia Royce, Susan Morgenstern, Carolyn Sutton, Suzanne Battaglia, Pamela May, Jake Drake, Minda Burr, Steve Brackenbury & Frank Ramos, Jason Brett & Lauren Streicher, Eddie & Jennifer King,

Troy Evans & Heather McLarty, Chris Tufty & Margot Ott, Cindy Ritt, Marian Hamlen, Sandra Wilson, Barry Caillier, Erik Krogh, Jeff & Ann Brown, Susie Singer Carter, and Don Priess.

There are also those amongst my fellow-authors' circle who've been particularly supportive and helpful. They include Mark Barry, Brenda Perlin, Jane Davis, Laura Diamond, Jenny Milchman, Junior Burke, Tracy Trivas, Geri Dunlap Clouston, Laurie E. Boris, and Kimberley A. Johnson.

Of course, there's always appreciation for my ten Amandes siblings—Peg, Mary, John, Paul, Tom, Eileen, Gerry, Louise, Vince, and Grace—and the many beloved spouses, nieces, and nephews sprouting from that hearty group, all of whom never fail to embrace creativity, doggedness, political activism, and vital humor.

To my dearest stepdaughter, Jennie Wilke Willens and her gang: hubby Jake, Gracie, and Ryan, who, along with the circle of Willens family, remain so lovingly connected to our family and my creative world.

Last, I want to thank the many people in my social and social media circles who have stayed involved, supportive, and interested in my work over all these many years. Whether fellow writers, artists of other mediums, readers, cultural activists, tangential friends met online, or extended friends and family in life, some of whom remain in far-flung places, the list is too long to name, but your connection and interaction with me on this journey is so very valued. Buying my books, reading my articles, sharing my perspective, reviewing my work, clicking "like," "love," "friend," and "follower" have all contributed to my very real sense of community, my faith that what I'm creating, what I believe is important to convey through my work, is seen, heard, and appreciated. Thank you . . . I am truly grateful to you all.

ABOUT THE AUTHOR

Photo credit: Maureen Grammer

An accomplished writer in several genres of the medium, Lorraine Devon Wilke, a Chicago native and one of eleven children, has built a library of expertly crafted work with a signature style that exudes intelligence, depth, and humor. Whether screenplay or stage play, article or editorial, short story or novel, her work captures the edge and emotion of real life, incorporating original plots, jump-off-the-page dialogue, and thought-provoking themes.

In 2010 she launched her "arts & politics" blog, *Rock+Paper+Music*, and from 2011 to 2018 she was a popular contributor at *HuffPost* and other news and media sites. Known for her "sass and sensibility," her work has been reprinted and excerpted in academic tomes, nonfiction books, and literary journals; a catalogue of her articles and essays can be found at *Contently.com*. Both her award-winning novels, *After the Sucker Punch* and *Hysterical Love*, are available at Amazon and Barnes & Noble.

Having left Illinois decades ago with a rock band heading west, Devon Wilke landed in Los Angeles where she still lives with her husband, attorney/writer/producer, Pete Wilke, with her son, Dillon Wilke, and other extended family nearby. She's working on a fourth novel, a rock & roll dramedy titled, *A Minor Rebellion*, while continuing her endeavors as a photographer, singer-songwriter, and actress.

To learn more visit @ www.lorrainedevonwilke.com.

READING GROUP/BOOK CLUB GUIDE

The questions and talking points that follow are intended to enrich your group's discussions about *The Alchemy of Noise*.

1. Despite the focal points of race, privilege, and police profiling, the foundation of this story involves the universal experience of falling in love, with all its joy, pain, and passion. Did you find Chris and Sidonie's relationship believable? Were you rooting for them? Did you think they would endure or were you expecting the obstacles they faced to ultimately thwart them?

2. Some believe that modern society as a whole no longer finds interracial relationships controversial, while others either witness, or struggle themselves, with some of the related conflicts detailed in the book. Discuss your own thinking, or the thinking of those around you, on the topic of mixed-race couples.

3. What was your reaction to the various confrontations with the police in the story, including Officer Mike? Have you had experiences that would allow you to relate to those characterizations, or were they improbable or inflammatory to you? Did they change your opinion of the police and their interactions with people of color?

4. The character of Sidonie Frame is bright, well educated, and generally aware, yet she's culturally insulated by the lack of diversity in her surroundings and the limitations of her own experiences. What were your impressions of her "learning curve" with Chris concerning race and could you relate to that process?

5. Vanessa Hawkins is a powerful, complex, and challenging character, someone who articulates viewpoints shared by many but misunderstood by others. As an articulate spokesperson on issues of prejudice and privilege, she stirs both admiration and controversy. What are your thoughts on Vanessa, her views, and the matter of "white privilege"?

6. Do you think race might determine a reader's response to Chris Hawkins's experiences throughout the story? Did you find those moments—whether the microaggressions of assuming he's the cabbie or the extreme violence of his arrest—believable? Upsetting? Did they change or deepen your perspective on what black men in America experience, or confirm what you already knew and/or have experienced yourself, whether as a witness or victim of racism?

7. Sidonie's sister, Karen, is compassionate, open-minded, and supportive, yet gave up a more socially conscious career as a public defender to immerse herself in a life of privilege and wealth via a lucrative civil law practice. Did you find her admirable or self-serving? Or both?

8. The two mothers in *The Alchemy of Noise* could not be more disparate: Delores Hawkins has experienced tremendous loss and the causticness of racism, yet exudes equanimity and wisdom. Marian Frame, on the other hand, has lived a largely sheltered life, with divorce being her greatest grief, yet seems to lack character and personal conviction. Discuss the impact of these contrasting characters within the story and on their respective children.

9. One of the most devastating plot points is the moment Sidonie briefly considers the fear that Chris could be a rapist. Though it is fleeting, it's a stunning loss of faith in someone she loves. Was it forgivable? Was there ever a moment in which you suspected Chris could be the criminal they were looking for?

10. Sidonie's best friend, Patsy, delivers a tirade of blatant racist tropes after hearing about Sidonie and Chris's relationship, which fractures the women's friendship. Was her later explanation valid? Was she forgivable in your eyes?

11. There's a current debate in literary circles concerning "cultural appropriation" and "whose voice gets to tell stories of race" (as mentioned in the Author's Note). What are your thoughts on this

issue, particularly after reading a book by a white author inclusive of depictions of black life and black characters? Did you feel this author met the standard of authenticity and balance?

12. One of the book's sensitivity readers commented, "The book is a sort of Racism 101, an eye-opener for allies." If a black reader, do you agree? If a white reader, did you find the story educational from that aspect, perhaps even illuminating?

MORE ABOUT LORRAINE'S OTHER BOOKS

Hysterical Love, a novel

Dan McDowell, a thirty-three-year-old portrait photographer wobbling toward an early midlife crisis, is unceremoniously dumped by his fiancée after mentioning a years-earlier "ex-girlfriend overlap." Bunking next door at best friend Bob's for far longer than anticipated, Dan finds himself lost in existential confusion. His life is further upended when his father takes ill and Dan reads an old story written by this enigmatic man about a long-lost love who haunts him still. Perplexed and inspired by this revelation—and incapable of fixing his own romantic dilemma—Dan sets off on a wild ride beset with detours, twists, and semi-hilarious peril to find this woman of his father's dreams, convinced she holds the keys to happiness for them all. A funny, thought-provoking tale of self-discovery and finding the true meaning of love.

2017 New Apple Books Solo Medalist Winner in General Fiction

2017 American Book Fest Best Book Awards,
Finalist in General Fiction

2015 indieB.R.A.G. Medallion Honoree

Kirkus Reviews:

"Wilke is a skilled writer, able to plausibly inhabit Dan's young male perspective. . . . A well-written, engaging, sometimes-frustrating tale of reaching adulthood a little late."

Literary Fiction Book Review:

"Devon Wilke manages to convey the male psyche with a good-natured humor that seems eminently believable. *Hysterical Love* is a deftly told tale."

Readers' Favorite Book Reviews:

"I just finished reading *Hysterical Love*, the newest novel by Lorraine Devon Wilke, and I must say, I simply adored it! Her writing style is witty, pointed and funny, even hilarious at times."

WE Magazine for Women:

Chosen as one of the "8 Books Worth Reading This Summer, 2015."

Barb Taub/UK Book Blog:

"I never found a writer who was as good as DH Lawrence, but who could also get into a man's head and tell that story. Until now. Wilke is a kind of genius. Or a damn good writer doing a better job of getting into the head of the opposite sex than DH Lawrence anyway. She combines humor, terrific writing, and some none-too-gently acquired truths into a different kind of relationship story."

A Woman's Wisdom/**UK Book Blog:**

"This is one of those books which exceeded all my expectations. I was expecting a romance with a couple of twists but what I got was something far deeper and more satisfying. If you want a book with many layers and to be thoroughly entertained by a cracking story then this one is for you."

Crossroads Reviews:

"So worth the read. If you want a great laugh then pick this one up. The story was great, as were the characters. Unpredictable in so many ways. One to stick with you."

⁓

After the Sucker Punch, a novel

They buried her father at noon, at five she found his journals, and in the time it took to read one and a half pages, her world turned upside down . . . he thought she was a failure, a posthumous indictment that proves an existential knockout.

Tessa Curzio—thirty-six, emerging writer, ex-rocker, lapsed Catholic, defected Scientologist, and fourth child in a family of eight complicated people—attempts to transcend, but his damning words skew everything from her current relationship and the truth of her family, to her overall sense of self. In the tumultuous year that follows, it's her little-known aunt, a nun and counselor, who lovingly strong-arms Tessa onto a journey of discovery and reinvention in a trip that's not always pretty—or particularly wise—but leads to unexpected truths.

After the Sucker Punch takes an irreverent look at father-daughter relationships through the unique prism of Tessa's saga and its exploration of family, faith, cults, creativity, new love and old, and the struggle to define oneself against the inexplicable perceptions of a deceased parent. Told with both sass and sensibility, it's a story wrapped in contemporary culture with a very classic heart.

2015 Independent Author Network,
Finalist, Book of the Year Award

2014 indieB.R.A.G. Medallion Honoree

2014 IndieAuthorNews Top 50 Indie Books

2015 Rosie Amber's Beach Reads Blog Tour Top 5 Beach Reads

Publishers Weekly/BookLife:

"A realistic and profound journey of realization and forgiveness . . . a solid novel that admirably explores the fragile, fraught relationship between parent and child."

Kirkus Reviews:

"Wilke writes with razor-sharp wit and radiant flair, and the prose's high quality is the novel's principal strength. She also sensitively portrays how real love and affection can survive and even flourish in an otherwise dysfunctional family."

Tracy Trivas, author, *The Wish Stealers* (Simon & Schuster):

"With bare-bone honesty and fiery dialogue, Wilke explores the loaded relationship between parents and their adult-children, examining the brave and lonely journey of self-discovery, reinvention, and healing . . . raw and brave."

Junior Burke, author, *Something Gorgeous* (farfalla press/McMillan & Parrish):

"A keenly executed character study. The novel is tightly structured and holds its complex elements with a sure and skillful grip. The dialogue pops . . . a thoroughly engaging and enjoyable read."

Mark Barry, Green Wizard Publishing/UK:

"A great, sweeping, beautifully written, page-turning read, gripping from page one. A family saga with ambition and class. Meant to be absorbed over time, savoured by lamplight."

SELECTED TITLES FROM SHE WRITES PRESS

She Writes Press is an independent publishing company
founded to serve women writers everywhere.
Visit us at www.shewritespress.com.

In a Silent Way by Mary Jo Hetzel. $16.95, 978-1-63152-135-5. When Jeanna Kendall—a young white teacher at a progressive urban school—becomes involved with a community activist group, she finds herself grappling with issues of racism, sexism, and oppression of various shades in both her professional and personal life.

Appetite by Sheila Grinell. $16.95, 978-1-63152-022-8. When twenty-five-year-old Jenn Adler brings home a guru fiancé from Bangalore, her parents must come to grips with the impending marriage—and its effect on their own relationship.

American Family by Catherine Marshall-Smith. $16.95, 978-1631521638. Partners Richard and Michael, recovering alcoholics, struggle to gain custody of Richard's biological daughter from her grandparents after her mother's death only to discover they— and she—are fundamentalist Christians.

Again and Again by Ellen Bravo. $16.95, 978-1-63152-939-9. When the man who raped her roommate in college becomes a Senate candidate, women's rights leader Deborah Borenstein must make a choice—one that could determine control of the Senate, the course of a friendship, and the fate of a marriage.

Shelter Us by Laura Diamond. $16.95, 978-1-63152-970-2. Lawyer-turned-stay-at-home-mom Sarah Shaw is still struggling to find a steady happiness after the death of her infant daughter when she meets a young homeless mother and toddler she can't get out of her mind—and becomes determined to rescue them.

True Stories at the Smoky View by Jill McCroskey Coupe. $16.95, 978-1-63152-051-8. The lives of a librarian and a ten-year-old boy are changed forever when they become stranded by a blizzard in a Tennessee motel and join forces in a very personal search for justice.